30119 028 788 64 6

KU-410-705

12|20
WAL

PARIS
BY
STARLIGHT

ALSO BY ROBERT DINSDALE

The Harrowing
Little Exiles
Gingerbread
The Toymakers

PARIS
BY
STARLIGHT

ROBERT DINSDALE

1 3 5 7 9 10 8 6 4 2

Del Rey
20 Vauxhall Bridge Road,
London SW1V 2SA

Penguin
Random House
UK

Del Rey is part of the Penguin Random House group of companies
whose addresses can be found at global.penguinrandomhouse.com

Copyright © Robert Dinsdale 2020

Robert Dinsdale has asserted his right to be identified as
the author of this work in accordance with the Copyright,
Designs and Patents Act 1988

This novel is a work of fiction. Names and characters are
the product of the author's imagination and any resemblance to
actual persons, living or dead, is entirely coincidental.

www.penguin.co.uk

A CIP catalogue record for this book is available from
the British Library

Hardback ISBN 9781529100457
Trade Paperback ISBN 9781529100464

Typeset in 10/14.5 pt ITC Galliard Std
by Integra Software Services Pvt. Ltd, Pondicherry

Printed and bound in Great Britain by Clays Ltd, Elcograf S.p.A.

Penguin Random House is committed to a sustainable future for
our business, our readers and our planet. This book is made from
Forest Stewardship Council® certified paper.

FSC
www.fsc.org
MIX
Paper from
responsible sources
FSC® C018179

For my parents, who have been reading my writing for thirty years; and for Esther, who is just beginning

See the small girl: she is waiting, as we all once waited, for her father to come and tell her bedtime stories.

Teeth brushed, hair combed; Esmé is the very picture of a model child. Tonight she is in her unicorn pyjamas – though unicorns, those magical beasts which once consumed her every thought, have (for reasons obvious to every parent in Paris) fallen out of fashion of late. With her bear in her hands, she sits impatiently at the end of the bed.

Patience, her parents tell her, is a virtue. But if virtue feels like this, well, surely it is overrated. Her father has been too long in coming tonight, so it is hardly Esmé's fault when her eyes start roaming the nursery floor. Boredom is satisfied by so few things, now that she is almost seven years old. A turn on the rocking horse does so little to help. Settling her dolls in their wooden bunks and telling them a story of their own lasts barely five minutes. She upends boxes, puts together puzzles, makes an unholy mess and tidies it into her toybox again, but none of it will do. Something else is nagging at her. Something else demanding to be done.

She stands on the sheepskin rug and turns to the nursery window.

The curtains are already drawn, but by pulling a cord Esmé can draw them back. Hidden behind are the shutters that her father built to 'block out the night'. She unfastens the latch and lets them roll back. On the other side, the window is covered in thick black felt, glued down in every corner. What it might be like, to lift just a corner, to catch a glimpse of the night-time world . . .

Such things are forbidden. And yet . . . the stories Esmé loves – the ones her father takes such delight in spinning for her each night – aren't they full to bursting with courageous girls doing forbidden things?

'Esmé?'

It is her father's voice. When she turns, her face flushing a guilt-ridden red, she sees him standing there, across an ocean of all the books and toys he ever bought her. In his hands are a glass of milk, a bedtime biscuit, the threadbare cardigan she has been taking to bed with her since she was a babe.

She closes the shutter and goes to him. He has told her about the window before. She is not supposed to need telling twice. But her father's admonishment is all in his eyes; he is too weary to scold her, so together they go to the bed and settle down in the blankets.

Once upon a time . . .

Words to soothe even the most troubled of souls. Esmé knows her father has been tormented of late. It is whatever is happening out there in the Parisian night, taking its toll on the man she loves more than anyone else. But she snuggles close and lets his words wash over her, and now she is safe, where she belongs – and she believes he feels safe as well, safe from everything that exists beyond the nursery walls. That feeling of sanctuary in arms: if only you or I were innocent enough to feel it again.

After he is done, they make their ritual of goodnights, kisses and hugs.

'I love you, Esmé. Get some good sleep; your mama is coming in the morning.'

Goodnight is hardly goodnight; chances are, he'll wake up to find that she's crawled into his bed some time in the smallest hours.

After he has gone, Esmé turns in bed. The window is right there, right where she left it, and this presents the most tantalis- ing conundrum of all. For an age, she tries to think of other things. In the morning there will be school. Élodie, who lives in the apartment downstairs, is to receive a bichon frise for her birthday. But these things can hardly keep away the idea which battles back to the top of her mind.

Ideas: such terrible, untrustworthy things. She hardly knows it when she gets out of bed. She is thinking nothing as she steals back to the curtains, unlatches the shutter, and sets to work at the blackout again.

First one inch, then a second and a third. Soon there is enough space for Esmé to slide her head between the blackout and the window pane itself.

She looks out upon Paris: this wonderful city of lights.

Esmé and her father live on the fifth storey, with only the apartment eaves above their heads. On the other side of Rue Saint-Rustique, the rooftops are lower, so that Esmé can peer down upon their gables and the flat terraces in between.

Once, there was nothing to see here but roof slates and gutters. Now . . . fountains of colour erupt.

Tonight, the gutters are a shimmering meadow of silver and gold, a thousand tiny flowers with their faces lifted up to drink in the light of the stars. Vines, replete with glowing petals and bells, tumble from chimneystacks and drainage pipes. A single tree, heavy in leaf – and those leaves webbed with veins which capture the starlight itself – has grown up through the roof slates, and its strange flame-coloured fruits dangle in clumps from its branches. One of the vagabond people is collecting windfall, piling them high in a basket and carrying them across one of the rope bridges between the rooftops, off to the night market – on whichever patch of abandoned ground it is being held tonight.

Esmé gazes out. From the rooftops of Rue Saint-Rustique, all the way to the great basilica of the Sacré-Cœur, the night-time world is waking up. Were her father to find her now, there would be no stories for a week – but Esmé wouldn't care; there is enough

3

enchantment in the city at night to make her wonder if she'll need stories ever again. She likes the way the flowers turn to drink in the starlight; how, as the sun sets and the stars rise, each petal burns a different colour: incandescent emeralds, sapphires and diamond white. She likes watching the tiny finches as they flit from flower head to flower head, long beaks dipping to take in the nectar, and how their plumage flares first silver, then gold, depending on the flowers from which they drank.

Esmé can resist it no longer. She strains at the window latch until it opens. She should not do it (her father would be furious), but if she leans out of the window just so, she can take in a southern view of the city. She holds on tight.

On scattered rooftops, from here to the Seine and beyond: jungles of moonlight, iridescent gardens all drinking in the stars. Here and there are little columns of smoke; the vagrant peoples are stoking their rooftop cookfires tonight. From somewhere, she hears singing in a language she does not understand – but music is universal, and music like this will linger in her head for days.

Her gaze is drawn up and ever upwards, until at last her eyes land on what she has been desperate to see. Hold on to the window ledge with her; let us look that way too. The Tour Eiffel, that stalwart of the Parisian night, still stands sentry over the river, just as it has for one hundred years, but tonight the vines that grow around its lattice are in the full blossom of midnight. Each of their faces turn upwards to drink in the moonlight. Together they turn the tower into a radiant beacon, the city's single, shimmering crown.

All of this, she thinks, happening in *her* Paris. Why it frightens her father enough to put up blackout blinds, she will never know.

Foolish adults! Her pragmatic mother. Her practical father. Once upon a time, they told her that magic did not exist.

BOOK ONE

PARIS, NOT SO VERY LONG AGO

Settle down. Pull your covers tight. Look to the window, and out into night. Darkness has fallen, the foul are abroad – but out there lies a world that will soon be restored. So let me tell you the tales of when we were born, between sunset and morning, between nightfall and dawn. Let me speak of the star that once shone in the sky, of the kingdoms of moonlight, the flowers-by-night. Let us travel together, through time's lonely mist, to that long ago age where enchantment exists.

Settle down. Pull your covers tight. Look to the window, and out into night ...

Opening lines of the Nocturne, era unknown

1

****

THE MIDNIGHT GIRL

It is said that you cannot truly know a city until you walk its streets after dark, but Isabelle had been tramping the streets of Paris every night for six long months, and still she found herself perplexed at its every corner.

Too often, it was the Métro that tricked her. The Métro could turn a country girl around, disgorging her in some corner of Paris where the sights were familiar but the smells and sounds all wrong. Tonight she emerged on the Rue des Martyrs and, taking in the vast, empty sky above, knew that she had somehow got twisted around. Sitting in the carriage, lost in a melody, hands straining at the list in her hands – that endless, regurgitating list of every place she meant to visit – she'd lingered a stop too long, scrambled off a stop too early, taken the bad advice of the guard at the gate. Now, as she heaved her harp up the stairs and onto the boulevard, the darkness was drawing in.

By the time she'd picked her way to La Cave de Denis, the music had already started. Most of the night's revellers had been bound for Le Bus Palladium – she'd already crossed *that* place off her list – but here couples still queued at the cellar door. Isabelle, who was no inveterate queue-jumper, felt a rush of shame as she hoisted her harp to the head of the queue and begged the door-man to let her in.

'You'll have missed your spot.'

Isabelle knew it. 'But I have to try …'

The doorman shrugged, and Isabelle staggered down the narrow stair.

She'd seen a dozen places like La Cave de Denis. Paris, she had discovered, was a world replete with cellars and catacombs and repurposed sewers: the dead arteries of the city, where its people came to play. La Cave de Denis was made up of a dozen tributaries, lined with cubbyholes where couples drank cocktails, and at the end of each a bulbous stone cellar with a stage lit up in lights. At the various confluxes between the passageways, Isabelle could hear the music of some accordionist mingling with the chorus of lutes coming from one of the other stages; a bluesy stomp on the piano echoed out to touch the edges of some fiddler's jig.

At the heart of the warren, she found its overseer. Denis was not his name, just the honorary title bestowed upon whoever had inherited the bar since it first opened. This particular Denis was the kind of man, Isabelle thought, who naturally gravitated towards cellars. His eyes were altogether too small, even magnified as they were behind thick spectacles – and these, together with his inconspicuous ears, gave him the appearance of a mole. Even his velvety hair and oversized hands afforded him the look of something subterranean.

'I traded your spot,' he said, nose crinkling up like the rodent from which he was surely descended, 'for a man who plays spoons. Spoons! He's brought his own washboard.' Kneading his hands on his apron, he admired the case at Isabelle's side. 'I'd rather have you playing your harp. I liked your recordings. It reminded me of when I used to come here myself. They had a harpist here during the war. Just called himself "Le Harpiste", like there was only one in the whole of Paris! You've got to admire arrogance like that.'

Denis took a stride along one of the passageways, as if to lead Isabelle on. But Isabelle herself remained.

'Please, before we go ...'

In the pocket of her green woollen coat, alongside the crumpled list, there lay a birthday card. She produced it now, its corners worn with the passing years. On its front was a picture of a frog princess, great jewels on her webbed fingers – but Isabelle opened it to reveal the photograph that had been hidden inside.

'His name is Hector. He would be ... forty-five years old.'

'Strange,' grinned Denis, 'he doesn't look a day more than twenty-three.'

'It's an old picture.' It always felt wrong when somebody else's fingers touched the face in the picture, with its wild blond curls – which perfectly matched her own – and big, luminous eyes. 'He'd be playing the mandolin, or ... the harp.'

Denis' eyes flashed between the picture and the case standing at Isabelle's side. 'You're the first harpist we've had in years, love.'

'He might have drifted through.'

Denis took off along the passage. 'I can look in the office for you. See if we booked a man named Hector ... but I'd just be playing along, girl. Everything that happens in these cellars gets stored up here.' He tapped the side of his head. 'And I've never seen the man in my life.'

Isabelle paused, letting Denis drift on. Later, she would take out her list and cross off yet another name. 'La Cave de Denis'. But her heart didn't sink – not yet. There were still a thousand bars to go.

The stage in La Cave's smallest chamber barely had space for Isabelle to arrange her stool and harp. She'd played to smaller audiences, but there was something about the intimacy of a place like this that unnerved her. Perhaps it was the way that the music, with nowhere to go, was bound to get caught in the confines of the narrow space, smothering her where she sat. Or perhaps it was only the way that the spoon player – who had been summarily dismissed from stage – remained in the room, eyeing her with malevolence from the corner by the bar.

Without introduction, she closed her eyes and began.

You had to let your fingers do the work. Where your fingers ventured, the heart and soul were bound to follow. The whole world existed in those opening notes. Plucking the first string, rolling her wrist so that the melody began to take shape; in this way, her fingers charted all the years of her life, from the first lesson she'd taken, sitting at her father's knee, to the day she'd come back to Paris, hoping to find him.

The melody beat its wings and prepared to take flight.

She dared to open her eyes – but, as she did so, her fingers lost their way. One poorly plucked string was all it took to obliterate the *feeling* of the song. She slowed down, retreated to the oasis she kept inside her, ventured out to find the melody again.

There it was. She dove towards it, fingers working like a spider spinning silk. But every time she thought she'd snagged it, it tore away from her. It was taunting her. It was … tempting her. Leading her into the outer dark.

Her fingers snatched for it one last time. She rolled her wrists, thinking that all the years she'd sat caressing these strings would ripple out, through her fingers, and bind her back to the song, but it was already too late. The melody dived away from her. Her fingers clawed at discordant strings. She stuttered. She stopped. She looked around.

The room was peering at her, with that curious cocktail of pity and horror with which she was becoming so familiar.

In the corner, the spoon player smiled.

'Well, naturally, I can't pay you. You understand that.'

Isabelle stood at the bar where all the many passages of La Cave de Denis conjoined, while Denis polished glasses.

'It just wouldn't do. I'd have performers turning up, playing half a song, taking their packet and going off to another job. They'd be running a racket all around the Place Pigalle. Imagine, you could play eight halls in one night, and scarcely a song between them ...'

Isabelle's shame was a palpable thing. It lit up the hidden corners of her. 'I can't explain it. Sometimes, my fingers ...'

If it had happened only once, perhaps she might have forgiven herself. But five, six, seven times ... that terrible litany kept replaying in her mind. First, at the Chapel of Sainte-Ursule, where the students from the Sorbonne had tried valiantly to hide their smirks; then, at the riverside restaurant beneath Notre-Dame, where the tourists stared fixedly at their dinner. Now, she felt both Denis' pity and his scorn, and she wasn't sure which was worse.

'I'll make it up to you. Denis, I'm already late on my rent ...'

Denis' round shoulders rolled in an enormous, affected shrug. Strange, how a gesture so outwardly cuddly could feel like a dagger in the side.

'Well, there is *something* you could do.'

It wasn't the first time Isabelle had heard those words (men in Paris were the same as men the world over), but Denis was not standing there with that expectant look in his eyes. Isabelle's eyes were drawn down; until this moment, she hadn't noticed the platinum wedding band on his ring finger, his hand so doughy it almost swallowed it up.

'This way,' he said, and led her through a small door behind the bar.

In a cramped office, where racks of old wine gathered dust, there sat a girl. Isabelle took in her long hair, matted all the way into the small of her back. Her complexion was dark, her eyes unusually large. It took a moment for Isabelle to realise that this was because of the way her skin had receded; evidently, the girl hadn't eaten properly in days. She sat with her hands folded in her lap, as coiled as a spring.

'She's been sneaking into our kitchen, ferreting in the bins out back. Been at it for days, but she pushed her luck tonight. Well, a little mite like this, she ought to be ashamed. We called the gendarmes, of course, but – can you credit it – they haven't turned up. Seems they've better things to do than looking after some runaway who can't even speak a word of French. If they haven't come to cart her off by closing, I'll have to put her back on the streets. And, well, you can imagine how ...'

Isabelle shot him a look so pointed that it pierced every one of Denis' rolls of blubber.

'Of course, if you wanted to get paid for tonight, *you* might do me the service. I'm always happy to pay for problems solved.' He lifted his spectacles to polish them, revealing minuscule black eyes. 'Well, it's yours if you want it. There's a station not five hundred yards from here. You just have to cross the Place Pigalle.'

Isabelle crouched at the girl's side. She could see, in the minute tremors that worked up and down her body, how focused she was on holding herself still. There was something practised in it, as if going unnoticed was a talent hard won.

'You rotten ... ' She checked herself, and looked back at Denis – who was already extending an envelope with her evening's pay in his hand. 'She's frightened. She's alone. She's ... '

'Your problem now.'

Denis foisted the envelope upon her. The fool, Isabelle thought; she'd have done this job for free.

*

Pancakes.

You couldn't go wrong with pancakes.

By the way the girl was devouring them, Isabelle counted them the very last pancakes on Earth. Across the canteen table, she watched with mounting incredulity as the girl found yet more corners of her mouth in which to cram the thick, fluffy batter, the whipped cream and honey. Once she was done, she painted a mahogany smile across her face with a mug of steaming malt chocolate, and then – at Isabelle's request – set about devouring the last of Isabelle's own hot griddled toast. Even then, her eyes searched out for more – so Isabelle took up the envelope Denis had given her and placed another order at the bar.

The Café Infini, after midnight, was not a place she ought to have brought a young girl. Its windows reflected the lights of the sex shop across the Boulevard de Clichy, and the air was thick with a sweet, botanical haze. Yet, no sooner had they emerged from La Cave de Denis, the rain had started falling, driving both Isabelle and the girl, and all the night's revellers, off the streets. Now, they lounged in the café's booths, partygoers side by side with the shift workers and down-and-outs who ordinarily haunted the Infini after hours. Around them, voices stirred in languages Isabelle did not understand. Somebody was bawling in the corner. Somebody else had fallen asleep. The night, in all its ordinary idiosyncrasies, rolled on.

'You're going to have to help me ... somehow,' Isabelle said, presenting another stack of pancakes. Above the girl's head, Isabelle caught her own eyes looking back at her from the window, her face distorted by the downpour. Her hair, tangled and blond, had been brought alive by the rain – the lion's mane, her mother used to call it – but in her eyes her weariness showed. She had (or so her mother said) her father's eyes: empty and blue. Tonight, her mascara had run. She'd always been a dirty child: her hair longer and thicker, more striking, than any of the other girls, but her body covered in faded yellow bruises from all the trees she'd climbed. She'd grown up long and lean, all angles and points; it was only when the music started flowing through her that she'd felt as if she had any elegance at all. Now, she looked at the harp, occupying the space next to the girl, with something approaching disdain. Twenty-three years old, and elegance already a thing of the past. This gulf that was opening up between them, it was like a war between sisters.

'We'll have to find a way. I'm going to need to know ... something. It's not like I can take you home.'

Home. The word echoed with so many different meanings. It was the attic apartment by the cemetery gates, right here in Paris. It was the place, far away, where the mountains met the sea. It was the birthday card folded up in her coat pocket, and the man whose fingers had left their inky prints as he signed his name.

'I'm Isabelle,' she said. 'Is – a – belle.'

The girl looked up, face still smeared in chocolate sauce. Her eyes were diametrically opposed to Isabelle's: deep and dark.

'Arina,' the girl said.

'Arina, I'm not going to take you to the gendarmes. I couldn't. But ...' How to say it, without words? How to communicate anything at all? There was only one way Isabelle knew of transcending all language, but music could not ask a question as specific as this; all music could do was plumb a feeling. Besides, her fingers had betrayed her once already. She dared not ask them again. 'Denis said you've been rooting in La Cave's trash cans for nights on end. So you must be back and forth. You must ... know. Arina, where have you been sleeping?'

She had to have people. A girl like this was not raised on the streets of Paris. She had to come here from somewhere, and surely that meant she had to be brought. So, Isabelle thought, she was ... separated from them. She'd strayed and got lost. There were enough beggar girls on the Métro. Their families sent them out, caps in hand, and it was easy to see how a scared girl might get herself turned around. You did not have to be ten years old for the city to play you false; Isabelle, who had grown up in the mountains and open air, was played false almost every night.

'Arina, wait here.'

The girl's ebony eyes stayed on her as she returned to the counter, bickered with a man turning skewers of chicken over a grill, and returned with pencil and paper.

'You need to show me.' And Isabelle herself began to draw, if only to show the girl what to do. Here was the mountainous sky-line that she'd looked out on each morning as a girl; here the little house on the outskirts of Saint-André, to which her mother had whisked her off in those weeks after her father left. Here was the crab apple tree at the bottom of the garden, from whose boughs Isabelle had tumbled too many times; and here were two stick figures: Isabelle and her mother. 'Home,' she said – and, turning the page, pleaded with Arina to take the pencil in her hand.

The girl's eyes focused, and somehow Isabelle knew that she understood. Perhaps she had fragments of French after all; or perhaps it was only the way the stick figures had been holding stick hands.

The girl worked with a confidence Isabelle had not expected. On the page, shapes took form. But these were not buildings. This was no mountain range, nor a range of tenements marking some suburb in the city's outermost reaches. These were ... stars. A dozen stars, rendered with the wobbly precision of a child's hand, and hanging between them a crescent moon.

The girl was finished. Proudly, she presented the page to Isabelle.

It was the sky at night; the starry vaults of the heavens – and beneath them, nothing at all.

Quickly, the girl whipped back the page. Between the stars, she scribbled stick boys and girls, and a figure whom Isabelle took for a grandmother, carrying her cane.

'This is where you live?'

The girl's eyes were wide and imploring, but to Isabelle it was hopeless.

'You come from ... the night.'

A row was erupting in some other corner of the Infini, trays clattering as one of the night workers rose to his feet in an explosion of invective. Isabelle hardened. Outside, the rain was growing wilder – but, with its every booth overflowing, the Café Infini was no real sanctuary tonight.

'There has to be something else. Look ...' Reaching over the table, she delved into the pocket of the coat and produced a torn Métro stub. 'Which station? Arina, you must have ridden the ...'

The girl was paying no attention, for another thought had occurred to her. The pencil was back in her fist, and Isabelle watched her draw a building with three great domes sitting under the stencilled stars.

There it was.

Isabelle needed nothing further. She'd walked beneath this basilica herself. She'd played her harp in its grounds at summer's end, while children squabbled over an old carousel. Back then her fingers hadn't seized up. The music had soared.

'And you can find your way from here?'

The girl stared blankly at her, but Isabelle was already on her feet. Just as well – for the raised voices behind them were rapidly turning into something more fierce. In the rain-streaked mirror of the window, she saw somebody's fist fly.

Isabelle had the girl's hand in her own. Soon they were at the open door of the Café Infini, the rain rampaging along the boulevard beyond.

One coat between them, thought Isabelle as they stepped out into the squall.

She prayed it was not far.

*

Alone among the buildings north of the boulevard, the Sacré-Cœur did not cower from the storm.

By the time they reached the rails beneath the basilica, Isabelle was no longer leading the girl; now, the girl was leading her. Flashes of memory seemed to be steering her. She paused at the junction of each road, squinting at the sky as if she might discern some clue in the churning cloud, and then moved on. Past the grounds of the basilica they came, past the old carousel sitting empty in the rain, past torn hoardings strung up above, advertising nothing.

Some way east of the Sacré-Cœur, the girl turned north. She had, Isabelle decided, scented home. For some time, they followed a broadening thoroughfare, the tenement blocks squatting on either side like ugly, uprooted teeth. Then, past a construction site where the skeleton of some new block arose, the girl picked a new route, beckoning Isabelle to follow.

How many hours since she had struggled onto stage at La Cave de Denis? She could feel the rain in her boots turning the flesh around her ankles to dough. Still cocooned in her coat, the girl remained dry, but Isabelle herself was so drenched that she no longer noticed the rain.

The further they came, the louder the sounds of the freight trains shunting along the railway tracks, somewhere to the east. The hum of engines in a car park, somewhere beyond the ring of buildings they approached, spoke of some vast bus depot, its fleet idling and ready to course out into the night.

At last, the avenue came to its end. The tenements they approached, half obscured by the barriers of a temporary roadworks, were arranged in a horseshoe around an empty, grey expanse, where a cigarette store had boards in its window and the lights of an all-night pharmacy looked to have been extinguished for years. Here the girl stopped.

'This is home?'

But the girl, knowing no words, only beckoned her on.

At least, through a side door – smashed off its hinges by some reprobate in weeks gone by – the stairwell was dry. It was dark in here. The bottom of the stairwell was a fenland of old newspapers turned to mulch. The scat of the tower block's rodents gathered in seams wherever wall met wall.

The girl pointed up, so Isabelle followed her up.

Soon, the stairwell echoed with their footfall. Past the second storey, Isabelle was able to gaze up and further up. If the thought struck her that she was being lured into some trap – Arina sent out into the world as bait – her fears were allayed by the eagerness on the girl's face, the way it widened in joy upon seeing the lights on the tower block's uppermost storey. Twisted garlands of silver and gold, it took Isabelle some time to realise that they came from fairy lights twisted around a bannister rail like vines.

There was but one apartment here, with cleaning cupboards locked shut on either side, and a further doorway leading – onward and upward – to the roof.

'Go on, Arina.' Isabelle had paused to catch her breath at the top of the stair, lifting the harp from her shoulder. Now she watched the girl go to the door. There was a new nervousness in her, as if she knew she'd been gone too long, but it did not prevent her from opening the apartment.

Moments later, a cascade of hands were reaching out, drawing her in. What began as a single cry of relief erupted into a joyous chorus – all of it in a language Isabelle did not understand.

Through the door, Isabelle saw Arina buried in arms. Then, as the crowd of figures jostling her drew back, the girl was left in the arms of one figure alone. By the look of her, she was Arina's grandmother, or great-grandmother – or perhaps she belonged to some generation even further back. Barely as big as the child, she wore a patchwork shawl, in which her tiny frame seemed little more than a collection of sticks, and her head craned forward on its crooked neck. Tight white curls made a waterfall around her face, disguising deep crevices and lines.

It was the woman who saw Isabelle first. She had one paper-thin hand cupped around Arina's face, and her tiny eyes were glistening with tears – so, when they revolved to see the stranger standing in the doorway, perhaps she thought she was seeing a mirage. But soon Arina was beckoning for Isabelle to cross the threshold – and Isabelle found herself drawn in.

It was warm in here, though perhaps that was only because of the presence of so many bodies. As she carried the harp through, Isabelle counted two girls scarcely older than Arina, two others older still, and in the corner a woman nearing forty, with a squalling toddler in her lap. There were chairs and beds, right here in the same room, and in the air reefs of both steam and smoke. The apartment was smaller than it had any right to be, an overlooked corner of the tower block in which bedrooms, kitchen and study had been crammed, with two side doors into a cramped bathroom and walk-in wardrobe, set deep into the building's eaves. In the main room, a single pot was still simmering on a stove. The smells of fish and shrimp were strong, so too the smells of salts and spice.

Arina was chuntering to her grandmother, and at once the diminutive woman tottered forward to take Isabelle's hand. Soon the old woman's papery lips were being pressed against her palm. Some of the other children, sensing humiliation, rushed forward as if to prise her away – but the grandmother's gratitude was stronger than their indignation. Clinging to Isabelle, she cleared a space at a small table – cluttered with trinkets, old crockery, bobbins and needles and thread – and barked out for one of the other girls to bring a bowl from the stove. Soon, Isabelle was presented with a steaming broth.

Arina and her grandmother both mimed for Isabelle to begin eating.

'I'm Isabelle,' she said. The smells rising up to envelop her were intoxicating. 'Does anyone speak ...'

'No French,' one of the older girls said. The only one who seemed undisturbed by their guest, she had retired to one of the beds on the edges of the room and lay down, as if to sleep. 'Levon only one speak good French.'

Isabelle's eyes darted around the room. The toddler was latched to its mother's breast, so it cried no more, but there was certainly no man, nor boy, named Levon here.

Nervously, Arina guided Isabelle's hand to the spoon at her side.

There was a thing Isabelle's mother told her, on the day she took the night train to Paris. Never rely, she had said, on the kindness of strangers. She'd hated those words then, and she hated them now. It was the kindness of loved ones you couldn't rely on; strangers were full of the stuff.

She'd done them a service, hadn't she? Why not accept a service from them?

So she tucked in.

A half-cooked sausage from a street vendor would have brought Isabelle's empty stomach back to life; this dish touched places of her she hadn't even known were hungry. The taste was of warm salt and smoke, of ginger and earth. The fish, which melted the moment it touched her tongue, was only plaice, but the broth in which it sat was like silk; it seemed to spread out into her, soothing her from fingers to toes. With a dozen eyes on her, she finished the bowl; another was there within seconds.

Arina and one of the younger girls had left the table. Now, they sat cross-legged on the floor, inspecting the harp in its case. Isabelle thought: I could play it now. It wouldn't matter, then, that they have so little French. Wherever they come from – whatever they're doing here, all eight of them in this apartment scarcely big enough for two – wouldn't matter. They'd understand music. All of them would.

If the thought of returning to the broth was enticing, it was eclipsed, all of a sudden, by the thought of what her fingers could do. Hang La Cave de Denis. The music hadn't been with her, then, but she felt certain it was with her now. 'Wait,' she said, for Arina and one of the other girls had started unfastening the buckles on the case, the fabric sloughing down around the harp like a bath gown being unfurled. 'Let me …'

But she was not yet on her feet when the apartment door burst open, and every pair of eyes revolved to see a young man – his shirtsleeves sodden, his wild hair heavy with rain – stagger into the room.

2

. . . .

HALF A WORLD AWAY

He was still standing in the doorway, shaking the rain from his coiled black curls – like a dog just out of a river – when the children threw themselves at him, enveloping him in arms. To Isabelle, it seemed like a mighty giant being borne down – though, in truth, the new arrival was only a little older than she was, with a chubby face and rounded shoulders, and something almost puppyish about his look. The others scrabbled to cling on to him, and he scrabbled to hold himself aloft.

'Levon!'

In everything that followed, it was the only word Isabelle understood. The rest was a cacophony with so many voices that she doubted she would have heard a thing, even had she known what language this was. She stared dumbly, aware of the grandmother in one corner of her vision and the mother with her babe in arms in the other.

Of the children, only Arina had remained behind. She was still standing by Isabelle's harp when the man named Levon fought his way out and, with rainwater still streaming into his eyes, looked down at her. Isabelle saw the way Arina drew into herself, uncertain where to look. Moments later, as the rest of the apartment watched, Levon dropped to his knees and clutched her fiercely by the shoulders. In that moment, Isabelle wasn't sure whether it was anger or relief that was sputtering out of him, as heavy as artillery. Then he heaved the poor girl with love against his chest – and released her only when she started squealing, freshly sodden by the rain on Levon's clothes.

Arina's grandmother had unearthed a towel from one of the piles of old laundry on the bed. She set about tousling Levon's hair dry, and Levon – though resisting the fuss at first – seemed resigned to letting her. Arina had brought him a fresh checked shirt and was helping lever his feet out of his boots when Isabelle became aware they were speaking about her. Levon's eyes, as black as his hair, kept landing on her, unable to comprehend this oddity in their room.

Finally, the grandmother left his side, hurrying to the stove to serve up another dish from the pot.

'I believe we owe you our thanks,' the man named Levon said, 'but you really mustn't be here.'

The French was heavily accented, but it was still the language Isabelle knew. Sounds that were supposed to be long were too short; sounds that should have been clipped went on and on. Somebody had put the French language through a press and this had come out the other side.

The grandmother barked at Levon from across the room; Levon fired back in their own language, then turned on Isabelle once more. His fieriness, she thought, was at odds with the way he looked. It was like being admonished by a teddy bear sitting up on a nursery shelf.

'You'll have to leave. And speak nothing of tonight, not to a soul.'

Isabelle could hear a fresh wave of rain moving against the side of the building. 'Leave?'

Levon had the harp in his arms and was presenting it as if it was her reward for a job well done, when voices started assailing him from all sides. Arina, straining on his arm, was evidently pleading; his grandmother, remonstrating with a single outstretched finger.

The baby, dissatisfied with its milk, had set up crying again – and, in the middle of it all, Levon stood like a lighthouse in a storm.

'What is it?'

The newcomer's face kept ghosting from indignation to confusion, then back again.

'She wants to clean your clothes.'

Isabelle's face creased. 'Excuse me?'

'My grandmother,' Levon said, with mounting despair, 'she's saying you can't possibly go back out in dirty clothes. She wants to ... clean them.' At first, it had seemed his anger was directed at her; now it spiralled outwards, without any direction at all. He fired off a volley of words at his grandmother, but none of them made her relent. 'She's going to get you spares.'

Isabelle rose to her heels. The thought of disrobing, in front of this family of strangers, chilled her more than the rainwater still soaking her clothes.

Levon's grandmother was a whirlwind of issuing orders, and soon Arina and the other girls were ferreting in the bags between beds, an ornate chest of drawers, the second room where – or so Isabelle presumed – the mother and child must have slept.

Levon continued, 'She says there's a hole in your coat. She can fix it for you.'

'But it doesn't need ...'

'She's seen it,' he said, with an air of defeat. 'You may as well give in. Here, Arina's found you a ...' Levon stopped. 'What is it?' Arina had reappeared at Isabelle's side, and in her hands was a dress with an elaborate floral design. 'By God, it's a ... nursing gown. My aunt wore it when she was with child.' He hung his head, and for the second time this evening had the appearance of a dog shaking itself dry. 'You'll have to put it on. I'll get you out of here, but ... Look.' He gestured for her to come out from behind the table and, clearing a way through his chattering family, guided her to the back door. 'There's a lock on the inside. Just ...' His eyes were like saucers, and they pleaded with her.

I ought to be afraid, thought Isabelle. An hour of forced marching into parts of Paris I don't know, all these strangers staring at me – and now being bustled into a locked back room. I ought to be in tatters.

But it was Levon, who'd walked into the apartment so full of fury and mellowed under the barrage of his family, who seemed in tatters now. 'Please,' he whispered, though the word came out half mangled. All of those intricate sentences, and he managed to botch something as simple as 'please'.

Isabelle stepped backwards through the door, and watched Levon's face recede as he left her in the dark.

She reached out and slid the bolt.

It was a small room, dominated by the single bed and crib that ran alongside it. Aside from that, there was only the small dresser that stood beneath the window, where ragged blinds obscured the rolling rooftops and the freight yard underneath.

Though there was no bulb in the light fitting, the room was not impenetrably dark. What she thought, at first, was a lamp sitting on the window ledge revealed itself, instead, to be a terracotta pot, and inside it an outburst of waxy leaves. Cradled by those leaves was the head of a single flower. It took her a moment to understand that the flower itself was the source of the light in the room: its petals were radiating a soft silver glow. She lifted the hanging bell with a finger. The flower head was almost translucent, but the veins that made a web across each petal were like pale silver filaments.

Voices flurried up on the other side of the door, startling Isabelle.

They were arguing, she thought.

What were they arguing about?

Instinct drove Isabelle to lift the ragged window blinds, revealing more of the rain-lashed freight yard below. There was, she realised now, a rickety fire escape clinging to the edge of the building. But the thought that she might heave herself onto it and disappear into the darkness beneath was only fleeting. She hadn't been afraid when she brought Arina here. She wouldn't be afraid now. What was there to be afraid of in seaweed wrapped around fish, and strangers insisting on doing your darning? And, besides, wasn't it Levon himself who was afraid?

Isabelle had always been a practical girl. Too practical to chase pipe dreams in Paris, her mother had once said. So there was nothing else for it now, she decided, but to get on with the task at hand.

The dress was altogether too large, like a bedsheet in which somebody had hacked holes for arms, but at least it was dry. Yet, when she stepped into it, she fancied she'd have been better off in her wet things. Dresses had never flattered her, but this was a calamity: she looked halfway between some apparition and a wedding cake left out in the rain. The kindness of strangers, she thought, allowing herself a smile – sometimes, it wasn't worth a thing.

Through the door, voices continued to barrack Levon, so Isabelle slumped onto the bed. La Cave de Denis seemed, suddenly, such a long time ago.

There were books here. A dictionary of the French language, its spine broken and its corners disintegrating, sat at the summit of a pile of picture books with half-a-cent stickers declaring the name of whichever charity shop they'd been rescued from. Idly she reached for the first one and, only as she did so, did she notice another book, tucked behind the rest like it was someone's treasured possession.

This book was quite unlike the others. By its worn corners she took it to be as well travelled as the *dictionnaire* – but where that was bound in battered cloth and card, this was bound in hard leather, and its yellowing pages were thick and textured. Inscribed across the leather were letters she had never seen, stitched in gold leaf. A single star was embroidered beneath. To Isabelle, there was something wrong about that star; it was only as she traced it with her finger that she realised it was asymmetrical, like a child's lopsided drawing. She had never seen seven points on a star.

Outside the door, the voices had died down. She heard Levon heave a great sigh; then, for a time, there was silence.

She opened the book, but inside were yet more letters she had no hope of understanding. There were languages in the world that relied on grunts and whistles; there were languages written backwards, languages inscribed from bottom to top, languages never written down at all. This, it seemed, was a language of spirals, interlocking and dividing in uncounted ways. There were words here – she understood that much – but no words she had any hope of comprehending. At least, she discovered as she turned onward, there were pictures. These too were textured – some of them paintings in oil that rose in miniature landscapes from the paper. In the first, the same seven-pointed star hung in the sky, at the heart of some foreign constellation. In the second: a boy at his bedroom window, gazing up at a sky blanketed in stars. In the third, the same boy was setting off into a forest glade, his trail illuminated by steep banks of luminescent flowers.

Isabelle's eyes lifted to the dim glow of the flower on the ledge. Then she froze.

Footsteps were approaching.

She could look no further, for as she fingered the next page, where a group of fishermen were hauling off beneath a nocturnal sky, there came a knock at the door.

Isabelle fumbled the book back onto the bedside and slid back the bolt in the door. Through a crack, she saw Levon's face looming. He was not, she decided, altogether unhandsome – although he would have made a prettier picture if his eyes hadn't been glaring, trying to impart some message for which words would not suffice.

'Are you ready?'

Ready for what, she wondered. Ready, certainly, for her own bed. Ready, perhaps, to waste every cent she'd earned tonight paying for a taxicab back through the rain-streaked night.

When Levon opened his hands, Isabelle passed him a bundle of her wet clothes. After beating a retreat for a few short seconds, he returned with her green woollen coat. 'She's stitched it,' he announced – but Isabelle remained paralysed in the room. 'Please,' he whispered, with mounting urgency, 'she'll be ... upset.'

Isabelle thought of the way she looked in the nursing gown and thought: I'm *already* upset. But she took the coat all the same. At least it covered up most of the monstrosity.

When she followed him back through the door, the rest of the family were watching. A dozen eyes tracked her across the room. Arina and one of the other girls crouched by the harp, plucking tentatively at its strings.

By now, Levon was at the apartment door, stealing out onto the landing. Isabelle's eyes darted around. The grandmother stood by the stovetop. She smiled benignly, as if imploring her to follow.

'But ... my clothes. My harp.'

Levon called back, 'We're coming back. Five minutes, I promise. No more ...'

It was a horrible feeling, to be compelled – but Levon had gone through the door, and the old woman's smile propelled her after.

At the top of the stairwell, with footsteps echoing from several storeys below, Levon stopped. 'Look, here's how it is: I'm getting you out of here. But, first, my grandmother wants to give you a present. Something to say thank you.' If Isabelle had thought he was going to lead her back down through the block, she was wrong. He turned and put his shoulder against another door, revealing a dank staircase leading above. 'You shouldn't be here. It's one of my rules. I'm meant to be keeping them safe. But maybe since you were good enough not to take her to the gendarmes, maybe since you filled her full of all those pancakes, maybe that means you can ... forget all about us. My sister Arina, she was ...'

'Hungry,' interjected Isabelle.

'They're not supposed to be going out begging.' As he ploughed up the stairs, his hands bunched into fists. 'I'll make it work, that's what I tell them. I'll find ways. They haven't starved yet, have they? But no, they want to go out there, when they can't even speak ...' He stopped, because some other thought had distracted him. 'We're not beggars. Maybe we had to beg and steal and borrow to get here, but that isn't the same thing.'

At the top of the stairs, he forced open another door, and Isabelle felt the chill of the night reaching down to take her in its fist. She could feel the frenzy of wind and rain playing out behind him, clouds shifting across the Paris sky.

By the time she too emerged onto the rooftop, Levon had stalked ahead, wending his way between two air vents and past a concrete sarcophagus she took for a water tank. Bits of old scaffolding littered the floor; she picked her way across them, following in Levon's wake. The wind was wild up here, and perhaps that was the reason the rain came in such sudden gusts, with lulls in between. She held herself tightly. The rooftops of Paris stretched to the north, the south, the east, the west – but Isabelle had eyes only for the strange vista opening up in front of her.

The great horseshoe of the building was crowned in outgrowths of scaffolding, an outcrop of cables with slumped satellite dishes sitting on top, and storage crates abandoned by workmen.

All of it was covered in green.

The rain sluiced sideways into Isabelle as she followed Levon into the lee of the scaffolding. Green vines had erupted from cracks in the apartment roof and snaked their way up the lattice. Beyond that, bulrushes grew in an ocean of undulating green around a succession of storage crates. An expanse of rainwater was choked on its peripheries by pond weed, growing so deep that there seemed a veritable lake, right here on the apartment roof. And on the shore of that lake, a tree with a head of waxy leaves was clawing skyward; its roots disappeared into the apartment roof – while, underneath its boughs, terracotta pots, in various different shapes and sizes, spilled yet more flurries of green.

Isabelle turned on the spot.

'What is this place?'

'It's my grandmother's garden. She shouldn't be coming up here, but you've already seen: she isn't a woman who likes to be told. She's been coming up here ever since we reached Paris, and that's six months. If the superintendent were to know ... Well, any reason to get rid of us, and we'd be gone. The block's half empty, damned to demolition, but he'd get rid of us all the same. Nine of us in rooms meant for two, and not one of us with papers. Well, you can't get papers for a country that doesn't exist any more, can you? The superintendent, he could go to prison for that. It's only my weekly "offering" that keeps him from calling the gendarmes himself. I can scarcely keep up with that as it is – not if I'm going to feed them all too. And tonight ...' His frustration boiled over. Now he was on his knees, fingering the ragged weeds that grew out of one of the gutters. When these, seemingly, did not suffice, he moved along to where a succession of terracotta pots were overflowing with the same rampant green. 'I took a shift in the rail yards. Trek a few miles up the line and they'll take who they can get. But when Arina went missing, I had to go searching for her instead ...' Levon opened his hands, revealing them empty. 'Hang it. I'll find another way. It isn't the first time.'

Isabelle was still trying to believe what she was seeing, but Levon's words cut into her. She found her hand dropping to her coat pocket. Here lay the envelope Denis had given her, and what money she hadn't handed over at the Café Infini.

When Levon saw what she was suggesting, his big eyes narrowed. 'My grandmother wanted to make you a gift,' he said earthily, 'not take your charity. You've already done us a service. In fact,' and here his voice rose to a pitch, 'you took my sister for pancakes. You fed her for us. So ... I owe you. You'll just have to wait until I can make it right.'

'I didn't mean to offend,' said Isabelle. 'I'm—'

But Levon had already relented. 'I'm sorry. It's been a long ...' She thought he was going to say 'night', but it might easily have been 'year'. He bowed down, picked up one of the terracotta pots and handed it to Isabelle. 'Here, it's yours.'

She looked down. Buried amidst the foliage in the pot was the head of a single flower. It was only as she lifted it that she took it for the same kind of flower glimmering in the apartment downstairs. Its petals seemed to be waking up to the light. She could see their veins picked out like threads of silver.

'I haven't seen anything like it.'

'Oh, you wouldn't.' Levon's tone was almost dismissive. He tried to wheel her around, as if to make for the way back down. 'That's why she wants you to have it. A gift from the old country. Truth is, I'd barely seen a flower-by-night myself, not until we came here. They're vanishingly rare. When my grandmother thinks of the old country, she still thinks of what it was like when she was a girl – back when these things still grew here and there ...' His face crumpled in mock distaste. 'But a lot can happen in a hundred years. That world she thinks about, it's been gone since her own grandmother's day. Most of it's just stories, anyway. All those stories in that book of hers. Back when the People lived at night ...'

When the People lived at night. There was something so odd about the way he said it, as if he was disparaging some piece of history she did not know. 'Where *do* you come from, Levon? I asked your sister, but she only drew me a picture of ... moons and stars, and people – your family – gambolling between them.'

To Levon, it sounded familiar. 'It's a picture from my grand-mother's book. That Nocturne of hers. People up in the sky, like they're constellations. It's just more fairy stories – like flowers that follow you across half the world ...'

'Half the world?'

There was a story here, though perhaps he did not wish to tell it.

'My home is gone,' he said. 'Snuffed out, just like that. It's part of the Russias now. They just marched in and took it from us. We had to find somewhere, and here we are.' Dull and matter-of-fact: what a way to chronicle the history of a people. 'Everything my grandmother's been growing up here, she says it just followed her here, but that's nonsense talk. She must have been carrying stuff with her.' He rolled his eyes. 'Three thousand miles we came, eighteen months on the trail, and she had bulbs from her garden shed crammed in her pockets all along. I'd have strung her up, if I'd known. Off I was, foraging in hedgerows, rifling through trash cans, stealing from markets ... We might have roast them on the fire like chestnuts. It would have been something. But no – she won't admit to any of it. "They followed me, Levon. They made their own way, Levon, just like we did." I've tried telling her – life's not a fairy story. You'd think three thousand miles might have disabused her of that particular notion. But no – it's only made her ... *believe*. That's what she says all *this* is ...'

Levon opened his arms, as if to take in the entirety of the rooftop, the tussocks of weeds growing in the gutters, the blossoms that spilled from each pot, like some stately home gone to ruin. '... the power of belief: our new home, honouring the old. We brought bits of the old world with us, she says, lodged up in our heads and ... BOOM! Like the world just needs reminding how it used to be, and it ... remembers. Suddenly, there are flowers-by-night popping up all over the place. I told you,' he said, 'she's cracked. But anyone would be, after three thousand miles. I suppose I'm half cracked myself. So if she needs to tell all the old tales and plant these bulbs just to have a bit of the old country to cling on to, to build herself a memorial to what we lost, well, let her.' His face creased up. 'Unless the superintendent finds out she's clogging the gutters with all these weeds. Then we're done for. Sometimes, I come up here and uproot it all – but she only goes and plants it again. The way I see it, you've got to get on. The old country's gone. We're meant to be making it here.'

They didn't seem like weeds, not to Isabelle, but perhaps he had the right of it. Weeds were just strangers growing where they oughtn't. But that made Levon and his family weeds as well, and she was quite certain that wasn't true.

'I'm ranting. I'm sorry. You must think me a fool.' When Isabelle did not reply, Levon looked up at the parting cloud. 'Rain's letting up,' he said – and it was; across the rooftop, the weeds he hated were waking up to the light of the freshly revealed stars. Isabelle saw tiny stirrings of silver spilling out of each gutter. 'You should get going while you can. It's going to blow back over.' He saw her look of doubt and gestured at the sky in the east. 'It'll be a couple of hours before it's back. Trust me. Three thousand miles, and most of them by foot. I can read the weather much better than I can read French.'

Downstairs, Isabelle found her clothes quietly roasting over the grill. The floral dress, Levon explained, was a gift, to go along with the luminescent petals in her pot. She took the bundle of half-cooked clothes gratefully, and the wholehearted embrace of Levon's grandmother with slightly less grace. Arina's embrace was gentler, somehow.

Then, with the chorus of goodbyes – half-heard, misunderstood, in a language she did not understand – ringing in her ears, Isabelle followed Levon back out to the top of the stairwell. It was only now that she realised that what she'd taken as strings of fairy lights, twisted around the bannister rails, were actually vines in blossom, each of their flowers radiating the same silvery warmth as the pot in her hands.

Flowers-by-night, the boy had called them.

They say that lives turn on moments. We wake in the morning one person and, by midday, we're somebody else altogether; by fall of night, we've fallen in or out of love, broken hearts or had ours broken – or else taken the first step towards some private transformation only we will ever understand. Here in the stairwell, Isabelle's face was awash with the light of the flowers on the vine. She saw the way that same light framed Levon's face – half in shadow, half in silver – and was struck, suddenly, by the thought that, however far she'd come to find her father in Paris, others had come so much further. Half the world, he'd said, but something told her that was only half the story.

'I haven't said it. I've been brusque and rude. I kept that girl safe for three thousand miles, you see. It's my lasting shame that I didn't keep her safe tonight, that it had to be you. But I'm glad that it was.' Was Isabelle mistaken, or was he blushing – this boy who, only two hours ago, had put on his most fearsome face (it seemed so laughable now) and instructed her to leave? 'Thank you, Isabelle,' he said, 'from the bottom of my heart.'

By the time Isabelle went back to the night, the first Métros were starting to run. How small the city could seem, when you descended the stairs on one street corner and emerged, moments later, into a different quarter altogether; yet how vast the world when, like Arina's people, you had had to walk it.

Isabelle arose to a deserted boulevard and wended her way east, until she stood at the foot of her own apartment block. Six months had not, yet, made this place feel like home, but still she felt a sense of hands drawing her onward, willing her home to rest. It was, she understood, only exhaustion speaking. But there was something else moving in her too, something in the story Levon had told; of a home destroyed, a home that was desperate not to be forgotten.

She remembered, once, how *she* had had a home.

Isabelle's apartment was in the attic eaves. Inside, she set her harp in its place by the window and lifted the small terracotta pot from the bag she'd carried so carefully home.

The light of the flower had dulled. Perhaps it was the journey she'd taken it on, but now that she lifted it out of the bag it was not such a marvellous thing. Its petals were grey, its head drooped down, and to Isabelle it seemed no more remarkable than the multitude of weeds growing between the cracks of every sidewalk.

Yet, only moments after she turned out the light, she sensed a new radiance in the room. Her eyes were drawn, inexorably, to the terracotta pot, sitting on the window ledge where she'd left it. The change was almost imperceptible at first, but the spider's web of veins in each petal were slowly waking up, each thread becoming a faint luminescence that solidified and brightened. It was, she realised, as if the plant was responding to the darkness, calling out to the night. Isabelle came nearer, the better to see, and watched as the threads connected, as the luminescence spread across each petal. Now the flower was aglow. Its stalk seemed to stiffen as the silver light spread down into the earth.

Isabelle looked up, through the window. High above the cemetery, the sky was a chart of stars.

It would be like having a night light in the room, she decided. The thought brought her strange comfort; it had been twenty years since she'd had a night light, but the memory of that glowing rabbit which had once looked over her as she slept seemed unusually strong tonight. What a world it was, to contain such wonders.

The last thing she did, before she threw herself back onto the bed – so dog tired that even this thin, broken mattress felt like feathers – was to reach into her coat pocket for the list she'd secreted there. This was her rite: at the end of every failed evening, to scour out the name of the club she'd visited. The city was vast, but the city was not infinite. Somebody had to have heard of him.

And yet, when she reached into the pocket, she did not find the list she'd painstakingly researched and written all that time ago, nor the birthday card it had been slipped inside. The pocket was empty.

She thought of the girl, Arina, swallowed up in the coat as they'd made their way north.

She thought of her grandmother, taking to it with needle and thread.

She thought of the young man, Levon, the coat folded up in his hands as he stood at the bedroom door.

Then, for a time, she simply lay there, willing sleep to come.

And every time she opened her eyes, there was the flower: sitting on the window ledge, its face drinking in the glow of the stars.

3

* *

THE ORIGINS OF
ENCHANTMENT

Watch ...

You think you know Paris. You, who have made your own odysseys to the city, to walk hand in hand with your lover along the Seine. You, who have read your stories of the oddity at Notre-Dame, imagined the masked impresario making his home beneath the Opera House, or followed a desperate thief on his long road towards nobility. Yet the lives of cities change, just like the lives of people. No man or woman who has ever fallen in love would dare to suggest that the world remains the same, not even from morning to the fall of that same night. And the Paris you have clung on to for so long, it has been changing by degrees since you first set foot here. It is changing still.

So, now, set out:

Go past the Gare du Nord and follow the freight lines north, to that tower block where Isabelle brought her runaway girl. Soar above the tenements and see the tiny cauldrons of light on the rooftop, the hanging bells and splayed-out radials whose roots sink into the moss between the tiles.

Is this really the Paris you know?

Each of those flowers is shining from stigma to stem. Out of one of them emerges a fat bee, its furred body radiating light. Off it goes, off on its night flight, a tiny luminescent dot depositing pollen on the other rooftops around.

See how, soon, the other rooftops start shining as well? Rooftop to rooftop, enchantment spreading like the warning pyres of old.

Now tell me you know Paris.

No, neither you nor I know a thing.

*

'Dear Mother,' she wrote.

The proprietor of the Delicatessen Absolut did not ordinarily mind if Isabelle whiled her afternoons away at the table by the window. Sometimes, he brought her coffees and cakes she hadn't ordered, and this – Isabelle supposed – was because he once had a daughter of his own. Whenever she could, Isabelle slipped money into the jar on the counter – but today was not one of those days. What little she'd saved from La Cave de Denis was already gone. From now on, it would be hot buttered toast and past-their-best bananas for dinner each night. Her stomach was already growling in muted complaint.

The weekly missive she sent to her mother – who steadfastly refused to reinstall the phone she'd had removed when Isabelle's stepfather left – was refusing to be written. She'd already described in faltering words the way her fingers seized up at La Cave, but the thought of saying anything that really mattered seemed to dry all the ink in her pen. Sometimes she still longed to tell her mother what she was really doing in Paris – but her father was an empty hole at the heart of each letter, just as he'd been an empty hole at the heart of each birthday dinner, each Christmas morning, each bedtime since she'd been small. To speak of him now would be like invoking the ghost of someone long dead; you burned people out of your history by never speaking of them, and Isabelle hadn't heard her mother use the name 'Hector' since she was a girl.

So instead she did what she had never done:

'Mother,' she wrote, and rolled her eyes at the very idea of the words that came next. What a terrible bore she'd become – and how thrilled it would make her mother! 'I have met someone ...'

He'd been waiting for her three days later, when she was daring to think she might venture out onstage again.

There was an open spot at Le Palais Anglais, that little bistro sitting on the north bank of the river where the waters branched out around Notre-Dame. She'd seen this swindle before: five francs got you a spot on the stage, with a hundred doled out to whoever was crowned champion that night. Albert, who worked at the Absolut, said he'd lend her the entrance fee, but accepting money seemed so much more like charity than coffee and cake – and, besides, she could scrabble the spare change together herself. So, on the third night after shepherding Arina back through the storm, she appeared at the bistro doors, the harp over one shoulder, and trembled five francs into the hands of a disinterested maître d'.

Levon was already waiting inside.

At first, she wasn't sure it was him. A solitary figure was sitting at the counter, his big shoulders hunched over whatever drink he was nursing. Her fingers felt faint, somehow. Could fingers feel faint? Even gripping a pencil would be too much. How she was going to spin music with fingers like these, she did not know.

The figure looked up.

Now, there was no doubt it was Levon. Black curls fell around his round face. Wordlessly, he got to his feet, crossed the bistro floor and opened up the book over which he'd been hunched. Isabelle saw, now, that it was his weathered dictionnaire.

From its back pages he produced a yellowing envelope.

Isabelle took it in her hands, opened it up and saw the familiar child's scribble over the picture of the frog princess. Inside that, the picture of her father gazed out. A handwritten list, a hundred names long, slipped out and floated to the floor. It was Levon who caught it. He pressed it into her palm.

'It was in the apartment. When my bebia was stitching your coat ...' He shrugged, as if that alone finished the sentence.

'But ... how did you know?' She opened her arms around the bistro, as if this too finished the sentence.

Levon said, 'I went with Arina, back to the place she was thieving. They sent me to your apartment. The superintendent didn't want to know, but he sent me to a delicatessen, the Absolut. And then ...'

'So,' Isabelle said, with only a hint of reproach, 'you're stalking me.'

Levon's black eyes were blank. Then, moistening the tip of his thumb, he feverishly turned through the pages of his dictionary until he came to the section marked 'S'. A few pages later, his cheeks were burning red.

'I'm joking,' Isabelle said. She took the dictionary from him, flicked to 'J', and returned it with her finger pressed firmly to the page. 'J-O-K-I-N-G.'

Levon's cheeks burned; embarrassment at embarrassment was evidently the worst embarrassment of all. He turned back to where he'd been sitting, and the carrier bags of fresh produce – apples and potatoes, mountains of green leaves – that sat beneath his stool. 'I found a shift last night, so I've been on the forage for supplies. I have a few spare coins, if you want a drink ...'

He said it with a kind of forlorn hope, and this bewildered Isabelle more than anything else. How did a man who'd seen his old country burn, who'd shepherded his family across three thousand miles to a new beginning, get so embarrassed at asking a girl if she wanted a lemonade?

'I wouldn't want to waste your ...'

'Please, I can afford one more. Look –' he pointed at a near-empty glass '– I've still got most of mine.'

Isabelle rolled her eyes as, together, they went to the bar. 'There's nothing left!' she said, handing the barkeep back the empty glass. 'So ... we'll share.'

After they were seated, the single lemonade sitting between them and a disapproving barkeep glowering down, Levon dared to ask, 'Who is he?'

The face in the photograph was not so much older than they were now.

'His name is Hector.'

'Hector.'

'He's my father.'

Levon paused.

'It's been a while.'

'How long?' asked Levon. He turned the picture, which had been sitting on the counter between them, to face him. He hadn't noticed, until now, how it looked like her. They had the same wild, entangled manes of hair – but it was in the eyes that they were most alike, and to Levon that meant they were the same in soul as well.

'Seventeen years.'

'But that would mean—'

Isabelle, who had defended herself too often, was quick to cut in. 'I was six. But I remember.'

'He just ... left?'

There's never any 'just', thought Isabelle. That was the story her mother used to peddle: one evening he was there, and by morning he was gone. But what's true in a storybook isn't true for real life. What's good for a girl isn't good for a woman. And if a life could be boiled down to a single sentence, why, it wasn't much of a life at all.

'We used to live here in Paris. It was home, up until he left. After that, my mother moved us away, all the way to Saint-André. It was where her parents had gone, when they retired. And, after we were in the south, well, we never mentioned my father again. And my father, he didn't come looking ...'

'In the old country, our fathers left always.'

Isabelle said nothing.

'We would see them, of course, so maybe it is not the same. But they'd be gone, even so. The tradition was that they would stay at our mothers' sides until we were crowned a year old, and after that they'd go back to the landlocked sea, and the long-houses where all the other fishermen lived.'

'And your father ...'

'I am like you. I never knew him as "father". I called him by his given name: Hayk.'

'Hector and Hayk. They sound like a double act. Vaudeville stars of an age gone by.'

'You're looking for him, here,' said Levon. 'This is why you have your list.'

Isabelle's eyes roamed over the names and places. Six months of searching had yielded not a clue. She thought she'd been prepared for that, but the weight of it was heavier than she'd anticipated.

'I'd been planning this trip for years. I've been making this list since I was eighteen. Just names I scavenged from newspapers, the telephone listings, wherever I could. My mother wanted me to stay in Saint-André. Paris is full of rebels and thieves – that's what she'd say. But ...'

'The heart wants what it wants?'

It was stronger than that. The heart yearned. The head could be distracted, but the heart stayed the course.

'It was my father who taught me to play. There were no bed-time stories, not in my house. There was bedtime music. He'd have his lyre, or he'd have his lute, his mandolin or ... his harp. And there he'd be, at the bottom of my bed. I used to watch his fingers. The way that they danced.' Here she faltered, for suddenly she thought how naïve it must seem. 'I thought, if he was anywhere at all, he was still here, in Paris. Still playing in the clubs he used to play. The bars where he met my mother. I thought ...'

She hadn't meant to, but her voice had started to tremble. It had been an age since she last felt it like this; she was a woman grown, but there was nothing like a father to make you feel like a little girl.

'Your father,' she said, because at least this changed the subject. 'Hayk. Is he ...'

Levon uttered, 'Alive or dead. Lost or found. I don't know.'

Then we're the same, she thought.

'The last time I saw him was the day when the soldiers came. We were still asleep, but my father was up early, to catch the tide on the landlocked sea. It was he who came hammering at our door. All the villagers were scrambling onto the boats – we figured the soldiers wouldn't give chase to us if we were out on the water. I helped my mother and my sister aboard, and my father told me to get off, to go with him instead. But I didn't. That's the last time I saw him. The truth is, I don't know if he made it out of the old country or not.'

She could feel him tensing. She reached out, allowed her fingers to touch the back of his hand.

'The old country,' she said. 'You keep saying it. You haven't once told me where—'

'It's gone,' he said, simply. And then, as if it was a saying she ought to understand, 'Once there was a country ...'

'Gone? But it can't just ... go.'

'I don't see why not. It's happening all of the time. You've heard of Prussia. You've heard of Brittany. Bavaria. Just because your maps say something, doesn't mean it's built to last. Trust me, Isabelle. I've seen.'

For a time, there was silence.

'The soldiers came. They built a power station on the lake. Took the villages as barracks.'

There was more to this story. She could sense it in the edges of everything he said: three thousand miles of story he wasn't telling. She wanted to know more, but now was not the moment, so instead she asked, 'Why Paris?'

'What?'

'You came all this way. You must have had a destination in mind. You chose Paris.'

'Plenty of us didn't. They went to Copenhagen. Berlin. A thousand stayed in Ankara. Hundreds more in Budapest. Some of us tried to get into London – but London?' He snorted. 'London only wants what it wants. England for the English ...'

'And Paris?'

He lifted the dictionary. 'I found it in a hostel outside Ankara.'

Yes, she thought, it was just like this man – strange and glum and determined as he was – to decide the future of his family, the future of his family for generations to come, because he'd stumbled across a dog-eared dictionary some frazzled backpacker had left behind.

'My bebia wants to make you dinner,' he said. 'She said that, if I was to find you, I was to insist. You liked her fish. This time she'll make chicken. She wants to say thank you.'

Isabelle thought of the luminescent flower from the rooftop garden and grinned. 'People say thank you a lot where you come from.'

'It's a national competition. If you out-thank the other person, that makes you superior. I've seen my bebia grind people down with her thanks. She's very proud of her victories.'

'Then I don't suppose I have a choice.'

'I'll make it up to you, I promise.'

Isabelle spluttered. Lemonade and ice cascaded from her lips, all over the counter. 'I think apologising must be a national sport as well. Find the most innocuous thing – no, the kindest, most generous thing – and find a way to apologise for it. Levon, it's a chicken dinner! I've been eating toast for days.'

'She'll apologise for it too. Back home, we had chickens. She'd wring a neck every Friday night. I think it made her happier than anything else. That satisfying crunch! She doesn't understand why I can't just bring a live chicken back to the apartment to have its neck wrung. It doesn't taste the same, she says, not unless your hands do the killing.' Levon shrugged again; it was, Isabelle decided, the way he punctuated all his sentences. 'But that isn't what I meant. What I meant to say was – your list, it's incomplete.'

Isabelle fingered it, guardedly. 'Incomplete?'

'That is to say, all the places you're going, well, they're … ' He stopped. It wasn't just his language skills that were stopping him articulating this thought. It was, she understood, his fear of antagonising her. 'They're the same. All the same people go there. Nightly, from one to another, listening to the same music, seeing the same faces. But there are other places. I could show you …'

He shrugged again. Then, as if to fight his embarrassment, he bowed his head to the lemonade and, with his lips pursed around the straw, promptly drank half the glass.

'If you're looking for him, mightn't it be he's somewhere … else? If he's been in Paris all of his life, he'd be bored of the old French songs. But my People aren't the only refugees in Paris, and they make music too. In the Goutte d'Or, or in Issy-les-Moulineaux …' He stopped. 'I like music,' he said, with a final simplicity. 'My bebia goes up to her night garden. Me, I go to listen to the music – that is, until they realise I haven't paid and a big, burly Frenchman comes to throw me out. I was thinking we could go. Might be someone out there really has seen your father. But if he hasn't ... there's the music.'

*

Isabelle did not know if she was doing the right thing, not as she waited in the cold on the corner of the Rue Saint-Bruno, with the spires of the Catholic church piercing holes in the sky behind her. All she knew was that the prospect of another night alone with her harp did not fill her with joy. So instead she waited in the dark, watching the shadows shuffle by.

Levon was one of those shadows. He loped out of the grounds of the church.

The first thing he said, before hello, was, 'You didn't bring your harp.'

'I didn't know I was meant to.'

'There are spots. You might have played.'

Then it was a blessing, Isabelle thought, that she'd left it behind. Because Isabelle hadn't won the hundred francs at Le Palais Anglais. In the end, she hadn't even played. When the moment had come, she'd risen to make the short march to the stage ... and instead staggered out onto the darkening riverside. Even the gargoyles up on Notre-Dame were scoffing at her, she thought. What good was a harpist who dared not play?

At least she had her list, and at least she had Levon.

'Where are we going?'

For the first time since she'd met him, Levon seemed eager – puppyish, even.

'Here, I'll show you.'

A few streets further on, the Marché Dejean was almost closed, all of its stalls being folded away and crammed into the backs of waiting wagons. As Levon led Isabelle through the clutter left behind, she heard a dozen different languages, and breathed in scents from the furthest corners of the Earth. 'We should eat,' said Levon. 'I know a man ...' And he did, it seemed; the truth was, he knew faces in all corners of the faltering market – and, by the time they'd emerged on the other side, he'd scavenged a cardboard tray full of *akara* – the little black-eyed bean cakes sold by an older Nigerian lady, who seemed to have adopted Levon as a sometime-son – and two sticks of raw sugar cane. 'I come here so much. At the end of the day, you can find treasures just waiting in the gutters. And, well, they look out for each other, too – the people who don't belong ...'

The akara were not to Isabelle's taste, but she devoured them all the same. The sugar cane was rough and, like Levon, she had to tease long fibres out of her teeth (it was truly unbecoming), but it fizzed inside her and she felt more awake than she had in days.

'I can hardly tell you what it felt like to find this place.' They were following the narrow Rue Léon, past convenience stores where the shopkeepers were taking in baskets of plantain and cassava root, strings of cowpeas and okra. 'Maybe I shouldn't say how we got into Paris. Or ...' He relented; she'd brought Arina back, hadn't she? He could *trust* this girl. 'They left us in the freight terminal, right where we're living. I used to think of Paris like it is on the front of my dictionnaire: all those lovers, basking in the gardens at the Louvre ... But everywhere I looked – just freight yards and warehouses and decoupled bits of trains.' He grinned. 'Still looked like the richest place on Earth to me. Then, of course, I had to set about making it work. For days I just roamed around, trying to speak the language, asking for just about anything I could get – and ... I wasn't being careful enough. I'd spent so long thinking about getting us here that I hadn't thought, for one second, how to build a world when we arrived. I stopped into one of these places, asked the wrong guy, and he takes me into a back room and tells me: he's like me. No papers, nothing at all. And what in hell did I think I was doing, just brazening around, advertising the fact? Was I really that naïve? No, I said, not naïve. This man has no idea what we went through to get here. *No idea?* he laughed. *Boy, I crossed the ocean.* So did so many of his brothers. And they've been here for years. Thousands of people are, right here in the Goutte d'Or alone. They come from Algiers or they come from Tunis or … almost anywhere in the world. And, well, they bring it with them.'

They had stopped outside a nondescript little door on the corner, where grilles covered the windows and red lights shone inside. A sign above the door read 'Le Tangiers' in decorative, cursive script.

'I guess I thought we were the only ones. But people's worlds are collapsing all the time, aren't they? It doesn't have to be a war. Little worlds implode, just the same as big ones. And they all need somewhere to go. When I found that out, it … I don't know, it just touched me. I've been coming into the Goutte d'Or ever since. Sometimes there's work down here. But mostly it's just for the music.'

Le Tangiers was little more than a hollowed-out basement, stretching beneath three of the shop-fronts above. In other hands, Isabelle supposed, it would not have been so different from La Cave de Denis – but the red and orange lights in the alcoves, the way the floor stuck to the soles of her feet, marked this place out as somewhere else altogether.

So did the music.

The stage was set into one of the recesses in the wall. From that cavern, the sound of electric violins battled with bulbous stringed instruments Isabelle did not know, and undercutting it all the beat of tiny drums. The singer, moustachioed and round, sat on a stool in the middle of the music. His voice soared in a language neither she nor Levon could understand.

Isabelle's eyes roamed the room, and between the dancers – for the centre of Le Tangiers was a depression, where bodies snaked together, then came apart – she took in a group of black women with spherical shakers and reed pipes, a single elderly man with a narrow, long-necked instrument she took for a kind of lute, and even a pair of brothers cradling bow harps of their own.

From somewhere, there were drum machines. A synthesiser blasted out a bastardised calypso, and yet more dancers surged to the floor.

She followed after Levon, eager not to lose him in the throng. To see him here seemed, somehow, an aberration. But, she supposed, two meetings were hardly enough to know him well. He shuffled onward until, at last, he reached the calmness at the very back of the hall. Here, the curvature of the walls seemed to dull the music, separating them from the hullabaloo out on the floor.

And here a lean old man sat on a stool, his eyes closed as he listened to the music.

Levon tapped him on the shoulder.

He was not as slight as he had first appeared. His body seemed to unfold, revealing him a head taller than Levon. The prominent cheekbones that might have made him striking as a young man seemed odd protrusions in old age, making his eyes – black, like Levon's – more sunken still, and his mouth, when he smiled, was full of gaps where his teeth had rotted clean away. Even so, the way that he smiled was infectious. He rose from his seat and wrapped his spindly arms around Levon.

For a time, they chattered in their own language. Then, Levon turned around and said in French, 'Isabelle, this is Beyrek.' Isabelle sensed the old man's eyes revolving to find her. 'Beyrek, this is Isabelle. She's the one who found my sister, when she wandered off.'

'The French girl,' the man named Beyrek intoned in a voice as light as feathers.

'Beyrek's from the old country too.'

Beyrek had already taken Isabelle's hand. She fancied he was going to plant a kiss upon it, but instead he just held it lightly, his skin full of ridges. 'Charmed,' he ventured, as if he was trying out the word for the first time. 'I see, boy, that you're doing what you promised – finding yourself a Parisian wife.'

Levon, whose face was suddenly a more lurid shade of red than the lights, hissed, 'Beyrek!'

The old man slapped a skeletal thigh. 'You left your sense of humour out on the trail, boy. I've told you this before. It's lost out there, never coming back.'

'You left your sanity out there too,' Levon muttered. 'They can keep each other company.'

For a time, they exploded in a cacophony of their own language. Whether it was argument or not, Isabelle was not sure – for every time Levon looked incensed, the elder man burst out laughing. Eventually, exasperated, Levon broke away.

'Beyrek reached Paris three months ahead of us. He was one of the first.'

'A pioneer, madam,' Beyrek announced, with an ostentatious flourish of the hand.

'When I started coming here, here he was – just sitting here, like he is tonight ...'

'And every night since. Well, there were so few of us from the old country back then. I thought to find my own people – but these other lost souls, they'll do. Everyone's got to be somewhere.'

Levon reached into his coat and produced a roll of old newspaper. This he carefully unfurled. Lying inside was a single stem from one of his bebia's flowers-by-night, with its hanging, translucent petals at the end.

'A promise fulfilled,' Levon began.

Beyrek held the dead petals in his hand and shook his head sadly. 'But I wanted to see it living, boy. I wanted to see its light.' His fingers touched Isabelle's shoulder. 'I haven't seen one since I was a child – and even then, only once in my life. That this boy's bebia has them flourishing on a rooftop, so far away from home …'

'Home doesn't exist, Beyrek. *This* is home now. Here's your new world – you've just got to embrace it.'

Beyrek rolled his eyes until they landed on Isabelle. 'And yet the boy still comes to places like this, just to … belong. He's mightily confused.'

Levon was undeterred. 'I'll get you seeds,' he said. 'You can plant them yourself. Though, if my bebia's to be believed, you hardly need them. Just start honouring the old ways, she says, and they'll be flowering all around you. She's cracked …'

'This boy's bebia is a weaver of miracles,' Beyrek smiled – as much, Isabelle thought, to taunt Levon as to rhapsodise this old woman he'd never met. 'I should be grateful to meet a fine woman like this.'

'I'll arrange it,' said Levon, 'then she might stop asking me about having great-grandchildren.'

'She honours the old world in this too.'

The music flurried up again. A Ghanaian singer and two guitarists had taken to the stage, and from somewhere there was the sound of a horn. Isabelle had heard music like this before, but only in snatches. Here was a classical foxtrot, and here a calypso, and here something she hardly had the words to describe. The French horn pierced the quick, arpeggiated guitar lines with what seemed to Isabelle a boundless joy.

'Here,' said Levon, 'show him.'

Isabelle hesitated before she reached into her pocket. The thought seemed so unlikely: that her father might himself have sashayed through Le Tangiers.

ROBERT DINSDALE

'His name's Hector,' she said as she presented the photograph. 'He'd be older now. Forty-five. This photo, it's twenty years gone, but ...'

For a time, Beyrek studied the picture – and, as he did so, Isabelle was certain she could feel a kind of sadness deepening the lines on his face. Every contour grew more pronounced; every chasm penetrated further.

'So now I know why you bring her, Levon. You finally discovered – there are lost souls in Paris as well.' Beyrek turned the photograph and, shaking his head sadly, pressed it back into Isabelle's hand. 'Everyone's missing someone, my dear. This is the Modern World. Take Levon here. Has he told you what happened to his mother? Has he told you where his father is now – where his seven brothers? He would if he could, I've no doubt about that. This Levon you've discovered has a good soul – and if he remains a little confused as to who he is, what his place is in this world, well, perhaps that can be understood. Perhaps that can be forgiven, even.' He paused. 'I'm sorry, little one. I have no more seen this man than I have my own children. My own wife.'

The sadness that Isabelle felt as she slipped the photograph back into the card was not for herself. She was, she decided, inoculated against sadness now. But something was leaching out of the elder man; she felt his own sadness spinning its web around her.

'The old country,' she said. 'Levon says so little ...'

Beyrek shook his head wearily. It was, Isabelle found herself thinking, not the weariness of old age – but of continents. 'No, he wouldn't. This young man likes to believe we are, all of us, *tabula rasa*. But blank slates upon which we may write our own chronicles. Well, such is the attitude of the young.'

Isabelle had seen the way Levon tensed beside her.

'What good is pining after the old world? It's gone ... '

52

'Gone!' the old man scoffed. 'Gone, gone, gone! Levon, it's time to make yourself useful.' He reached into a pocket and flicked a coin up, so that it landed in Levon's hand. 'Your lady friend will need a drink, if she's to hear a story.'

Levon made eyes at Isabelle and muttered, 'He thinks *this* will buy him a drink,' and rolled the single coin round in his palm. But when nothing more was forthcoming, Levon disappeared all the same.

New musicians had come to the stage, and soon some folk singer's gentle voice rose into the scarlet dark. Mournful was not the right word for this music, for there was joy in it as well, but suddenly Isabelle was thinking of lands far away, lands that had once been home. Every exiled people had a music of their own.

'He tells you nothing, because he thinks he is young enough to live his life over. But we are none of us young enough to forget.'

It meant something to Isabelle. 'I was born right here in Paris. My mother took me away when I was six. A fresh start, she called it. But even now, seventeen years later ...'

'Pah!' beamed Beyrek. 'Then you hardly need telling at all!'

Isabelle's eyes had picked out Levon through the crowd. He was standing at the bar, spectacularly failing to get any attention, while all around him the crowd joined in with the singer's lament. All of a sudden, she had a plunging feeling inside. She might so easily not have gone to La Cave de Denis that night. Her fingers might have worked, and she might have remained up on stage, so that she would never have shepherded Arina back through the storm.

Lives turn on moments. It could all have been so different. And this was the feeling of falling in love.

'Please,' she said, 'I want to know what it was like. Where he comes from.'

Her gaze was still fixed on Levon. At the bar, he revolved, until he caught her eyes.

So Beyrek began his tale.

'Once,' he whispered, 'there was a country ...'

Look for it now, he said, and you'll find no trace of it remains. Countries like ours are small and insignificant enough that they have only ever troubled the most ardent mapmakers. They exist on the edges of your atlases, in the creases where one page meets the next, in writing so small and cross-hatch so smudged that the eye completely glazes over it. 'We're not the first,' Beyrek went on. 'We won't be the last. There have been countless countries like ours. There will be again. But ... people like big stories. They like warlords and wars. The little stories of little countries make little ripples.' He stopped, and touched the back of Isabelle's hand with his aged fingers. 'That's how whole worlds disappear. That's how it was on the great landlocked sea ...'

The music continued to swell in Le Tangiers but, as Isabelle listened, Beyrek's voice subsumed all.

In the long ago, he said, theirs was one of the great khanates of the south. Long before the Khanate of Kazan, long before the Golden Horde, long, long before there were written chronicles, a people grew tired of their nomadic existence and settled instead on the shores of a great landlocked sea. 'Here my ancestors found another way of living. Within a generation, we'd set our horses free and taken, instead, to the waves as fishermen. No more did we drink of our horses' blood. No more our horses' milk. This was a new age for a new world. And we called ourselves the People.'

'Why the People?' asked Isabelle.

And Beyrek said, with the warmest of smiles, 'It is what all people call themselves, in the beginning.'

The landlocked sea, Beyrek explained, was unlike any other sea in the world – for the fish that populated its waters lived not by day, but by night. With the coming of each night, when the stars rippled in reflection across the surface of the water, the fish of the landlocked sea would rise up to feed on the insects drawn down to those twinkling lights – and, soon, they themselves had developed a glittering glow to lure in the insects, even when no stars shone in the heavens. So too did the flowers which grew on the banks of the landlocked sea learn to shimmer, and so too the gulls and tiny songbirds who darted through the night-time air, feasting on the insects intoxicated by the light.

'Well, in those days,' Beyrek said, his eyes opening in wonder, 'a wayfarer who stumbled upon the Khanate of the Stars might have risen above one of the neighbouring hillsides, hungry and spent after long days of riding the Steppe, and looked out upon a paradise of lights. A land of wonder at midnight!' he laughed. And Isabelle thought she could see what was behind his eyes: a tiny, forgotten corner of the Earth where the constellations existed not across the blank canvasses above, but right here, around us.

Now that the People had their home, Beyrek went on, they no longer needed the bow and arrow, neither to hunt nor to wage wars. 'We kept our kings for a time. Our Ulduzkhan, the King of the Stars!' Beyrek puffed his chest out in pride, as if he himself was standing sentry at one of those ancient courts. 'He and his kindred ruled for generations … but these things never last. The world keeps turning. Somewhere along the way, who knows when, there came an age when the People no longer had need of kings or queens. And, from that day on, we lived without rulers. We were all of us equals on the landlocked sea. The grandchildren of dethroned kings took to the waves alongside the other men every twilight, hauling in their nets so that the People could be fed.'

Sometimes, out in the world, travellers heard whispers of the Khanate of the Stars. The Khanate is gone, they would say – the

Ulduzkhan never really existed, and nor did all those other figures out of legend – but the flowers-by-night are real; they still
open up at twilight, and the lightjars still make their nests in trees
that bear iridescent fruit. Were you to camp on the shores of the
landlocked sea, you would still see the silvery shoals turning
under water, in imitation of the stars themselves. Go there, and
visit the night markets; take a seat in the longhouses as their
storytellers speak from the Nocturne, their Book of Legends; linger by the village jetties at dusk and watch as the men wake from
their slumbers and head out onto the waves. If you linger until
the hour before dawn, you'll see them returning, spilling their
iridescent catch onto the wharfs.

But, more than any of this, you'll *feel* it. To live your life by the
pattern of the People, rising at dusk and retiring at dawn, is to live
out of step with the Modern Age, to understand that worlds exist
out there, just on the edges of our understanding, to know that
there is yet magic on this Earth.

'But everything changes,' Beyrek said.

His eyes had a new cast about them now. Gone was the wonder Isabelle had seen when he spoke about the shoals of glittering
fish. Now, his dark eyes had grown darker.

'The Modern Age,' he intoned. 'You must understand, my
girl, that pockets of the world move on at different times.
When it's day in one world, it's night in another. One country's
past is another's future. And while the People lived from one
night to the next, the daylight world was marching onward –
ever, ever onward . . .'

Death came to the landlocked sea.

Seven score years ago, four generations as the People marked
the passage of time, the luminous shoals began to darken and
disappear. At first, there were fewer shoals each season. Somebody noticed that the light beneath the waves was less vibrant
than it had been when he was a boy. One of the village women,

who took the young ones out to harvest nectar from the flowers-by-night, started saying the flowers were no longer as potent, that something unfathomable was fading out of the world. In the villages and towns, it was said that the younger generation were disrespecting the old ways, that this was the way the ocean had of calling its faithful back. But the demagogues were wrong. Magic might have been fading from the starlit world, but it was not because of the People.

It was because, in the daytime world, the century was turning – and along the rivers that fed into the landlocked sea, from Volgograd and Rostov-on-Don in the Russias of the north, the new age of industry was dawning.

Travellers spoke of great factories looming along the rivers, each of them pumping out their waste into the waters that fed the sea. No, magic wasn't fading because the People no longer deserved it. Magic was being choked. The lights of the People were being snuffed out by poison pumped into the water.

'It took but a single generation for the landlocked sea to stop shining. After that, the lights faded in the hills and fields around us. The lightjars stopped nesting. The flowers-by-night grew tussocky and sparse, until they barely shone at all. And, one by one, the People gave up the way of life we'd always known since time immemorial. What was once thought a heresy became a norm: the People started living by day. That's the world I myself was born into, Isabelle. A mere shadow of the magic that once was …'

Some vestiges of the old world lived on. There were always old weatherwomen who, driven mad by old age or the tribulations of their dastardly children, denounced the Modern Age and lived, instead, by night. There were mad soothsayers and defiant young men, oddballs and cranks, who still rose with the moon and turned their backs to the sun. But the rest of the People joined the daylight world their ancestors had long ago left behind. And from that day onward, the old Khanate of the Stars was no more. No magic, not here; now, just another string of fishing villages in a country so small that the mapmakers of the world barely shaded it in. Once all the old-timers were gone, all they really had, to remind them of what once had been, was the Nocturne, their Book of Legends, which their mothers would read to their children each night. The history of the People, millennia of culture and tradition – now just bedtime stories, to soothe a child to sleep.

'We lived like that for a hundred years. We might have lived like it a hundred more. Largely forgotten. Largely unseen.' Beyrek stopped. 'Then the soldiers came. For so long, they'd wanted to make industries of the landlocked sea, to raise their dams and power plants – and, if that meant enslaving the People, well, that was a price they were willing to pay. By then, of course, the People had forgotten how to fight ... What can fishermen do against tanks and guns? So, when they came, the People weren't ready. We piled onto boats, those of us who didn't take to the hills, and looked for ...'

Beyrek would have gone on. There was more he could tell. But now Levon was back, the drinks overflowing in his hands.

'It's the past, Beyrek. The past! By the Stars, if we all put as much time into dreaming of the future as we do dreaming about the past, we'd ... we'd ...' He stopped, for when his exasperation had reached its peak it had not exploded, but withered on his tongue. Such, Isabelle was discovering, was his way. 'Hang it, we're here for the music. Isabelle?' He reached out his hand, and Isabelle took it.

The heart of Le Tangiers was bustling as the new musician started to play. In the middle of the floor, with bodies buffeting them on either side, Isabelle said, 'You shouldn't be ashamed of where you come from. It sounds ... magical.'

'Oh, magic. Magic's a thing of the past, just like the old country.'

'But Levon, I've seen your bebia's night garden ...'

He had no answer for this, but he had no need to. The singer had taken to the stage and, in the voice of her own country, brought cheers from the crowd.

As the music cascaded around her, Isabelle's mind drifted from that land of midnight and stars, and turned to imagining her father in a place like this. This was not his music, she was certain of that. She remembered those bedtimes, and the courtly romances he had picked out on his mandolin. Melodies that conjured the palaces of medieval kings. Lullabies, from a different age. She could not picture Hector in Le Tangiers – but it was not this thought that preyed on her as the singer's song reached its zenith. No, the thought that would not leave her alone was much more harrowing: because seventeen years had passed between the present moment and the photograph in her hands – and, if all it took was a few fleeting days to end Levon's world, what might seventeen years have done to the father that she loved?

At the end of the night, Levon walked her back to the Métro station – and there they lingered, in the shadow of the Roman church. 'This place,' Levon finally said. 'Saint-Bernard, they call it.' He directed her gaze at the silhouette, ringed in a halo of stars. 'Only a few years ago, they were rounding up people like me. The gendarmes battering down doors and ... dragging us out, one by one, into their wagons. My People weren't in Paris then, of course. The old country hadn't quite vanished. But ... people from Tunis and Algiers, they hid behind those doors. Well, churches used to be sanctuaries, didn't they? So the church took them in.' Levon hesitated. 'You'd have taken us in, if that was your church, Isabelle. Just like you took in my sister. And that's how I know – the kind of person you are ...' He hesitated, uncertain of his words. 'I still remember the day we had to leave. My father was barracking us as we raced for the jetties and Arina, she was scared. I had to drag her out of the house before the soldiers set up their checkpoint. Well, there was only one road … But she's my sister. I'd have burned the old world myself, if only to protect her. That's why, when my father was telling me I was a coward, that I wasn't one of the women and children, that I should get off the boat and put up a stand with him, I turned away and took them all to sea. My father was the sort of man who had many children scattered up and down the landlocked sea. I was the only one among his sons not brave enough to go with him …' Only as he was saying the words did he realise how clumsy they were, but he was grappling after something – something as fleeting as a feeling – and he could not pin it down. 'I'm sorry I didn't tell you about the old country myself. I'm sorry I left it to Beyrek. He's like my bebia. They cling on to the past. They want to talk about it. Me, I just want to look to the future.'

'Levon, you sound like your grandmother. Too many apologies! And, besides, you showed me the music, didn't you?' Now it was Isabelle's turn to pause. 'There'll be another time, won't there? I mean, the music hall – there are more like it …'

'Oh, hundreds,' grinned Levon. 'Thousands. You're going to need a new list.'

4

························

THE DISCOVERY OF
STARLIGHT

It was peaceful in the night garden tonight.

The stars did not only wheel in the skies above Paris. They wheeled here, at Levon's bebia's feet. Emerald flowers-by-night had erupted along one of the gutters, and on the bank of the rooftop lake new bells were glowing silver and gold.

The young boy – his name was Aram, which was a good solid name, a name from the old country – was gambolling through the scaffolding where sapphire flowers-by-night had begun to snake around every length of steel. Levon's bebia watched as the little boy ducked his head to take in the scent, then recoiled spluttering with a face full of luminous pollen. Momentarily blinded, he stumbled in circles, until Levon's bebia swept him up in her arms.

'Yes,' she said in the language of the old world, 'you see it, don't you, boy? Your cousin won't ... but you can see the magic.'

Children always would, she thought as she set him down and proceeded to clear the radiant globules of pollen from his face with the hem of her dress. Very vaguely, she remembered being a little older than Aram, and her own bebia taking her down to a little cove off the landlocked sea, where a stand of the very last flowers-by-night survived. People said there was a vagabond down here who lived ferally, sleeping in some cavern by day and roaming the shoreline at night – and Levon's bebia was certain, now, that this was the secret, this the reason that the flowers-by-night had persisted in this one spot, and no other: because, every time somebody honoured the old ways, their honour was reflected in the world. 'You'll start living by night with me, won't you, Aram?' She grinned. Rather than being scoured clean, the pollen had worked its way into his cheeks and he now looked faintly luminous himself. Her own emerald child.

'Aram, look!'

Something had flitted up and out of the flowers-by-night. She directed the little boy's gaze – and together they watched as a tiny bird, barely as big as the two-year-old's fist, fluttered up, its long beak glittering with the nectar it had been drinking. Every last one of its feathers was as radiant as the stars.

'Oh Aram,' she said, 'it's a ...'

After that, the boy stepped back. Something peculiar was happening to his bebia. Moments ago, she'd been marvelling at the tiny bird. But now – Aram had no idea why – she was lying face down in the flowers-by-night, one arm reaching out while a hundred tiny tremors worked up and down her body. The boy had never seen the like of this before. He cocked his head to one side.

Then he started to cry.

*

Somehow, Paris did not seem the same to Isabelle after that night in Le Tangiers. She went to sleep in the glow of the silver flower-by-night, and woke to a different city. Where once all the avenues were leading to dead ends, now the map of Paris was opening up. Possibilities blossomed.

Three nights later, Levon took her into Issy-les-Moulineaux, where in a little den behind a shoe shop they listened to the music of Armenia and Georgia, folk songs played lightly by dulcimer and violin. Nobody had seen, nor heard of, Hector here – but perhaps that did not matter. This, Levon said, was as close to the music of his homeland as he had found and, tonight, it was enough for Isabelle to hear it with him.

There were other places. Bars in the Goutte d'Or where two Somali sisters sang dirges. Or beyond that, in the cellars of Seine-Saint-Denis, where Arabic pipes shared the stage with synthesisers and electric guitars. The klezmer at the Troika she was familiar with, but of the stomping rebetiko at Des Jardins she knew so little. And everywhere, though the story was the same – no sign of Hector, no sighting, no sound – there was Levon.

She was sitting in the Delicatessen Absolut, watching the rain stream down the window glass (Paris in the rain, such a particular kind of beauty) when the door opened and Levon reappeared. She was grateful to see him, and not only because the missive she'd been trying to write for her mother was faltering on the seventeenth attempt. There were only so many ways to avoid the reality of why she'd returned to the city. It was like writing letters from the trenches, she'd decided, everything she actually cared about redacted so that only the banalities remained. 'Dear Mother, Paris has buildings. The bakeries bake bread. There is water in the river, and you have to cross by bridge.' She didn't like the deceit, but the truth was harder still.

Yet, somehow, Levon's awkwardness put her at ease. He sauntered in, as sodden as a man who'd tumbled into the waters of the Seine, and began shaking himself dry. At the counter, the proprietor was already reaching for his mop.

'I'm going to need your help.'

Isabelle grinned. Here was the feeling. She could feel the anxiety sloughing off her; it was like shedding a skin.

'I know,' said Levon, sensing her amusement, 'it's not as if you haven't helped me already, is it? But ...' Levon stalled, and Isabelle saw all the colour drain out of his face. 'It's Bebia,' he whispered, 'she's fading fast.'

In a moment, she was on her feet. 'Levon ...'

Without meaning it, her arms were around him, and she was getting drenched too. Levon whispered into her ear, 'I can't take her to the doctors. Not one of them would have us. They'd be looking for papers and … she won't risk it, not if it means we might be rounded up and turfed out. She says it's nothing – but, Isabelle, it can't be nothing. She walked three thousand miles, with barely a cough, whether we were sleeping in hostels or open fields.' He hesitated, uncertain if he could give voice to what came next. 'That's how I know. If she made it through all that and she's failing now, it has to be … real.'

She'd been waiting to be taken back to the apartment, back to that promise of a chicken dinner and the magic of the night garden above, since before Le Tangiers, and now here it was. By the time they got there – Levon showing her the perfect way of dodging the Métro turnstiles, so that only the unwatched cameras in the wall ever found out – the apartment was near empty. Only Levon's aunt remained, carefully tending whatever was on the stove. 'Mariam,' Levon began, and asked her a question in their own language. As she replied, Mariam's eyes lifted to the ceiling above.

'She's sent the girls up to the garden,' he said, 'to give my bebia some sleep. Come on, I'll show you.'

Isabelle smiled at Levon's aunt as, nervously crossing the apartment floor, she followed Levon through the door in the corner.

In the cramped back bedroom, Levon's grandmother was curled in her bedsheets.

'She's sleeping?'

Levon whispered, 'It's daytime. She always sleeps at daytime. Well, it's like Beyrek told you. Honouring the old ways.'

'Is she getting out of bed at all?'

'She'd taken Aram up to her night garden, just after dusk. She must have been showing him the flowers-by-night … and the next thing anyone knows, Aram was bawling. Thank the stars that he was, because that's why Aunt Mariam went up there. My bebia, she'd collapsed.'

'A heart attack? But Levon ...'

Levon shook his head, as if to say he was powerless to know. He planted a single soft kiss on his bebia's brow and, taking the leather-bound book from her bedside, ushered Isabelle back out of the room.

'She says it's all in here, everything she needs.' He fingered the cover, the seven-pointed star that was embroidered in gold. 'The story of Tariel, who lost his heart's desire.' He turned through pages bedecked with a thousand different spirals, until he found the story he was seeking. Here a woodcut showed a young man on his knees in front of a star fallen to Earth. 'Tariel watches the Star fall,' said Levon, 'and knows it for his HEART'S DESIRE. Only, when the star stops shining – as it must, unless it's anchored in the heavens – his heart stops shining too. So he goes on a quest to find the only things that can mend a broken heart ...'

'But Levon,' Isabelle ventured, 'it's only a—'

'A story, I know.' Wearily, he snapped the book shut. 'But what am I to do? She won't let me summon a doctor. I've asked everyone I know where I can buy the right medicines, but this ... this is what she wants.' Turning back to the story, he started to read. 'Ground ginger root. That should be easy enough. The earth of the old country. Well, that's going to be harder. The pollen of a ruby-red flower-by-night.' He groaned. 'Even in the stories, it's the rarest one. Tariel has to go on a quest to find it in the Khanate Beneath – that great network of caverns underneath the land-locked sea, where the dead kings still rule. It's all just nonsense – I don't see how any of it helps. The egg of the smallest songbird. Honey from the Queen of the Bees. Blood given freely, from one who loves you. Well, now we're getting down to it. Honey and blood and the pollen of flowers that barely exist. I'll bet you're starting to see why I asked for help ...'

Every day, it seemed, brought some new quest or another. Stitch them all together, and it made up the story of your life: just one quest stacked on top of another.

'I'll help you, Levon.'

All of his bravado was sloughing away. So, she thought, she had an effect on him too ...

'She's my bebia,' he whispered. 'My mother's gone, Isabelle. I buried her myself. We made landfall on the western shore of the sea, but by then the chill was already in her lungs. She lasted as long as she could, but then we had to go on alone. And as for my father – only the stars know where he is, if he's even alive.' He paused. 'I need my bebia. I don't want her to ... '

But he never finished the thought, because Arina and the others were suddenly tumbling back into the apartment, and after that there weren't any words at all.

*

There seemed so little Isabelle could do.

Honey was easy to find, though whether it was queenly enough was a question without answer. Neither she, nor Levon, had the inclination to go climbing the trees in the Luxembourg Gardens searching for nests, so a single quail's egg from the market would have to do. Levon set Arina to scraping out the pollen of a bank of golden flowers-by-night that had sprouted, suddenly, from the leaf mulch in one of the gutters. But none of it was right, and the concoction they made looked more like a witch's brew than it did modern medicine.

'Blood from one who loves you,' Isabelle said. 'Well, that could be you, Levon.'

So he pricked his thumb and watched, dejectedly, as his blood marbled the potion.

'Beyrek says there are back-street doctors. There's a man from Senegal, studied medicine for seven years. But, here in Paris, he has to drive a taxi. If you pay him a fare, he'll do what he can. The problem is ...'

'You don't have the fare.'

'I've a shift at the Métropol tonight.' The blood had stopped beading on his thumb. 'Thanks to you, Isabelle.'

She'd played in the bar of the Hôtel Métropol the week she'd first arrived in Paris. None of the staff there had known Hector, nor any of the other musicians – but she'd played there several times since, and made the acquaintance of the head concierge, an older man who kept wondering, out loud, if Isabelle might like to accompany him for a drink in the bar. She hadn't (she never would), but at least he was good for something. The Hôtel Métropol had needed night porters – who doubled as night cleaners and, when the need was there, nightwatchmen – and Levon had needed steady, regular work. This was the kind of magic even a charlatan could perform.

They passed, together, into the back room where Levon's bebia was propped up in bed, Arina at her bedside and Aram in her lap. The magic of family, thought Isabelle.

'Did you make it, just like my Nocturne said?'

'Yes, bebia.'

'And your ... friend?'

Levon looked at Isabelle, who understood not a word, and smiled. 'She's been helping, bebia. She found me work, at the Métropol. And ...'

Levon's bebia took the mug like a chalice in her hands, and put it to her lips. 'I thought it might taste ... sweeter.'

Levon could hardly hide his shame.

'I'm going to bring you the doctor. The Senegalese.'

'You'll do nothing of the sort!' she spluttered, bringing the concoction back to her lips. 'What's good for Tariel is good for me.'

'Bebia, it's only a story …'

She shook her head fiercely. 'My night garden's real enough,' she slurped, 'and so is this.' Over the rim of her mug, she looked Isabelle up and down. 'Tell her to come closer.'

Levon sighed. 'She wants you to go closer, Isabelle.'

Isabelle smiled – there were grandmothers like this in all the untold corners of the Earth – but that did not quell the nerves as she crammed into the space between the wall and the bed.

'Maia,' the old woman said, and clasped a hand across her heart.

'Isabelle,' Isabelle replied.

Maia's eyes looked straight through her, landing on Levon again. 'I like her,' she declared, 'but you'll have to do something about this language of hers. And … all that hair! It needs a good brushing. Arina, fetch the girl a brush. Levon, you can brush it.'

'I'm not brushing her hair, bebia! She doesn't want me to brush her hair!'

'Nonsense. All a woman wants is a man tender enough to put braids in her hair. Wash the fish guts off his fingers, pour the hot tea, and pay her some attention. Arina, the brush!'

Arina tumbled for the doorway, but she needn't have bothered, for Levon already had his hand on Isabelle's forearm, teasing her away from the bedside.

In the apartment, where Levon's aunt Mariam and the other girls waited, Levon pulled on his work boots and reached for his coat. 'Don't let my bebia know where I'm going. She'll think my eyes have been opened, that I'm honouring the old world at last. She couldn't possibly understand the idea of a night shift …' He stopped. 'Are you sure about this?'

•

'I'm sure,' Isabelle promised. 'If anything happens, anything at all, I'll call an ambulance. I'll hide the rest of them up in the night garden, feed the paramedics some cock-and-bull story – just like we said.'

Levon's face darkened. 'What is ... cock-and-bull?'

As Levon's face darkened, Isabelle's lit up in mirth. There was, it seemed, perfect balance in the world. 'A pack of lies, Levon. I'll tell them I'm a neighbour, that I've been looking in on her. Once they're here, they'll have to look after her, papers or not.'

'Detained is better than dead.'

'Exactly. And we can figure out the rest later.'

Levon lifted himself, puffed out his chest. 'It won't come to it. She is strong.'

Isabelle watched him go. If strength was enough, she thought, then Levon would walk the Earth until all the seas had boiled dry. But strength carried you only so far. Strength gave out.

For a moment, she stood and breathed in the apartment. So this is it, she thought. Paris. The great adventure. A quest way-laid. You set out with one grail in mind, and end up with quite another.

A little cough interrupted her train of thought and, startled, she spun on the spot.

There, peering up with big doe eyes, was Arina. And in her hands: a hairbrush, thick with her bebia's hair.

There was work three nights a week at the Métropol. Three nights when Levon loaded laundry machines in the hotel cellars. Three nights when he ignored the catcalls of his overseer, kept his head down and carried on.

Three nights without Levon meant three nights when Isabelle came to the apartment to watch over Maia as she pottered up and down, or help her up the narrow stair to the night garden above. She was frailer in body than she'd been, but there was nothing frail about her soul. In the night garden, she seemed to come alive. Sometimes, Isabelle watched her bending down to breathe in the scent of her flowers. Or she'd coax Arina and the others to follow her up there, then sit them down to tell them stories from the Nocturne.

Isabelle needed no language to know how little Maia thought of this plot of Levon's, to have her watched at all times. On the first night, Maia made for the apartment door, intent on bustling up to the night garden alone, the very moment Isabelle's back was turned. On the second, she served Isabelle up a broth rich with chicken and ginger – and, as soon as Isabelle was eating, darted for the door. She was, Isabelle decided, the sprightliest sickly octogenarian she'd ever encountered. Her body might have been slowing down, but for everything it lost, her mind seemed to gain.

All that Isabelle could do was follow. Besides, there was such beauty in the night garden that she was happy to linger there, basking in the flowers' hypnotic glow. Each night, the scents seemed stronger, the colours more vivid. Sometimes, in the corner of her eye, she could see a dazzling rush of colour flit through the air, as if tiny birds were dancing just beyond the corners of her vision. Sometimes, she could hear the beating of miniature wings.

Maia kept her distance, but soon the girls gravitated towards Isabelle. They, at least, wanted to *know*. At dusk one evening, Arina tugged on her arm and bade her sit down on the floor, where the two other younger girls were waiting. The elder girls, out all day roaming – or begging, in spite of the law Levon tried to lay down – had not yet returned.

Arina had produced a chequered board, and on it began to arrange a collection of cardboard pieces, cut out from the edges of some box. Then, once the game was assembled, she advanced one of the pieces – and, with expectant eyes, urged Isabelle to do the same.

Draughts, Isabelle thought, and tried to play it as such – but the stern looks from Arina, and the laughter from the other girls, quickly dissuaded her of the notion.

Next, she moved one of the cardboard scraps as if it was a pawn, a knight, a rook, but the howls of derision only became more intense.

'So, not chess either . . .'

Arina picked up a scrap of cardboard. The word she said sounded like 'Ulduzkhan', which brought back memories of the story Beyrek had told.

Slowly, she pieced the game together. Pieces moved helter-skelter, seemingly according to whim, but after some time she perceived order in the chaos. The goal, she thought, was to join together the points of a constellation: the same seven-pointed star she saw stitched into the front of Maia's Nocturne.

Games were a universal language, but there was one other language that they might understand, thought Isabelle. So, on the third night, she carried her harp up the north road and played for them as the stars came out.

'Sometimes my fingers won't work,' she said as she stroked each string. 'You three are the biggest audience I've played for in weeks . . .'

The thought made her shudder. Her rent was already overdue. If I don't get out and start playing again, she thought, I'll lose the apartment. But, more than that, I'll lose Hector. I'll lose the hope.

She was not certain she was ready to lose hope yet, so she started playing.

As the first bars poured out of her, one of the old canons her father used to play, she saw the bedroom door open and Maia appear, with her Nocturne in her hands. There she lingered, just listening as the canon sailed up and all around them.

The girls' eyes were wide as they followed her fingers. She was speaking to them, she realised. In her own way, she was spinning them a tale.

An audience of four. Well, perhaps there was something she could build on here.

Music got her so far, but if she truly wanted to understand them – not just linger here, like some ghost in the family – she needed more.

By the end of the first week, she was starting to pick out words. By the end of the second, sentences were starting to make sense. In the third week, she made her first tentative forays in speaking their language herself – and, if it did not come as naturally as the language of music once had, they still knew to put milk in her tea when she asked, and to bring her pens and papers for their lessons ... and to stop brushing her hair, no matter what their bebia declared.

At least, she finally knew, they were not speaking about her – or, if they were, they were keeping it to themselves.

Piece by piece, she got the measure of this odd, unwieldy family. Mariam was Levon's aunt, and baby Aram – a newborn in arms as the old country burned – his cousin. Of the girls, Arina was the only one his sister by blood. Ana and Elen had been classmates of Arina's in their little school by the landlocked sea. In the madness of those first days, their parents had been left behind. The elder girls, Natia and Nino, had first found Levon's group in the camps outside Izmir, and again in the middle of the Aegean Sea, when the traffickers they'd paid for passage corralled two boats together for the second part of the crossing. Natia's father had remained in the old country; he was the kind of man who loved a lost cause, and instead of fleeing the soldiers' advance had taken – like Levon's father – to the hills. Nino's mother had been with them until Izmir. Nobody knew what had become of her. She'd left in the night, and the last reminder they had of her was the life savings she'd used to pay the traffickers at dawn.

By day, Natia and Nino went to explore the city. Sometimes, they begged. Levon had told them not to – but, then, Levon was not the sort of man who had to be obeyed. Natia's father had been one of those: fishing on the landlocked sea by day, drinking in the longhouses by night, then throwing orders around like mortar fire whenever he came home. Natia said she was sure she could find work, just the same as Levon, but Maia had forbidden it: there was only one sort of work for undocumented girls in a city like Paris, and none of them had crossed continents to become some rich man's slave for the night.

One night, as Isabelle helped Arina into bed, Maia looked on them with a quelling eye, before sloping up into the night garden.

'Bebia's angry,' said Arina. 'She wants us to start living by night as well.'

'Like in the old country ...'

'Did they used to live by night in Paris, as well?'

'Not here, little one.' She was getting used to the feeling of the words, but Arina was working hard at her French as well. They were spending an hour each night sitting over Levon's dictionnaire, and perhaps it was this that frustrated Maia most of all.

'She'd rather we were listening to her Nocturne ...'

'What's in that book?' Isabelle asked, as she tucked the covers in around the girl.

'It's just ... fairy stories,' Arina said. 'Do you have fairy stories in Paris?'

'Oh, almost everywhere.'

'Like what?'

'Well, there's ...' But the story that sprang straight to her mind was of Bluebeard, and the blood-soaked room at the back of his chateau, and all she could say was, 'I'd rather hear about a world as beautiful as yours used to be. All those lights ...'

Afterwards – once the girls were asleep, and Mariam waiting up for Natia and Nino to return from wherever they'd absconded to – Isabelle drifted up to the night garden, where she watched Maia trailing her fingers through the flowers-by-night. In her mind's eye, she saw a night garden as vast as the world. The pond became the edge of the great landlocked sea, the little outbursts of luminescent flowers became great banks of silver and gold. A world like this, captive in time, one of the world's last wonders. What it must have been like, to live by night …

'Maia,' she said. 'Bebia.' The old woman focused on Isabelle with narrowed eyes. 'Your Nocturne. I should like to hear it.'

Maia's eyes narrowed even further, as if this was a scarcely credible thing. But, moments later, they were sitting in the grove together, and the book was splayed open by the water's edge. And so it was that, with Maia's frail hand holding her own, Isabelle was led through the long-lost centuries of the Khanate of the Stars. She voyaged with Tamaz and Tariel. She took to the ocean waves with the first Star Sailors. She was there, on the landlocked sea, when Besarion and his Seven Brothers built their light sail and set off for the constellations – and grieved with their sweethearts and sisters, until the night they came back home.

'And always, in every story, the seven-pointed star …'

Maia thumbed through the pages, hovering over each picture and the star that shone in every sky: six shafts of light pointing upwards, and one shining down, illuminating the chosen People. 'Why?'

'Well, isn't it obvious?' She paused. 'Because, wherever they roamed, however distant they voyaged, not a soul among the People was ever lost. Not really. How could they be, when they had their own special star to guide them home?' Maia closed the Nocturne. 'All they ever had to do was look up, into the sky, to know who they were …'

It had been so long since the old woman smiled.

*

In the fifth week, Levon counted up what money he'd saved and resolved that he'd need to beg his overseer at the Métropol for a fourth night, even a fifth if they were willing. 'It's all the deductions they take. I'm still paying them for my uniform. And they make me pay for meals. I'd gladly go without eating, but ...'

It wasn't just the deductions the Métropol clawed back from Levon's pay packet. By the time he'd paid off the superintendent and brought home what forage he needed, there was only a pittance to set aside for the Senegalese. Isabelle watched him dropping what little he could into a glass jar each morning, but the pride he took in seeing the savings inch upward was tempered by his despair at how long it was taking.

Natia and Nino, too, had been adding coins to the collection. Arina said they rode the Métro up and down, until they got chased away – there was sport in it, yes, but there was frustration as well. Even if Maia wasn't their bebia by blood, they wanted to help.

'It's stifling in here for them,' Isabelle began. 'Levon, you can't imagine ...'

Levon stiffened. 'I've been in a jail cell, Isabelle. I can exactly imagine.'

For a time, there was silence.

'I'm sorry,' he whispered, 'I didn't mean to ...'

She put a finger to her lips.

'Time's running out,' he said. 'You don't know it until, suddenly, it's gone.'

His words were with her as she left the apartment that morning. They rattled in her head as she rode the Métro south. By the time she'd passed the Château Rouge, she fancied she could feel the very same frustration that was plaguing Natia and Nino. Just being there wasn't enough. Levon couldn't do it alone.

The city was still stirring, so the doors were firmly shut at La Cave de Denis. Isabelle lingered in one of the cafés, stretching out a single coffee until it was cold and bitter. Before midday, she watched as Denis himself waddled down the boulevard, and hurried to catch him before he vanished within.

'You?' he balked. 'Play here?' His piggy eyes blinked in extraordinary fashion. 'Dear, you were scared witless. I couldn't take the chance.'

'I need it, Denis.'

His round shoulders rolled. 'I do need a new barmaid.'

'Would you advance me? A week's pay?'

The very notion seemed outlandish. 'One week in arrears, and I can't say better than that.'

But nights spent here meant nights she couldn't be there for Levon in the apartment. Slowly, she backed away.

There was a slot at L'Avalanche, but not for two weeks. Le Chic Pigalle was fully booked up, and La Rive as well. Of the next places she tried, two would let her play – but would pay her only a pittance for the privilege, and most of that in free drinks at the bar. By the time evening was coming back, her stomach was empty, her thoughts distracted, and her pockets bare.

Perhaps that was why her eyes lit up when she saw the shopfront where the sign said 'Prêteur'.

Inside the pawnbroker's, the shop floor was cluttered. Glass cases displayed mismatched jewellery. On a wooden mannequin hung a vintage dress of preposterous lace, and behind that another glass case showed old Polaroid cameras racked up alongside watches of extravagant design.

In the corner, a circular buzz saw sat with its teeth bared, the guardian to a host of other power tools on the floor.

The pawnbroker was dressed fastidiously in a gabardine suit and navy bow tie. He was, Isabelle was surprised to see, scarcely her own age – but the man who kept flitting out of the little office behind the counter seemed to be the king here.

'Mademoiselle,' the younger man ventured.

'Sir, I'm looking for a loan.'

He was already reaching for the receipt book under the counter. 'We're always glad to be of service. Well, times can be tight, can they not?' His gold rings flashed in the strobing shop light. 'Everyone needs a little assistance, here and there. But if we're to make you a loan, we'll need you to stand something as a security. Of course, it is almost *never* truly required. But,' he smiled, 'there are traditions that must be honoured.'

It was only now that Isabelle paused. If there was anything that could stop her, here it was – for, in that moment, she was no longer in the pawnbroker's on Rue Feutrier. Now, she was five years old, tucked up in her covers, and her father was letting his fingers make their final, gentle roll across the strings of his harp. Then, with his familiar whisper of '*bonne nuit*', he slipped out of the room. He was already out on the landing, Isabelle hoping that tonight they would not argue like they sometimes did (that there would be no smashing of plates, that her father would not be sleeping in the *salon* when she woke up next morning), when she recognised the shape still sitting at the end of the bed. 'Papa!' she cried out – and he came running (because, in that once upon a time, he always came running). 'You left your harp ...' He liked to play it at night-time. Out on the balcony, with a beer at his side, watching the street below.

'No, my little thing, I don't have a harp.'

'But ...'

He came back to her and kissed her on the brow. Then, with his face so close to hers she could feel the prickle of his whiskers, he whispered in her ear the two words she would carry with her through all the long years to come: 'It's yours ...'

In the darkness of the pawnbroker's, Isabelle set the harp on the counter. 'It's vintage,' she said, 'Nineteen thirty-two. Thirty-six strings. Celtic.'

Moments later, money was changing hands.

By the time Isabelle reached the apartment, Maia was waking up. Isabelle could hear her spluttering through the walls. Without word, she crossed the floor, the eyes of all the girls upon her, and was sliding a roll of notes into Levon's glass jar when he emerged from the back bedroom, the mug that had been filled with Tariel's concoction making sticky trails down his arm.

He stopped. His eyes were on the jar. 'But ... how?'

'For the Senegalese. My present to you.'

'How did you get that money, Isabelle?' Levon's eyes were darting around.

'She doesn't have her harp!' Arina cried out.

Isabelle was silent. This, then, was the feeling of being found out. She felt naked. Or ... as if a piece of her had been cut away. You read about the aching sadnesses of children who'd left a beloved comforter on the Métro, or dropped it in the gutter. You just didn't realise that it happened to adults too, that you could be fully grown and yet still leave some piece of yourself on a pawnbroker's counter three miles away.

'For the Senegalese,' she said. 'For you.'

Levon crossed the room and put his arms around her. 'It's yours,' he whispered, and an echo reached her from seventeen years in the past. 'I don't know why you'd do that for me ...'

But he did, she thought. By the Stars – wasn't that what his People said? – there could be only one reason.

She'd just given him her soul.

The Hôtel Métropol could wait. Levon took off into the night and, two hours later, returned to the apartment with the man from Senegal.

The man's French was immaculate, his bearing calm and assured. He followed Levon and Isabelle until, together, they emerged into the grove of crystalline lights that was the night garden. At first the man from Senegal paused. It must, Isabelle decided, have been like walking into a dream. Since the first night she'd come here, the stands of flowers-by-night had grown deeper. Now they lined the edges of the rooftop, as if the apartment block had developed a halo of alternating silver and gold. In the middle of the garden, on the banks of the lake – now thick with bulrushes that rippled in the wind, spilling sapphire dust – the boughs of the spidery tree bore bulbous fruits with the brightness of flame. It was in a shelter under this tree that Maia was sitting. She'd spread out her blanket and, by the light of the flowers, she was reading her Nocturne.

'Bebia,' Levon began, 'this is Dr Senghor. He's come to help.'

She eyed them suspiciously, then returned her eyes to the Nocturne. 'I have all the help I need.'

'Bebia, be fair. Dr Senghor has come a long way.'

Levon went to her side, and there he crouched between the lights. Isabelle watched the sapphire dust from the bulrushes settle across his shoulders, giving him a luminous air. In the corner of her vision, the good doctor was taking it in as well.

'What is this place?'

'Levon says she brought bulbs from the old country, that she collected seeds and filled her pockets ...'

The Senegalese shook his head. 'You think different.'

The truth was, she didn't know what to think. Seeds made shoots. Shoots spread out. But not this quickly. Not with this magnificence. She looked around, and fancied she could see pinpoints of light on the rooftops of apartment blocks across the freight yard. Particles of light were borne up and eddied around on the wind like the sparks of a bonfire. It was like watching a new world being born.

In the bulrushes, Levon said, 'If not for you, bebia, then for me. Please.' He was begging; Isabelle could hear it in his voice. 'We love you.'

There is nothing like love to break down a wall. Maia had wanted nothing to do with any doctor, Senegalese or not, but Isabelle watched as she used Levon to hoist herself up out of her bivouac. Together, they skirted the edge of the lake until they were standing in front of Dr Senghor.

Maia's lips parted, and out came a mortar attack of words in her own language. At the end of the volley, Dr Senghor looked to Levon.

'She says she's survived the end of the world. She's lived near ninety years through wars and famine and pestilence. Yes, *pestilence*.' He shrugged, hopelessly. 'I don't know how else to translate it. She's given birth to three children, and outlived at least two.' Here, Levon took a breath, and, looking into his eyes, Isabelle knew that he was thinking of his own father – somewhere, out there, in the night. 'If she can survive all that, she says, what's going to stop her now?'

The answer was simple.

Maia had refused to be taken down below, so instead the good doctor opened up his bag of instruments, produced stethoscopes and thermometers, arm cuffs, pumps and dials, and conducted his examination right there in the garden. After it was done, she settled back down and returned to her Nocturne.

'She's old,' the Senegalese said, steering Isabelle and Levon to the top of the stairs. 'There isn't another way to say it. The body doesn't last.'

'It lasted this far,' Levon returned, half venomous – as if something so straightforward simply couldn't be correct.

'And it lasts no longer.' Doctors could be so matter-of-fact, just engineers of blood and bone – but at least there was sadness in the way the Senegalese spoke. 'She has been through much. I've seen it many times. The will is finite. We expend so much of it when our old worlds burn. Levon, your country ...'

'I know,' he whispered, 'I was there.'

'She made her last great odyssey. She had something to live for, seeing you all here. She is a proud woman, and perhaps she doesn't see it – but the soul says her story is done.' He paused. 'She's slowing down, Levon. She had no heart attack. She's ... tired. She's blessed and she's tired.'

For a time: silence in the night garden, all but for the flutter of tiny wings, somewhere beyond Isabelle's line of sight.

'What can we do?'

'Make her comfortable,' said the Senegalese. 'Let her have her final time.'

Levon looked past the doctor. There she sat, his bebia, in her shrine of lights. And it filled his heart, then: this idea that she wasn't going to die in some foreign country at all. No, he thought, she was going to die in a corner of the old country, one of those tiny sundered pieces that had somehow survived the fall, been cast adrift and wound up somewhere else – just like him. Something in him was unravelling out of the shape he'd made for it. Levon and Arina, Ana and Elen, Natia and Nino – maybe they were all young enough to start again, for the old country to become but a footnote in the long history of their lives. But his bebia deserved this – and there she was, illuminated in the grotto she'd somehow brought back to life.

Levon had the glass jar in his hands. He made as if to pass it to the Senegalese, but the doctor only closed his fists, refusing to take it. 'I've done nothing here tonight. I cannot help her, Levon. So I cannot take your money.'

'A token,' Levon insisted, with his fingers in the jar.

'Fare for the Métro,' the doctor replied – and, with the saddest of smiles, a deal was done.

After the Senegalese was gone, Isabelle and Levon watched Maia. Her head was nodding over the Nocturne, as if her day's sleep was still not enough.

'Take it,' Levon said, and handed Isabelle the jar. 'I won't forget what you did, but ... your harp. You should go for it now.'

'That doesn't matter.'

'It all matters,' Levon insisted, with words half broken, 'every last bit of it.' He stopped. He could not look her in the eye. 'And ... I want to hear you play. I've known you all these weeks, and I haven't yet heard it. I would hear it tonight, if I could. Everything's moving so fast.'

The stars were out, but the night was not yet so old that the doors of the pawnbroker's might not be open. Isabelle's hands closed around the jar and, as she took it, they locked onto Levon's fingers. There they stood, entangled together, until finally Levon teased himself away, back towards the glittering grove. Isabelle watched as he crouched beside his bebia. 'It's cold,' he was saying, in their own language. 'Bebia, please come. The girls will want their stories. What's it to be tonight? Which Star Sailor, bebia? What about the Ulduzkhan, who reached for the stars and fell from the mountain? Tell them the story of the seven-pointed star ... '

'Bah! That's *every* story, Levon. You'd know it, if only ...'

Levon was smiling. 'I know, bebia, I know. You could always tell where home was, every runaway who'd strayed too far from the sea, by looking to the seven-pointed star ...'

Some stories you had to cling on to, thought Isabelle – and, in a roundabout way, that brought her back to her father's harp.

The pawnbroker's was closing by the time she floundered up to the door, but she braved their disappointment and cradled her harp in her arms again as she rode the Métro back north.

Outside the block, Mariam was rocking Aram up and down in his pushchair, desperate for him to sleep. 'It's his bebia's blood in him,' Mariam muttered, giving Isabelle a despairing smile as she passed, 'I'm sure of it. He thinks he's a night person too. I'd walk him round the block if I dared ...'

Isabelle thought: I could play him a lullaby. But in her heart she dreamt of another audience tonight.

There was no sign of Levon in the apartment. When Isabelle opened the doors, Arina and Ana and Elen were circling their bebia on one of the stacks of mattresses, and the story she was pulling out of the Nocturne was of Inkar the Star Sailor, who had learnt the language of the seven-pointed star and wrested wisdom from her every midnight. 'He's gone above,' Arina mouthed, and soon Isabelle was back in the night garden as well, an old packing crate for a stool, the harp braced on her lap as her fingers described one of her father's old melodies – and Levon just listened.

'It's beautiful,' Levon said.

He meant it, Isabelle realised. She set the instrument down and went to join him on the edge of the lake-in-miniature. If she closed her eyes, she could almost feel the spray coming in from the landlocked sea, imagine it reaching out and over the horizon, its incandescent gulls wheeling overhead.

'I'm sorry about your bebia.'

'I was thinking about what the doctor said. How everyone gets a story, and then that story ends.' He crouched to skim a stone over the surface of the water, setting it to ripple. 'I thought I knew what my story was. Now, I'm not so sure ...'

The words echoed in her. She hadn't come to Paris to fall in love. There were other girls for that. They could have that story and run with it. Isabelle had a story of her own – a quest she'd been bent on since she was six years old. And yet, here she was, in a garden of captured moonlight, staring into his black and soulful eyes.

When he stood, she bent her head to meet his.

Yielding to it was soft and right. Here was something to melt into. Isabelle had had her share of kisses before, but this was new. It was like ... kissing Levon, she decided. Kissing Levon and nothing else.

She was still melting into it when, from somewhere else – somewhere that seemed so far away – she heard the clatter of footsteps. Breaking away from Levon, she turned to see Arina erupting from the rooftop stair.

'Levon, it's bebia. She's ...'

The girl's French disintegrated, and out frothed a torrent of words in that strange, spiralling language of their own. Isabelle understood so little, but she did not need to; Levon was already loping after Arina, back into the darkness of the block – and Isabelle's hand, still entwined in his, was drawing her after.

She was lying in the back bedroom, a whisper in the sheets.

'Bebia, can you hear me?'

The girls, who until this moment had been arrayed around the bed, drew back, so that Levon could kneel at her side. He reached up to take her hand – but, the moment he touched her, something sparked inside her, and she batted the hand away. 'I have a little time yet,' she laughed. There was death in that laughter. 'Help me up, you lot. There's much I have to say.'

'Bebia, you're tired. You're not yourself. You should rest. Somebody,' he snapped, turning on the girls at the foot of the bed, 'bring her hot tea.'

'Oh, hot tea!' his grandmother crowed, even while Arina and the others rushed off to brew it. 'I don't need hot tea! I'm dying.' To Levon's grandmother, the logic of it seemed unassailable. 'Here, help me up, boy. I'll not die lying down.' What strength she had left was already expended. In the end, Levon and Isabelle lifted her together, buttressing her on either side with pillows. 'There, that's better.' One of the girls had reappeared with a mug of hot tea. She eyed it suspiciously and, with a roll of her eyes, instructed her to set it down. 'Tell them to go, would you, boy? I'd have a quiet word.'

'Bebia, you need to rest ...'

'Rest!' she grunted, as if the notion was preposterous. 'If I close my eyes now, I'll not open them again, and then how will I tell you what to do with the rest of your life?' She rolled her eyes from Levon to the girls. 'I'll lay this on you girls, should I? Go and fetch me my flowers-by-night. I'll take them with me. Don't pluck the whole lot – I don't need to be greedy. Just a little light to get me where I'm going.' She paused. 'Oh, don't look so horrified! I'll not go anywhere 'til you're back. We crossed half the world, didn't we? I can last another half-hour.'

Arina gave a defiant nod, and it seemed to Isabelle that she was grateful for the mission. In a moment she was gone, drawing the other girls with her.

'Do you want me to—'

Isabelle didn't get the chance to finish that sentence, for Maia cut her off. In her own language, she stuttered at Levon and, in turn, Levon said, 'She says that you should hear everything she has to say. She says you're ... one of the family. She says I should stop being a – what was it, bebia?' His grandmother repeated a single scalding word and, flushing red, Levon said, 'A ... coward, and tell you that I love you.' He spat back at her in their own language, and Isabelle was pleased to see the way Maia's lips curled in a smile. 'She also says that she's going to speak her own language now, because that's what damn well suits her, and if you can't keep up, well, you should just ... pretend. Oh, Bebia,' he said with that familiar despair, 'you're not really going anywhere, are you? You're still burning as brightly as your flowers-by-night ...'

Isabelle saw the way Levon was trembling. Sometimes, he could look so much like Arina. She knelt with him and took his hand, completing the chain.

'You're to live by night, Levon.'

Levon only stared.

'You heard me, didn't you, boy? You're to live by night, and never forget who we are. Never forget where we come from. Oh, don't look at me like that. I know what you've been up to. It isn't enough for you to learn French and fall in love with this French girl – beautiful as she is. You want to ... *be* French. You want to be anything other than what we are. But I'm telling you, boy, it isn't happening. You think the old country's gone, but it isn't. It isn't gone, because it's in every one of us. Maybe there won't be an atlas on the Earth that records its passing, but ... it's here, all around us, wherever we breathe it out. Wherever we carry the old stories. Don't you remember the story of Davit the Daydreamer?'

Levon sighed. By the Stars, he knew it word for word. All those times she'd told it, out on the trail ...

'He tried living by day.'

'Though his father forbade it. And what happened?'

'Well, he faded clean away, didn't he, Bebia? He just stopped existing.'

'And there you have it,' she said. 'Levon, my boy. You're the one who got us here. You're the one who found the way and fed us. But don't be Davit the Daydreamer. Don't let us fade away, not now that we've made it. The world doesn't want you to. Some things *want* to abide. All you have to do is look at my garden up there and ... '

Levon was weary. 'Bebia,' he said, 'you *planted* that garden.'

'I planted not a thing. You still don't understand it, do you? Here, pass me my book ...'

The Nocturne was sitting on the crate at the bedside, hidden behind that much-maligned mug of hot tea. Isabelle set it gently in Maia's lap.

'Children's stories. Fables. Well, that's what you think, isn't it? Too big for stories, aren't you, boy? Well, what if I was to tell you they're not *just* stories?'

'Bebia, they're not ... real.'

'Oh, *real*!' she scoffed. 'What's "real"? Was there a Davit the Daydreamer? Did he really just ... disappear? I reckon not. But it doesn't mean the story isn't real. Levon, you were *there*, out on the trail. Every night, didn't we sit down with this book? Didn't we find ourselves a hole and ...'

Levon thought: perhaps *you* did, but I was out finding shelter, finding food, meeting the bastards we needed just to get ahead ...

'I know what you're thinking, boy. I have the eye, remember. You're thinking that stories don't matter, not when we're still living hand to mouth, day to day. Not while there's empty bellies. But souls need nourishing too. You might have kept our bodies fed on the way here. You honoured that promise, Levon. I'm proud of you for it. But ... it's my Nocturne that kept our souls fed. Without my Nocturne to make us feel one, we'd have scattered to the winds. This book isn't the history of our people. It's nothing as throwaway as that! It's the ... feeling of our people. It's the feeling of *us*.' She grappled with his hand again, her skin like paper-thin bark. 'We need that feeling. So ... live at night, Levon. Live like our forefathers did. Keep telling the Nocturne, so the little ones – and their little ones – never forget. If you do it, boy, oh, what wonders you'll see ...'

She's cracked, thought Levon. He'd said it to Isabelle from the start, but now she was seeing it for herself. Cracked, if she thought any of it mattered. Cracked, if she thought that her night garden proved anything. A few overgrown window boxes. A scattering of seeds germinating in places they did not belong ...

'Bebia, I can't,' he whispered, but Isabelle heard the way his voice wavered. 'This isn't the old country any more. They need to live lives. Find work. Forge friendships. Maybe even marry, start having families of their own. You can't just imagine a place and bring it back.'

Maia's voice had a new curtness. 'You're being a fool. You've never been a fool before.' She fixed her eyes on Isabelle. 'If he can't see it, why, you'll have to make him. Here, help me up.'

'Bebia, you're—'

'I'm still alive, aren't I?' she snapped. 'I'm still your elder. You'll have to teach them this as well, boy. In the old country, we respected the elders. So help me up, and help me now.'

Levon took her in his arms. Bearing her out of bed was like carrying one of the girls had been, out there on the trail. She was as light as a child as she directed him to the window. There, at her instruction, Isabelle rolled up the blind. The city, in all its empty ordinariness, stretched into the north.

'I've heard some foolish things in my time, but never from my own flesh and blood. What do you think this is? Paris, and London, Volgograd and Baku. You're going to tell me they're cities, aren't you? But they're not. They're … ideas. That's all. All of it, Levon, the whole wide world! It's only Paris because everyone who comes here thinks it's Paris. It's only Paris because it makes you dream of learning and lights and walking with someone you love in the rain. Paris doesn't exist, Levon. It's all up here.' She'd been using her hand to steady herself, but when she lifted it to touch the side of her head, she stumbled. 'I didn't plant my night garden, Levon, but it's there all the same. I didn't make those flowers wake up to the stars, but they did it. They did it because I haven't forgotten what the world used to be like, what it might be like again. It leeches out of you, all that belief – it has to go somewhere. All those people out there, they might not know it, but they're doing the same thing. They imagined Notre-Dame, didn't they? They imagined the Sacré-Cœur. The money you go out there to earn, it's just paper – paper and ideas! It's only worth a thing because you imagine it is. Passports and countries, kings and queens, good and evil, it's all just things we imagine – and imagine so hard they come to life …' Finally, she allowed Isabelle and Levon to guide her back to the bed. 'You don't see it yet, but you will. The world, and everything in it, is just this extraordinary outburst of the imagination. By the Stars, that isn't being foolish, that's just ... being alive.'

As Levon watched, his grandmother sank back into the sheets and closed her eyes. She was sleeping, he told himself. And didn't she deserve her rest? Three thousand miles had taken a toll on them all.

At that moment, Arina reappeared in the bedroom doorway, the girls crowding her shoulder. In her hands hung a bouquet of flowers-by-night, all of them radiating the light they'd soaked up, silver and gold and emerald green.

'Levon,' Arina whispered, on seeing their grandmother laid back in her sheets, 'has she ...?'

'No,' said Levon, 'not yet.'

But she had – and, when Levon turned back to where his grandmother lay, he saw that, in her final moments, her eyes had reopened, and the very last thing she saw on this Earth was the cluster of flowers-by-night, pulsating with the light of the old country, the light of her people, guiding her home.

*

Beneath a night vast and covered in stars, Levon's family gathered.

Isabelle was the last to arrive. By the time she rose up from the derelict stairs, the rooftop grove was alive with the light of the flowers-by-night. In the days since she'd been here, they seemed to have grown wilder, more abundant. She walked in their glow.

The family were waiting by the tree that had erupted from the rooftop slates. There was Levon, in a hand-me-down suit stolen from one of his hotel's lost-and-founds. There was Arina, dressed in black, and beside her Ana and Elen, the three of them holding hands in a tight circle. Mariam crouched with Aram by an outburst of sapphire flowers-by-night, while the elder girls stood windward of the concrete sarcophagus, wrapped in their honorary grandmother's shawl.

What was left of their grandmother herself was in the tiny package in Levon's hands. There'd been little of her in life, but there was even less in death: just a handful of ash, the sum total of a human life. Even that, thought Levon, was borrowed; he'd be paying the night guard at the crematorium for months to come.

Isabelle reached out and took Levon's hand.

'Are you ready?'

Levon nodded – and she saw, then, that in his other hand was his grandmother's Nocturne, a paper shred poking out as if to mark a page.

In a few moments, Isabelle was ready too. Arina had brought her a stool and she settled there with the harp in her lap.

Illuminated by the diamond-white flowers-by-night, the family formed a half-circle around the tree, with Levon standing alone in its centre. He looked so ... alone, thought Isabelle. And suddenly she was thinking of all those stories he'd told her: their nights out on the trail, nights like this, out under the stars, or in the cities of tents – and through it all, their grandmother telling the stories from the Nocturne.

Now, it was in Levon's hands. How clumsy he looked, holding it.

In an uncertain voice, he began to read. Something startled in Isabelle, for she had expected him to speak in French – but of course he had gone back to their own language, with all its strange cadences and sounds.

Past the forests of midnight, so the old stories say, a boy lived alone where dark magic held sway. He'd been vilified, exiled, spat on and stoned – for he was a pauper, who just hadn't known, that a pauper can't ask for the hand of a Queen, that

a pauper must live life unheard and unseen. So they'd driven
him off from our glittering tide, to an anchorage deep in the
radiant wild.

'This is not how it was, in that time long ago. We were braver
back then. We were noble and bold. So the start of this tale is
a terrible thing: a lost, lonely pauper, who couldn't be King.

'Come sail with me, come sail with me, out across the land-
locked sea ...'

After that, the story broke free. Isabelle had heard this tale
before – it was one of Maia's favourites, the story of the boy who
fell in love with the moon – but hearing it spun by Levon, her
Levon, made it strange and new.

Soon, his eyes lifted to meet hers – and she knew that her time
had come. She had to trust to her fingers tonight.

The melody she began with was meant for a medieval lyre, but
it matched the mood. It was simple and thoughtful and, when it
slowed it came almost to a silence, long and respectful, before
rising back up. At its height, when it was tinkling joyfully into the
air, it had always put Isabelle in mind of the sky at night. Memory
was bound up with music, but this one more than any – for whenever she dared her fingers to venture here, she was back in the old
apartment – and there was her father, sitting in the chair by the
window. It was he who'd taught her to play it. Six years old, the
week before he left.

Somehow, it seemed fitting to be playing it tonight. Was anything as bittersweet as a death?

The music was soaring. She opened her eyes. There was
Levon's family, because – no matter what blood was between
them – family it surely was. And it struck her, suddenly, that –
even though her father's face was there when she closed her

eyes – she had not thought about the list in her coat pocket in weeks, perhaps even months.

She'd come to Paris looking for family. She'd thought to find it in the corner of some smoky jazz cellar, the repurposed cata-combs where the ageing musicians went to play.

She had been wrong, because here they were.

The thought was only just crystallising when Levon's voice rose up, reaching the ending of his story. The boy who fell in love with the moon could not have her, for she was forever marooned in the night-time sky. Instead, he spent the long years of his life staring into her reflection in the waters of the landlocked sea – for the heartache of gazing at her directly was too much to bear.

So caught up in the story was she that she did not, at first, realise that her fingers had stopped spinning her father's lullaby. It was only as Levon came to the story's bittersweet ending, then opened up the tiny urn in which his grandmother lay, that she became aware that the melody she played was no longer so ach-ingly familiar.

Sometimes, the fingers remembered what the head and heart had long ago forgotten. They remembered arpeggios and studies you last played sitting at your father's knee, or tunes you'd picked out listening to the radio that used to buzz relentlessly in the corner of your mama's kitchenette. All the old melodies, every one you ever breathed in, still existed somewhere between the fingers and the heart. But this … this was something new.

Soft and mournful, a melody in the minor key. Her left hand reached high, finding notes that fell like rainfall; her right remained low, describing a strong, sombre bass line. Uncertain where the melody was leading her, Isabelle tensed – but the music carried on. This was not like being on stage at La Cave de Denis. Here in the night garden, it was as if her fingers were unable to stop. This new melody rose and fell like the tides on whose waters Levon's people had once travelled. It broke down. It slowed. It rose up, as though it was breaking victorious through the waves. And then it began again, each iteration slower, more mournful, more ... longing, than the last.

Under the crooked tree, Levon had taken a pinch of ash out of the urn and, opening his fingertips, let it vanish into the air. There was so little of her left. As Isabelle watched, he poured a measure of it into the palm of his hand. Arina, who until now had been holding herself proudly, buried her face in Mariam's shoulder, while the other girls steeled themselves to watch. To bear witness. To honour, Isabelle thought, how far they'd all come.

Levon whispered, 'The final night has fallen. There will be another night.'

Was Isabelle wrong, or did the words really match the melody her fingers had discovered?

The grey sifted through Levon's fingers and down, tumbling over the flowers-by-night in sapphire, emerald, silver and gold.

The melody Isabelle had been playing was slowing down at last. She allowed her fingers to spin out the last of it. The elegy was done. She looked around. The children's tears were not yet over, but Levon was crouching down, trailing his fingers – and the last of the dust – through the reeds by the water's edge.

For a time: silence.

It was Mariam who spoke first. Aram had been soothed by Isabelle's melody, so that he slept up against her shoulder. Softly, she said, 'It's time for bed, girls. Your bebia will be here in the morning. She's with us always now.'

Soon, Mariam was leading the girls back into the darkness of the apartment stairs.

'Wait,' Levon whispered.

Not one of them heard. The girls disappeared below, and then it was only Levon and Isabelle in the night garden.

'Your music,' Levon said, standing at last, 'I remember it. When I was a boy, and my father took me out on the lakes, there was a man who worked down by the jetties. Father said he was once a fisherman too, but he near drowned and, after that, nobody could coax him back to the water. He was scorned for that. Spat on and sullied. They called him less than a man. But, every dawn, when they'd set out, there he'd be – with this little zither on his lap and a cap open in front of him. He said ...' Levon stopped, for the idea was too preposterous to give it voice. '... they were melodies his grandfather taught him. Melodies from the old times. But if that's so, how can you ...?'

Isabelle tried to put herself back in the song. 'I don't know where it came from,' she whispered.

But Levon knew. His eyes revolved, until he was gazing at the stand of flowers-by-night over which his grandmother had settled. She was gone, he thought, but the old country was still here, flowering from roof tiles where they should not be flowering; growing where there was no earth to succour them; forcing its way back in through the cracks in the world.

He turned and took flight through the night garden, back through the door and into the block below.

By the time Isabelle caught him, he was standing in the apartment door.

In the crowded room, Arina was already in bed. The other girls were settling themselves, the lights down low.

And Levon thought:

It's gone now. If I let it be gone, then it's gone. Oh, maybe they'll tell the old stories for a while; maybe one day they'll even look back and feel a flicker of what those stories meant to them, then tell their children what vestiges they can remember. Even you, their children will say – even *you*, mama, had a once upon a time. But memory fades. Life demands other things. Without bebia to remind them, what's to cling on to? They can meet people. Have families. Be whoever they want to be.

Arina reached and snuffed out one of the lamps.

Levon took a step deeper into the darkness. He knew it had to be destroyed. All of these months since they'd come to Paris, he'd been waiting to destroy it. Now, he supposed, was his chance. It was the weight of history that had been holding his bebia down. But it was *her* history. It wasn't theirs. In seven years, Arina would have lived in Paris as long as she ever lived in the old country. Another few years, and Levon would be the same. What's a child-hood when stacked against the long chronicle of a life?

It wouldn't take much. The Nocturne could be lost. They'd need to move soon, spread out into the city – just as soon as he could get the girls papers – and then, why, they'd hardly be a family at all, much less a people. The old world had been fading for generations anyway. Old traditions, old religions, they were like old dogs: they limped on until somebody put them out of their misery.

And yet …

He could still feel her papery hand. He could still remember what she said. *You're feeding their bodies, boy, but it's my Nocturne feeding their souls.*

'Stop,' he cried out.

All was still in the room. Save for Aram fidgeting in Mariam's arms, there was nothing to stop – for nowhere did anybody move.

He marched between the beds, into the room where his bebia had died, and brought the pot with its single flower-by-night back into the room. There he placed it in the middle of the floor and beckoned the girls to come down. 'Arina. Ana. Elen. Natia and Nino. Mariam …'

Arina had picked herself up, the covers drawn around her. 'What is it, Levon?'

'It isn't … bedtime, little one. We don't go to bed, not at night.'

95

On hearing the words, the girls' eyes narrowed in suspicion.

'Levon,' Mariam ventured, 'what do you mean?'

'It's what bebia wanted, isn't it, Levon?' asked Arina, her little voice filled with awe.

Now, Isabelle floated into the room. The girls were all dropping out of the beds, dragging blankets with them, and forming a circle around the glowing flower on the ground. Uncertain whether or not it was allowed, she sank down to join them.

'It's not about bebia,' said Levon, 'not any more. Bebia's gone, little ones.' He touched the Nocturne, which he laid on the ground between them. 'Gone into Endless Night, like the stories say. This is about ... us.' What words would come next, he could not say. But perhaps that was OK. Perhaps it was like the music that had poured out of Isabelle; the words would just come, and Levon could be their vessel.

'I wanted to leave it behind,' he said, and his eyes looked luminous in the flower's light. 'All of it – every last bit. Somewhere between here and there, I just knew it had to go. Izmir or Tirana. Trying to get across Lake Skadar at night. There she was, every time I looked up, telling you stories from that book of hers – and me, in the corner of whatever camp we could find, with my head in my dictionary, forcing myself to think with all those new words because ... well, I watched the world burn once, and I was damn well going to be part of a world that couldn't just burn. I was going to join it, with everything in my heart.' He stopped, gazed into each of the girls' eyes in turn. 'I promised my father I'd look after you all. I thought I'd found my way. The old country burned. The world wouldn't remember it, so ... why should we? It's all just accidents of birth, I thought. Once, we were one thing. Now, we could be another ...' He paused. 'I hadn't reckoned on bebia and her night garden. I hadn't thought that bits of the old world might still exist. In our hearts, she said. Truth is, I didn't believe it, not until tonight. But ... our hearts, they're a part of the world too. How could I ever think to destroy that? It would be like destroying each of you.'

And then, he thought, there was the music – music that had been dead for a lifetime, music that had soared over them in the night garden tonight, three thousand miles and two hundred years from the places it used to flourish.

For a time, there was only silence. He could feel the girls' eyes on him, every last one. He reached out and clasped their hands.

'Leaving it behind, starting again, it could never be enough. We could stay here a lifetime. Build houses of our own. Be mothers and fathers and bebias ourselves. But we'd still be us, wouldn't we? I love you all,' he whispered, his eyes resting momentarily on Isabelle. 'I wouldn't change you for the world. We survived it. We got here. But I was wrong. We didn't get here to start again. That isn't really what I want.'

Levon tightened his hold on their hands, drawing them inches closer – so that, though his next words were but whispers, they touched each of the girls in turn.

'So we're going to live by night.'

Up in the night garden, the night was becalmed.

Then: everything changed.

Levon and Isabelle were not there to see what happened next. They were downstairs, gathered with the children, the Nocturne lying open on the apartment floor between them as they read aloud the stories of Davit the Daydreamer, of Tamaz who followed the Seventh Star, of Ketevan and her Night Maidens, who served at the courts of the princes of old. So lost were they in the old stories that they did not see as a thousand shoots rose from the gutters and roof slates, and banks of yet more flowers-by-night turned their eager faces up to the stars. They did not see the lightjars – tiny birds, whose feathers burned brilliant with the nectar they drank – suddenly emerge from the new trees where they'd been nesting. They were not there to marvel at the nocturnal water rats, extinct for a generation, who drank at the water's edge, nor to see the vines – replete with luminous leaves – that spiralled up each length of scaffolding, or choked the air vents, or turned the concrete sarcophagus into a mountain of shimmering green. They did not see the rarest ruby-red flowers-by-night blossoming on the vine.

But what they did see was more magical still.

Down in the apartment, Aram grew restless. Perhaps it was the story of Siran, who searched for the sword at the bottom of the sea, that inspired him – for, as Levon spun the story, he picked himself up and charged across the crowded apartment floor, brandishing his bebia's old wooden spoon in fury.

Mariam hurried close behind – the mother locked in her eternal battle to stop her son impaling himself on door handles – when, at last, Aram crashed into the room where his bebia had breathed her last.

By the time Mariam caught him, his face was pressed up against the window. The skies of Paris at night were clear, but his face was turned upward – not at the glowing vines still cascading from the rooftop above, but at something higher, deeper, even brighter than that.

'Look!' he said. 'Look!'

So Mariam did. Then, 'Levon,' she breathed. 'Isabelle ...'

The story of Siran died behind them. Levon and Isabelle hurried into the room, and soon the rest of the family-by-night were crowded around. All of them gazed up, above the freight yard and the rolling rooftops of Paris. All of them saw what had not been there before.

A new star hung in the sky above Paris tonight.

Brighter, more vivid than all the rest, its light shone out in seven striking spires.

AN INTERLUDE

SOMEWHERE ON THE TRAIL

See ...

The border fence is new, built eight feet high and capped with turrets of barbed wire. But the man called Hayk has got through worse. In the beginning, the boats were so overflowing that, as they took to the landlocked sea, men perished in the very same waters their ancestors had sailed since the days of the Khanate. At Ankara, soldiers had opened fire on the column of men marching through. When the 'humanitarians' resolved to send them back to their conquered home, Hayk had cast himself out of one of the freighters, shattering his arm in two places so that he'd worn it in a sling for six weeks. After all of this, a razor-wire fence means so little.

The night is full of terrors, but Hayk knows fear. Hayk near drowned as a boy. Hayk was beaten by his father. Hayk was clubbed down by the soldiers when they caught him leading a sortie against their squadrons camped up along the landlocked sea. If anyone can turn fear to his advantage, it is a man like Hayk.

Besides, he thinks, he doesn't have to outrun the border guards. He only has to outrun his fellow refugees.

There they all are, lurking in the darkness around him. Most of the forest on this length of escarpment has been burned away. Fewer places, you see, for a refugee to hide. But between the outcrops that remain, hunkered in black scrubland with dirt and ash smeared into their faces, are the men who have sneaked out of the camp. It is always the men. Women and children you can barter through, but against men you must raise fences and build walls.

Hayk bides his time. He has the patience of continents. The first man to break for it is somewhere on his left. A shadow streaks through the darkness, scrambles up and over the fence. He gets over, and then he is swallowed up in the pitch black of the other side: Hungary, and the free world beyond.

His triumph gives others fresh cause. Hayk holds himself as they stream out of the dark. Some stumble as they take to the wire. Others heave themselves to the top, brace themselves there, and reach back to help their brothers up. Yes, the People help each other, thinks Hayk. Here's how they can help me.

His time has come. He charges for the fence. The first across, he thinks, will be the first to get caught. Leave it too late, and the border guards sweep in. But lose yourself in the heart of it, and there's a chance you can get through.

'Please!' he cries out to the man balanced precariously on the top of the fence. He reaches out his good arm, and the man – faltering, for his fellows are already streaking into the Hungarian dark – cannot ignore the plea. He steels himself, helps Hayk scramble up – until they are both balanced above the razor wire, ready to crash down on the other side.

Then come the lights.

Voices cry out. It is a language Hayk does not understand, but he has no need to. The language of order, the language of force, is the same the world over. It comes with megaphones and dazzling bright lights.

Engines are gunning on the Hungarian side of the border. There's every chance he's left this too late, but there isn't a bone in his body that means to retreat. Before the lights land on them, he and the other refugee crash to earth on the Hungarian side of the fence. Then, hoisting each other up, they run.

Engines to the left of them. Engines to the right. Most likely, thinks Hayk, they have guns. He hears the first reports somewhere behind him and knows the transports are arcing around – but the cover of trees is only three hundred yards away and, if he can reach it, perhaps he can yet win through.

At some point, he becomes aware that there are footsteps pounding behind him. Over his shoulder, the shadow men closing in, long batons in hand.

There's only one way out of this. 'Brother,' he says to the man lurching beside him, 'they're too close …'

'Just keep running, you dog!'

Dog, thinks Hayk. *Dog*. Well, this will make it easier.

He stops, waits, kicks out with the flat of his boot, shattering the other man's knee.

He doesn't have to outrun the border guards. He just has to outrun his fellow refugees.

The man is on the ground, screaming curses in the language of the old country, but the damage is already done. He'll pick himself up, perhaps even begin running again – but in moments the border guards will be on him, while Hayk himself will get away.

'You dog!' the man is bawling. 'You dog!'

Hayk dares to look back, the whisper of a smile showing on his face, and sees the border guards heaving the other off into the night. It's only the smallest sacrifice Hayk has made. This one, he can live with.

Blackness.

Hayk realises, suddenly, that he too is on the floor, and that the lights circling in his eyes are not the stars wheeling around in the heavens, but explosions of light where something has hit him. He knows the feeling of pain. It blossoms across his temple, spreading in fractures across his face.

Faces appear above him. Border guards, where he had thought they were none. But, oh, they have been wily, he thinks. This wasn't a chance encounter. This was an ambush.

He rolls, but the shock is still reverberating around his body. He is helpless as they lift him by his arms, helpless as they cast him into the back of their transport, helpless as the night surges past in fits and starts of colour, as doors open and close, as other men haul him, like the worthless sack of stones that he is, through a succession of gates and doors.

Here they leave him, behind one final door, brutalised and alone. But look at him, down there in the darkness. Catch a glimpse as he picks himself up from the metal grille where he has landed. Is he weeping for his lost country, weeping for himself, as he heaves himself to his feet?

No, he is smiling.

This isn't the first detention centre he's found himself in. What about Odessa? What about Bucharest? Just pit stops along the way, he thinks. Just places to nurse your wounds and gather your thoughts. Nothing lasts forever. The old country didn't, so why should this?

There must be twenty men in the cell, and only six of them in cots of their own. Some are sandwiched together. Others lie in nests on the floor. Two sleep sitting up, propped against each other like prisoners-of-war – which is, Hayk observes, precisely what they are, if only they were clever enough to know it.

He shakes one man awake. The man is not alert enough – Hayk could have killed him in his sleep – and tries to bat the newcomer away, uttering curses and oaths. It is enough for Hayk to deduce that he is one of the People. So are all of the people in these pens. He snorts at this, turning over every sleeping face. Not one of them is the face he is hoping to see. Not one of them his last-born son. But no matter: every detention centre he reaches, every detention centre he escapes, is one detention centre closer to the West. He'll do it over and over, if that's what he has to do.

One of the sleeping men has made the mistake of taking the boots off his feet. No possession is more prized out here than a pair of sturdy boots. Without good boots, you never get far.

Hayk's own boots are worn thin, threadbare and full of holes. He eases them off swollen feet and helps himself to the boots sitting at the end of the bed. He helps himself to other things too: one man has stockpiled rations; another has a bottle of water, which eases its way down Hayk's hoarse throat. Well, he thinks, if you don't look after what belongs to you, somebody else just comes along and takes it.

And that, he decides, is the lesson of the old country itself. Open and unprotected, a country of fishermen's sons without a soldiery of its own, lulled into thinking they owned the land-locked sea because of some old fables and traditions. How a civil-isation as old as theirs could be so foolish, Hayk will never know. Nor will he ever forgive.

There is but one window in this cell. He picks his way to it. Up in the sky, through its bars, the clouds shift and come apart.

See ...

Hayk knows the heavens well. All the sons of the People do. He knows the Great Bears and Charioteers; he knows the Herds-man and the Archer. The People have not lived by starlight for generations, but the old knowledge abides.

And that is why his heart, which has been brutalised for so long, burns with new life when he looks out into the night.

The night, they say, is full of terrors. But, if the Nocturne is to be believed, it was once bright and full of joy. The night was when enchantment happened, when the People knew that they were special – for they were the ones entrusted with all of the magic left in the world.

'Wake up! Wake up, you dogs!' He bursts into wild, uncon-trolled laughter, and wraps his fists around the bars that cage him. 'It's night-time, you wretches, and the People – the true-blood People – don't sleep by night. Up, up! Come, you dogs, come and see!'

It is funny, he thinks, but he never thought about the Khanate of the Stars before the old world burned. Just bedtime stories. Just the Nocturne that his mother Maia used to keep.

It is only now, out in the modern world with the old country vanished, that it seems to matter at all.

But oh how it matters . . .

Soon, the other detainees are awake and clamouring at the bars. Jostling each other, they snap and scrap for a place, but none of them will uproot Hayk.

Hayk is staring with them, up into the night-time sky. He remembers, too vividly, the way the world came to its end.

But here, he thinks, is the start of another.

For a seven-pointed star is rising in the West.

BOOK TWO

PARIS, THE CITY OF LIGHTS

In the time of enchantment, before you were born, a young man named Tamaz made landfall at dawn – and said to his fellows, who crowded the shore, 'The night's a fantasia, but don't you want more? More than just sailing our ocean each night? More than just basking in silver starlight? The world's so much vaster than our stories say. I'll set off next nightfall for lands far away.'

'One piece of wisdom,' his captain then breathed, 'before you set off on adventures like these. Through all of your dark times, one truth you must know: all that you love still exists long ago …'

From 'The Story of Tamaz', the Nocturne

5

....

THE MUSIC OF THE NIGHT

The rumour first reached the tenements in Kreuzberg, Berlin. Some young fool had started living by night.

A moronic endeavour, somebody said. It's been hundreds of years since the old-timers last lived by night. This is the Modern Age. Now there's Economics. There's Science. What good could be done by looking back at things that ceased to exist all those aeons ago – if, indeed, they ever existed at all? Live by night! somebody scoffed. The very idea!

And yet ...

We did it once, somebody said. I remember how my great-grandfather would speak of that midnight world. The banks of the lakes would wake up at nightfall, and the flowers-by-night were like fields of starlight itself. The birds glowed with the nectar they drank. The lakes came alive with endless schools of the *bakhtat*, glimmering just below the surface. My bebia used to say that *her* bebia had one of the last surviving water dogs, from the days before the sea was poisoned. And I remember the old stories too. My grandfather knew the best tales.

What might it be like, to catch a glimpse of that world again?

It's only one boy living at night, they said. It doesn't mean a thing.

Oh, but it did. It meant a thing to the old-timers who'd found their way to Copenhagen. It meant a thing to the refugees still sitting in the camps outside Ankara, the detention centre at

Budapest. It meant everything to the families scrabbling their pennies together in Munich and Berlin, anxiously waiting to discover if they might be being moved on. The very idea that somebody remembered. The idea that anybody cared.

They say there are flowers-by-night growing in the gutters of Paris. They say that, should you look up when you walk the Champs-Élysées by night, you can see luminescent dots darting in and out of every roof terrace – and that these are the lightjars of old, brought back to life by the power of belief.

The old country wasn't destroyed after all. It was ... broken into a billion tiny pieces, and each one of those pieces buried in one of us. It's the job of a people, they said, to restore what was broken. It can't all be left to one boy.

His name is Levon, somebody said. It's a good solid name. A name from the old world. And yet ... it's going to take us all, if we're to be a people again. One boy cannot do it alone.

So come, they said in Copenhagen. Come soon, they said in Kreuzberg, Berlin. Stop plotting your ways across the English Channel. Stop clinging to the landing gear of their aeroplanes and freezing to death, thirty-thousand feet high. There's a new home now. It's where we belong.

Come one, come all, they said, to Paris-by-Starlight.

*

Midnight at the Hôtel Métropol. Levon's shift had barely begun when the girl from the reception desk came to find him. There he was, his face in the toilet bowl while he fought to remove some particularly truculent stain, and her shadow fell across him.

'There's more of them here for you. I had to turn them out – there's not a reservation among them. But there they are, with all their suitcases and packs ...' Levon squinted up at her, and saw that she was caught somewhere in that no man's land between 'amused' and 'thoroughly pissed off'. 'Look, if M. Fortier sees them loitering, he'll know who to go after. Well, they've got your look, haven't they? All your people do. Just see them off. They can't be bothering actual guests.'

Stripping off his rubber gloves, Levon got to his feet. 'Thank you, Fae.'

She rolled her eyes and slipped back to the restroom door. 'How many more of you are there?' she said, when she was almost out of sight.

'I don't know. The old country wasn't big, but ...'

A whole people, he wanted to say. *The whole People*. But the girl was already gone.

The Hôtel Métropol sat on the corner of the Rue Castex, only a short stroll from the Place de la Bastille. A perfect place, people used to say, for weekenders coming to Paris – but the truth was it was shabbier than the hotels around, and what had once been fashionably irregular had fallen, in the past years, into real disrepair. The old-time staff said that M. Fortier used to care. During the war, the Métropol had hidden artists and musicians, kept a runaway in its cellars for weeks on end, poisoned one Nazi and then another (the chef had been positively medieval), but in his later years M. Fortier was more interested in how his horses were racing than the reputation of his family hotel. Consequently, the carpets were ragged, the rooms looked a decade out of date, and half of the staff had no documentation to prove they had any right to be in Paris at all. The night manager himself was from Tunis, and the cleaning staff almost entirely made up of the People.

After midnight, the reception hall was still. Levon walked through and out into the Parisian night. As he set foot on the Rue Castex, he saw a single luminescent bell, shimmering in sapphire where it had forced its way up through a crack between two paving stones. Carefully (and though it prompted a pang of regret), he ground it beneath his heel. It was happening too often. He'd found a tussock growing in one of the window boxes on the second storey only last night. His bebia would have told him it was because of the cleaning staff – all of them of the People, and all of them living by night – but, if M. Fortier were to find out, he might not find it quite as joyful. One man's magic was another man's madness.

On the other side of the hotel's black iron rails there was a bench, and there the family had set up camp: a mother and a father and, between them, two teenage children, one with a babe in arms.

They looked tired, thought Levon. Tired and drawn. He approached them cautiously.

'You're him, aren't you? You're Levon?'

Levon nodded.

'So you can get us in – a bed, even for a night?'

Levon looked back at the face of the hotel. 'I'm sorry. If I could ...'

The man's face was crumpling when Levon turned back to face him. 'We've come so far.'

'I know, brother.' So had all of those who kept turning up at the Hôtel Métropol, as if Levon had all of the answers. They'd have heard his name in some whisper and latched on to it. The way they said it: so loaded with expectation. 'Where have you come from?'

'We were in Utrecht. We heard they were letting the People settle. Only, there were too many of us there. I spent the summer picking fruit, but since then – nothing. And then we heard ...' The man, whose words were turning to a frenzy, gathered himself. 'We have it right, haven't we? You're the one?'

It wasn't the first time he'd heard those words either – and every time, just like now, he longed for his bebia. If she were here, he'd have turned them over to her, let her tell them how no soul worked alone, how the old country existed in each and every one of its People – how it had been waiting, just waiting, for its People to summon it back. But four months had flown since they scattered her ashes in her night garden, and sometimes Levon struggled to remember her voice.

So his would have to do.

'I can't get you into the Métropol, but I won't leave you behind. Wait here.' He scurried back inside, made his excuses to Fae – who cared not one jot, for she was watching soap operas on the television behind reception – and then returned to the night. 'Follow me,' he said, shouldering one of their packs, 'it isn't far.'

The night markets moved.

Levon was never certain where the People gathered each night. Truth was, he wasn't certain when the first night market had been held, nor who the first traders had been. Such things existed where once they had not – and this simple truth had to be enough. But if you followed the whispers, you could ordinarily stumble upon one or other of the nocturnal bazaars. Some were little more than a few traders spreading out their wares on woven blankets. Any place would do: the Squares Léon and Saint-Bernard in the Goutte d'Or, or the edges of the Luxembourg Gardens; but better still were the vagrant patches of ground outside the heart of the city, the places that Paris's vagabonds already knew well. If you wanted homespun clothes, you could find them in the night markets. If you wanted fake passports or star charts, or the fermented spirits of the landlocked sea, there was somebody who could help. And the more People who arrived in Paris, the more vibrant the bazaars became.

When he reached the Place des Vosges, tonight's market was already being routed. A trio of police officers gathered on the edges of the square, writing out a penalty notice to some dejected refugee in front of the griddle he'd set up. There had been ten or more stalls set up here – they'd burned brightly beneath the trees, in the lee of the impressive townhouses that bordered the square – but most were already being packed away.

'I'm sorry,' said Levon, 'I thought we'd find someone here who could ...'

'Police are the same the world over,' the man said sadly.

But they weren't, thought Levon. He'd seen police with batons beating the People at the Serbian frontier. Yet here, the police officers were sharing a jubilant expression, gazing upwards into the trees. From the boughs of one of the horse chestnuts there exploded a flurry of emerald lights. Like sparks of green fire, five or six lightjars darted upwards, fanning out across the manicured lawns. Such joy on the gendarmes' faces, thought Levon. They were like children chasing butterflies.

The family were staring too. The mother of the child, if mother she was – for didn't the families of the People slot together in different ways now? – pointed as one of the lightjars pirouetted directly above.

'So it's true,' the father said. 'You really did it!'

'I didn't do anything,' Levon insisted. 'It's just the ... turning of the world.'

'Might we find work here, in the bazaar? I was a shipwright on the landlocked sea. There's no call for ships in Paris, but it's carpentry like everything else. I have a trade.'

'Rooms first, work second.' Levon shepherded them cautiously along the edge of the square; enchanted by the lightjars the police might have been, but they still had a job to do. 'Did you get your papers in Utrecht?'

When the newcomer next spoke, he sounded fearful. So did they all, thought Levon – but the fear, he had learned, was not absolute. Even now, after everything, it could be ground down. Out there, you thought that it had become a part of you, that being afraid was the same thing as being alive. It got so you needed the fear. It anchored you. You became fear's shadow, stalking it across the continent, unable to separate yourself from the aching terror you felt. It did not occur to you, when you were out there, that there'd be a time when you wouldn't feel fear again. But here in Paris was a sanctuary of the most magical kind.

'The wait for papers was always so long. And the bureaucracy! Any chance to move you on, and they took it. We had friends – there one day, gone the next, and we never did find out where they were sent. I couldn't take my girls into a system like that.'

Levon understood. 'Then stick to the People. There's enough of us now. The People will look after you.' He stopped – because, no matter how many times he'd said it, the emotion of it still moved in him. 'You made it,' he whispered, with the most exalted look. 'You're home.'

And here home was.

The superintendent never looked happy to meet more refugees from the old country, but inwardly he was always smiling. Levon could see it in his eyes: he'd lived his life a pauper, but now – courtesy of the special payments he received from each new resident – he was a prince.

'When the border patrol comes knocking, you'll find me sunning myself on the Côte d'Azur,' he grinned. 'They won't catch me, you can count on that!' He had a slithering way about him, but there was a heart hidden in there. Dripping with effluent it might have been, but countless were the times he'd forgone his payments and accepted dried fish, flame fruit from the night garden above, or just stories from the old country instead.

The block had grown busier as the seasons advanced. As the superintendent led them into an apartment vacated some time ago by an elderly artiste, neighbours watched from the stairwell. These were families of the People as well. Sixteen families called the block home, but that was only a fraction of the People who'd reached Paris.

'Two thousand, maybe more,' said Levon, but it wasn't as if there'd been a census. More came with the fall of each night. Wasn't that what the people hanging out of the doors in the stair-well were doing? Scouring each new face for signs of people they'd left behind, people they'd thought never to see again – until the world reminded them that, sometimes, miracles do hap-pen.

'Might you have family here?' he asked as, leaving their packs in the apartment, they tramped further up.

The family were quiet, until finally the man said, 'My brothers. My sister. Cousins. Scattered to the winds.'

And so the story went on. Levon himself found it easier to pretend that he didn't have a father, that the rabble of half-brothers he'd had – always a distant presence in his life, even when he was young – had simply slipped out of existence, that when the old country burned so did all of his memories. Patent nonsense, he thought, but some deceptions were more useful than others.

Some things, of course, refused to be forgotten.

They came up the last stair and Levon led them out into the night garden above.

The grotto was aglow, a wilderness of lights. The luminous creepers – a myriad of different sapphires, cyans and darker blues – had grown up to form an archway through which Levon and the family came. Beyond it, the horse-shoe shape of the block was ringed in flame-coloured flowers of a thousand different hues. The lake at its heart was banked in undulating emerald reeds; the dust they cast into the air gave the appearance of a ghostly green mist, obscuring the orchard beyond. Here, half a dozen spidery trees were heavy with bulbous fruits. A shifting mass of dragon-flies, their lace-like wings emanating a soft silver light, moved in unison across the surface of the water.

The People were here as well. Somebody had constructed a small gazebo on the windward side of the orchard, and in its shelter Mariam stood before a group of the block's children – and, in her hands, Maia's copy of the Nocturne. Here were Arina and Ana and Elen, but so many others as well: boys and girls, and even a young man who looked too old for schooling. Beyond them, others were taking in the delights of the garden at night. The flowers of the old country had no fear of this Parisian winter; even in the depths of the season there was the light of the stars to keep them nourished. Warmth went hand in hand with light; here in the night garden, it was as seasonable as spring.

'Come,' he said, 'I'll show you.'

They skirted the school – where Arina waved furiously as Levon passed, and the story of Davit the Daydreamer was in full flight – and came to the edge of the rooftop, where shimmering vines cascaded over the edge. Here yet more lightjars danced, disappearing off the precipice to the bright flowers budding below. Not a soul had seen one of the nighthawks that, in the stories of the Nocturne, hunted the lightjars – but it seemed that the lightjars themselves remembered, and made their nests where none could see.

Levon stared into the suburbs of the north. Out there, the city fractured; you could see the long fallows of the motorways and railway lines, the low-lying suburbs punctuated by occasional eruptions of tower blocks, funnels and spires. The night was clear, and crowning some of those tower blocks were other gardens just like this. Levon liked to think of them as tiny crucibles of belief – as if, wherever the People had found a place to call their own, the world had responded in kind. His bebia was still with him, in every thought like this.

'It started here, but it's not as if we own it. It's just the old world, rippling out, starting again – little pockets in the night.

The park-keepers, the street-sweepers, they weed it out when they find flowers-by-night popping up in the city parks … but up here, where nobody wanders? Well, up here, it's the old world – incandescent. There are so many forgotten places. Look – out there, and there, and there …'

'It's how I imagined the landlocked sea used to be,' the father began, dreamily. 'You'd be on the waves in the dead of night, the shimmering waters all around – and there, on the shore, bastions of light, just like these rooftops, where the villages used to be. By the Stars, young man, what you've done …'

Levon could hear no more of this. He was no more the champion of this resurgent world than he was a hero plucked out of the pages of the Nocturne. But sometimes people needed explanation. Stories needed a face.

'The orchards are for everyone. Take what you need. And here …' He called out, and Arina came scuttling out of the school with a bundle of pages in her hand. They'd been stitched up in golden thread, and onto the raggedy book's cover had been stencilled the same seven-pointed star that was now suspended directly overhead. 'For you.'

The mother of the family took it and traced the star with her fingertip. 'The Nocturne …'

'My bebia brought her bebia's copy with her, out onto the trail. She said: it isn't the history of the People. It's the *feeling* of them. Now, my family are making copies, so that everyone might remember. This one's for you.'

'I remember these. My own grandmother used to tell them.' She flicked through the pages and began to read its cursive, spiralling script:

In times unremembered, when the People were free, two lovers were wed by the shores of our sea – and decided one night, in the luminous wild, they would lie down together and bring

forth a child. They would raise it together, this boy or this girl,
and make gifts to it of all the joys in the world. The lightjars
and moon moths, wherever they roam. This feeling of wonder.
This feeling of home. So this is the tale of when Two became
Three, down by the shores of the glittering sea.

Forget, for a moment, this man was your King, and focus
instead on the love the night brings ...

It was hardly a religious text. Just bedtime stories. But the reverence they gave it, even this raggedy copy transcribed in the apartment downstairs, was itself a wonder to behold.

'How can we repay you?'

Levon shrugged his big round shoulders. 'Don't repay me. Repay them. The ones who come after. There are thousands of us still lost. Thousands more need homes.' He had thought about this much, along the way. It was funny how you could forget there was such a thing as 'the future'. 'Look after each other. Keep the magic alive. Don't we deserve a little enchantment, after everything that's happened?'

The family turned their faces, again, to the kaleidoscope of lights that made up the garden. 'A little enchantment,' they seemed to be saying, 'goes a long way.'

Levon left them gazing out, and walked with Arina back to the gazebo where the class was in full session. Mariam was in her element. It was easy to forget she'd been a teacher in the old country; losing Aram's father somewhere in the Aegean still haunted her – but seeing the ease she had with the children, Levon was reminded: it wasn't just the old world that the Nocturne could restore; it was the old you.

Arina scurried after him, back into the apartment where half-finished copies of the Nocturne were waiting to be stitched together. He'd thought to find Natia and Nino here, but of course they were out roaming the night, looking for more People of their same age.

The apartment had changed since his bebia went into the final night. The back bedroom where she'd breathed her last was now the place where Levon laid his head. Natia and Nino had taken a room in an apartment on the other side of the stairwell, with another couple who'd reached Paris via Dortmund and Cologne. By some strange mercy, Ana and Elen had found an elderly cousin on one of their forays to the night market, and now they lived two storeys below. Miracles, thought Levon, stacked upon miracles. The seven-pointed star was calling them home. Now, in the apartment's main room, the beds had been rearranged so that the apartment could become their own little hive of industry: the stories of the Nocturne being told and retold, its woodcuts and portraits being reproduced in pencil, pen and crayon.

Levon went to the stovetop, where the remnants of the breakfast hash remained in a pot. 'I need to get back to the Métropol before Fae rats me out,' he said, wolfing it back, 'and you should be in school—'

'Levon!'

Arina's protest was only half-hearted; the fact was, she enjoyed her schooling as much as any child who has crossed continents, not knowing where they're bound.

'Here,' he said, digging into his pockets, 'take these for the class – and make sure Aram gets his share.' And he produced a brown paper parcel filled with spirals of the salt-water *sudjukh* they sold in the night market. In the Nocturne, Tamaz filled his knapsack with these sweet snakes, made from the powdered roots of the flowers-by-night, and these were the things that sustained him on his voyages far from home. Not even Beyrek could remember a time when they'd been sold in the old country, and the secret of their concoction was not hidden in the pages of the Nocturne itself, but by their taste it was hard to believe these weren't the same sweets that the sailors of old had taken out on the dark water, or that lovers had shared as they lay together in fields of shimmering starlight, overlooking a shoreline where radiant orbs eddied and danced.

Arina began chewing on the first spiral. As she took in its flavour, her face lit up in delight. There was nothing else like it – not in the old country, and not in the new. 'Where was the night market tonight?'

'They'd set up in the Place des Vosges, but they were being moved on. They'll be in some waste ground by now ...'

'Isabelle says she'll take us down to the bazaars one night, that we could even have a stall. There she'll be, selling her guidebook – and us, right there, with copies of the Nocturne too. Beyrek's going to help.'

Levon, filled with a sudden joy at the idea, clapped his little sister around the shoulder. 'I love you, Arina,' he said, and meant it.

There was a copy of Isabelle's guide lying on the kitchenette counter. Levon picked it up. *Paris-by-Starlight* was emblazoned across the page. Since the People had started arriving, it had seemed important to Levon that they know the Nocturne. But it was Isabelle who'd known it was important that the people of Paris knew too. The pamphlet in Levon's hands was her attempt to guide them into the new nocturnal world. How else, she'd said, could the people of Paris know how lucky they were?

He loved looking at her handwriting, the knowledge that it was her fingers that had caressed the page. Opening it at random, he read:

We people of Paris have always known magic. And yet something more enchanting still has come to our city at night. Come to Paris and go to the night markets, hear the voices of a lost world, gather at Montmartre and look above to find the Seventh Star hanging in the sky, or simply go to the nightspots where the music of a lost country is being revived. Paris has always been a home for runaways, but now we welcome an entire runaway world. And in nightspots like the Ambergris, L'Oasis, Le Tangiers ...

Here Levon stopped reading. His eyes lingered on the last words.

Le Tangiers, he thought. Yes, of course – she'd be there now.

*

Le Tangiers was alive.

There were newcomers in the cellar bar tonight. You could always tell newcomers by the look in their eyes: half trepidation, half disbelief. They'd drift around Paris after dark, following the scents of whatever was being cooked up in the night markets, or just gathering around the stands of flowers-by-night that had taken root under the motorway bridges. Sometimes, they'd have to wander for nights, breathing it all in, before they understood that this was real, not some mirage sent to test them. Only then would they dare gravitate to places like Le Tangiers – where, against all the experience of a lifetime, their arrival in Paris was being celebrated each night.

Even Isabelle, who waited in the wings of the tiny stage, could detect those who had just come in from the trail. From her darkened alcove she watched two young men come down the basement stairs and, parting the curtains, enter the bar. Their faces were contortions of delight – ugly, because they doubted what they were seeing; beautiful, because they were daring it to be true. She watched as Beyrek angled his way through the crowd to greet them.

It wasn't only the People who came to Le Tangiers. Half of the room was speaking the soft, spiralling language of their old country, but among them were revellers from every corner of Paris. Some of them had come to sample the fermented spirit that the People made from the same flame fruit that flourished in Levon's night garden; its taste – which was fiery and sweet, and left a faint luminescence on the lips – had already drawn in connoisseurs and curious students. Now they came to see what other treasures the People had brought with them.

Among those treasures was the music.

Beyrek loped onto the stage and, with a deference normally afforded for people of much greater stardom, Le Tangiers fell into a reverential silence. The pride that he carried every time he stood before his People was towering. She had seen it iron out the lines in his face a hundred times. Tonight, he was wearing one of the loose-fitting black *chokha* that they'd started selling in the night markets; in the Nocturne, sailors had gone to the landlocked sea wearing these same satin shirts, their captains with the emblem of the seven-pointed star embroidered on its sleeves. Beyrek himself wore the stars tonight: captain not of his own fishing vessel, but of Le Tangiers.

'People of the night,' he said, and repeated the same in French – so that all the Parisians among the People felt the same thrill of the world reborn, 'it gives me the greatest pleasure to introduce the Rose of the Evening ...'

At the edge of the stage, Isabelle dared to believe. Here was the feeling she'd been chasing ever since she came to Paris: the feeling that some indefinable pieces of her had at last become one, that everything was right and she didn't have to *try*. As if her own seven-pointed star had risen in the sky.

She stepped out onto the stage.

The Rose of the Evening, they called her. That was a name straight out of the Nocturne too. There she was, in the background of every fable, spanning whole centuries of life under the Khanate of the Stars. When Tamaz travelled far from home, the Rose of the Evening was playing the music of the old country in every wayfarer's inn through which he voyaged; when Ketevan and her Night Maidens served in the court of the Princes of the Night, there she was, spinning the music with which they soothed the young herald to sleep; when Davit the Daydreamer dared to live by day, the Rose of the Evening appeared to tempt him back; when Tariel ventured into the Khanate Beneath, her music haunted him from every crevasse under the landlocked sea. Beyrek said that the Nocturne neglected her, that the Rose was as vital to the feeling of the People as any of the adventurers whose lives the Nocturne chronicled. She deserved a story of her own – and this story was being spun right here in Le Tangiers.

Isabelle started to play.

In music, a moment that was fleeting in life could be stretched into an eternity. You spun it out in the way your fingers danced. Since that night in the moonlit grove, Isabelle had let the music guide her. She followed it, now – first into movements she'd discovered before, and then beyond the horizon, into the unknown melodies and counter-melodies, runs and refrains, that were waiting out there. Each melody brought with it a story. She closed her eyes and could see herself, soaring through a sky jewelled in stars. Or she was cantering on horseback through glades of rippling emerald reeds, kicking up a radiant dust behind her as a lonely tower, strangled in glowing sapphire vines, promised sanctuary up ahead.

Sometimes they danced in Le Tangiers – but, more often, they stood as they stood now: mesmerised by the Rose of the Evening, whose harp (or was it her heart?) was summoning back the spirit of an elder age.

The sensation of a song ending was at once a sadness and a release. After some time, Isabelle felt the music escaping from her. She grappled after it – but the music had broken free. She opened her eyes, to find herself not in a meadow of silver flowers-by-night, but in the cellar with a hundred faces coming out of the spell she'd been weaving.

The room broke into applause – and, for a moment, it was like the waves crashing over the landlocked sea. Then all of the fantasia – if fantasia it really was – was swept away, and Isabelle felt herself grounded again, back in the bar. Her fingers ached. Her body was spent. There was something about letting the music pour out of her that left her battered and bruised, as if the sea had been tossing her around.

The applause sustained her, but the fact was she needed a drink.

By the time she'd reached the bar, so had half of Le Tangiers – but that didn't matter; there were more than enough revellers willing to stand her a drink. She took hers to a corner and looked out over Le Tangiers.

Natia and Nino – who would rather be here than almost any-where in Paris – had welcomed the strangers and sat with them by the bar, while a French boy tried to inveigle his way between them, desperate for Natia's attention. Poor lost boy – he stood no chance. Beyond them, Eldar and Aysel – who'd been living rough in Stuttgart when they first heard whispers of Paris-by-Starlight – were deep in conversation with an elderly man, Kevork, who had spent his life travelling the edges of the landlocked sea. Here, thought Isabelle, was the old world entire.

Beyond Kevork, a middle-aged man with tousled blond hair and an inscrutable look was cautiously putting a glass of crushed ice and fermented flame fruit to his lips. Isabelle's eyes lingered on him, though she could not say why. He wasn't the only Parisi-an in the bar tonight; it was just that he was the only one who looked out of place.

Isabelle had little time to think on it, for in a moment Beyrek was beside her.

'It was beautiful, Isabelle. That movement, I haven't heard it before.'

She smiled, as if to say: neither have I.

'I'm tired, Beyrek. It exhausts me.'

'Then come!'

There was food for her behind the bar. Nightly, Beyrek went out into the night market – wherever it was – and brought back the dishes of the old country they were serving up. There was an old fisherwoman's wife who had teased out the taste of Beyrek's childhood – the salt, the spice, the freshness of seaweed – and brought it even further to life with the essences she was extracting from the flowers-by-night. 'Like they used to eat, in ages gone by,' Beyrek said as he served Isabelle. 'This will see you right.'

As she ate, people intermittently approached. Some of them she knew from nights gone by. At first, she'd been fearful when she was approached. How dare *she*, she wondered, play their music to them? But they came to her with love, or marvelling at the images they'd seen across the backs of their eyes, and questions about the music she played. In four months, she had known no hatred – only wonder – and perhaps it was this that had freed up her fingers. She doubted them no longer.

Tonight, one of the listeners asked her if she taught.

'I used to play, when I was a girl. I had an old oud, and there were melodies I could pluck. But … it was all the songs they'd brought in from the Russias. Or from English travellers. I should like to play something of the old country – the actual old country, before the sea was poisoned, when there was still … magic in the world.'

And Isabelle said, 'Come to our night garden. Then you'll see – there's magic yet …'

'I mean magic like there is in your music. I close my eyes and I can see it: the whole world, like it used to be. Before pollution and corruption and soldiers and war. I should like to play those songs for myself. I feel brittle,' she said suddenly, 'brittle and alone. My husband died on the trail. Once, I had a daughter. Now, I'm cleaning shop floors three thousand miles away from home … I should like a little magic.'

Isabelle stood and, daring to wrap her arms around the woman, felt some of her brittleness soften. And though the softening was slight, this meant more than all the music in the world. She'd been meaning to say: I couldn't possibly teach you; I don't know how I do it myself. But instead she said, 'Find me here on Friday night, before the show starts. I'll show you what I can.' And the woman – too fearful to voice her thanks, in case she lost control of her words – nodded and was gone.

'They're ready for the Rose,' Beyrek said, and she followed his gaze back to the stage.

Isabelle nodded. 'One more voyage, before I really am spent,' she said – and wondered where the music would take her this time.

She turned to the bar to order a glass of water – but, when she turned back, already feeling some gentle rainfalling melody, she was not alone. The man with the tousled blond hair was standing in front of her, and the look on his face was of a child come before its parents to confess some terrible wrong. He hung, six feet away, as if he might be repelled if he got too close.

Up on the stage, Beyrek was bringing the crowd back to a reverential silence. 'Ladies and gentlemen. One more time, for the Rose of the Evening …'

But there was no Rose. The stage remained empty. Isabelle was still at the back of the bar, staring at this stranger with the wild blond hair, the eyes that seemed fractionally too large.

'I came for the harpist,' he said – and to Isabelle his voice was like the music she'd been discovering, like pulling at the fragments of a history long forgotten. Suddenly, a hundred thousand memories were scrabbling out of the deepest recesses of her mind: an old world being restored. 'I had no idea it was you. It ... is you, isn't it?'

Isabelle had no words.

'I haven't played music of my own in a lifetime. But I still like to hear it. The harp. The mandolin. I go to the places I used to play, and pretend I'm still one of them – that life didn't happen, that things didn't change. And in the bars they were talking about you, about the Rose of the Evening, about the new music ...'

Le Tangiers was still silent. One by one, the crowd were revolving to find Isabelle.

'You know me,' the stranger whispered, his entreaty barely audible, even in the silent bar.

'Hector,' Isabelle replied. And then, cautiously – because, even though the word sounded wrong, she had wanted, for so long, to say it: 'Dad.'

6

OLD WORLDS, OLD INCANTATIONS

Watch ...

The winter sun is setting over the Paris you know. Its last light touches the pinnacle of the Tour Eiffel. Its final rays turn the great basilica at the Sacré-Cœur to butter and gold. All along the Champs-Élysées, the shadows lengthen until they dominate the avenue. For the briefest of moments, the sunlight is seen as narrow ribbons of fire cresting every rooftop in the city. Then it is gone ...

... and a whole new world wakes up.

In the waste grounds of the city's far-flung places, tiny blossoms turn their faces to the sky. Under the motorway flyovers where the tent cities sprawl, lightjars emerge from their diurnal roosts to zip, like tiny comets, through the night. On overlooked grass verges, sapphire sits side by side with silver, while in demolition sites not meant for the eyes of good, honest Parisian folk, vagabonds are setting up stalls.

And in the back bedroom of an apartment block, somewhere in the city's north – with the rumble of the railway to the east and the freight yards somewhere behind – a young man wraps his arms around his lover and whispers into her ear, 'Then you did it. Everything you set out to do. Only, now you got what you wanted, the real adventure begins ...'

Levon kissed Isabelle gently. 'When we were out there, getting into Paris was the only thing I thought about. Even eating, when

I ate at all, was just about getting enough fuel to get me through the next ten miles. Then, when we got here, it was like … another world ending. I'd wander the city, up and down, thinking: What next? Well, what next was life …'

'Nearly eighteen years.' The flowers-by-night on the ledge were waking up. She watched, as she did each evening, the light spreading through each petal and leaf. 'You're chasing a dream, and then, there it is.'

Dreams of flesh and blood. She'd rehearsed their meeting countless thousands of times, and yet, when it came to it, she had no words. Hector said he'd been thinking about leaving all evening. The moment he watched the Rose of the Evening walk up on stage, his heart had turned against him. He wanted to leave and he wanted to stay and, the surer he got that it was Isabelle up on stage, the more trapped he was between the two. 'And the harp,' he'd said, 'you're playing my harp …'

She'd still had to go back to the stage, still had to be the Rose of the Evening. It was the first time, since the music had come to her, that she'd faltered – for how could the music of that long ago land flow through her when she was suddenly thrust into her own Golden Age, her father watching as she tentatively reached for each string?

Yes: dreams of flesh and blood. But the dream was easier somehow. The dream could be controlled.

By now, Levon was pulling on his boxer shorts, his roughspun trousers, his work boots. He'd grown rangier in the last months, but there was still something puppyish about him.

'Where will you meet him?'

'I can hardly bring him here.' She looked around the narrow room and laughed. For three months she'd been living here. When she thought back on her old apartment, now, it was only as she'd think of a bus depot where she was transiting from one coach to another – just a port of call, until she got to where she was truly meant to be. 'I'm to go to their house. He's married. He has a son. To think – I'd have been eight, still wondering if he'd turn up in the mountains to find me, and he was here in Paris, holding his newborn son . . .'

She didn't intend it, but there was bitterness behind her words. Hector walked out on her, she thought, but he didn't walk out on *him* – whoever this *him* was.

'This son,' Levon said gently, 'is your brother.'

'Half-brother.'

Levon shrugged. 'You get to know that families are all kinds of things,' he said. 'And, besides, you already have one – right here.'

He opened the door, and Isabelle heard the riot of voices on the other side.

It was Arina who was most excited – for Christmas was coming to Paris.

The children were speaking of it in the night garden. They'd celebrated Christmas for generations in the old country. Some traditions travel far, and there they remain. Most of them had celebrated Christmas on the long trek west as well. But there was something, Isabelle thought, about a first Christmas in a new home that solidified a life. She could still remember that first Christmas in Saint-André, how snow had capped the Pyrenees, how she'd sat and watched its slow, flickering fall deep into the night, wondering if this was the moment when her father might return.

Mariam was late in coming to the lessons, but not one of the children seemed to mind. There they were, breakfasting on the edge of the rooftop lake, faces glowing with juice. There were new children here tonight, though that in itself was nothing new. The citizens of Paris-by-Starlight swelled with every moonrise. As Levon and Isabelle crossed the rooftop grove, they saw one young boy, scarcely older than Aram, tucked up on his elder sister's knee, his thumb in his mouth and his eyes screwed shut.

There were still travellers coming in from the trail, then. That harrowed look was too familiar, but at least in the night garden it faded fast.

'The snows are coming,' Levon said – and thought, with a sinking sensation, of those still out there. The stragglers who kept tramping into the city. His own father – if, somehow, he survived. 'I've got to go. M. Fortier's just looking for a reason to get rid of me.' He took three steps away, their hands still intertwined. 'Isabelle, your father. I mean to say ...'

'I know,' she whispered. 'Be careful.'

She'd been thinking the same herself – that love tendered did not mean love received, that hoping too much meant there was too much at risk – but Levon said, 'I was going to say ... good luck. You deserve everything, Isabelle.'

Then he tumbled back through the lights.

After he had gone, Isabelle looked up and saw clouds drifting in from the east. When they obscured the stars, the night garden would glow less vividly – but the snow never settled here, for the flowers made their own warmth. Lightjars were darting in and out of the rainbow foliage that cascaded over the rooftop's edges.

'Isabelle, look!'

Arina had gambolled through the flowers to meet her. How different she looked to the thin waif who'd set about her pancakes with such gusto five months ago. It wasn't only that she was more rounded; her face was changing shape, inching its way from girl to woman grown.

In her hand hung the oldest copy of the Nocturne, the one Maia had treasured. Where she was clinging to it, the pages were sticky with the pulp of the flame fruit she'd been eating. Isabelle dropped quickly to her knees and took the book, carefully dabbing its corners dry.

'Arina, you must be more ...'

It wasn't the only copy of the Nocturne in Paris-by-Starlight, but there still seemed something totemic about the book. Its pages were ingrained with the dirt of centuries. Its pictures had endured the fingertips of generations. The copies they'd been making, to circulate among the People coming to Paris, might have been cleaner and crisper, but not one of them had been lived in as deeply as this book. Without it, she thought, there would be no Paris-by-Starlight at all.

'But, Isabelle, you have to see …'

After smearing her hands dry, Arina took the book back and turned carefully through its brittle pages. 'Mariam started telling everyone the Christmas story. A star in the sky, and a manger, and all those shepherds. But I started thinking … well, that isn't *our* story, is it? Not really. Mariam says stories travel, just like people do, but I remembered my bebia used to sit us down every Christmas and tell us a story of her own.' She smiled. 'New stars in the sky – I bet *they* got that from us!' She stopped. 'Here it is!'

Isabelle began to read the words in their own arcane script. After a few moments, when she was still lingering over the same symbols (did a clockwise swirl change the meaning of that word?), Arina stepped in. 'It's the Night of Seven Stars,' she said, eyes still prowling the page. 'Once a year, the Seventh Star aligns with all the others in its constellation. When they line up, the star shines bright as the sun in the midnight sky. That's the star the lost sailors followed, when they brought back the Princess of the Night. She'd been lost at sea for a year and a day, but they never gave up. The star guided them home – and, every year, people gave gifts and made feasts to remember her by. She was the most gracious Empress of the Night …' She beamed up at Isabelle. 'That's it, isn't it? Back in the old days, there wasn't Christmas in the old country at all. There was this. So that's what we should be doing, isn't it? The Night of Seven Stars …'

Isabelle stared into the Nocturne. On the page, the story ended with an etching of the sailors bearing the baby back home.

'But . . . how?' she wondered. 'How would we celebrate?'

Arina shrugged. This seemed so elementary to her. 'Well, it's like everything else, isn't it? Paris-by-Starlight – it's going to remember.'

*

The night market was somewhere near. Levon was still breathing in the scents of its braziers, all the musk and spice of the old country, as he crashed through the tradesmen's entrance at the Hôtel Métropol.

The December darkness was growing deeper by the day, and in the Métropol plans were afoot for their Christmas celebrations. Somebody had heaved a Norwegian fir into the little reception area, and there it stood, filling the hotel with its pine-needle scent. When Levon hurried through, Fae was on her knees, trying gallantly to unravel a tangle of lights.

'Do you want some help?'

Fae only grunted in reply. 'You don't have time. M. Fortier's looking for you.'

Levon's eyes were drawn to the door behind the reception desk.

'He's in the wine cellar,' Faye muttered. She wasn't acknowledging the fact, but Levon could see that she'd somehow entangled her forearm in the wires and was systematically failing to tease it out.

'The wine cellar?'

'You'll see . . .'

He saw it the moment he descended the stair.

The wine cellar at the Hôtel Métropol was accessed by a crooked stairway behind the brasserie. Levon was barely halfway down when

he saw the glow from beneath. By the time he reached the bottom –
where the slight, hunched figure of M. Fortier was waiting – the
light, violet and indigo and luminescent mauve, was blinding.

M. Fortier had sensed the new arrival on his shoulder. 'It
wasn't here last night. Where does it come from, boy?'

From an age long ago. From the pages of the Nocturne. From
the hopes and beliefs of a people far from home. There was no
answer that M. Fortier could possibly believe, so instead Levon
said, 'I'm not certain, sir.'

Racks of wine, some of the bottles pre-dating the hotel's glory
years, sat gathering dust along the cellar walls – but between
them had arisen flowers-by-night more enormous than any Levon
had seen in the nocturnal city above. Great bells of prismatic purple reached as high as his knee, their leathery petals furled back to
reveal a stamen crowned with glowing orange orbs. Each of the
great flowers seemed to have erupted, fully formed, from the
stones that lined the cellar floor – and, in their halos, dragonflies
the size of a fist danced.

'There's more, boy.'

'More?'

M. Fortier was a slight creature, but what he lacked in physi-
cality was more than compensated for by the intensity in his eyes.
He lifted his spectacles and appraised Levon fiercely. Then he
commanded him to follow.

At the back of the cellar, where the amethyst glow was at its
softest, a dusty rack of wine was set into an alcove. M. Fortier
heaved the rack back, revealing a further cavity in the wall.
Through there was darkness, punctuated by yet more lights.

'How much do you know about Paris?'

Levon said, 'Not as much as you, sir.'

'Well, at least you have a wise head on your shoulders. This
hotel's been in my family for generations. You've heard the
stories, I dare say. About what we did here during the War.'

'You provided sanctuary. For the Resistance.'

'My papa knew how to keep men hidden.' He stepped back. 'Well, go ahead. I'll follow.'

Levon felt his way into the darkness. The tunnel roof was low and, with hands braced against each wall, he guided himself down the narrowing slope. It was when he came to the first kink in the tunnel that he saw the light: another giant bell, this one with petals of fiery vermilion, obscuring the way ahead. Pools of moisture had formed in the cracks where it had erupted, and in these miniature lagoons a multitude of golden frogs glowed.

'The *carrières* de Paris,' M. Fortier said. 'Don't ask me how old they are. My history doesn't go back that far. There are quarries like this all over our city. Any fool who comes to Paris knows the Catacombs – but, well, you have to be a true Parisian to know the carrières.'

Levon followed the tunnel around. Sometimes, there was water at his feet; sometimes, he had to duck around yet more kinks and corners. Levon was not by nature given to fear, but in time the echo of M. Fortier's footsteps gave rise to a subtle kind of dread.

Noises echoed in the black portals up ahead. Sometimes, Levon startled. Sometimes, he heard the beating of wings. Something shimmered as it scurried across the tunnel floor, but it had vanished into a hole before Levon could discern whether it was flesh and blood or figment of his imagination. Soon, the flowers-by-night that grew along the tunnels were growing more populous, obscuring the way ahead in landfalls of luminous leaf. The walls themselves shimmered in spectral patterns where the trails of some underworld slug had crossed the stone.

Levon felt the whisper of wind across his face. Three strides later, beyond an outburst of glowing indigo petals, the tunnel disgorged them into an expanse more cavernous than any he had known.

Levon gazed, daunted, across a wonderland of lights. Out there were banks of sapphire and mauve. Silver flecks in fields of gold. A wind had risen from somewhere, and it set the enormous flowers-by-night to ripple, like undulating fields of grain.

How deep the flurries of colour reached, Levon could not say. There were blacknesses between them too, and in those blacknesses other lights darted. But these were no lightjars – of that, at least, Levon could be certain. He heard the hum of insects he had never seen – not, at least, outside the pages of his bebia's Nocturne. In places, great stalactites reached down from the cavern roof to meet their counterparts rising from the bedrock below.

Something crowed – a bird? – in the blackness, and then was gone.

M. Fortier fought his way through the flowers behind him. It was only then that Levon realised that the cavern floor was a spider's web of miniature waterways, each cutting their interconnected rivulets in the stone. He saw the electric flash of a shoal of tiny fish, each one of them a spark in the darkness.

M. Fortier had floated onward. Now he crouched by a single great golden flower, sinking his arm into its bowl. As he taunted the petals, they convulsed; the golden bell snapped shut, too late to envelop his wrist.

'The thing to understand, boy, is that this wasn't here before. I don't speak solely of the flowers. I don't mean the dragonflies and frogs, not even whatever those rats are, chittering out there in the darkness. I don't even mean that beast I've been hearing, because there's something cantering – yes, *cantering*! – through these caverns. Levon, I mean the *caverns themselves*. Trust me, boy. I used to get sent down here with bread and soup. I'd bring messages. We had two British airmen holed up in here for half the War. My papa never admitted as much, but we had more than one Nazi in these tunnels who never saw the light of Paris again. I know these tunnels. This was my world.' He paused. 'Not now.'

They turned, together, to survey the underworld expanse.

Levon could not be certain how deep the cavern stretched. He heard the susurration of waves, and wondered if, somewhere, in the middle of all those lights, the multitude of waterways conjoined to become an underworld lake. What wonders might those waters have given birth to? he wondered. Once, there was a country ...

'That look on your face. You know what this is, don't you?'

Levon didn't, but he could hazard a guess.

'They used to call it the ... Khanate Beneath.'

'The *what*?'

'It's just a story,' said Levon. 'A place under the landlocked sea where the dead kings used to rule. A second kingdom, where it was *always* night, and the magic of the world above didn't have to fade with the day. But that's all it was – just a story.' He paused, trying to imagine the world he had left behind. 'There *were* caverns. Sea caves, like you'd find anywhere in the world. Moorings for smugglers. Hideaways for lovers. When we were boys, we might camp there. But, in the stories, they were the lands of the dead. The Khanate Beneath ...'

Stories, thought Levon. Wasn't it time he stopped dismissing it as *just stories*? Every night gave birth to some new wonder in the city above. Was it really so incredible to think that the old country was manifesting here, too, in the stones beneath Paris? Memories knew no borders. This magic, whatever it was, just wanted to exist. It just wanted to find a new home. And, in that, it was not so very different from him.

'What would you have me do, sir?'

M. Fortier had stepped into one of the waterways. He marvelled at the way a flotilla of tiny sparks, each one the beating heart of some larvae, parted around him, re-forming on the other side.

'*Do*, boy? Yes, I've been thinking on this. I've been dreaming. At first I thought ... lock the cellar door. Get the exterminators in. Burn out the rot. Protect the Hôtel Métropol, just like your father did, and his father before him. But it doesn't work like that, does it, Levon? I could brick up the cellar. I could bring in a truck, pour cement into the carrières and pretend they'd never existed. But this ... magic ...' He had to roll the word around his mouth before spitting it out; it sounded so distasteful. '... doesn't play by those rules. I've been into your night markets. I've seen the water rats, shining down by the Seine. A nest of your lightjars up in the hotel gutters. Whatever this magic is, it finds a way.'

Something soared through the cavernous dark. Levon saw it lit up in snatches, whenever it crested a stand of the ravenous flowers-by-night. What beasts did Tariel do battle with, when he dared venture into the Khanate Beneath?

'So no,' said M. Fortier – and it was, perhaps, the first time that Levon had seen the old man glimmer with mischief, 'I won't be sealing the cellar doors. What could that ever achieve? Something like this, you can't look the other way. It's like my papa used to say about the War: if you tried to pretend it wasn't happening, then everything was forfeit; all you could really do was look it in the eye. And, well, this old hotel, it's been flagging for years. That's my fault, I shouldn't wonder. I've had my eye on other things. Well, no more. When people come to Paris, they come for magic. They come for its wonders. They come for romance. So let's give it to them.' He paused. 'Levon, I'm giving you a promotion. There'll still be toilets that need your scrubbing, young man, but from now on, you have new duties as well. From now on, you're the hotel's tour guide – into this ... Khanate Beneath.'

*

Two Métro rides, one city bus, and a half-hour meander through the southern suburb of Créteil, but none of it was enough to keep Isabelle's heart from beating out of time.

Levon had been right. The snow was starting to fall. Across the rooftops of Champeval thin rags were tumbling from the clouds. There were apartment blocks here – from one of them she saw the unmistakable glow of a cascade of flowers-by-night – but, apart from that, the low-lying houses of Champeval appeared untouched by the arrival of the People. She might have been a hundred miles from the heart of Paris-by-Starlight, and for some reason the thought unnerved her. Somewhere along the way, she'd started thinking of that little back room in the unlicensed apartment as home.

Home ...

She reached the Rue Saint-Christophe just as the snow clouds were hardening, and the single amber flower-by-night she'd brought in a pot was already fading to a faint glimmer. So much for her welcoming gift. Now, its glow only reminded her of the new family she'd left in the north, and she had to use all her will-power not to turn around.

The house was whitewashed and small, with two windows set into its attic eaves and a chimneypot trailing grey. Though the upstairs shutters were closed, downstairs the lights were bright. As she stood in the frigid night, she supposed that they ought to have been inviting – and she wanted to believe in that too. But the railing that ran around the property seemed a barrier to keep her out. She'd been standing at it for seventeen years.

Home, she thought. How many homes could you have in a lifetime?

The last time she'd seen her father was in that cramped little apartment in Montmartre, where they used to live. Reason dictated that things would have changed in the seventeen years since, but in her dreams he had still been there, rolling up his cigarettes between pieces of the old instruments he was putting back together, a tangle of catgut and nylon strings at his feet, the radio playing jazz from one of the pirate stations he adored. She'd never thought he was going to ... grow up.

It was now or never. She thought of the Nocturne. Tariel went into the Khanate Beneath, didn't he? People from the old country were always venturing out on odysseys of their own. Levon and Arina, Mariam and Maia, they'd crossed continents. All she had to do was knock on that door.

So that was what she did.

It felt wrong to be crossing the railing. Not for the first time, she thought of her mother and all the lies she'd have to tell. One day, she'd tell her the truth – but first she had to discover exactly what that truth was.

Light spilled out of the opening door, and there stood Hector.

'Isabelle, you came.'

She nodded and, because the words she'd been rehearsing had completely evaporated away, offered up the flower-by-night instead. Hector took it dumbly, and welcomed her within.

She had not known what to expect, but as she stepped through the doors she was quite certain this was not it. In her dreams (how childish it all seemed), her father lived in a museum of old stringed instruments. He had lathes at which he crafted his own. His bed was a hammock suspended between the shells of two enormous double basses. In fact, there was laundry on a clothes horse in the hall, a pile of *Pariscope* magazines waiting to be recycled, and newspapers laid out to catch dirty boots.

'Come,' he said, shuffling deeper in, 'let me introduce you.'

Isabelle waited before following. Taking off her coat filled her with a dread she had not been expecting, but taking off her boots was worse. Stupid, but it felt like locking a door. At least with her boots on, she might turn tail and flee. She had to tell herself that this was what she'd come here for. Seventeen years had flown by, and this was a girlhood dream. But, confronted with it, even this had lost its potency. She'd had other dreams too. She'd wanted to fly a hot-air balloon over the mountains into Spain. She'd wanted to ride a wild pony across the Camargue, because that was what the girl Lucky did in the stories she used to read. Girlhood dreams did not have to become manifest. Most of the time they stayed where they belonged.

It was too late to turn around now, so she left the harp in its case and followed down the hall. As she passed the bottom of the stairs, she was distinctly aware of a figure watching from its uppermost step. Eyes were on her, but her eyes were not upon it. Hector was standing in the doorway at the end of the hall, and seventeen years were drawing her towards him.

The kitchen was small but cosy, built around a square dining table. A sink was piled haphazardly with crockery, counters were cluttered with kettles and pressure cookers and altogether too many pans – but there was, nevertheless, something that screamed 'home' about the place. The air was heavy with steam, and in that reef stood a woman to whom Hector had already given the flower-by-night. As Isabelle stepped nervously in, she was placing it on the ledge.

'Isabelle,' Hector said, with a stiff formality that hardly suited him, 'this is Adaline ... my wife.'

Her eyes had dropped, without meaning to, to Hector's hand – and the silver band he was wearing there. He had never, she remembered now, married Isabelle's mother. 'He's a musician,' she used to say, with an air of exaggerated exasperation. 'It wouldn't be good for his *music* to settle down.' And yet, there he was, with his wedding ring on one hand and the other lightly touching the small of his wife's back.

Adaline was some years younger than Hector. Her black hair was a stark contrast to Hector's blond, and where his was a tangled mane, hers framed her face in straight, severe lines. Isabelle's first thought was: she's severe around the lips as well. They're pursed, as if she's eaten something sour. But her eyes were the same blue as her father's, striking and faraway, and something in this endeared her to Isabelle. When she spoke, the sourness wasn't there at all.

'You're very welcome, Isabelle,' she said, and took her hands. 'Very welcome. Isn't she, Hector?'

Hector said, 'I should say so.'

'I hope you like lamb.'

Isabelle, who loathed it with a passion, said, 'More than anything. It smells delicious.'

'I'm afraid there's still a while to go. The slower you go with lamb the better. But don't let me stop you! You two should get acquainted.'

Hector shrugged sadly at her. He'd heard it too: *acquainted*, as if one of them hadn't given rise to the other. But not a word more was spoken, and as he tramped out of the room, Isabelle followed.

In the salon a fire crackled in a grate. An easel sat in the corner, displaying a landscape half finished, and Adaline's books lined the wall – all pristine hardcovers, a library of primers and exhibition catalogues she'd picked up across a lifetime of visiting galleries. 'I used to go with her,' Hector said, when he returned with two glasses of red wine. 'When we met, that's what we'd do. She'd come to see me play, and I'd trot around the exhibitions with her. We went to Barcelona for Gaudi. Gauguin right here in Paris. Do you like art?'

Isabelle said, 'Bruegel. My mother bought me a print. *Hunters in the Snow*.'

There was a painful silence. She'd known, of course, that those two words – 'my mother', as impersonal as if Hector had never known her – would provoke something, but she hadn't known it would be pain. She saw it ghost across his face, evidence of some old scar.

'How is your mother?'

'She's good. She got married.' Hector's eyes opened fractionally wider. Her eyes had been browsing the books, because looking directly at Hector sent too many possibilities tumbling through her mind. But she turned to him now. 'I'm sorry. This is awkward, isn't it?'

'It isn't,' he said, willing it to be true.

'It is. That's why I brought this.' She'd brought the harp into the salon while Hector was pouring wine. Now she got down on her knees and disrobed it. 'Music can cut through anything, can't it? I remember you and Mum. You'd argue like dogs, but then I'd hear your playing one of your old ragtime records and, if I peeked through the door, the pair of you would be dancing in the kitchen.'

She barely knew if it was real or imagined. Six-year-olds don't have memories. All they have are fables. But there was beauty in it. She thought Hector might see the beauty too, but by the look on his face, all he remembered was the fighting. Different fables, for different times.

Conversations were like minefields. You had to find a safe way through one. She said, 'Mum doesn't know I'm here. Well, she knows I'm in Paris. She thinks I came for the music. Not that I was searching for ... '

Too late, she realised what she'd done. 'You were ... looking for me?'

Isabelle was glad when she heard a declarative splutter come from the doorway. She and Hector both looked up, and there stood a boy of some fifteen years, a concoction of arms and legs too long for his body so that he looked, to Isabelle, like a stick insect in human form. What Isabelle first took to be a suit revealed itself the uniform of his local college. His hair was as black as his mother's but as feral as his father's, his eyes the same cerulean blue that Isabelle saw each time she looked in the mirror.

'Isabelle, this is—'

'Alexandre,' the boy shrugged. 'So, you're the sister.'

'I suppose I am.'

'Well,' said Alexandre, 'that's a turn up for the books. A sister!' He took a tentative step into the room – as if, Isabelle thought, it wasn't his – and stopped. 'She looks like you, Dad.'

'Alexandre …'

'Well, she does.' He loped across the room – he had the same lolloping gait as their father too – and ceremoniously planted kisses on each of Isabelle's cheeks. 'Well, you do.'

After the formalities were done, Isabelle said, 'I'm pleased to meet you,' and tried to sound like she meant it. The boy had retreated into a curious silence, and kept shifting from the back of a sofa, to the door, to stoking the fire in the grate as his father marvelled at the harp Isabelle had placed between them.

'By God, I remember playing it for you, the evening you were born.' He crouched down to inspect it. 'And then that Christmas, your first on this Earth …' Hector paused, suddenly chastened. 'Listen to me, getting sentimental. I'll expect you don't remember any of it.'

Isabelle tightened, involuntarily. If she remembered none of it, she wondered, why did he think she was here at all?

'I remember Christmas morning, when you were four years old. You, crawling in between your mother and me with that stocking we'd left out. Eating cake for breakfast and playing "Petit Papa Noël" on the harpsichord …'

As he spoke the words, he was spinning it back into existence. In her mind's eye, Isabelle saw her mother kiss her father. Not in her wildest dreams would she ever have imagined such a thing, so it had to be real.

Hector's hands were reaching out, as if to take hold of the harp. 'May I?'

She had fantasised about this moment, but now that it was here the fantasy felt foolish; it was only a man, and the instrument in his hands was only her harp. Yet, as he took it, something in the fantasy took flight. She'd been waiting to be underwhelmed, but as he struck the first note she felt a rush of memories so vivid that she thought, for the first time, that she understood how Maia must have felt on first seeing the flowers-by-night erupt around her. Here, right now, her own old world was resurgent – for there was her father (not Hector, but her father), and his harp still slotted perfectly into his arms.

He played a lullaby.

'No bedtime stories in our home,' Hector whispered. 'Only bedtime music.'

He began to sing. At first, his voice was just following the music his fingers made as they weaved up and down. Then, fragment by fragment, he remembered the words.

> 'Everybody's good in the neighbourhood,
> It's time to go to sleep ...'

Isabelle had to hold on to herself, for at once she was six years old. Her adult self hovered like a ghost, somewhere on her shoulder, their hands conjoined – and, though she wanted to let go, the six-year-old Isabelle clung on for dear life, refusing to be stranded back there in the past.

It was Alexandre's voice that saved her. Throughout, he'd been lurking in the salon door. Now he blurted out, 'Mother's been calling you for hours. Come on, Pa, you know what she's like ...'

Hector stood, looking suddenly sheepish. The spell was broken, as spells always are. Isabelle watched him lope out of the salon, and soon she followed after.

'I remember that one,' said Alexandre as she passed him in the door. 'Every night, over and over and over again – by God, you think he'd have learned some new ones! But no ... *Everybody's good in the neighbourhood. It's time to go to sleep.* It still sends a shiver down my spine.' By the look of him, he'd been expecting camaraderie, but all he received was silence. Embarrassed, he muttered, 'He wanted me to learn, but I was never any good. Here, I'll show you through. She's made Pa's favourite. Navarin, with shank of lamb. I bet you'll have eaten that too.'

But no, thought Isabelle as she followed him through. Back in the long ago, Hector had been a vegetarian. France's very first – or so her mother used to say. 'Don't go thinking about him, Issy. He'll have wasted away by now. A man can't live on onion soup and Pinot Noir.'

The smells drifting in from the kitchen were meaty and strong.

Five places had been laid at the table. The fifth was occupied by a man twice Hector's age who had about him the look of a deflated balloon: altogether too much skin, and hardly enough person to fill it. Even his clothes suggested a man who had once been more significant in size; the grey corded cardigan hung about him like a shroud, and the gold watch on his wrist hung like a bangle, the totem of some earlier age.

'This is Isabelle, Pa,' Adaline began as she lifted the lid from the earthenware pot in the middle of the table, revealing a casserole with a spine of five great protruding bones. 'Remember, I told you – Hector's girl.'

The old man revolved to look at Hector, who was taking his seat beside him. That look was supposed to be knowing, perhaps even congratulatory – the shared devilry of two villains at play – but Hector was not open to receive. Instead, the old man cackled to himself and set about helping himself to a bone.

'Isabelle, this is my father, Victor,' Adaline began, with more kindness than the old man was showing his lamb. 'You've been living with us six years now, haven't you, Pa?' She lifted her voice at the end; evidently the elder man was deaf. Insolent, too, because he was already smearing the lamb across his face before anyone else had been served. 'Well,' Adaline sighed, as she served Isabelle, 'you've got to look after your own, don't you?'

At those words, Hector shifted uncomfortably in his seat.

'Shall we?'

And dinner was served.

Conversation stuttered, stopped, and then stuttered again. By the time the main course was through, Isabelle had heard about Adaline's work at the local school, Alexandre's desperation for college to come to an end, and the startling rate of Hector's car insurance. The old man seemed to be content in his own ravenous silence. She'd quite run out of questions by the time the first dishes were being cleared away, and after that there was no way to avoid being quizzed on her own time in Paris. It did not seem right to tell them what she had really come here for, so instead she concocted half-truths and half-lies. She'd come to Paris seeking her fortune. She'd come to Paris for an old flame. She'd come to learn new music, the music of the city, the kind they never played in the village bistro and bars around Saint-André.

'And you found it,' said Hector. 'Isabelle, when I heard you playing ... They call her the Rose of the Evening, Adaline, after an old story of theirs. To think that my little girl ...'

Isabelle hardened at the words. *My little girl*. Through long years she'd dreamt of him saying those words; now that he was here, and now that he did, it felt like theft.

'Where do they come from, these people?' Adaline was revolving around to deposit the earthenware dish in the sink, when her eyes landed on the terracotta pot in the window. The flower in the pot was hungrily drinking in the light of the nightscape beyond. Its amber halo grew.

'They come from ...' Isabelle remembered Arina's words, and echoed them now, ' ... the night.'

There was a clattering as Victor impatiently threw his spoon into his bowl, awaiting dessert.

'They call it the landlocked sea,' Isabelle went on, wary of the way Victor was watching her, 'or at least they did. A tiny country, hardly worth a mention. Except ...' Words would not suffice, so she gestured instead at the flower-by-night. 'They say there was magic in the world. Once, their whole nation flowered just like that. But then the landlocked sea was poisoned. The magic ebbed away. One by one, the lights went out, until ... well, it's like Levon says: nations are ending all the time. The landlocked sea's part of the Russias now. They sent soldiers in. They're building power stations on the shores.'

'So they come here,' snorted Victor, 'and pretend Paris is theirs instead.'

Adaline had been marvelling at the glowing flowers on the ledge for so long that whatever was baking in the oven had started to burn. The smell of warm, baking coffee was turning suddenly bitter – but so startled was she at Victor's words that she fumbled as she lifted out a tray filled with bubbling ramekins.

'Pa, we talked about this ...'

'The Chabons have lived on Rue Alfred since I was a boy. That's longer than you've been alive, and twice over. But since those neighbours moved in, they put blackouts in their windows at night. That hasn't happened since we drove the Nazis out. Nobody asked them, did they?'

Adaline arranged the desserts around the table. At least, as she shared them around, Victor had something else to occupy his mind.

The coating of Isabelle's own dessert had turned to cinder toffee and, when she broke it, a geyser of gooey coffee erupted upwards. The scent of it was close to an assault. And no sooner was she thinking about that than she realised she could smell everything else in the kitchen just as vividly. The lemon detergent that was pooling, right now, in the earthenware pot. The perfume Adaline was wearing, the medicated shampoo she'd used to scrub whatever was left of Victor's hair. Even the pollen of the flower-by-night, which rose in a misty halo around its petals.

Her stomach convulsed.

'Who's Levon?' Alexandre piped up.

'What?'

'You said Levon. He's one of these People, is he?'

The smell of the coffee was too much. She watched Alexandre chewing and felt as if it was billowing out in a cloud to consume her. The knots that had been constricting her stomach tightened yet further, propelling her up and out of her seat. 'I'm sorry,' was all she could muster, and then she was stumbling out into the hallway, looking in vain for a bathroom door.

Moments later, she was braced against the sink, emptying her stomach into the basin. People said that purging felt good. It was only the body's response to a poison, designed to restore the body's balance. But people were wrong.

Too late, she realised she'd left the bathroom door ajar. Through the crack, she could see along the hallway and straight into the kitchen where the family – *her family*, they'd tried to tell her – gathered.

She was splashing cold water over her face when fingers knocked gently on the door.

'Isabelle?'

It was Hector. She dried herself, turned to push open the door.

'Isabelle, you're unwell.'

'It wasn't the food. Please,' she floundered, 'tell Adaline, it wasn't the …'

She was pushing past him now, darting into the salon where she'd left the harp behind, then pirouetting around needlessly until she was almost at the front door. 'I'm sorry,' she stuttered, 'I wasn't supposed to stay. I'm playing. Tonight. At Le Tangiers … '

Hector reached for his own coat. 'I could come …'

But Isabelle only shook her head.

The rest of the family had gathered in the hall. Isabelle was acutely aware of them watching as she opened the front door, only to discover that the snow had returned. In the open doorway, Hector tried to take her hand – and, though she let him, something close to disgust rippled up her arm. What she was disgusted at, she did not know. Certainly it was not the touch of his fingers. Something in the touch felt like betrayal – but that could not possibly have been right, for she had no-one to betray but herself.

'Come back for Christmas.'

Haltingly, she said, 'I don't know. Hector …'

And he nodded dumbly, because seventeen years of shame were not to be undone in one stocking under a tree, no matter how much he meant it.

'Please, I've got to go.'

The snow was thicker now. It obscured her footprints as she ran.

She was late to Le Tangiers. Beyrek had near given up on her, filling the stage with storytellers and fire-eaters instead. But when the Rose of the Evening appeared, the restless crowd grew quiet. With the touch of Hector's fingertips still upon her, she took her place upon the stage. At first she thought that her fingers would betray her, or that the harp would not connect with her in the way that it should – for *his* fingers had been the last to stroke its strings, and perhaps something in the harp remembered the master it had once had. Yet, the moment she started playing, all of those fears disappeared. The music that came to her was not just the music of the old country, with all its mournful nocturnal airs, but the music of her own old country as well: those long-ago Christmases when they'd been together – her mother, her father, and Isabelle herself. Her fingers found the sound of tinkling sleigh bells, and without meaning to she had woven it into the movements that came to her, straight out of the Nocturne. Her Golden Age, and the Golden Age of the People, mingling together in the smoky air.

For a moment, the music broke. She looked out over the mesmerised figures in Le Tangiers. Two Golden Ages might have swirled around in her music, but only one of those Golden Ages was manifest in Paris tonight. On the rooftops, the night gardens flourished. In the demolition grounds, the night markets thrived. Lightjars made their nests in the eaves of shopfronts up and down the Champs-Élysées, while down here in the dark the People felt the harmony of the landlocked sea. The old country, living and breathing again.

But of the love and warmth of her own old country, there was nothing left – and no amount of belief, she finally understood, was enough to summon it back.

7

THE NOCTURNE BELOW

Emmanuel Caron has had the privilege of being head park-keeper at the Jardin des Tuileries for half of his adult life, and there is not a thing in Paris that makes him feel more alive than parading the hexagonal ponds every twilight, doffing his cap ostentatiously to the statue of Theseus as he slays the Minotaur, or secretly petting the stone Pegasus on which Mercury is taking to the skies. Tonight is no different. His hat pulled down around his ears, he takes a promenade from the Louvre to the Place de la Concorde. In this place of fallen kings, Emmanuel Caron himself feels just a tiny bit royal. A sacrilege, you might say, for a Frenchman – but Emmanuel cares not one jot, for this is his private playground. One day he will bring his little girl Esmé here at the fall of night, and take joy in it together.

The snow does not often settle in these Gardens, but tonight it dusts the banks of the grand alley. Emmanuel strolls along the elevated terrace, naked trees on either side, and marvels at the way the snow, thin as it is, captures the moonlight so exquisitely. Here, even as darkness hardens, it might almost be day.

Strange, he thinks, but the snow is reflecting other lights as well: lights he has never seen before, lights of violet, red and blue.

He goes between the trees, so that he is facing the Grand Carré in the eastern quarter of the Gardens. A few steps further, he approaches the source of this new light.

He is not the only one. Two clerks, on their way home from work, have stopped to gaze upon it. A father and his two children, out to make games in the dark, are crouched alongside it too. And there – one of the vagabond People who have lately come to Paris is lurking a little further off, between the trees.

'The Gardens are closing for the night,' Emmanuel proclaims. He'd rather not linger here. For hours already, he's been dreaming of home, where his little Esmé will be waiting: the games they will play and the stories they'll tell before bedtime comes around.

But the figures do not move.

It is only as Emmanuel comes closer that he recognises the true source of the light. What he had idly taken as a Christmas lantern is a great flower sprouted, suddenly, from the earth. He is quite certain this flower was not here when he walked his rounds yesterday evening, for there are few things more memorable in life than a single flower, the height of a grown man's thigh, pulsating with soft purple light. But he cannot deny how enchanting it is. The flower is comprised of six tall petals – meaty, like the flesh of a cactus – which together comprise a tall funnel. In the heart of that funnel, a single tall protuberance is ringed by other fleshy orbs, and each one of them pulsing a different colour, from gold to silver to vermilion to the white of stars.

'What is this?' he begins.

The little crowd fans out, so that Emmanuel can inspect the aberration. Emmanuel is a quiet man. He likes solitude, and being with his daughter, and reading his mystery novels in the little apartment they share. But this does not mean he knows nothing of the People who, denied their own country, are making the Parisian night their own. One evening, they held their night market right here in the Jardin – and only the arrival of the gendarmes prevented it becoming a bustling bazaar.

But he has never seen anything quite like this.

As he is watching, the petals swell and convulse. It seems, to Emmanuel the park-keeper, as if the flower itself is taking a deep breath.

Then it exhales.

There is a subtle pop, and the tip of the petals open, casting a multitude of lights up into the air. Upwards they arc, upwards and ever upwards, charting their paths high above Emmanuel's head so that they land, a scattering of minuscule stars, between the trees all around. Then the flower, its petals splayed out, loses its lustre; the petals fall flat to the ground, and to Emmanuel it seems it is breathing its last.

But: in death, life. He turns on the spot, to see the children fanning out, chasing down the multi-coloured stars the flower has cast out. There they are, on the ground all around him: balls of pure light, as big as a child's fist. Seed pods, he thinks, radiating new life. The children pluck them up, faces full of joy, and cast them at each other like snowballs, trailing luminous vapour in the air like the contrails left by aeroplanes above.

Emmanuel ought to tell them to stop. That is what his overseer would tell him. But, tonight, he just stands here and marvels at the criss-crossing trails of light.

No, Emmanuel could no more stop this game than he could tell his little Esmé that he is cancelling Christmas. Whoever the People are, he will never forget the splendid absurdity of a night like this.

In the darkness of the trees, the vagabond is beaming.

*

'So there,' said Levon, 'just like I told you.'

Isabelle turned her eyes against the strafing snow, towards the cauldrons of multi-coloured lights peppering the tents and bivouacs beyond. A few steps through the trees, the snow and wind could no longer touch them – for, high above, the motorway flyovers looped against themselves, giving the impression of some enormous cavern roof. Now, at last, Isabelle could get her bearings. Beyond the trees, clustered in depressions against the banks of the lower roads and the forested islands in between, a city of tents sprawled. There was little order here, no rhyme or reason. It might have been one settlement or it might have been a thousand miniature ones, each one ranged up against its neighbours. She watched lightjars darting through the frigid air, plummeting down to the outcrops of flowers-by-night which grew at the opening of every tent, like the embers of cookfires. She saw the People there, wrapped up against the cold.

The flyovers above were choked with traffic, even before dawn. Isabelle could hear the dull roar of a million guttering engines. This place was not so very far from the splendour at the centre of Paris, but it might have been a different world.

'They've been here for weeks. Some of them paid the traffickers, I'll bet, just like we did. Thinking there's a home at the end of the road – not daring to think there might just be another camp. They were bedding in by the Canal Saint-Martin. But down there there's people to make complaints. So the gendarmes turned up and started asking for papers and, after that, they came here. The mayoralty must know they're here – see, they've brought cabins, portable toilets – but just ... not care.'

They'd crossed the railway lines to reach this place. It wasn't hard in the witching hours, when only the freight trains slipped in and out of the sidings. On the eastern side, great demolition sites yawned open, and here the evening's night market was being held. The stalls proliferated, braziers burned with delicacies from the old world, while some storyteller told the fable of the last of the Ulduzkhans for a crowd of children who hadn't yet found schools. Some of the stragglers from the camps had been in that night market, looking for forage. Now, between the tents, the vagabond People were eating glowing tubers out of rattan containers, or merely folded up inside leaves from the flowers-by-night.

'Why are we here, Levon?'

When Levon shrugged, he was wearing the same boyish smile that made Isabelle think she'd known him all her life.

'Because it's Christmas,' he said.

'The Night of Seven Stars,' she corrected.

'One and the same,' shrugged Levon, and led her into the tents.

They hadn't yet crossed the first line of tents when somebody called his name. 'Here he comes,' a voice chirruped out of the dark, 'the Ulduzkhan himself!'

Levon rolled his eyes. 'Ignore them. That's Khazak. I'm trying to get him shifts at the Métropol, but he won't clean himself up. Khazak!' he called out. 'Gather everyone.'

The young man named Khazak – a head taller than Levon, with crooked teeth that told the story of the truncheon that had been beaten into his face – came closer and, ignoring Isabelle, said, 'They've been in again tonight.'

'Who?' whispered Isabelle, but Khazak went on, 'They just brazen in here like it's theirs. They got my brother off his face, smoking whatever shit they're pushing, and now they say he owes them for the honour. They're getting bolder. Treating *us* like their own personal night markets. Well, it's not like we can ever go running to the police, is it?' Khazak paused. 'I told you, Levon. We need our own police. Protect the People, so far from home.' For a time, there was silence, until finally Khazak added, 'There's eighteen more boys from the old country turned up. Rode the freight train straight into Paris, if you can believe it. They'll need protecting from these pushers too. It's like I said: three thousand miles out there, nearly two years dreaming of the gold at the end of the rainbow and … well, you end up thinking almost anything's gold after that. Even that cheap junk they're selling.'

Levon dwelled on it for a moment. 'Just round everybody up, Khazak.'

'I'll tell them the Ulduzkhan's come, shall I?'

Levon snapped, 'You'll tell them no such thing!' Then he found his calmness again. 'Don't go riling them up, Khazak. I've found a way.'

As the man named Khazak slipped back into the tents, Levon led Isabelle on.

'Why did he call you Ulduzkhan, Levon?'

'He's a fool, that's why.'

Isabelle gave him a pointed look.

'He thinks *I* did this. That I clicked my fingers, or spoke some secret words handed down to me by Destiny and just ... made all this happen.' The frustration that was rippling through Levon found its way out through his leg; wheeling backwards, he kicked out and sent the heads of an outcrop of diamond-white flowers-by-night flying, describing luminescent trails in the air. 'Ulduz-khan, the last King of the Stars. From my bebia's Nocturne ... But it didn't end well for the last Ulduzkhan, not in the fables. Khazak ought to read that story more closely. The last Ulduz-khan got greedy. He wanted to hold the Seventh Star in his arms himself, so he climbed to the top of the highest mountain and planted a starlight grove there. Only, when he couldn't reach the star, even from that grove, he kept on building the mountain higher. His people quarried stone and bore it up the mountain-side. They coaxed the trees and flowers up and ever upwards.' Levon shrugged. 'Eventually, he got too high. He reached out for the star ... and fell from the mountain.'

'That's the gloomiest story in the whole of the Nocturne.'

'It's a different age, Isabelle. We don't need an Ulduzkhan.'

'But they're counting on you, all the same.'

'I suppose it's just my turn.' Levon realised how sour he sounded and forced himself to laugh instead. 'I'm glad I have you, Isabelle. Everyone's counting on somebody, and they're counting on somebody else. But ... it's like dominoes. One person steps out, and the whole thing comes crashing down.' He stopped, for something had caught his eye. 'Look!' he called out. 'Nighthawks!' And when Isabelle turned her face upward, she saw them too: three different shapes in the darkness, waiting to pick off lightjars as they tumbled from flower to flower.

They weaved on, until they reached a dell in the middle of the motorway island that had become a pasture of cyan blooms. On the edge of the glade, pressed up against one of the flyover turrets, an elderly man sat outside a bivouac made of branches.

'Levon?'

Levon turned, instinctively stepping between Isabelle and the stranger. History called out in him: three thousand miles away, in another lifetime, he'd known this voice. The face that appeared, spectral in the light, was hidden behind the fronds of an ice-white beard. That beard was more significant than the man to which it belonged, for the figure behind it was wizened and slight, wrapped in one of the traditional chokhas that the sailors used to wear. A fur stole lay over his shoulders, keeping out the wind, but aside from that the man had only the warmth of the flowers-by-night to sustain him. He was draped in them too. He had taken stems and stitched one into another, so that he was wearing a garland just like the mothers who'd once gone to the shore to wish their sons good fortune on their maiden voyages. He'd chosen the flowers so that they cloaked him in alternating amber and blue, with an ouroboros of scarlet over his heart.

As he stumbled forward, Isabelle saw that lightjars were drinking from the garland itself. They took off and danced, then darted back down, using the elderly man as a roost.

Finally, Levon knew this face.

'Master Atesh?'

'Levon!'

The old man threw open his arms, scattering the multitude of lightjars from his shoulders as if he was one of the Nocturne's own enchanters, casting a spell. They buzzed around him, until the bravest among them dared to settle again.

When they did, they found themselves fluttering madly for safety, because Levon had put his arms around the old man. 'Master Atesh. By the Seventh Star, Master, you made it ...'

Isabelle saw the men come apart, then re-join. When Levon finally stepped back, one of the lightjars was sitting, dazed, on his shoulder. Two others, darts of shrieking aquamarine, dived down to revive their fallen sister and flanked her as they took off, searching for less perilous roosts.

'Levon, how long have you ...'

'Master Atesh, I thought you'd ...'

The conversation turned in circles, until Levon finally blurted out, 'Nearly a year, Master Atesh.'

'Then you're one of the fortunate ones. Some are out there still.'

'And you, Master?'

'Less than you. Since the dying days of summer. I meant to make the crossing to England, but ...' The man named Master Atesh needed to say nothing further, for Levon already knew: why risk the journey to the island nation, when the island nation always turned you away?

Levon stepped back, inviting Isabelle in. As she joined them, she sensed a phalanx of shadows moving through the tents: rags of People were coming down, gravitating towards the sunken glade.

'Master Atesh, this is Isabelle. The Rose of the Evening.'

The old man narrowed his eyes, as if in deliberation. 'I remember this fable.'

'She's a friend, Master. A friend to the People. And much more to me.' Momentarily, there was silence. Levon's eyes looked up. He too had seen the advancing People. 'Isabelle, I know Master Atesh from the old country. He taught us until we were old enough to join our fathers on the landlocked sea. Master Atesh taught our fathers and our grandfathers and—'

The old man brought a single finger to his lips. 'By the Stars, I'm not that old.'

'You taught my father though, didn't you, Master?'

'I remember your father well. A strong boy. A strong man. By the Stars, he was determined. A principled boy, at ten years of age. I wasn't in the least surprised when he became the captain of his own boat. People liked your father, Levon. They were drawn to him.'

'My father might have been strong, but it didn't help him in the end, did it, Master?'

Master Atesh was silent, but from the cyan glade another voice called out: Khazak was calling them down.

'What do you mean, boy?'

'My father was the one who got us onto the boats. I can still remember it. The sea and the spray, and Arina screaming for our mother. But, after that, he wouldn't get on himself. Said he was going to stand and fight, with all of my brothers, with the other captains and their crews. He wanted me to go with him, and when I didn't ... Well, you remember what he was like.'

Master Atesh nodded, solemnly. 'Take pride. You made it, Levon.'

That statement: as vast as the world.

'But my father did not.'

Khazak's voice rose up again, louder this time, more insistent. 'Ulduzkhan!' he was cackling. 'Your People await!'

Levon braced himself against the word, but his eyes remained locked on Master Atesh.

'Your father did not perish in the old country, Levon.'

Between them, the silence continued.

'Your father *did* make it out. I know it for a fact. The last time I saw your father, he was in a detention centre on the Serbian frontier. He'd tried to make the crossing. He failed. He was wearing another man's boots. I sat with him, boy, and we spoke about the old times – and, when I was moved on the next day, he was still there. Languishing, yes. Rotting, perhaps. But alive, Levon. Your father is alive.'

A hand fell on Levon's shoulder, whirling him around. Perhaps he had spooked himself with the recollection of that day the old country vanished, for Isabelle saw his hands turn suddenly to fists. It was only now, seeing Levon – her Levon, who could never hurt a fly – with his fists clenched that she felt the panic, the uncertainty, the fear that had throbbed in him since then.

It was only Khazak who had reached out. 'Don't keep them waiting, Levon. They're hungry. Hungry men are quick to ire.'

Levon and Isabelle turned, to see the waiting host.

They came from far and farther still. Men and women and – between them, in arms, or hoisted high on shoulders – the children they'd brought from that vanished country, or the ones they'd birthed on the way. They were old and young. Mothers and fathers. Brothers and sisters. Clots of friends, who'd formed families of their own. Too many of them, thought Levon as he reached their edges, and all of them looking impatiently at him.

He held on to Isabelle's hand.

Find the words, he thought. Find the words like she – and he looked sidelong at her, marvelling that she was here with him at all – finds the music.

'I know what you're thinking,' he ventured, and his voice was frail until he saw, standing between the People, a flower-by-night bigger even than the ones he'd seen beneath the Hôtel Métropol. It was pulsating in indigo, with ribbons of some lighter hue running through it. 'Because I thought it too. You're thinking: we crossed half the world ... and this is it? Half the world, only to end up in a tent beneath a flyover, winter drawing in, and men coming to sell us drugs, or prostitute us. We treated dogs better in the old country.'

There were voices of assent in the crowd.

'But it doesn't have to be this way. You've seen what's happening out there in the Parisian night. I don't claim to understand it. But when I see the flowers-by-night, or I listen to Isabelle, the Rose of the Evening, spinning music from centuries ago – with not a soul to teach her its refrains – I know that my bebia was right. The old country survives in us. It's coming back to us now.

'People, the Night of Seven Stars is coming.' He saw empty faces, and hurried on: 'You don't know what it is yet, but you will. In the stories of our People, a princess was lost – and sailors set out, onto the landlocked sea and into the imaginary oceans beyond, to bring her back. By the time they found her, they too were lost in Endless Night – but the six wandering stars lined up behind the Seventh, and shone a light so bright that they found their way home.'

'Home!' somebody snorted, from deep in the crowd. 'This isn't home, you fool. This is the End Times. I've read the Nocturne too. My bebia had half a copy, buried at the bottom of her chest. Haven't you read the final tale? The stars wink out one by one, Levon. The People have nowhere to go!'

'No,' said Levon, who had read the very same tale but cared not a thing for a story so desolate. 'Because that isn't the final story at all. Our stars already winked out ... but now they're burning again. This isn't the End Times,' he uttered, and felt Isabelle's head on his shoulder as he held himself, rigidly, for everyone to see. 'We're writing a new story now, and it has but one line. *We are the People, and the People look after each other.*'

For a moment, he held his breath. It seemed, too, that the crowd were holding their own.

'Listen to me,' he begged, 'I know of a place.'

And here it was.

Isabelle felt the walls closing in as Levon heaved the wine rack away from the wall. As she took her first steps after him, down into the darkness beneath the Hôtel Métropol, the feeling only intensified. The crowd of bodies at her back, a procession three hundred strong, would have panicked her, had she not been clasping Levon's hand. Such a foolish thing – the Isabelle of six months ago would not have countenanced it – but holding his hand put her at ease. And that nausea she was feeling, surely that was only because she hadn't eaten since twilight; ten hours had gone by, but she couldn't stomach a thing.

Levon stepped into the cavernous expanse first. There he waited above a depression where great flowers of pink and silver, threaded with gold, grew out of the silt. Isabelle stopped beside him, wondering at the rainbow fields that stretched into the darkness beyond.

The People were fanning out around them. Among them, Khazak and his circle fell silent. Master Atesh, around whom flame-red lightjars still pirouetted and dived, cast open his arms, and streams of the tiny birds flocked out into the cavern air.

'The Khanate Beneath,' said Levon. 'I've been into the outer tunnels. It cares nothing for the Métro or for the sewers or the rest of the carrières de Paris. There are ... things out there. Look to Tariel's story, and you'll know what they are. Some of the flowers will look to eat you, so watch your children as you're hacking them down. The rest of them – well, the old world provides ...' Levon's hand darted into the upturned sapphire bell over which he loomed, and came back out with one of its grains of luminous nectar, the size of his fist. This he bit into, and let the sweetness trickle down his throat. 'M. Fortier wants to bring peo-ple down here. Where we see survival, he sees … opportunity. It's our job to scout the tunnels. To open it up. To … bring life back to our land of the dead. If we can do this, we can stay.'

The People moved past him, threading their way between the outcrops of flowers. Soon, they were vanishing into cracks in the cavern walls. Some were depositing their packs on stone islands. Tents were being erected wherever the cavern floor allowed, while some resourceful fellow had produced a fishing line from his haversack and had set about reeling in a glowing, golden eel.

After some time, only Isabelle and Levon were left by the tun-nel's jaws.

'It's places like this that the People will find their home, isn't it?' Levon began. 'Like the gardens on the rooftops, or the dem-olition grounds, or the vacant tenements … wherever the other people aren't. The forgotten, untended little places. We'll make those our own.'

Isabelle imagined the caverns stretching out, enveloping the Métro lines and sewers, breaking into every catacomb and forgot-ten quarry on which the city had once been built.

'They think *I'm* showing them the way. Isabelle, they're cracked. The Nocturne's showing us. I'm just plodding after.'

'I hardly think so. Plodding? *You*? You brought those girls across half the world …'

'Yes,' Levon muttered, 'by *plodding*. One foot in front of another, over and over again. Plod, plod, plod.' And he showed her exactly how, tramping his feet ridiculously up and down.

Isabelle put her arms around his waist. 'I like it when you plod.'

'If you like a man who plods, you're going to have a happy life, Isabelle.'

There was something more that she wanted to say, but for a time they were silent.

Soon, Levon had crouched down, trailing his fingers through a glittering pool. A shoal of tiny fish, like so many glittering fragments of quartz, parted around him and zigzagged on.

'Levon, your father ...'

Levon was looking at his reflection in the water. There his face was pitted in darting lights. With a wry smile, he wondered if this was what plague had looked like in the old country: blisters of bubbling light opening up on every face.

'I look like him,' he said. 'I never thought I did. I was a mama's boy. Well, we all were, back in the old country. But I never thought I looked like him, not until now ...' He whirled his fingers, as if to break the reflection was to break up the thought.

'He's out there, somewhere.'

'Perhaps.'

'But then ...'

Levon looked over his shoulder, at Isabelle looking back down. 'There's a world out there. Where would I even begin to start searching? No,' and Levon's voice echoed across the cavernous walls, 'if he's out there, he'll have seen the seven-pointed star. The People are coming to Paris-by-Starlight. It's like my bebia believed: the star is guiding them home. Well, let it guide him too. As for me, I've ... got work to do.' He said the last reluctantly, but Isabelle had not imagined the twinkle of pride that lit up his eyes. This work: the work of building a new home, so far away from the one that they'd lost. For the first time, she understood how proud of it he was. 'Only one of us has a father here in Paris,' he said as he stood.

He hadn't meant it as a rebuke, not really, but she took it that way, reeling back when he tried to take her hand.

'No, wait. I meant to say ...' Levon was glad when she relented and let him hold her. 'You spent your life on this quest, Isabelle. You built your life around it. You think it means something that we came three thousand miles? Isabelle, you came seventeen years.'

'I thought I'd feel more than I did,' she whispered. 'Something. Anything. But I was just sitting there, in a house full of strangers, eating their food, drinking their ...'

'Much like that night you brought Arina home to us.'

'That's different.'

'How?'

She did not like to think she was given to sentimentality, but still she said, 'It was the start of something. With Hector ... it's like the end.'

Levon shook his head. 'Your quest isn't over. Why, it's barely begun. So you didn't love him, there and then? By the Stars, he isn't your baby.' Isabelle hardened at the word and Levon, fearing he'd lost her again, hurried on, 'What I mean is – you're not meant to love him straight away. I shouldn't think you even have to like him. Just knowing him ought to be enough.'

Still she seemed coiled, as if uncertain what to say. There was a time, before the music of the People came to her, that her fingers had seized up whenever she stepped onto a stage. But she was not on stage now. All she had was Levon. If only he might make her laugh, for just one moment ...

'You know, Tariel didn't give up, not when he was on his quest.'

Here it was: Isabelle spluttered with laughter. 'Do shut up about bloody Tariel!'

'Well, he didn't, did he?' Levon insisted, joining in with the laughter. 'Listen to me. Please. Paris-by-Starlight or not, we were going to have to make our home here. Whether the old world ushered us along or passed completely out of memory, this was it. There wasn't a new road to travel. Here was Paris: the end of the quest. If the old world hadn't come with us, well, we'd have had to build one ourselves. It might not have been *this* ...' And he opened his arms, as if to take in not only the Khanate Beneath but everything that was happening, up there on the surface. '... but it would have been ours. And your father ... well, maybe there isn't gold at the end of the rainbow. Maybe he doesn't have a chest filled with all the birthday cards he didn't send. Maybe there were years when he didn't think of you at all. I don't know. But I do know that he's there, and he wanted you for Christmas.'

A great roar of excitement flurried up from somewhere in the cavern. Some enterprising stranger, it seemed, had netted a fat, golden fish.

As December deepened, the People stumbled across more of the gargantuan flowers on their midnight forays. Levon thought they were migrating upwards from the Khanate Beneath, where the People from the flyover encampment had set about turning the underworld into a permanent bazaar. Some of them spoke of how they missed the sky at night; but, as each new group pushed into the tunnels, they discovered more spiral stairs and jagged pathways leading back above: into the cellars of townhouses, the archives of the Petit Palais, a demolition site where the steel frame of a stillborn tenement was being overtaken by shining silver vines. Nobody knew if the Khanate Beneath was still growing. 'It grows further, the deeper we travel,' Master Atesh pronounced – and, from that evening on, this was what the People believed, that the Khanate Beneath would have no real end as long as its People kept exploring. Sometimes, at night, its creatures ventured out into the city above – so that theatregoers would marvel at great silver toads hopping in procession across the Avenue Montaigne, or glittering dragonflies which, upon being seen, would shrink into tiny spots of flame and then promptly vanish, leaving behind only trails of buzzing vermilion light.

It was not only around those hidden doorways into the Khanate Beneath that the great flowers grew. In the heart of the Jardin des Tuileries, where once a lone flower stood, the people of Paris gazed over a field of thigh-high blossoms. At the Arc de Triomphe, where avenues branched in every direction, the flowers sprouted with the twilight and retreated into the paving stones by dawn – so that the sunlit world betrayed none of the mystery nor majesty of the night. In the gardens of the Louvre: a single scarlet blossom, radiating its blood-red glow. At the Tour Eiffel: three golden cups brimming with fire. From Petit-Montrouge to the parks of Villette, the citizens of both day and night stopped to wonder.

'They're called winterlights,' Arina told Isabelle, up in the night garden where an upturned bell of aquamarine was opening up. Her bebia's copy of the Nocturne was in her lap, and she traced the spiral writing of one of its lesser tales with the tip of her finger. 'They're not the same as in the Khanate Beneath, not if I'm reading it right. When the constellations are coming together, the winterlights blossom. On the Night of Seven Stars, they light the world.' She stopped, turned curiously to Isabelle. 'What do you think it means?'

But Isabelle had no way of knowing. She stared at the drawing on the page, where an old crone stood among flowers half her height, her face turned up in communion with the stars.

'What do you think she's waiting for?'

'Oh, that's easy,' said Arina. 'She's the lost princess's nursemaid. She's waiting for the sailors to bring her home.'

'Home for Christmas ...'

'For the Night of Seven Stars.'

The longing Isabelle felt wasn't only seeping out of that picture. Never mind the People and the fables from the Nocturne. Plain old Christmas had a magic all of its own. She imagined the lost princess being brought out of Endless Night, back to her family who had waited so long – and suddenly she was thinking of Hector and Alexandre, of Adaline and her father. It mattered not at all that the pieces didn't quite fit; this feeling of longing was contorting them so that they slotted precisely together.

Every bit of her revolted against it. Every bit – except for her heart. That, after all, was where the magic was vested. It was like Levon had said: she was going to have to do it. The magic compelled her.

There was no denying Christmas, after all.

8

. . . .

THIS NIGHT OF SEVEN STARS

It was Alexandre who heard the knock at the door.

At first, he tried to ignore it. Certainly it was not for him, because Alexandre didn't have a friend in the world good enough to come knocking on Christmas morning. Probably it was M. Chabon, one of the elderly neighbours, coming to wish his grandfather Christmas cheer – but this was the sort of thing Alexandre felt that he should not have to indulge, not on a morning like this. He'd already opened the gifts from his mother and father: the leather jacket he'd ogled in a store uptown, video games, and the comic books he devoured each holiday, pretending he was still a much younger boy. The magic set was a gift from a distant aunt, who really did seem to think he was perpetually eight years old. Not that Alexandre minded: he'd already mastered the card tricks, and was studiously practising making a coin disappear in one hand and reappear in another. Sometimes, eight years old was the happiest place to be.

When the knocking came again, Alexandre rose in frustration. His parents had disappeared on their Christmas morning walk, and there was precious little hope that Victor would hear it. The old man was probably having his morning nap. If Alexandre had had the patience, he'd have continued to wait until whoever it was sloped away, back to their own Christmas – but instead he risked a peek around the shutters … and saw his sister standing there.

The sight of Isabelle – or was it Isabella? – panicked Alexandre, though he did not know why. Soon he found himself whirling across the room, stashing magic sets and comic books where they might not be seen. By the time he'd reached the front door he was quite out of breath. They'd have chided him for that at school. He'd tried out as a long-distance runner but the games master said he was too idle, and ought to take up a sport more fitted to him – like knitting.

Cautiously, he opened the door.

'It's you.'

Isabelle. She looked more like his father than Alexandre himself did, and this could only have been nature's way of laughing at him. It was almost, Alexandre thought, as though she didn't have a mother of her own. The hair, the eyes, the dreamy faraway look – it all came from his father, as if the man had somehow contrived to have a daughter with himself, then abandon her along the way.

'Alexandre,' Isabelle began, 'happy Christmas.'

He'd only opened the door a fraction, but now he felt obliged to step back and welcome her within. God knew what his mother was going to say, but there was a greater authority than her – and that was the authority of not feeling awkward.

'Dad's out,' Alexandre said as she closed the door behind her. 'He takes Mum strolling every Christmas morning. I don't know why. It's a thing they used to do. Come in, I guess. I can make you hot cocoa. Well, it's Christmas ...'

The house had been festooned since she was last here. The tree in front of the hearth was small but decorated with an artist's precision, strung up with a multitude of minuscule white lights. The rest of the hearth was dominated by a wooden nativity scene, in which a variety of scruffy felt farm animals (and one particularly inappropriate elephant) had been placed. The trinkets, Isabelle thought, of Alexandre's childhood. Cards lined the walls on long lengths of string, just as her mother used to do, and a child's sculpture of a snowman – with black eyes big enough to give it an alien air – stood sentry on the mantel.

'Here, please ...'

Isabelle had brought a satchel bulging with four presents. As she handed the first to Alexandre, his eyes caught the stocking still hanging on the hearth. Promptly, he pulled it down. 'It's my mother,' he murmured. 'She still thinks I'm eight years old.'

Together they sat. 'I'm afraid it's not exciting. I wasn't sure what you'd like.'

He tore at the corner, revealing a silver picture frame with nothing inside it.

'Does Hector ...' As she drew out the second gift, she caught herself. 'Our father, does he still drink chartreuse?'

Alexandre considered it dumbly. Then, extending his hand, he took hold of the bottle. 'I think he'd prefer the picture frame.' And before Isabelle could properly understand, an exchange had taken place. 'They'll be back soon. Look, let's make that cocoa. My grandfather might ... '

As if Alexandre's words were some magical rite, the old man appeared in the doorway. Standing upright, he was much smaller than Isabelle had imagined. The years had diminished him, so that it seemed only his clothes – the same corded cardigan he'd been wearing last time, and slippers like two enormous sledges – gave him presence at all.

'Grandfather, you remember Isabelle. My sister.'

If the old man did, he didn't seem interested. 'I was expecting M. Chabon.'

'I haven't seen him, Grandfather.'

'He comes every year.'

'Not this.'

'You'll have to take me there, boy. He may have slipped.'

'Oh, Grandfather! If he's slipped, he has his wife to take care of him.'

'There's every chance she's slipped as well. The pair of them, stranded on their kitchen floor. You'd leave them there all Christmas, would you? No, I'll get my coat. Boy, fetch my stick.'

The groan that rolled around the back of Alexandre's throat was well practised. He rose sluggishly and went to meet his grandfather in the salon door. But fortune favoured him today: no sooner had he got there than came the sound of the front door opening, of footsteps and clapping hands. 'I can smell the capon already.' That was her father's voice. 'It needs basting. I'll bet Alexandre hasn't ...' And that was Adaline.

The dread took hold of Isabelle again. This time she was prepared for it. She told herself she was not on stage, that she was not here to perform, and for now this was enough: she swallowed the dread back down.

Alexandre was already out in the hall, ignoring his grandfather's clamour. 'Mum,' he was saying. 'Dad. We have a guest.'

Isabelle heard the dull thud of boots as they dropped to the ground.

Hector appeared in the salon doorway, his lion's mane tangled even further by the hat he'd just taken off, his blue eyes full of disbelief.

'You're here.'

'Well,' Isabelle ventured, and reminded herself of everything Levon had said: the quest she'd been on, only just beginning, 'it's Christmas-time. I thought we could try.'

Isabelle's second dinner with her father brought back more memories than the first. The roasted capon had the same smells of butter and sage that she remembered, like the memory of a dream, from seventeen, eighteen, nineteen years in the past. The rabbit terrine that Adaline had made was a new addition, but it suited the meal perfectly well. When Adaline explained that, when she was a girl, they'd adhered to the old ways – the *réveillon* on Christmas Eve, the shoes left in the hearth to be filled with chocolate candies – and that her mother's rabbit had been the centrepiece of the evening meal, she got to thinking about the Christmases she'd spent since, with her mother and first stepfather, and the stepfather after that. Traditions from each filtered down, she thought. Her first stepfather had eaten goose, and this had persisted into her second stepfather's time as well. She was quite certain that the potatoes she was eating now were according to her mother's own recipe (the wild garlic was the tell), and that Hector had, in some unknowing way, brought this into his new family. One family, she thought, always bleeding into the next.

Memories were fragile things. 'Do you still sing?'

Hector, whose face was full of capon, spluttered, 'For Christmas?'

'You used to do carols, with the Yule log.'

'I did when Alexandre was small. But Alexandre ... well, you're too big for that now, aren't you?'

'Sing if you want, Dad.'

'I don't have the voice for it. I only really sing when I'm out on the bins, and even then the boys tell me to shut up. They just don't know good music ...'

Hector had worked a number of jobs – too many, Isabelle's mother used to say, for a man who can't settle on how he pays his way can hardly be expected to settle on anything else – but, since Alexandre was young, he'd worked on the municipal refuse trucks. 'A noble profession,' he'd explained with a wink, 'for the civic good ...'

'But Isabelle – you should sing. Did I tell you, Adaline, how they call her the Rose of the Evening? These People ...'

Something told her that speaking of the People was not the wisest course to take, so Isabelle quietly let the conversation drift.

After that, they spoke about Christmases past: how, when he was a boy, Alexandre had hated nothing more than visiting Victor and his wife's house, for fear that Père Noël would miss him at home. Or how, when he was ten, Alexandre had unearthed the Christmas presents his parents had kept hidden in their attic crawlspace, and had already been playing with his remote-controlled cars for two full weeks before they appeared, miraculously, in the hearth upon Christmas night. Hector told the story of how, out on the refuse trucks at the end of one December, he'd rescued enough fir trees to make a five-year-old Alexandre a pine forest in the back yard. And Isabelle thought, with a bitterness she did not like to feel: I would have liked that too, in my own once upon a time …

It was wise for Isabelle to ignore her own Christmases. Her first stepfather had taken them to Saint-Tropez one year, and Isabelle had spent Christmas morning on the beach with another girl from the hotel. Her second stepfather was a traditionalist, and believed in both the réveillon and Christmas Mass – and her mother had followed him so slavishly into religion that Isabelle had felt sinful for refusing to go. There were Christmases at home and there were Christmases away and perhaps that was why she felt so little betrayal at not being with her mother this year: traditions evaporated just like families. Without them, there was so little to miss.

'That's enough!' Victor announced. 'We've dithered too long already. M. Chabon could be curled up at the bottom of his stairs. I'll go to him myself, if I must.'

The old man was up and on his feet, guiding himself by the kitchen work surfaces towards the door, when Adaline rushed to catch him. 'Papa …'

'Don't argue with me, Adaline. I might be decrepit, but I remain your father. M. Chabon would come to me, were I in trouble. I'll be damned if I'm not going to do him the honour of the same …'

Adaline rolled her eyes at Hector, who only nodded, accepting defeat. 'Help your mother, Alexandre.'

As Alexandre followed his mother into the hall, Hector laboured to his feet and – if only to be a devil – snatched one of the sugared pastries Adaline had made from the counter, broke it in half and crammed one segment into his mouth. The other he offered to Isabelle, as if some deal was being made.

With one eye on the commotion out in the hall, he said, 'Isabelle, did you ... tell your mother where you are today?'

It was difficult to give it voice, so instead Isabelle only shook her head. 'She thought I might come home for Christmas. I told her I was spending it with Levon.'

'He's ...'

'One of the People. But they don't celebrate Christmas ... at least – not this year.'

A voice came from out in the hall: Victor barracking them to hurry. 'Time waits for no man!'

Hector rolled his eyes dramatically. 'The hours I've spent indulging that man.'

She was about to go after them, out into the hall, when Hector said, 'I'd have got you a gift, Isabelle, if I'd known you would ...'

She wished he hadn't said it. Now that he had, an ugly thought reared up inside her. Apologise for not giving me a gift now, she thought, but not a present, not a card, not in seventeen whole years. After she'd articulated the thought, it was so hard to think of anything else. What had felt like the hand of fate when she was a girl – she and her father, divided by destiny – felt more like a laziness now. Destiny she could understand, but laziness was so difficult to forgive.

'Here.' He'd reached into a pocket and drawn out a roll of banknotes, twenties and tens. 'You could buy yourself what you want.'

She tried to push the hand away – 'I don't ...' – but in that same moment Adaline reappeared. 'Let's get this over with,' she said. 'Then we can have a night.'

She would have said more, but her eyes had drifted down to the banknotes in Hector's hand. She shot him a look like poison, and stalked back to her father in the hall.

The night had deepened.

The moment Hector opened the door, Isabelle could feel its bitterness. No doubt there would be warmth in the night gardens, or wherever the People gathered, but here in Créteil the frost was settling in.

Victor moved slowly, and the family at his pace. With their breath billowing around them, they inched along the avenue, around the corner – and there, right in front of the house to which they were headed, stood the Chabons themselves.

Victor called out with triumph, as if some victory had been won, but his elation was short-lived, for soon he saw that the Chabons were not alone. M. Chabon, a year Victor's junior but twice his stature, was standing with his wife Cecily in the middle of the avenue, and around him milled a motley collection of neighbours and their families, all gathered in consternation.

'Something's wrong,' Victor ventured.

'Nothing's wrong, Pa.' Adaline was sterner than she'd been inside, and perhaps this was evidence that she was feeling it too.

But whatever could have been wrong on a Christmas night?

It was Isabelle who knew it first. Halfway to the crowd, she perceived the light emanating from its centre: strobing scarlet and amber, the colours of danger. But if only they knew the magic this really meant. She hurried on, ahead of Hector and the rest, and came between two of the neighbours, who were keeping their children – twin girls, dressed in matching pink snow suits – close. In the middle of the crowd, a single thigh-high blossom had broken up through the asphalt. The light in its heart was the colour of claret, turning to sunset along every edge.

'Can you believe it?' somebody was saying. 'Two hours ago, when we walked Papillon – nothing! And now this ...'

'It comes every night,' somebody else piped up, 'but not like this. I've seen it happen. Forces its way up after dark, and back down again at dawn.'

'It's because of *them*.' That was Victor's voice. He'd finally reached the crowd, Adaline trailing exasperatedly alongside, and reached out to clasp M. Chabon's hand. Then he gesticulated at the little house alongside the Chabons, where flowers-by-night crowded the window boxes and a tree in the garden was heavy with incandescent fruits. 'They do this, don't they?'

There began a faint muttering among the neighbours, until finally one of the children crouched down alongside the flower – and, lit up entirely in its ruby-red halo, said, 'But mama, isn't it pretty?'

'Pretty unusual,' somebody said.

'Pretty strange.'

'From pretty far away.'

'What I think you mean, gentlemen,' came a more sober kind of voice, 'is that being pretty doesn't count for a great deal. By God, I've known pretty women in my life. Poison, the whole lot of them! Yes, mark my words, poison comes in pretty packages.'

'Well, it can't stay here.' One of the neighbours, a man in his fortieth year with a porcine barrel of a belly, put his arms around the blossom as if he might heave it bodily from the ground. When it would not budge, he redoubled his efforts – and Isabelle was quite certain that the redness flushing his cheeks was as much from embarrassment as it was the light of the flower. 'I'll have to fetch my shovel,' he finally relented. 'Margo, my shovel!'

In the crowd, his wife threw her nose in the air. 'He used to call me "*ma chérie*", and now he calls me ... shovel.'

'I'll fetch it myself, shall I?'

'Don't bother fetching it at all,' somebody else piped up. '*They're* the ones who put this here, so *they're* the ones who should fix it. Somebody go and knock them up ... '

At this, Victor's voice re-joined the fray. He reached out to grasp Alexandre's elbow. 'Run to it, boy. Give them a knock. They'll be Christmassing in there and thinking nothing of this, when it's all their ...'

Alexandre was already loping towards the house when Isabelle said, 'They're not celebrating Christmas at all.'

She'd said it louder than she meant, but now that the faces in the crowd were turning to take her in, she did not mean to retreat.

'It's their Night of Seven Stars. That's what they're celebrating in there. The night their lost princess came back from Endless Night.'

For a moment, there was silence. Then, the woman who'd been so incensed at her husband demanding she go for a shovel, said, 'And who, mademoiselle, are you, to fancy yourself such an expert in all of this?'

Isabelle opened her mouth to respond, but a second voice sailed over her: 'She's my daughter,' Hector announced.

Isabelle sensed her moment. How foolish, to be buoyed up by a father she barely knew – but it felt like his wind was in her sails, and this was the feeling of a lifetime. 'They call them winterlights. They used to blossom in the old country, back when there was still ... magic in the world.'

'Magic!' somebody exhaled, breaking into a throaty laugh.

'Every winter,' Isabelle went on, 'before the Night of Seven Stars.'

'Seven Stars,' Victor uttered. 'Of course, she means Christmas.'

But no, thought Isabelle. They couldn't deny what was happening in the Parisian night. She looked up, and saw the seven-pointed star beached in the sky. Where the clouds shifted and came apart, its light was stronger than any. You couldn't refute enchantment, not when it spilled its light across you.

As she stared, she became aware of the constellation in which the star shone. Throughout the long December nights, its stars had been growing clustered, just as the story of the Nocturne pronounced – and there they were, ringing the seventh in a dia-mond halo, so that the light of one star was almost indistinct from the next. The thrill Isabelle felt upon seeing it, like a shining crown in the heavens, did not last long – for here, down on Earth, a shovel had been found, and one of the men was brandishing it at the flower's basin, preparing to carve it apart.

She looked back, at her father standing with his arm around Adaline's shoulder. 'Hector,' she whispered – but he did not hear, and already the man had brought back the shovel, like an axe, to strike his first blow.

'Please,' she said, wheeling around.

It was then that she saw the rippling light.

It was as if the flower itself understood. Or perhaps it was responding, not to the shovel, but to the shining crown in the heavens – the stars, so many thousands of miles distant, finally lining up. Pulses of scarlet light moved along each petal's veins, rising up the deep curve of the plant and escaping, like a blood red haze, from its upturned face. It was the ripples that gave the man pause. Then, as the light grew faster, more frenzied, he took a step back. His neighbours, too, had fallen silent. Soon the petals themselves were moving, bucking and convulsing and making the enormous blossom tremble. It seemed to Isabelle that something was moving in the plant, something deep beneath the surface. She took a step forward, as if she might stare into its cup – but she was too late. At that moment, each of the six flaming petals furled open, and as they fell the burning stamen in the heart of the flower exploded.

The petals fell back, the flower exhaled, and the pillar of rainbow orbs that had stood at its centre erupted upwards, like some geyser was breaking. Each of the glowing orbs – fruits, she had thought, though that seemed foolish now – shot upwards and out, describing great arcs over their heads with whistles and high-pitched shrieks, like rockets being fired.

The neighbours were reeling around, as if they might scatter for cover, but none of them knew where – for the orbs of gold and silver, emerald and ruby, sapphire, magenta and aquamarine were surrounding them now. The light of the unfurled petals was dying, steam rising from the frosted earth where they lay, and together the neighbours turned to watch the rainbow orbs as, having reached the top of their flights, they began to plummet back to earth. Hector had reached for Alexandre, wrenching him close as if to keep him safe. Adaline was clinging to her father. Mothers rushed to their children. Wives buried their faces in their husbands' breasts. One particularly sozzled old man clapped his hands over his eyes, as if he'd already seen too much. Isabelle alone watched the rainbows fall with her eyes open wide. Not seeing the beauty in this had to be a wilful act. You had to choose to be blind.

Isabelle chose to see.

The stars were crashing back to earth. Isabelle fixed her eyes on a cyan orb, hurtling down out of the heavens – but the ball of light never touched the ground. Somewhere in its descent, the ball itself arrested its course. Too far away to see, Isabelle cantered down the road, past banks of parked cars, until at last she saw what had stopped the cyan orb.

It had sprouted wings.

Now it was hovering there, shaking off whatever its luminous casing had been – and, as that casing evaporated away, cyan snowfall settling across the street, she saw a single lightjar unfold. Its wings beat fiercely to keep it aloft. Its eyes blinked and blinked again, freeing themselves of the caul in which it had been wrapped. Its beak, built for drinking nectar from deep within the flowers-by-night, sprung out from a tiny spiral into a long, elegant reed. Then, only seconds into its life, it darted into the sky.

Isabelle turned on the spot. Back down the street, some of the neighbours had dared to open their eyes. Now they saw the magic, she thought. Now they would marvel at what the People had brought to Paris. In the air all around them, the other rainbow orbs were opening up. Out of each, a lightjar hatched mid-flight. A rainbow of hatchlings was taking to the skies. There they zipped around, revelling in their freedom, revelling in life. Soon they were criss-crossing the street in exuberant array, and soon after that they had come together, a flock of a hundred different hues.

Isabelle made haste back to where her family was standing. The faces around her were etched in confusion – but she did not see fear here, not any longer. She took hold of Hector's hand, so that he might look at her. 'We need to go.'

'Go? Where?'

'Trust me,' she said, and the joy burst onto her face with the same undeniable flourish as the winterlight had when it erupted. 'We can't miss it. Is the Métro still running?'

Hector took in the bank of faces in front of him. Victor's was the only one still set in anything resembling a scowl. Adaline's eyes were bewildered and bright. Alexandre looked as if he'd just woken from a dream. 'Forget the Métro,' said Hector – and, reaching into his pocket, brought out a fist of jangling keys. 'We'll take my car.'

On Christmas night, the seven stars conjoined.

In the Jardin des Tuileries, Emmanuel the park-keeper hoisted his daughter Esmé onto his shoulders and looked up as the seven-pointed star burned with fresh fire. Along the Champs-Élysées, where the winter fair was in full swing, revellers stepped off the carousels to discover the night as bright as day. Families closing their shutters gazed up at the sky. Solitary dog-walkers paused to pet their pooches and felt a new white light falling across them. Skaters on the city's ice rinks drew spirals around each other as, momentarily, they felt the touch of magic from above.

And wherever the winterlights were growing, on the open plateaux in front of the Tour Eiffel or down by the banks of the Seine – in demolition grounds and hotel forecourts, on terraces and balconies where, until now, only window boxes had flourished, in the forgotten country beneath the motorway flyovers where refugees had once camped – passersby stopped, their eyes drawn to the convulsing flowers.

Emmanuel the park-keeper had seen this before. But the wonder of children playing snowballs with orbs that left colourful comet trails in the air was nothing against what happened next. 'Watch, Esmé!' he gasped – and Esmé, who had rarely seen her father as overjoyed, scrambled down from his shoulders to get a closer look. The winterlights that had appeared, like miracles, in the Jardin were glowing with a light that seemed alive, a light that seemed ready to spill out. On the Champs-Élysées, an enormous indigo flower looked full to bursting with pent-up light. And in the night garden, where Arina sat in the crook of Mariam's shoulder with little Aram on her lap, a pure white winterlight started to thrum.

By the time Hector's rickety motorcar had reached the embankment, the first winterlights were coming to life. From somewhere there came a shriek, and Isabelle caught sight of miniature comets arcing over the rooftops, then sprouting wings and soaring even further high. 'There!' she called out, and Hector banked the car in that direction, to the vocal displeasure of Victor, who sat in the back, squashed up between his daughter and grandson.

North and further north. Over the ring road, where the lanes lay unnervingly silent, and into older Paris beyond. The sound of rockets could be heard over the old town. Fireworks, the city-dwellers must have thought – but these were not fireworks at all.

When they came to the open air of the embankment, Isabelle saw pin pricks of light over the northern arrondissements. But it hasn't really started yet, she told herself. There are too many winterlights. It's just waking up . . .

Isabelle directed Hector to the Hôtel Métropol and there, before the car had slewed to a stop, she scrambled out. Pounding through the doors, she ignored the protests of Fae at reception, and hurried past, into the wine cellar and down, down, down into the Khanate Beneath.

'Levon!' she gasped, for there he was, among the rest of the vagabond People and their bustling bazaar. 'Levon, you have to come . . .'

They burst, together, back to the night. A smaller winterlight, out on the Place de la Bastille, sent a spray of silver orbs fountaining upward. As the lightjars hatched, the glittering casings fell like snowfall along the Rue Castex.

Isabelle and Levon spiralled around together, cocooned in a dream. 'I want to see it with them,' she said, and thought of Arina, Mariam, Natia and Nino, all the People of the apartment block that had become her home. 'I want to see it with you.'

Levon nodded. 'One moment.' He was gone for seconds, back into the Métropol, and when he reappeared, so too did all the vagabond People. Soon they were streaming out onto the Place de la Bastille, where a succession of bigger winterlights were still thrumming with unspent light, their moments yet to come.

Isabelle opened the car door. 'Hector, this is Levon. Levon, this is my . . . father.'

The man behind the wheel looked sheepish, as if perhaps he did not belong in his own automobile. There were others in the back, and they gripped each other as Isabelle cajoled Levon inside, then somehow found the space to sit alongside him up front.

'Hector!' Adaline exclaimed. 'This is really too much. It's Christmas night! We should be at home.'

Hector waited until Isabelle had slammed the door shut, then gunned the engine back to life.

Some time later, with the fountains of light still shooting upwards at increasing intervals, the car reached the great horseshoe of the apartment block. Levon and Isabelle were almost at its doors before the rest of the family had unfolded themselves.

They stopped.

'Hector, you don't really expect us to go up there?' Adaline looked at the face of the building with something approaching disgust. 'My father's near eighty years old.'

He crossed the car to kiss her on the cheek. 'I know, Adaline. But ... I have to.'

It was only Hector who followed them up the stairs. If Isabelle cared at all, she did not show it. The way up was long, but she did not stop, not even as Hector lagged behind. She waited for him at the very top – and then, together, they burst into the night garden.

'Isabelle! Levon!'

Arina leapt up, the Nocturne still in her hands, to fling her arms around them both. 'It's the Night of Seven Stars! I told you we'd know – I told you it would show us how!'

Isabelle carried Arina into the heart of the night garden, where the whole apartment block gazed out into the night. It had started happening seconds before. All over the city, from the industrial vistas of the north to the minarets and turrets of the old town, the winterlights were coming into blossom. Seeing it up close was a wonder, but seeing it en masse was a miracle all of its own. Parabolas of green and red, vermilion and gold, bright white and metallic silver were being charted in all corners of Paris. The strobing lights made them look like domes being cast over the city: big and small, tall and flat, domes inside domes, lights inside lights, like standing inside a Christmas tree and seeing the fairy lights being strung up from within.

Then, in fits and starts, the perfect parabolas of those blossoms began to break down. Hurtling lights stopped mid-flight, so that from a distance they seemed to be hovering, just the same as the stars up in the sky. Isabelle held on to Levon's hand, and saw the points of light dart in different directions. Lightjars exploded into life across the night sky. It seemed to Isabelle that a million rainbows were turning in spirals across the city.

In the streets of Paris, from the most opulent townhouses to the campsites where the down-and-outs stayed, people were staring up at the same enchantment. The Christmas lights along the Champs-Élysées paled by comparison – but so too did the rest of life. For a minute, the shifting dome held its form, as everywhere the freshly hatched lightjars grew accustomed to this new world. Then it began to break and come apart. Flocks formed of different colours, and either sailed down to earth, seeking the nectar of the flowers-by-night that would sustain them, or returned – perhaps grieving – to the winterlights that had nurtured and cast them out. After that, shimmering formations of single colour could be seen above. In the night garden around Isabelle, lightjars of pure white had landed, to peck disconsolately at the winterlight that had birthed them, and flutter among the People who'd gathered to watch.

Tears had come to Arina's eyes. She cradled her bebia's Nocturne as if she couldn't let go. 'It's the first one, isn't it? The first

Night of Seven Stars since the old times. Oh, Isabelle, if only bebia was here to see it ...'

'She'd have loved every moment.'

'She knew it was coming,' Levon added, crouching to wipe the tears from Arina's cheek. 'She's out there in the night, right now, looking down on us and laughing.' He needled her with a finger. '*I told you so, Levon!* That's what she's thinking ...'

Isabelle looked around, and there was Hector, dumbfounded and alone. She gave him a wan smile, and opened the circle she'd formed with Levon and Arina to welcome him in. Two stuttering steps towards her, he halted. An expression she could not decipher had flickered across his face, and then died. His blue eyes, which had taken in the same wonder, looked suddenly sad.

'Is it ... real?' he asked her.

'Every bit of it,' she beamed. But it only occurred to her afterwards that, perhaps, he didn't mean the lights at all: that he meant her, right here, back in his life, sharing all this with him. 'Hector ...'

He hated it when she called him Hector. She saw it in the way his face contorted, even though he tried to suppress it. 'Dad, isn't it magical? That all of this even exists. Hector, look!'

Her father started, for a lightjar had landed in the unruly mess of his hair, and was even now pulling at strands of it.

She could not contain her laughter as he tried to bat it away. The bird, with a scornful look, rocketed upwards, to find its brethren in the skies above.

'Hector,' she said, 'it's new beginnings, isn't it? Christmas. The Night of Seven Stars.' Rebirth, she thought, in the very middle of winter. 'It's here for all of us, whether we're of the People or not!'

*

In the gardens of the Louvre, where a winterlight the colour of year-old marmalade had just birthed a flock of lightjars with pie-bald plumage, the Paris Presbyterian Carollers had regrouped. Some of their younger members could not be contained. Now they stood on the fringes of the group, gawping and pointing at the fluttering points of light. Tonight, their mischief could be forgiven. Even the adults in the garden had to remind themselves that they'd been building to this concert since autumn drew its cowl across the city. And so they began.

'O holy night, the stars are brightly shining ... '

Some of the adults stopped there. They turned their eyes upward – where, through the shimmering flock of lightjars, the seven-pointed star still reigned supreme.

'A thrill of hope,' the others continued, 'the weary world rejoices ... '

It was then that the choir leader, a stern man in his sixties who had lived half his life alone, realised that it was not only his singers lending their voices to the carol. The children who'd scattered across the garden were still singing. So too were the families who'd gathered to watch. Their eyes might have been gazing on other wonders tonight, but their voices were as one. He fancied he could feel some enchantment rippling out from here, the very heart of the city, running through every ventricle and along every vein, touching everyone in every quarter of Paris. But this was not the magic of song – no matter how much he believed in that particular power. This was the magic from above. The wonder of this Night of Seven Stars, bringing everyone together.

'A thrill of hope,' the singers repeated, 'the weary world rejoices ... '

Well, all of Paris – no matter from which corner of the planet its people came – was rejoicing tonight. Everywhere was love.

*

ROBERT DINSDALE

AN OPEN LETTER FROM THE MAYORALTY
OF PARIS

This Noël we the citizens of Paris witnessed a moment few of us
will ever forget.

Moments like this are markers in History, but too often they
come in our darkest times. Paris has known too many of these.
We remember them for the loved ones we lost, or the torments
we endured. But on Christmas night we lived through a
moment we will recollect for its reminder that there is love and
beauty – and, dare we say it, even magic – left in the world. And
that, though our species contains divergences too many to mention, the wonder at a beautiful thing will always bring us
together. Hate and fear might divide us, but magic and love
unites.

So, while we can never forget the purgatories that Paris has
survived, let us also not forget that our city has been a bastion of
imagination and enlightenment since time immemorial. That
Paris has always welcomed the brave and the good from the four
corners of the Earth. That we are a city of playwrights and per-
fumiers, of artists and artisans, inventors and scholars. And that
we have always celebrated ourselves as a City of the World.

It is in this same spirit that, on this New Year's Eve, we are
proud to proclaim a General Amnesty to the refugees and set-
tlers who call themselves 'the People', who came this year to
Paris in the wake of their old country's collapse – in search of a
new place that they might call 'home'. Home: the most magical
word of all.

People of Paris, I ask that you join me in welcoming our new friends and neighbours, that we might celebrate each other and share the magic of both our peoples for the generations to come.

To all the many peoples of Paris: a happy New Year!

AN INTERLUDE

SOMEWHERE ON THE TRAIL

See . . .

Hayk is late to the rendezvous, and by the time he reaches the outpost – an abandoned barn in the corner of some rain-washed Serbian field – the traffickers are already gone. It isn't the first time he's been ripped off, and he doubts very much it will be the last, so it does not unduly bother him. Nor is he alone in this dilemma. When he crashes through what's left of the door, he sees a figure hunched in the corner. It startles when he appears, and the look on its face is one of horror. Hayk is not unduly bothered by this either. He caught himself in the window of a broken harvester, sinking into the mud out there, and a creature more feral he has never seen. His beard has grown tangled, the thatch above his eyes gives him the look of the forest, and his face is still marked with blood where the last smugglers set upon him. Fools! They thought he had coin enough to pay for a passport. But they left with no such impression. The ones that left at all.

Outside, the rain comes down. December, deep December . . .

The woman – for it is a woman hunched into the corner, bent over a little wind-up radio – darts for a knife she has laid out. As for Hayk, he hardly cares. She will not come for him. Or, if she does, she will not get far. He can see that she's trembling.

He settles himself idly in the opposite corner, where the ground is dry. 'They cut and run on you too?' he says, in the language of the old country.

The language soothes her. She sets down the knife.

'Just took my money and ran.'

Hayk has an apple in his bag. He lifts it, sinks his teeth into it – then tosses her the other half. 'Here, have this as well.' 'This' is a packet of the marshmallow cakes he's been devouring at every pit stop: light and cheap and full of the sugars his body craves. 'Eat,' he says. 'You're wasting away.'

So she eats.

It used to be that you met lots of the People out on the trail, but in the months since Hayk was ejected from the last detention centre, dumped back in some further province so that he could begin his trek all over again, the world has shifted. To walk in caravan, like they used to, is to get rounded up. To seek the company of the People is to invite disaster. There are refugees from other places out here, all drifting west – the world is nothing if not full of people aching for home – but Hayk tried putting his faith in people once. He will have no such weakness again.

But then . . .

This woman, she is alone too. Unlucky, Hayk thinks – or else as cunning as he. He offers her another marshmallow cake, and asks, 'Where are you headed?'

The woman is suspicious of the marshmallow cake and says, 'Paris-by-Starlight.'

'I've heard of this place too.'

'One border left,' the woman begins. 'After that, they won't look for papers again. You can ride all the way into Paris-by-Starlight. Begin again. My husband's there . . .'

Hayk grins, inwardly. Yes, she's cunning all right. She wears no wedding band on her finger and yet she speaks about a 'husband', because she thinks Hayk is like any of those other bastards out here, who say they'll take you from one country into the next, if only you give up your life's savings, if only you spread open your legs.

'My wife as well. Anahit. My mother, Maia. My daughter. The last of my sons.' Hayk stops. 'If they survived.'

The woman nods, sadly. 'This is the big "if" of our People.'

'How many have you lost?'

'Too many.'

'On the day the soldiers came.'

'Then, and every day thereafter.'

They sit in companionable silence, the rain sluicing down, until at last the woman says, 'How do you mean to do it ... to get into Paris-by-Starlight?'

Hayk stands. From the doorway of the barn he can see so little: only the curtains of grey that turn the once-green field into a churning dark mass. Stupid, but it's in moments like these that he feels most alive. He can forget the day the soldiers came. He can forget herding his family onto the boat and turning tail with the rest, to head for the hills. He forgets the sorties they made and the chaos they tried to provoke as, one after another, they were captured or killed, or just gave up the fight to join the great exodus west. All of that evaporates, and life becomes elemental. This must be, he thinks, how men of old used to feel – the prehistoric men, their lives measured from campfire to campfire, from empty belly to full.

If you ignore the marshmallows.

'I'm going to make the river crossing. I already forced the fences and got sent back. I'm done with smugglers and all the shit they serve up. I'm going to walk the river.' He does not turn around as he adds, 'You can come with me, if you wish. Two bodies brave the current better than one.' Besides, he can always use a sacrificial lamb.

The woman is on her feet, the wind-up radio crackling with some litany about the storm sweeping Eastern Europe.

'Of course,' she says, 'it would be dangerous to walk into the river now. They speak of the winds. Of floods.'

Hayk lets the rain lash his blistered his face, his open eyes.

'The floods are our friends. The border guards will be off balance. Their eyes on other things. What kind of a fool,' he grins, 'would try and ford a river in flood?'

The Danube: grey and wild, and as wide as the oceans.

Go to an official border crossing north or south of here, and the battles are pitched. Two dozen border police can hold back a flood a thousand strong. In history, they would call this a glorious rearguard, a victory for the ages, if only those thousand hadn't been penniless refugees, women and children. Yet, come to places like this one – lonely and wild, forested on one side and farmland on the other – and the only battle to be fought is with the elements. The river police make this their route, but not now. You'd have to be mad to step into these waters tonight.

'You can't see the other side,' the woman (who still declines to share her name) says.

'But it's there,' says Hayk. He has lashed a plastic barrel, dragged out of some farmyard, to a wooden pallet, and this he drags into the water. 'People used to think the world was flat, and they still set sail. Have a little faith. The other side's waiting for us.'

And so it is.

Hayk's been stranded at sea before. The glowing serpents that once lived in the landlocked sea might have been extinct for generations, but that doesn't mean the water didn't have treacheries of its own. When he was seventeen, still a second mate, a freak storm robbed the boat he was fishing with of its sails, so that he and his crew had to row their way back in the night. Or there was the time, just after he'd become captain, when the crew got steaming drunk and, in their stupor, lost the sextants and star charts overboard. Disasters befall every seaman. You don't fight against them. You just learn to cope.

Or, 'Disasters don't befall me. I befall them,' Hayk laughs, as they turn and turn again across the roiling river.

It takes three hours to make the crossing, but at last they fetch up on the opposite shore. Croatia, they call it, but the difference between one country and the next is hardly the difference between 'day' and 'night'. Everywhere the same, and just imaginary lines dividing them. At least when wayfarers stumbled upon the old country, in days gone by, they truly stepped into a different world.

Hayk stirs a little fire in the shelter of a hedgerow. It does little to warm them, but it lifts their spirits. After that: off into the outer dark, with only their haversacks on their shoulders (towed behind the raft in bin liners), in search of a way further west.

It takes seven days to find that passage. The border is replete with army vehicles, coursing up and down the Danube, but Hayk is prepared for this – so they forage a little from the hedgerows, steal a little from the service stations, and remain hidden during the day. 'Well,' Hayk remarks, 'the People – the true People – should always travel by night.'

Without money, finding a way further is hard. But there are ways. The thought occurs that he might hold up one of the service stations, and he makes plans to enact this exact plot – but, when he's on the brink of it, he decides he's had enough of wasting the months of his life in prison cells. If the old world really is waiting at the end of the line, he wants to see it soon. He wants to live everything that was lost.

'We could just walk,' the woman says one night when, having begged enough, they've taken a bed in a hostel.

'Can you go that far?'

'I've come this,' she mutters, irate that he'd doubt her.

He curls around her, in the single bed they've bought. 'Are you ready to tell me your name?'

'Not yet.'

He holds her, because this seems right, but he doesn't touch her in the way men do, because this does not. Besides, that part of Hayk is spent now. His body is made for walking, and nothing else.

So they walk a little. Ten miles a day. Twenty. They hitch-hike when they can. Three hundred miles in the back of a lorry delivering cornmeal. Two hundred in an empty horsebox. Sometimes they sleep in hedgerows and sometimes under tarpaulins in the motorway lay-bys. Sometimes the going is easy, but mostly it's empty and hungry. In this way, days become weeks. But none of it matters, not to Hayk: the borders are gone. The road goes on and on – and it's leading him home.

Paris creeps up on them. In days of yore, you would stand on a hillside and see the border fires of whichever township you approached from a distance. You'd see a cathedral, rising out of the wild. Now: just the motorways growing more densely, the suburbs a blight on the landscape. Industry, thinks Hayk, was what first drove the lights out of the old world. It was industry that poisoned enchantment. And if this is Paris, well, it is hiding its enchantments well.

It's hiding them so well, in fact, that for the first days, Hayk and his companion think little of this fabled Paris-by-Starlight. So consumed are they in the new bounties the streets have to offer – for here you can forage and steal so much more easily than in the last thousand miles – that the first signs of Paris-by-Starlight take them quite by surprise. Then, one night, tramping beneath the rumbling lanes of the Boulevard Périphérique, they spy a smattering of lightjars, miniature comets in magenta and mauve, turning overhead. Hayk and his companion share a look of paradise reborn.

It will not be their last.

Beyond the ring-road, the nocturnal world is awake. Two cities abound here, though their streets and monuments and parklands are one and the same. When darkness falls, flowers that have been biding their time during the day light up in radiant array. Out come the lightjars, and the nighthawks to hunt them. Something canters along, further up the road, just out of your sight, forever searching for the shores of a sea that is no longer there. A little deeper in, and you begin to hear voices in a language that feels like home. On some rooftop, children are taking their lessons, singing nursery rhymes and lullabies that have not been given voice in hundreds of years. On another rooftop, the night market is in full swing. Hayk and his companion climb a rickety stairway and pirouette through it, and the sensory overload is almost too much to fathom. Hayk eats roasted water rats that his grandfather's grandfather could barely remember. He drinks the spirit of the vermilion flowers-by-night and feels its iridescent warmth restoring every crevice. An old-timer from the landlocked sea recognises, in Hayk, a man who has only just reached his destination, and offers him a bed in one of their flop-houses. 'Or go down to the Nexus,' somebody says, 'which the people of Paris-by-Day call the Hôtel Métropol. They'll find a home for you there. Never a sight have you seen, stranger! Did your bebia ever tell you of the Khanate Beneath?'

They take the long way, for this city of Paris-by-Starlight is full of wonders – and by dawn it will be gone. Along the river they wander, where the gargoyles of Notre-Dame glow indigo in a strange new moss. Further along, where the Tour Eiffel is entangled, each night, by a rainbow of vines, and in those vines the civilisations of lightjars and dragonflies, lace-winged bears and blackweathers who last made their homes on the landlocked sea. Somebody is farming in the Luxembourg Gardens. Somebody else has her apiaries buzzing across the city's rooftops, fat furry bees of the night heavy with luminous pollen.

At last they stand before the face of the Hôtel Métropol. Hayk knows straight away why this is so special. Each window in the hotel's face is a halo of light. Flowers and vines from the old country spill out of each, so that – of all the buildings along the Rue Castex – this stands sentry against the night. Inside, the jungle scent hits him like a wave. Flowers-by-night have burst through every tile on the floor. A painting above the reception desk seems to sprout them around its circumference, so that it is itself a portal into the old world. Sweetness and stickiness roll over him, until a girl named Fae directs him down through what was once a cellar – now an underground grove, where bulbous lights grow on reeds and eyeballs growing on stalks wink at him as he passes – into the caverns below.

'The Khanate Beneath,' Hayk's companion whispers.

Citizens of Paris-by-Starlight bustle through an underworld that seems to stretch forever, its outlands replete with luminous mangroves. On every rocky island the People have built their bazaar. There are permanent homes here, woven from the longest reeds. Rope bridges lead from outcrop to outcrop, and the air is alive with noise. People, Hayk laughs. The People everywhere.

'You'll be off to find this husband then, will you?' Hayk asks, still doubting that the man exists.

Pointedly, his companion reaches into her pocket and produces a silver wedding band. This she slips onto a finger.

Hayk roars with laughter. So, he thinks, not cunning at all. She wanted only to make sure her totem was not stolen, or that she was not forced to trade it out there on the trail. To Hayk this is as much a marvel as everything he has been seeing in Paris-by-Starlight tonight: some people still tell the truth.

'My name is Milena. Look to me if you get sick. I was a doctor in the old country.' Then, with a wistful air, she adds, 'Maybe I can be a doctor again. Maybe Paris-by-Starlight needs its own doctors.'

Moments later she is on one of the rafts, being directed out into the cavern. A doctor, thinks Hayk – and, lifting his hand, marvels at the two stumps of fingers on his right hand, where the border guard's dog wrestled him to the ground. Yes, this world is full of wonders.

As he is standing there, an old man whirls past, buffeting his shoulder as he come. Hayk turns around, reining in the impulse to claw him to the ground. It is only one of the People. His heart hammers. You see enemies in every corner, Hayk. But look around you. The old world is being honoured here tonight. Somewhere, here, you have people too . . .

'Stop.'

The old man looks back. 'Citizen?'

'I'm searching,' Hayk says.

'For what?'

'My life,' Hayk says, and the words make him quake. They're so simple. So true. And they open up a yawning abyss within him.

'Come,' the old man says, 'I think I know what you seek.'

There are lost people boards, right here in the Khanate Beneath. The old man punts him out to one of the nearest islands, where a woven reed wall is covered with notes.

'That's why they call this the Nexus. The meeting place. A place for connections to be made. People looking for husbands and wives and daughters and sons.'

But no matter how much Hayk scours the boards he sees no names he recognises here. No missive, pinned up in the desperate hope he might see. All these People, crying out for connection, but not for him.

'Who rules this place?' he says, and the question startles the old man.

'Rules?' he wonders. '*Rules*? But, citizen, this is Paris-by-Starlight. There isn't a ruler here.'

Hayk turns on the spot. All of the colours, all of the lights, all of the sights and smells and sounds. He remembers lying in a hedgerow, starving and beaten up and the border guards still tramping up and down. All the hallucinations he'd had then, vivid from fever, are nothing compared to this – for how could a place like Paris-by-Starlight exist unless it had its King of the Stars, like the khanate of old?

'No ruler? But that's why the old country was overrun. Because we were weak.'

'There's the Ulduzkhan,' the man shrugs, 'but ...'

'But what?'

'He doesn't fancy himself leader, though he's the one who dreamed it back into life.'

Hayk utters, 'Where do I find this man?' His eyes dart around the Khanate Beneath, but the old man only says, 'He isn't here, but he isn't far.'

'Where then?'

The man squirms, uncomfortably. Somewhere out in the cavern there's a shriek as one of the last winterlights, dormant since the Night of Seven Stars, finally unfurls. 'Well,' the man continues, and his eyes elevate upwards, towards the cavern roof. 'It's the damnedest thing. The Ulduzkhan, he's cleaning out the toilets, in the hotel upstairs.'

BOOK THREE

PARIS, NOT SO VERY FAR FROM NOW

Tariel watched as the star fell to Earth. His heart was too full. He feared it would burst. He had never before suffered feelings like these. He begged understanding. He begged for reprieve. When his prayers went unanswered, he fled before dawn (and braved purest sunshine 'til darkness returned) — by which time he'd fought through the emerald glade, through forests of scarlet, the diamond-white haze; and, reaching the dell where the star was on fire, he knew down inside this was his Heart's Desire. 'I'll save you,' he told her, 'my beautiful star. Set you back in the heavens. You've fallen too far.'

Though the star did not answer, just gazed up above, Tariel knew that he'd fallen in Love.

From 'The Story of Tariel', the Nocturne

BOOK THREE

PARIS IS NOT SO VERY FAR FROM NOW

AN ORDINARY ENCHANTMENT

Dr Senghor had profited handsomely from the People's coming. As the People flocked into the city, they'd needed a doctor, somebody they could trust. And so, every nightfall, just as the flowers-by-night were opening up and the lightjars taking flight, the Senegalese had set up a station in the night garden and waited for the People who needed him most. If only the things he saw – the infections festering in old wounds, the after-effects of malnutrition and exhaustion – had been unfamiliar; but Dr Senghor had made a journey of his own, and seen countless others who had done the same. The injuries done to the People were the injuries done to exiles the world over, so he did what he could and was proud when he saw the People thriving, this 'Paris-by-Starlight' of theirs spreading from rooftop to waste ground, to the very aether of Paris itself.

But as much as they'd needed him then, they needed him no longer. By the time their winterlights were exploding across the firmament of Paris, a display of fireworks more magical than any Bastille Day, there were doctors enough among the People to tend to the swelling population. Some had undergone formal training, but more plied the things they'd spirited up out of the Nocturne – and, in spite of Dr Senghor's suspicions, they seemed to work. You could argue with the idea of enchantment, but you could not argue with its effects. Dr Senghor had seen broken men restored by the tinctures they derived from their flowers-by-night.

He'd heard a baby's croup cough fade away. Hedgerow magic, the healers in the Nocturne called it. They had this in Senegal too, but Dr Senghor had always put his faith in science.

Which made it all the more confusing when, answering a call one night, he heard a voice he'd half forgotten on the end of the line, and now found himself tramping up the stairs of that same apartment block where he'd once made nightly appearances, wondering what, by the very Stars, had changed.

The apartment block was transformed. The central staircase, which had once echoed with lonely footfalls, was now a glowing pillar, where every railing was tightly wound in vines. To the Senegalese it was like ascending through a rainbow. By the time he reached the top, he was quite dizzy – and grateful when, on rapping at the door, a face instantly appeared. Mariam – whose boy Aram had grown immensely in the months since his last visit – welcomed him in, and shut out the vividness in the stairwell.

'I can only think you need me for a miracle migraine cure.'

Mariam smiled. The Senegalese was not a man who often made jokes, and of this one he seemed enormously proud. 'She's in the back room,' she said. 'She's been sleeping.'

But when Dr Senghor looked round, Isabelle was standing at the bedroom door, her scarecrow's hair ragged and wild. 'Come through,' she said – and the Senegalese, with the sensation that something was seriously wrong, did not hesitate to follow.

'You already know what this is.'

The Senegalese stood at the end of the bed while Isabelle dressed, one hand cradling her belly.

'As far as I can tell, everything's as it needs to be. I could take bloods,' he shrugged, 'but, Isabelle, you're French. There are hospitals for you. Physicians. You don't need a back-street doctor. You need a ... midwife.'

Isabelle said, 'I'm scared.'

Dr Senghor was used to scared people. He was used to being scared. He laid down his instruments and folded his hand over hers. 'Your body is a marvellous thing. You think all this – flowers of starlight and new stars in the sky – is a miracle? Isabelle, your body's building a new human being.'

'I've been being sick. I can't stand the smell of coffee. I used to drink three cups by midday! Mariam brought back jars from the night market, things the People had pickled and preserved. I could smell vinegar through the glass. I made her throw them away.'

Dr Senghor had begun packing his instruments away. 'I didn't say the body was perfect.'

'How long have I got?'

'*Got?* The way you speak! You haven't been handed a prison sentence. You're—'

'Please,' she said, and now that she was fully dressed began holding herself again, 'how far along am I?'

'I couldn't tell you for certain, not without bloods. But, Isabelle, you'll have a child by summer.'

She sat back on the bed, and the images that coursed across the backs of her eyes were of her own days as a child. Right here in Paris, her mother dangling from one hand and her father from the other. Hector's voice as he sang her lullabies each night. *No bedtime stories in our home. Only bedtime music.*

'I'm not ready,' she whispered.

It was why she'd been putting it off, until she could put it off no longer. It was why, she realised now, she'd summoned the Senegalese instead of taking herself into one of the daytime city's doctors. The thought of holding a child, let alone the thought of what was happening in her body, was unutterable. To visit a doctor was to make it real. As long as it remained here, in Paris-by-Starlight, a little piece of her could believe it was part of the fantasia. But now ...

'What should I do?'

'Visit a doctor.'

'It's why I sent for you.'

'They'll have ultrasounds. There are systems. Isabelle, you can't think to do this...'

'But *he's* of the People, isn't he?' She held herself. She felt certain it was a 'he': a blue-eyed Levon, with a stubborn streak wider than continents. 'Paris-by-Starlight's his home. So it should be a doctor of the night ...'

'Paris-by-Starlight doesn't have hospitals. It doesn't have operating theatres.' Dr Senghor reached into his bag and pulled out a tiny plastic jar. 'Vitamins,' he said. 'Take vitamins. Drink lots of water. Rest, when you need it. And eat, even if you're feeling sick. More than toast.' He hesitated before going on. 'Look to your body, Isabelle. It will tell you if you need help.'

Dr Senghor opened the door and crossed the apartment, back to the kaleidoscope in the stairwell.

He passed through emerald and red, through indigo and blue, wondering that anybody could live in such a riot of colour, and soon he heard the toll of footsteps coming from the opposite direction. He stopped, looked over the bannister rail into the levels below. From here he could see two figures, grown men idling at the bottom of the stairwell. 'I told you,' one of them said in French, 'look at it. It's where it all started.'

'And nobody stopped them?'

'Can't stop them, can you? It's politics.'

Dr Senghor remained still. Down below, the men were strobed by bands of different colour.

'General Amnesty!' one of the men muttered, with barely concealed contempt. 'It's a licence to do what they please, and why? All because it's beautiful?'

'I've heard that one before,' the other joined in. 'My first wife was beautiful. Beautiful is poison.'

'What is it they say? Pretty girls make graves.'

'If only ...'

There came another sound: the click of a door being opened.

'Wait,' one of the figures said, 'here one comes.'

The Senegalese wasted no further time. There was a scalpel in his bag. A scalpel would be protection enough, whatever these men were about. He unfastened the top of his case and, in loping strides, made it to the bottom of the stairwell.

Stairwells: such dank and lonely places. He remembered when this one had been fouled in cardboard mulch and rat spoor, but now all that was gone. There were ruby flowers growing and fat bees buzzing where the rat droppings used to be.

A third man had entered the stairwell, and now the two Frenchmen stared at him. 'Levon!' Dr Senghor hailed the new arrival from where he stood on the stairs. 'You're home.'

Levon's eyes did not leave the two strangers, not even at the Senegalese's insistence. He made them a mute hello and sidled past – and the two men, sensing some change in the atmosphere, shoved their hands in their pockets and slipped through the door, back to the coming dawn.

Levon had the dogged weariness of night's end about him. Twelve hours at the Hôtel Métropol could do that to a man.

'Dr Senghor, what are you doing here?'

The Senegalese did not answer. His eyes were still fixed on the two men, beating their retreat.

'Trouble, Levon?'

'They think to trap lightjars, and turn them into pets. They think there's a racket to be made. But lightjars don't trap so easily.'

To Dr Senghor, who had been called every slur under the sun, this did not seem the real reason men like that would venture here, but for a time he said nothing. 'You should go upstairs, boy.'

'Sir, has something happened?'

'Oh,' the Senegalese said, and ran his hands along the bannister rail, disrupting the lace-winged bears and glowing bumbles who were feeding there, 'something quite beautiful.'

Levon took the stairs three at a time, rising through the spectrum until he was at the very top. Somebody had left the apartment door ajar. He pushed it gently, so that he could see within, and stood nervously on the threshold – for there was Isabelle, smothered in Mariam's arms.

'You silly girl. All this crying. You know you're not truly upset, don't you? It's your body, playing tricks. Hormones going haywire. I used to sob if I put too much milk in my coffee.'

Isabelle lifted herself from Mariam's arms.

'Who have you told?'

Isabelle said, 'You're the only one.'

'Not your mother.'

She shook her head.

'Your father.'

Isabelle spluttered, 'I've seen him *once* seen Seven Stars. He wouldn't …' She stopped. 'Well, why should I tell him? Why should I care? Seventeen years meant nothing to him. He knew where I was all that time. It wasn't him who had to go on odysseys. It wasn't him who had a "quest". So he's going to be a …' Isabelle stopped herself again. She'd been lost in this rabbit hole too many times since Hector sashayed into Le Tangiers – but now, and forever hereafter, there was something more important in which to lose her mind. 'Do you think he'll be angry?'

She'd started trembling again. Levon saw it from the door.

'Your father?'

'Not my father. Levon.'

Levon flushed crimson. He'd been eavesdropping all along, but only now that his name was mentioned did it feel a sacrilegious thing.

Mariam had stepped back from Isabelle, her face opening in a smile. The distance she'd put between them was only so that she could look Isabelle up and down, to try and decipher if she was serious or making some joke. 'Levon? Angry?' The two words seemed to slide off each other, like oil over water. 'I saw that boy with his face pressed up against the border wire, and he wasn't angry. He was only ticking over, thinking about it quietly – even while they wrenched his hands behind his back. No, Isabelle. Levon, angry ... about *this*? If you'd known Levon in the old country, you couldn't think such a thing. If you'd known Levon's mother. Anahit. My sister. You see, Levon wasn't made for the old country – not really. All the men out on the landlocked sea, or drinking in the longhouses, while the women and children got on with the ordinary business of life. He'd have made a decent fist of it, if that was what had happened – but it wouldn't have been him. No, Levon was a ... mama's boy. You'll think it's an insult. People do over here. But I don't mean it that way. I pray that Aram is a mama's boy too! Somebody who cares. Somebody who thinks that family matters. That children aren't for siring and then ditching until they come of age. Isabelle, he's not going to be angry. He's going to be excited! A new chapter for all of us. Hang all the magic in Paris-by-Starlight – this is what Levon's been waiting for, ever since we arrived.'

It was enough to dry Isabelle's tears. She kneaded her eyes, thought herself completely ridiculous, and turned to where Aram was building blocks on the apartment floor. 'Well, what do you think, little man?' she said, sweeping him – quite against his wishes – into her arms. 'How would you like to stop being the baby of the family? You could consider it a promotion.'

She whirled him around until he giggled – and only when she stopped did she realise that a second set of eyes were watching her.

Levon was there, his eyes wide as saucers, in the door. But he was smiling, she realised. He'd been smiling all along.

*

He'd started taking the long route home, and that had helped for a while, but now that they'd realised what he'd done, they were more vicious than ever. Try to avoid them, would he? Well, Alexandre would pay for that.

It had seemed a sensible plan. He wouldn't take a different bus; he'd just catch it in the opposite direction and ride it back around, so that by the time it deposited him at home it was a full hour later, and the streets already empty. Alexandre didn't mind. His father was ordinarily home early, but ever since Isabelle had appeared he'd been occupying himself with the trunk of old instruments he used to play – and, because his mother worked after-hours at her college, it was ordinarily left to Alexandre to sit with the old man, or make him pots of coffee, or take him on his evening perambulations up to M. Chabon's and back. Alexandre loved Victor, but he was pleased to miss that. Besides, when the bus ran counter-clockwise around the old lake at Créteil, there were so few passengers that he could luxuriate in the empty seats. He'd bring out his magic set and practise turning one coin into two, or fanning a deck of cards. He could make a golf ball levitate and a stuffed rabbit disappear, but if the other boys saw him they'd call him a baby and take his toys away.

This time, they were waiting for him when he finally disembarked. There were still orange barriers erected at the site where the winterlight had burst through the asphalt; one of the neighbours had complained that the pothole was ruining the suspension on her car. As Alexandre passed, he couldn't help thinking about the magic of seeing the first lightjars taking flight, nor the helter-skelter ride across the city when the whole firmament was alive with magic. But the boys waiting on the corner had other designs.

A stone arced overhead and landed at his feet.

'Raphaël, it nearly hit my head.'

Raphaël was the tallest of the three. His father worked in the mayor's office, which meant he was certainly superior to Alexandre's father, who only emptied the mayor's trash. He was sitting on the wall where the streets converged, with his cousin Antonin and Suzanne, who lived three roads over and had been going with Raphaël since New Year. The boys at college said that, if you waited long enough, everyone got their turn romancing Suzanne – but Alexandre was not sure there was time enough in the world for his turn to come.

'Next one will hit you square,' Antonin called out, before adding, as an afterthought, '*faggot*.'

He walked a little further on.

'You get the bus with us tomorrow, Alex?' Suzanne smiled.

That smile was false. He knew it was false. And yet still it warmed a little part of him. It caused him to turn. Half an inch – no more – over his shoulder, and he saw that she was waving. The waving was false too, but it called out to him nevertheless. He hated this about himself more than any other thing. Raphaël and Antonin he might have shrugged off, but the yearning for a girl like Suzanne remained.

They were still talking about him as he hurried down the street, careful not to run lest they think he was running away.

He crashed through the front door, and – though this was no baron's castle – felt the immediate relief of his own four walls. Tramping past the living room – where Hector was surrounded by lengths of wood and coils of catgut – he made straight for the kitchen to ferret around for some snack. Here Victor was sitting, with his shoebox of old newspaper clippings, like he did most afternoons – constantly sifting and rearranging them, as if, Alexandre thought, he was panning for gold.

'Dad's still making his lyre, is he?'

Victor nodded. 'I should say so.'

'Mum will be impressed.'

This got the old man's attention. They shared a knowing smile. Sometimes, the best way to bond with someone was to root around in the fragilities of somebody else. Adaline was tolerating Hector's newfound obsession in her usual way: by saying nothing, and hardly acknowledging its existence at all. But over the past three weeks, this had become a Herculean endeavour. It was Christmas that had changed things. Isabelle turning up with gifts, while there were none for her in return: it had opened up a wound Adaline had thought long closed. 'Your father thinks that one present, if it's magnificent enough, might make up for seventeen years of birthdays and Christmases,' she'd said one night, when, exhausted after a long day, she'd let her guard slip.

'How many has he built now?'

'Seven false starts. The man's determined, I'll give him that.'

Alexandre thought: He never honed a gift for my Christmases. You didn't need to learn a craft to wrap plastic guns and figurines.

Into the silence that followed, Victor suddenly said, 'What are you doing tonight, boy?'

Alexandre shrugged. 'What do you think I'm doing, grandpa?' The image of Suzanne flashed into his mind, but that was only his mind taunting itself. He thrust his hand in his pocket and pulled out an endless string of rainbow handkerchiefs. Then he took a bow.

'It's my Reunion night,' said Victor.

'Oh yes.'

'But your mother's working. And him in there … Well, he's not bothered, is he? He doesn't want to ferry me around when he's got the heart of a long-lost daughter to win back!' Here he cackled. He just couldn't help himself. 'You could come, if you liked. You're old enough to drive, are you?'

'You know I'm not.'

'It's a couple of bus rides. Alexandre, they don't let me go alone.'

'You get lost, grandpa.'

The old man looked glum. Anger, Alexandre could understand. Fire and brimstone he didn't mind. All the endless chatter about Paris and what the city used to be like, back in the good old days – when all the decent, honest folk of Paris had to contend with were Nazis and nightly bombings. All of this he was inured to – but when his grandfather looked glum, everything was lost. Eighty years old was no age to be, when all you really wanted to do was *remember*.

'I'll come grandpa,' he said, and turned to look in an empty cupboard. 'Assuming they have snacks.'

There was a public hall, just north of the Château de Vincennes – they'd had winterlights here on the Night of Seven Stars – and here, once a month, Victor and his friends met to reminisce, pore over old photographs, and launch fierce critiques of each other's baked goods.

At least, Alexandre thought, his grandfather hadn't lied about the snacks.

He was helping himself to a twisted pastry spun in sugar when the old men gathered. They were all men, Alexandre noted. His grandfather was a widower, but most of these other men had left wives at home. Alexandre's mother would have smiled at that. If there was one thing grown women wanted, she said, it was getting their husbands out of the house. The real revelation was seeing that his grandfather had so many friends. It was easy to think of him as a belligerent, silent old sod – because, at home, that was exactly who he was. But here the old men seemed eager for his company. They clasped his hand and clapped him on the back, and one even wrapped his arms around him. After that, they sat in a circle and Victor spread out the clippings from his shoebox – and then, just like that, they were fifty years ago, stalking fearfully through a very different Parisian night.

Soon, the red wine started to flow.

There were chairs lined up on the edge of the room, and here Alexandre sat. He'd brought his magic set and, as he practised fanning his cards, he became dimly aware of the hall door opening and another old man being ushered in. Still Alexandre did not look up. Magic – real magic, not like whatever had coursed across Paris over Christmas – demanded absolute concentration. He was concentrating so hard that he barely looked up when a figure deposited itself into the chair beside him, and shards of sugary pastry began to shower down.

'What are you doing there?'

The old men were deep in their conversation: Paris, at the fall of '44, and the secret celebrations of Christmas that year. But this was no old man's voice. The cards erupted out of Alexandre's hands in a geyser, and so did his frustration. He'd been so close.

He looked up.

Another boy had slipped into the seat beside him. Tall and rangy, a head taller and perhaps five years older than Alexandre, his black hair was cut in a military fuzz. He sat, slumped, in the chair with a practised kind of contempt. Alexandre had seen this before: Raphaël and Antonin. They had the same eyes as well.

'Nothing,' Alexandre muttered.

'Show me.'

'What?'

'I said show me. What, are you deaf?' The boy threw his arms apart, in mock exasperation. 'Go on, don't be shy about it. I haven't got all day.' He paused, thinking. 'All night, I suppose, while this ol' lot jabber on. But, look, I want to see, OK?'

All Alexandre could do was shift uneasily in his seat. Then, as if sensing his hesitation, the new boy shoved what was left of his pastry into his mouth, got down on his own hands and knees, and started gathering the fallen cards. When he pushed them back into Alexandre's hands, the instruction was clear: get on with it.

As Alexandre sorted the deck, the boy said, 'So which one of these wraiths you here with?'

'Wraiths?'

'This lot. You know. Wraiths. Skeletons. Zombies. The living deeeeeeaaaaaaaaad.' He stretched out the last word until he started laughing. 'That's mine, right there. Valentin, the old romantic.'

'That one's mine. Victor. He's my grandpa.'

'I got stuck with mine,' the newcomer sighed. 'Community service, isn't it? I had my hand in the till at the delicatessen, so they stuck me with farming out old men for a hundred hours. Honestly, you've no idea how long a hundred hours is. Here, I'm Étienne.' Étienne put out his hand, expecting Alexandre to shake it – and Alexandre, who was still trying to figure out whatever ruse this was, just shook his head. 'They got you spooked good and proper, haven't they? What is it, all this talk of the old days?'

Alexandre laughed, then checked himself. 'Actually, I kind of like them talking about the old days. It feels real.' He paused. 'Sorry, that was a dumb thing to say.'

'No, I hear it. I hear it. So ... are you going to show me this card trick or not?'

Alexandre felt the same rush of warmth he'd felt on seeing Suzanne waving to him earlier that day. He tried not to hate himself for it, this time. Suzanne wasn't genuine – but perhaps this boy, this Étienne, was. 'You really want to see?'

'I'm not going to,' Étienne groaned, 'if you don't get on with the bastard thing ...'

As Alexandre showed him, he felt snatches of conversation sailing over him. At first, nothing piqued his interest. Victor was regaling them all with the story of how he met his wife Marie at the tail end of the War, when he'd been appointed to run a message to a farm outside Reims, but this was a story Alexandre already knew well. It was only when he heard the words 'Hôtel Métropol' that he lost focus on the trick and began to listen in.

'Nobody knew a thing about the Fortiers. Not even the Colonel.'

'Oh, Mathieu, you have your head in the clouds! Of course the Colonel knew. What you mean is he didn't show it. That's quite a different thing ...'

From what Alexandre could gather, this 'Hôtel Métropol' had, once upon a time, been a kind of sorting house, a nexus where messages got left or cyphers put together. 'And that rumour about the wine cellar!' one of Victor's friends laughed. 'They said there was a wine rack, and if you took the right bottle off at the right time, it swung backwards on hinges, and down you went into the catacomb below.'

Alexandre pulled his chair a fraction closer. This seemed the sort of thing he'd read in one of his comic books: a secret passage to a secret lair. And his grandfather had been a part of it too. 'See,' he told Étienne, 'I told you there was real stuff here.' It felt good, he realised, to have it in his history; to have his very own Once Upon a Time.

'I know it for a fact,' Victor announced. 'I took a message there once, on behalf of the Colonel.'

'Lies!' someone laughed. 'Victor's telling stories again.'

'I am not. They had Berliners in the hotel restaurant, and I walked straight through and down. Not one of them knew what I was doing ...'

At once, the other old men chorused, 'And that's how Victor won the war!'

There was a moment when Alexandre thought his grandfather might bite back. He thought of Raphaël and Antonin, perched on that wall. But instead Victor only joined the laughter, and started pouring more wine. 'You old rascals! You're just jealous you weren't trusted by the Fortiers. M. Fortier was a true hero of the Resistance. I won't hear a word against him!'

'No,' one of the other men added, 'but as for his son ...'

The mood darkened.

'That place is holy. There ought to be a plaque. Instead ...'

'Fortier's just opened it up. Told these People they can have it for their bazaar – and all for nothing.'

'Not for nothing,' interjected a man with features of craggy nobility. 'Fortier will be making a packet. It's just he'll be hoarding for himself. The way he treated that hotel, after his father ... It's the lack of honour that bothers me. It's not as if he doesn't know what that place meant.'

'A shining beacon, on a dark, dark night. The most special place in Paris, not that anyone knows it. And now it's gone. Oh, I know people still go there. There are these People making it their home. They invite you in, if you want to go and see their light shows or eat that foreign food. But it isn't the same. They had a British airman in the carrières all War.'

Victor, who had by now poured all the wine, said, 'You won't catch me going down in the dark. No, not again. I'll remember it how it's dear to me. They can't take that.'

'Imagine,' one of the other old men snorted, 'the sort of people who'd even *want* to live at night. Well, we did it ourselves for a time, didn't we? When we had to. Paris at night – that was the time for secrets. But people who'd choose it? It's enough to make you shudder. As if they've got something to hide ...'

'Well,' whispered Étienne, who had drawn his chair closer, 'they've got that part right.'

'Yeah?'

'The only reason to live at night's if you can't stand the day.'

'Yeah,' Alexandre said again, though he scarcely understood Étienne's meaning.

'Stands to reason they've got something to hide. Any fool could see it, if they weren't so blinded by fancy flowers and light-jars. People get confounded by the pretty shit. Me, I know what's underneath. I tried. I really did. I wanted to give them the bene-fit, just like everybody else. Even at Christmas, with all that show-ing off – well, I thought, that's *something*. *That's* a Christmas we'll never forget. Only, I guess we won't be allowed to call it Christmas when we look back on it. It'll be "Night of Seven Stars" this and "Night of Seven Stars" that, and if you call it Christmas they'll, I don't know, disappear you into that Khanate Beneath. It's a land for their dead, don't you know?'

Alexandre said, 'We were right there in the middle of it. We were driving straight across Paris ...'

'Then you got a front-row ticket to the new world,' Étienne muttered. 'Look, I guess it sounds like I'm mouthing off. And I guess I am. My mouth always got me in the shit. But the thing is – I'm right, and just 'cause it's unpalatable, don't make it untrue. I used to have this girl, you see.' Étienne stopped. 'Don't give me that look, Alex. I can see you giving me that look!'

Alexandre – who was giving him no deliberate look – would have replied, but Étienne was already marching on, 'Élise. You'd have liked her, Alex. Unless you're one of them faggots, and I can tell you're not, because you haven't once put a hand in my lap yet!' Étienne shrieked with laughter. 'I'm messing with you, Alex. I'm joking! But Élise, she'd have done it for you. We'd been going together six, seven months, when these People turned up. And I decided – well, I'll take her to one of their night markets. That'll do the trick. It's romantic, you see, because it's all starry and shit. And it's got that edge too – because this was before the General Amnesty, so they were still illegal, their night markets, still floating about from patch to patch. Well, we had a blast, me and Élise. All those flowers lighting up the stalls, and the strangest things you ever saw to buy. They had these fish in a tank, and when they skewered one for the griddle, its light fizzled out, just like *that*.

'Well, there was another stall. I got talking to one of them – as much as I could; his French was pretty awful. Said he'd been in Paris nearly a year, but you wouldn't have thought it. I reckon, if I got dumped in another country, I'd make more of an effort … but that's just me. Anyway, Alex, you're side-tracking me! Stop side-tracking me! This man, he was selling … moonshine, I guess you'd call it. Liqueur they got from those flowers. Had it in red and gold and sapphire blue. Whatever colour of flower you could find, he'd have it in liqueur. Me and Élise, we always liked a drink, so I got us a bottle, took it down to the bypass where I live – and we had at it.'

'What was it like?'

'It was *good*, Alex. Nectar, with just a bit of a kick. We drank the whole thing. I had a banging headache the next morning, but I figured it was worth it. Or at least I did, until Élise ditched me. Three days later, she just turned up on the doorstep. She'd written a letter. Said we weren't right. I argued it, of course – but she was done. I didn't figure why until a whole week later. See, Alex, she'd found someone else. That's what girls will do to you. I can't say I was surprised. Not until I saw her with him. And there he was, this fellow – calling himself Khazak. One of the "People".'

'Oh …'

'*Oh* is exactly right. And he wasn't good-looking. He didn't have charm. Just another one of those vagabond types, can't even be bothered to get up during the day.' He paused, shaking his head ruefully. 'It took me an age to figure it out. An *age*, Alex! Because it was that liqueur they sold us. Christ, I walked willingly into their trap. They tricked her into drinking it, and it addled her. A love potion.'

For a second, the story seemed to be spinning apart. Alexandre's face creased. 'You're not serious.'

'I am.' Étienne's voice had hardened. He reached out, gripped Alexandre by the wrist. 'You're going to tell me love potions don't exist, aren't you? Well, dumbass, you said it yourself – you were there in the middle of it, on this Night of Seven Stars. Tell me magic doesn't exist! We all saw it, didn't we? With our own eyes! Yeah, that's right. If they can carve caverns out of the earth they can mix up a potion easily enough. They magicked Élise into taking up with one of them. And if that isn't a crime, then I don't know what is.'

Alexandre tore his hand away. If Étienne noticed the tension with which he'd done it, he didn't show it; he'd already dropped the same hand around Alexandre's shoulder, as if they'd known each other for years.

'It's not really a crime though, is it? Not if she ...'

'You need to put your thinking cap back on, Alex. Everybody knows: love potions, they're for creeps. If you need a potion to take someone back to your bed, that makes you a degenerate in my eye. And the eye of every loyal, decent Frenchman. This is Paris. The city of lovers! If you're relying on love potions here, there's got to be something wrong. No, these old folk, they've got it right. Your grandpa over there, he'll tell you. There was a time we used to care about our city. People risked their lives for it. This old lot might look like useless, but they were heroes when they weren't much older than us. They had something to believe in. Paris for the Parisians. Honestly, this General Amnesty! It's just Vichy all over again.'

After that, they sat in companionable silence, Étienne's arm still draped around Alexandre's shoulder.

'My sister's with one of the People,' Alexandre finally piped up. 'She lives by night with him, in a tower block up north.'

To this, Étienne just shook his head sadly. 'Well, there you go, Alex. There's your evidence, right there. What right-thinking French girl would just up and *choose* to never see the sun? Alex, I'm sorry to be the one to break this to you – but she'll have been the victim of a love potion too.'

*

Into the approaching dawn, there staggered a man.

The sun coming up over the railway line was no sight for a man of the People, but he'd come this far – if he lived a few brief hours of daylight, it did not make him Davit the Daydreamer. It only made him desperate. Desperate to reach the end of the trail. Desperate to meet this man they called Ulduzkhan.

The old town vanished, somewhere behind him, as the demolition sites grew up along the railway track. This, he decided, was more like the cities he'd dragged himself through, out there on the trail. Freight terminals and gas stations, the city's untended places, fit only for wayfarers moving through the night.

Hunger was gnawing at him, so he stopped in the mouth of one of the demolition sites to eat what little he had stowed in his pack. Propped up against the iron hoardings, he watched the nocturnal world prepare its retreat. There had been lightjars too many to mention, wheeling in flocks over the domes at the Sacré-Cœur. Now, something else nosed its way out of the building site. A dog, its fur shimmering, its eyes luminous green.

The dog came to him. All dogs did. He exuded trust. It occurred to him that he could snap the dog's neck – and there was a time that he would have done this, then roasted it on a fire he himself had kindled. Enough meat on a dog this size to sustain him a week. But those days, or so he'd been told, were near their end. All he needed was to lay his eyes on this man, this Ulduz-khan, and he would let himself believe.

The dog was lithe and light and, when he cupped its head in his hands, it submitted. It smelt of salt, thought the man. It smelt of the landlocked sea. As he petted the dumb thing, his fingers caught on ridges of muscle just beneath the line of its jaw. Sensitive, perhaps, the mutt tried to pull away – but the man whispered to it gently, calmed it, probed further. With his fingers, he parted the fur.

He staggered back.

Gills, he thought. Ridges like that could only be gills.

And he thought of the old sailors' stories, of the water dogs that used to follow the fishing boats, the glowing hounds who dove for their masters, stirring up the fattest, brightest shoals from the ocean's uttermost depths.

'Come with me,' he told the dog – and the water dog, recognising the voice of its master reborn, trotted after him – until, at last, they stood before the grounds of a great horseshoe-shaped tower, where curtains of glowing vines hung down from the rooftop like hair, and through the doors all the colours of the rainbow shone.

*

At the bottom of the rooftop stair, Levon took Isabelle's hand.

At the end of every night, the People of the apartment block gathered to eat. All were welcome in the rooftop grove. Trestle tables were lifted between the trees where the flame fruit grew. Cookfires had been conjured. Near a hundred of the People ate together, and spoke of their long nights.

Isabelle and Levon walked up the stair.

The rest of his family were here. Mariam ate with Aram and Arina at the end of one table. Ana and Elen squabbled at its other end. Even Natia and Nino, still joined at the hip – but joined, by the other, to the boyfriends they'd found at the bar-in-the-bazaar where they worked. All of the odyssey was here – even Maia, for there she was, in the fluttering of every lightjar in the trees.

They stood together and watched the People mill. Up above, the seven-pointed star was fading as the daylight world was restored. But there was light in it yet.

'People,' Levon began, and climbed the headland of earth at the miniature ocean's edge. 'People, please. Isabelle and I have something to say.'

Levon was never loud enough. That was just his way. In the end, it took Arina – who bouldered over to his side and bellowed, 'Everyone, shut it!' – for the grove to descend into respectful silence.

Isabelle crouched with Arina and put her arms around her shoulders. 'They should call *you* Ulduzkhan!'

'What's going on, Is?'

But Isabelle only smiled, and pressed a finger to her lips.

By now, the People in the night garden had turned their eyes on Levon, but Levon was still. He closed his eyes, and what he saw was not the future echo of his son or daughter gambolling through this night garden, nor showing him the infinite wonder of the seven-pointed star; it was those first days, after they'd beached on the western shore of the landlocked sea, how tiny and cold and frail Aram had looked as they'd taken to the trail for the very first time. All those nights, in hedgerows and encampments, shut up in the backs of wagons, listening to the jackboots tramping past. These were the things that echoed in him now.

He felt Isabelle at his side. Her hand curling into his.

'You tell them,' he whispered.

She said, 'You're choking. It's like me and my harp. Just breathe it, Levon. This is what you came here for.'

He'd spent too long chasing the right words around his own head. Isabelle had given him up for lost. When he came back to his senses, she was already saying:

'I'm having a baby.'

There was a moment of silence in the rooftop grove. Then the cheering began.

'Isabelle!' Arina exclaimed. Levon saw her grappling, with uncontrolled delight, with Isabelle's shoulders, hoisting herself up to be hugged. 'Does it mean ... am I going to be an aunt?'

'Yes,' Isabelle laughed. 'Oh, Arina, yes. We'll feed him pancakes together, you and me, every night.'

The men had gathered round Levon. Some of them were embracing him. But above it all, Levon could hear the trilling of a single white lightjar. He forgave himself a moment of sentimentality and decided that he could hear, in that birdsong, the voice of his bebia. *Oh*, she'd said, *what wonders you'll see ...*

At last, with the dawn already upon them, the People began to drift away from the mound where Levon and Isabelle stood, Arina still sandwiched between them. It was a tide of joy that carried them through the scaffolding, back down the rooftop stair – but something was obstructing them as they left.

It took Isabelle a moment to understand that a figure was standing there, with a dog snaking around his legs. As the People pushed past, she saw him more clearly. The man stood a head taller than the rest. His face, which was weather-beaten and lined, had the piebald look of one which has, until recently, been covered in outgrowths of feral beard. His eyes, one of which bulged under the protrusions of some old wound, were fixed on her and her alone.

'I am looking,' the man declared, in the language of the old country, 'for the Ulduzkhan.'

Isabelle turned to find Levon, and realised that he'd drifted off. He was down in the glade now, with Mariam's arms around him, Arina hanging off his shoulders.

The man's voice silenced their celebration. Slowly, they lifted themselves up, coming back through ferns edged in glitter to stand at her side.

'Please,' the man continued – and, for the first time, Isabelle sensed the desperation in his voice. He was starving, she realised; his body was distended, and his eyes as big only because his face so gaunt. A man, she thought, who'd only just come in from the wild. She'd have gone to him, pulled flame fruit from the trees to feed him, all the magical bounty of Paris-by-Starlight – but something stayed her. It was the way he held his own body. It rippled with violence.

'The Ulduzkhan,' he uttered. 'I was told this was his palace. Please.'

Isabelle reached for Levon's hand. 'He means you ...' But when she took it, she found that he was shaking.

'I'm no Ulduzkhan.'

'Can't you see he's frightened?' Isabelle whispered.

Levon could. It was written in scars across his body. It was there in the way his eyes kept darting into every corner, as if expecting ambush or attack. But it was not the only thing that Levon saw. He untangled his fingers from Isabelle and stepped down from the mound, crossing the gap between them and the stranger in three long strides. Three long strides – but it might as well have been three thousand miles.

At last, he stood in the shadow of the man. Levon was scarcely as big as his shoulder – but, seeing them so close, Isabelle saw what she had not seen before. Their black, coiled hair was exactly the same. And, if you ignored the protrusion, their eyes reflected each other like mirrors.

'Ulduzkhan?' the stranger ventured.

Levon drew a long breath.

'No, father,' he said, 'there is no Ulduzkhan, not here. There's only me. Your son. Levon.'

10

* *

THE RETURN OF THE NATIVE

Under the covers in the back bedroom, Isabelle put her arms around Arina.

'It didn't look like him,' she kept saying. 'Only half of him, Isabelle. He used to be my father.'

Isabelle ought to have had words for that. She thought of Hector, so different and yet so disappointingly the same, and only tightened her hold on the shivering girl. She thought: You come to the end of one quest, and end up on another; just the story of a life.

'Tell me what you remember about him.'

Arina said, 'Not much.'

'Oh, but there must be something. I was six when I last saw my father. I didn't have much either. But I guess I had a ... feeling.'

'I have a feeling now, Isabelle.'

Daylight was shedding through the window blinds. Isabelle turned her shoulder against it. She could feel the razor line of Arina's fingernails where she held her. You couldn't brace a body until it stopped quaking, so instead Isabelle just let the girl tremble.

'What feeling, Arina?'

And Arina said, so softly she could barely be heard: 'I want my mother.'

*

A part of Levon had wanted him to sleep in the apartment, in a bed thick with eiderdowns – the kind of bed, he supposed, that his father hadn't slept in since the old country fell. That was nearly three years ago, but you could still see its shadow across Hayk's skin, like disease in a dying tree's bark. But another part of him, the greater part, couldn't brook a man so feral stepping inside the same walls where Isabelle and Arina lay their heads. The man who'd forced his way up the rooftop stair, demanding the Ulduzkhan, was both his father and yet not his father. Three years, thought Levon, was a lifetime and more.

His father had made no complaint. Exhaustion and starvation were his constant companions and, as he took in his old family, arrayed around him like border guards pinning him down, he'd said barely a word. Mariam, his sister-in-law, had brought him food, Arina – nervous, but with Isabelle at her side – had drawn water from the pool, and as a family they'd sat him on the earth of the rooftop grove. As he'd eaten, he'd stared above, his eyes fixed on that place where the seven-pointed star hung each night, until their heavy lids had closed. And Levon realised: he needs the sky. He isn't a man for buildings and bedsides. If less than a year could conjure the mystery that was Paris-by-Starlight, what might three do the soul of a man?

All day long, the water dog slept across him, as if keeping its master safe from harm.

Now the dark of night was falling again. Levon stood alone in the night garden as the freshly revealed stars brought it back into life.

The water dog sensed it too. When it stirred, it nosed its way to the edge of the pool and considered its reflection. Then, real-ising afresh that this was not the landlocked sea for which all its kind pined, it set up a mournful lament.

Whether it was that lament, or the increasing intensity of the garden, that woke his father, Levon did not now. From a distance, he watched as the gnarled man rose. For a time, he sat there, shaking in the beauty of the garden. Then he crawled, on hands and knees, to the same water from which the dog was lapping. His hand shot down, and came back clutching an eel, pulsing with sapphire light. Until that moment, Levon had not known that such fish had manifested in his bebia's pool.

Their eyes met across the garden.

'Do you know me now?' Levon asked.

'And last night,' Hayk said, 'though I thought it a dream.' Before Levon could stop him, his teeth sank into the wriggling eel, which continued to thrash even as he slurped at its sinews. 'I came looking for a king, but instead I found ghosts.' He stopped to rip more flesh from the eel. 'I dreamt about my mother last night. Tell me, where is she? I saw the rest of you, but my mother . . .'

Levon faced his father from the other side of the pool. Three years ago, he'd borne Arina off a boat on the western shore of the landlocked sea. Frigid and afraid, they'd joined the procession tramping into the setting sun, their father left behind on the ocean's eastern edge. Somehow, he still seemed as far away.

'She perished, didn't she?'

His father's rage was barely concealed. Here was a man, thought Levon, still many thousands of leagues from Paris.

'She passed away right here, right in front of my eyes, with all the magic of the old world only just waking up around her. She's here, in her garden. She's the one who started living by night. The one who believed that the old ways were still out there, just biding their time.'

A single white lightjar erupted from the foliage of the tree beneath which Hayk slumped. He watched as it rocketed up into the gathering dark.

'My mother,' Hayk laughed, the last of the eel trailing from his lips, 'the Ulduzkhan.'

Yes, thought Levon. This, at least, was closer to the truth.

'Hayk,' he said. 'Come with me. Please.'

His father drew his sleeve across his lips, sated for a little while. 'I will,' he nodded, 'but I'll be bringing the dog.'

Father and son walked out into the night.

The daytime world was not done with yet. The French folk of Paris were still gathering for drinks along the pavement cafés, heading out together to take dinner and drink champagne. But all around them, Paris-by-Starlight was coming to life.

There were night gardens flourishing all the way along the Rue René Clair. Tonight, Levon followed his nose while Hayk tramped beside him, the water dog snaking between. In one of the gardens, children gathered for school. In another: a tiny night market stood among the trees, where an enchantress was performing the Nocturne's Festivity of Light in a cloud of lightjars she herself had trained. By the time they reached the old town, night was absolute and the People were abroad.

'It just woke up,' Levon tried to explain. 'Just like ... it needed reminding. Bebia had been living by night for months, with only little flourishes around her. But it was enough to make her believe. So I made her a promise. We started living by night. Our world came back into flower ...'

'I saw the seven-pointed star when it rose. We all did, from the detention centre. And I remembered her stories.' Hayk gave a guttural laugh. 'By the Stars, she used to fill my head with that nonsense. Davit the Daydreamer. Ketevan. Endless Night, in a world where magic used to exist. And you'd think: fairy tales! Just legends for a dark night. Well, all people have them, don't they? The stories that separate them from the others. Stories to make us special. Because we are the People.' He sank to his haunches to cling on to the water dog. It seemed, to Levon, that the great man was clinging too tight. 'Who knew that our stories were real?'

They wandered on, eating the sweet tubers of the flowers-by-night, until some time later they came to the Champ de Mars. Here, the People had come out to play. A theatre troupe had formed and, in a great ring of spectators, played out the old world's fall – and the rebirth of the new. Up above them, the Tour Eiffel was a pillar of light against the black of the sky. At night, the vines that had been slowly sprouting along its every strut came to life. Now, when the wind blew, the colours shifted and swirled as if in some fever dream.

There had been silence too long. Levon said, though he had not planned it, 'It's been three years, but I haven't forgotten that day on the shore.'

Hayk grunted.

'I know you thought me a coward, but I got them here safely, father.' The last word felt so improper on his tongue. He'd never been 'father'; he'd been 'Hayk'. Hayk: that distant presence, spoken of but seen so fleetingly, year after year, season to season's end. 'I did what I said I was going to do. I looked after them all.'

Hayk rose to his feet, and something in the motion – like an eruption – made the water dog cower. 'It's funny the way you say it, like it's something to be proud of. Because I don't see her here. Your mother.'

A pair of silver-blue lightjars came between them, tussling over some glowing strand they'd uncovered.

There were two voices in Levon. One of them wanted to ask his forgiveness, but the other was stronger.

'She made it over the landlocked sea. There were those who didn't. You'll remember it, Hayk, just like me. The wind. The hail. The ice. There were already too many of us on that boat, but I held on to her and Arina all those miles in the dark. And the screaming and the panic and not knowing where, by the Stars, we were – or who, by the Stars, we'd left behind. Aram, months old, in Aunt Mariam's arms, and her husband at the tiller, trying to guide us. Of course, *you* weren't there, so *you* wouldn't know. You were off playing soldier with the rest of your sons. The good brothers.'

Hayk bristled with violence, but he said not a word.

'Oh, my mother made it over the landlocked sea, but it was still the landlocked sea that killed her. It was in her lungs. The cold never left her. Day on day, tramping and wet and hungry and …' Levon stopped. He had seen a look flickering on his father's face, and wondered, perhaps, if some moment of understanding was being reached.

'What became of her?'

'I buried her,' Levon breathed, and looked at his hands, dirty and treacherous and still, it seemed, lined with the filth of that solitary hour. 'Kissed her cold body and laid her down at the side of some road. I couldn't even tell you where. She's gone.'

Hayk turned, without word, to the glowing spire of the Tour Eiffel. Some birds, soaring condors of brightness, had made their eyrie at its very top. Everywhere that the daylight world slept, Paris-by-Starlight: alive, alive, alive …

And to his son he said not a word.

Night hardened in the Champ de Mars, but there was so much of Paris-by-Starlight left to see. They ventured into the Hôtel Métropol, where the wine cellars had all been decanted and claimed by the starlit wild. They punted in boats across the underworld pools of the Khanate Beneath, and emerged by one of the outer stairs into a bazaar where a healer was administering ointments she'd refined according to the stories of the Nocturne.

'I think it's those stories that do it,' said Levon. 'They remind you what the world used to be like, and then the world reflects it back at us.'

'Stories like ... the Ulduzkhan.'

The word hung heavily between them as they made the final journey, north again, into the Goutte d'Or and the staircase ringed in golden blooms. The words 'Le Tangiers' still hung above the entrance, but they were no longer needed. Every citizen in Paris-by-Starlight knew where this was. It was said that the Khanate Beneath now rumbled underneath, that there was a way down below if you lifted up the stage panels and crawled into the dark.

'Ulduzkhan,' said Beyrek, as they joined the old man at the bar. 'Well, it's as you've said, Levon. These are Modern Times. No place for conquerors and kings, like the days of old. Here, we must do without kings. We must live *together*.'

'If only you'd been here for the Night of Seven Stars, Hayk, then you'd see. All the people of Paris-by-Day came tumbling out of their homes to watch the winterlights blossom. It was so beautiful that they welcomed us in. Told us we could stay. That this was our home too ...'

The water dog had not left Hayk's side. As they took their places at the bar, it settled at his feet. Hayk's hand started shaking as he lifted a tankard of some frothing nectar to his lips. There were too many people here. Crowds. There was so little safety in crowds.

'Yet they still call you Ulduzkhan, boy. My son – the leader of a new world ...'

There was movement on stage. Levon stared. Isabelle's harp was already waiting there, on the seat in the spotlight. The chair was a throne of vibrant pink blossoms, still pulsing with the light of the stars beyond the cellar walls.

Something landed on his shoulder. He startled, turned around, and was more startled still to discover it was his father's meaty hand. Only now did he realise that two of its fingers were gone, hacked down to uneven stumps.

'You led them here, Levon.'

'What?'

'Three thousand miles you roamed.' Something had changed in his voice. His body still bristled, but not with violence. If a body could bristle with contrition, here it was. 'That's true leading. Let them name you Ulduzkhan if they wish.'

Levon felt his father's hand like a lead weight. 'I'm no leader. I just foraged a lot.'

'You kept them together. It's more than I ...'

His voice trailed off, then – for in that same moment the Rose of the Evening had walked out onto stage.

Levon could see the way her belly filled the lace dress she was wearing, how her shape was subtly changing by the day. And the music that poured out of her, that was changing too. Every night it took her into new starscapes.

'The music just found her,' Levon whispered. 'She may not have been born one of the People, but it decided that she was the one who was going to bring it back. Right there in the night garden, putting my bebia to rest, it soared up and all around us. That's how I knew ... this new world doesn't need kings. The old world isn't in her blood but it touched her all the same. If it could do that, well, it wasn't just for the People. The magic, the beauty, it's for everybody.'

As he spoke the final words, Levon took his eyes off Isabelle and turned to where his father was sitting. While he'd been lost in the music, his father had reached down and borne the great water dog aloft, so that now the mutt was cradled in his lap. On another man, it might have looked ridiculous: a wolf as a lapdog. But on Hayk, it seemed right, somehow.

It was the only thing that was right about this picture.

Hayk's hands were straining in the dog's fur, if only to stop them from shaking. Every muscle in his neck was wrought like thick rope. As the music washed over him, drawing him back into elder times of enchantment, tears leaked out of his rigid mask of a face. He did nothing to dry them. He made no sound. He simply sat there, watching the Rose of the Evening. Listening to songs of a fallen country. Songs from an elder time. Songs from an age of fable, when all was good and all was right – and there was yet a place on this Earth that a man like Hayk could call home. As the Rose of the Evening spun her web from one song to the next, the quaking of his body changed. No longer was he quaking without. By brute force, he turned it inwards – so that not a soul could see. Instead, all that the milling faces in Le Tangiers saw was a scarred man, older than his years, sobbing in silence at the back of the bar. And because there was no shortage of men like these in Paris-by-Starlight, not a soul seemed to mind.

Fire.

He pounded the shoreline road, with the inferno raging behind. A great flock of lightjars lifted themselves out of the reeds where they'd been feeding, but they were too late; as the host took flight, sparks from the inferno caught up with them, incinerating them as they flew. Thousands burned in tumbling fury, until he was pounding his way through a rain of tiny charred carcasses.

Everywhere, the People were fleeing too. Boats. There were boats on the landlocked sea – but they too were aflame, and mamas were lining up with their children to leap into the waters and drown. Inland, streams of the People emerged from their houses, took one look at the advancing flames and ran into the night. 'You can stop this!' he was yelling. 'We have water! Water, everywhere! Help me,' he begged – for, suddenly, there was a pail in his hand and he was floundering to the edge of the broiling sea to fill it. 'If we stand together, we can save it!' But nobody would stand with him. They'd grown up fishermen and fishermen's wives. What use them against the curtains of flame? 'Cowards!' he bawled. The very sky above him was alight. 'You're too weak! Stand up and fight, you dogs! Stand up and ...'

He woke, to sunlight spilling over the rooftop grove.

His mouth was dry as bone, so he plunged it into his mother's pool and reared up, scared and alone. An Empire in flames, he thought. There was an Empire in flames ...

Staggering down the rooftop stairs, hands braced against either wall, he reeled off a list of names. Anahit, once upon a time his lover. Maia, his mother. Aram, father of Aram. Tigran and Gor, Alex and Edgar, Andranik and Artur and shy, brave Mher – seven half-brothers, seven good sons, all of them gone. His head was on fire with it. It needed quenching.

The apartment door was open. Flimsy thing, it wouldn't have barred his way even had it been locked. Entering, he knew, was a transgression. But he'd robbed and killed and he was still wearing another man's boots, so striding into the quarters where his children slept was not the thing that would, one day, damn him to hell.

Inside was still. The daylight filtering into the room illuminated the bed where Arina lay sleeping. He did not want to linger over her, but it was hard not to: his sleeping angel. He'd paid them so little attention when the old world existed. Now, to find them beached here in the new, was a feeling unlike any other. That it had been Levon, who forsook his own father at the landlocked sea, who had guided them here – this was a sensation somewhere between indignity and guilt. He coiled up, inside himself again. The inferno of his dreams – it did not need to chase him any longer, because somehow it had become him.

If only to stop himself from sitting at her side – for what if she woke and saw the monster there? – his eyes roamed the room. The other beds were empty, but a table was piled high with papers: each one of them a copy being made of the Nocturne. He sifted through the landslide. Some of these copies were in French. There was a typewriter, and from it lolled the story of Besarion and his Seven Brothers: how Besarion built his sailing ship out of starlight and set off for the constellations.

Besarion knew there was no coming back. Besarion gathered his men. Besarion told them to bid their farewells. Besarion bade his, and then – though three men deserted, and one was struck dumb, and another rebelled at the thought – he lifted the prow of their boat to the moon and whispered, 'It's time we left port. This quest is not bringing you home, my boys. Say goodbye to the glittering sea. Your sweethearts will miss you, your mothers will grieve – but let's hoist the mainsail, let's try and believe, that the stars are a-waiting for us to sail through, that the comets are singing for this stalwart crew. If there's magic down here, then there's magic up there – for Besarion's boys, in the glittering air . . .'

Hayk gathered sheets of paper in his fist, then paused. No, these would not do. Copies were copies. Hayk needed more.

Inexorably, he was drawn back to his daughter. She lay curled in the sheets, but did not flinch as he approached. This, too, was cause for guilt. Here she was, sleeping soundly in this enchanted world. But it was not down to Hayk. Nothing, none of this, was because of him. He hadn't saved the old world, and he hadn't helped build the new.

Lying at his daughter's side was the weatherworn copy of the Nocturne he remembered from when he was a boy.

Up in the night garden, he opened the first page:

Settle down. Pull your covers tight. Look to the window, and out into night. Darkness has fallen, the foul are abroad – but out there lies a world that will soon be restored ...

Stories to get drawn into. Stories to make the nightmares go away. He read a little, then read a little more, and then, finally, realised he was not reading stories at all. He was reading spells. This Nocturne was a memory of magic. Read out its incantations, he thought, and it brought back what was lost. Lightjars and flowers-by-night. Winterlights and water dogs.

Anahit, he thought.

Maia.

Aram, father of Aram. Tigran and Gor. Alex and Edgar. Andranik and Artur and shy, brave Mher.

And me.

With this last thought, his eyes lifted from the Nocturne and took in his upturned hands. The stumps of his missing fingers. The crevices where once men's warm blood ran.

*

As Paris-by-Starlight awoke, Lucien and Léon were waiting at the Métro station on the Rue de Liège. They'd already drunk the half-bottle of cognac they'd taken from Léon's father's cabinet, and this was enough to steel them against the late-winter chill – so they stood there in their shirtsleeves, growing more impatient with every second that passed.

'They're good boys,' Étienne said as he harried Alexandre up the narrow Métro stair to join them. 'And Lucien, he's ... *connected*. You'll like them, Alex. They've got a bit of the devil in them – just like you and me!'

Alexandre – who had, until that moment, never thought he had a devil, nor any sort of demon, inside him – felt another rush of warmth. The devil in him. Stupid, but he liked the sound of that.

In the gathering dark of the Rue de Liège, Étienne made the introductions. 'Alexandre, this here's Lucien. Léon's his brother. Don't call them twins though, because they'll lose their shit. Léon's younger by exactly ten months – which means their mother was just gagging to get on with it. Well, some women are like that, aren't they, boys?'

If the brothers noticed that Étienne was making a slight on their mother, they didn't seem to care. Alexandre thought: I wouldn't let him make a slight on *my* mother. But he laughed all the same.

'This is Alex. The boy I been telling you about. He's been out of sorts, but he's one of us, so we'll see him straight. Needs some cheering up. That's on us.'

Alexandre thought again about why he was here. He'd seen Étienne a second time at his grandfather's reunion, and a third time in the car park outside – where Étienne was idling around, jabbering on about the kind of car he was going to get when he'd found the money. 'If you don't care about the car you drive, you can't care about anything. A car tells the world what you're about. Don't it, Alex?' After that, Alexandre had wondered about inviting Étienne back to his house one afternoon – and counted himself lucky that he hadn't found the courage to ask. It only later occurred to him that posing a question like this was the act of a child. He was glad, therefore, when it was Étienne who suggested Alexandre come and meet his friends. 'You're in want of friends, Alex. That's the thing eating at you. You just haven't found your people yet. But Lucien and Léon, they know people that two boys like us ought to meet ...'

Lucien and Léon were older than him, perhaps of an age with Étienne, with hair the colour of sunsets and long bodies that, right now, were loping off up the road. 'It's up here tonight,

Étienne, just like I told you,' the one named Lucien was saying –
and Étienne, grinning, hustled Alexandre to follow.

'Here, Alex, you've never been to a night market, have you?
Well, take a look at this.'

Some way further on, the road ended in a great roundabout
suspended, on turrets, above the railway below. On each corner
of the roundabout sat scrubby parklands. It was in one of these
scrublands, where sapphire vines turned the ring of iron railings
into a bank of glowing swords, that the night market thrived.

Alexandre looked through a gap in the railings. The vagabond
People were too many to count. Their strange language, of music
and whispers, was filling the square. Their stalls had been hastily
erected, built out of wheelbarrows, canvas tents, picnic tables and
chairs. Grills and braziers sent columns of sweet-smelling smoke
into the air.

'That one's selling potions,' Étienne said, with certainty in his
voice. He'd lifted his chin to gesture at one of the older People,
who'd filled his stall with glass bottles.

'A man looks like that needs all the love potions he can make!'
Lucien laughed. 'Hey, Alex, I wager you don't dare walk in there
and take a swig.'

Alexandre remained dumb.

'Cut it out, Lucien. Alex is all right.'

'What? It isn't hard, is it? Look, there's normal folk wandering
in and out. Plenty of Parisians in there already! Alex has got two
legs, hasn't he? What say he just brazens in there, takes a swig
from a bottle, and sets it straight back down?'

'Don't listen to them, Alex,' said Étienne. 'You take a suck on
that, you're liable to fall in love. I don't want to be dragging you
home, explaining to your grandpa why you're shacking up with
some eighty-year-old man who doesn't speak a word of French.'

There was a silence while the boys watched through the railings. One of the vagabond People had woven glowing amber

flowers around batons and was performing an elaborate juggling act, while a horseshoe of Parisians watched.

A figure moved behind the juggler, marching straight towards the potion-maker's stall. His arms were rigid at his side, his eyes fixed on his prize.

'By God, he's doing it!' Lucien and Léon turned to each other, each a smirking mirror of the other. 'Étienne, your boy's got balls!'

Alexandre was no longer behind them. Now he stood on the other side of the sapphire rails, reaching out to take one of the apothecary's bottles. Without word, he pressed the ruby liqueur to his lips. The bottle stoppered again, he placed it down and, with outstretched hand – the world's most dictatorial mime – he demanded another. Emerald, he took. Then amber. It was only as he reached for the fourth bottle, a phial of the purest silver, that the apothecary began to remonstrate.

'Come on!' beamed Étienne 'Now's the moment …'

'Young man,' the apothecary began in halting French, 'enough! This liqueur is made by the labour of these hands. Would you rob from me without so much as a thank you?'

Alexandre, it seemed, was committed to his mime – or perhaps it was only that, if he opened his mouth to speak, all his bravado would vanish. He arched his eyebrows in righteous fury, darted first for one bottle, and then for another. The apothecary could not possibly hold on to all his wares at once. Soon, Alexandre clutched a phial of molten gold. He was wrenching out its stopper when the familiar voice of Étienne called out, 'Now, Alex! Let's get gone!' And, torn out of his act, he turned to see Étienne and the blond brothers haring out of the night market, a bundle clutched in their hands.

The juggling act had stopped. All of the traders turned to wave fists and shriek at the scarpering boys. And Alexandre – who found himself suddenly beached in a sea of angry People (land-locked, the satirists might say) – felt all his bravery vanish.

There was a gap in the crowd. He darted for it, up and out of the market.

Their cries followed him up the Rue de Liège, until – upon nearing the Métro station – he saw Étienne hailing him from some alleyway between the shopfronts. In the darkness between the buildings, flowers-by-night grew in a mossy carpet. He propped himself against a wall, feet firmly planted in the cascading blues and mauve, and gulped in great breaths of air.

'Well, I'm not in love,' he announced.

'You're a bona-fide madman,' Étienne announced, with towering pride. 'What a discovery! And look ...'

Lucien and Léon were shredding papers, scattering them about their feet to obscure the lights of the flowers.

'What is it?'

'It's in French. That's what it is.' Lucien thrust a bundle of papers at Alexandre, who saw the word 'NOCTURNE' stencilled above a crude image of a star.

'You were golden, Alex! Golden! They were so busy wondering what in hell you were doing that they hardly saw us. Look, Léon got himself some food.' Léon stood by the trashcans, suspiciously picking his way through a cone of luminous white tubers. 'And Lucien got these. It's one of their storybooks. But why in hell they're putting it in French, who knows ...'

'Isn't it obvious?' spat Lucien. 'People like this can't keep themselves to themselves. My uncle Maxime is going to be fuming.'

Étienne whispered, 'Maxime's the one we ought to meet, Alex. Only you've got to *earn* a meeting with a man like Maxime.'

Before Alexandre could ask how, Étienne whipped the book out of his hand and brandished it aloft. 'People in Paris used to be proud, didn't they, Alex? Well, we heard enough of it from the old folks. All the things your grandpa did, Alex – and all so that

Paris could be safe! Used to be, we had our own things to celebrate. My old man – wherever he is – he used to do the parades on Bastille Day. People used to *care* about Bastille Day, didn't they? That was *our* day. Now it's just fireworks and concerts. You hardly even watch the parade on TV.' He kicked out at a clump of flowers-by-night, so that their glowing heads went flying. 'Who's going to care about fireworks and parades this summer, when their heads are full of that Night of Seven Stars?'

'He's right,' Lucien muttered darkly. 'All you got to do is look at all those folk cooing in their night market. It doesn't take much to titillate a simple mind. People care more about flowers lighting up the night than they do their own families and friends.'

'It's like *that*,' said Étienne. He lifted a finger, directing it deeper into the alleyway, and when Alexandre gazed after it he could see a pair of glowing, golden eyes. As he focused further, he saw that they belonged to some mongrel dog, its hide dusted with a billion tiny grains of light. 'You know what that is, Alex?'

By now, Alexandre had recovered his breath – but, as Étienne's words washed over him, he could still feel the beating of his heart, and this confused him, because he ought to have left his nervousness in the night market. What was there be nervous about, standing here with boys who only wanted to be his friends?

'Well, I'll tell you,' Étienne went on. 'I should know, because it happened to Élise. You remember me telling you about Élise? You see, there was one thing Élise loved more than me – and that was her mother's dog. Can't say I thought much of the thing, myself. A cocker spaniel. They called it Anaïs, which is no name for a dog – but that's just the sort of family they were. Well, Élise's mother, she figured Anaïs wasn't going to last forever, so she should have its puppies. And that's what she did. They found some pure-bred spaniel to sire them, shut them up in a room for a few hours, and the job was done. Only, two months later, when the poor bitch is lying there, tongue lolling out, pushing its puppies out into the world, it isn't cocker spaniels that come out at all. It's these *things*. Water dogs, they call them. Used to go out on this landlocked sea of theirs with all their sailors. Here, I'll show you …'

Étienne got to his knees and coaxed the water dog near. At first, the mongrel was suspicious. But Étienne was patient and, when it came close, he dared to run his fingers through its hair. Trusting, now, the dog pressed its wet nose to his palm.

Then Étienne's arm was around it, and he was parting the fur at the nape of its neck.

'See,' Étienne said. '*Gills.*'

Alexandre recoiled. But he was the only one. The blond brothers were on their haunches too, staring intently at the furrows in the mutt's neck.

'Now, I know for a fact that Élise's dog didn't go near one of these. Élise's parents wouldn't have let it happen. So tell me, how did their dog give birth to … this? What sort of witchcraft is it that rips ordinary things out of their wombs and brings back creatures of the night instead? Yes,' he said – and Alexandre realised, then, that he was not holding the water dog in a loving embrace, but hemming it in instead, his arms locked tight, 'these People might have their enchantments – but, if you ask me, you'd be a fool to get sucked in. Everybody thinks the Night of Seven Stars was so beautiful, don't they? Well, we used to have a name, here in Paris, for this sort of person, didn't we, Alex?'

Alexandre was still.

'Think!' Étienne compelled him. 'What did your grandpa call them? Scum, he said. Cowards …'

In that moment, Alexandre himself felt like the dog: hemmed in, compelled, controlled.

'Collaborators,' he whispered.

'Exactly! And what did the good people of Paris do to collaborators?' Étienne turned, taking in the blond brothers as well.

'They taught them a lesson. Sent them a sign. So maybe that's what these People need now.' He stroked the dog again. He stroked it into submission. 'A sign.'

Alexandre wanted to ask: what kind of a sign? But the way the boys were already crowding the dog opened up too many ideas inside him, and slowly he stepped back.

'Get in here, Alex,' Étienne said, 'it's only a dog.'

'It's scared, Étienne.'

'So are we,' Léon muttered, darkly. 'So's every right-thinking Frenchman.'

'Let him leave, Étienne,' Lucien said, as Alexandre – still walking backwards – reached the apex of the alleyway. 'Who is he, anyway? Marching into the night market's one thing, but tomfoolery like that isn't going to impress my uncle. It's like you said ...' And Alexandre had to strain to hear the rest, for he was already stepping back out onto the Rue de Liège. '... it has to be a sign.'

Later that night, in the eerie light before dawn, the vagabond People dismantled their night market and tramped, in procession, back along the Rue de Liège. Some of them were drunk. Some of them high on the spirits of the night. Many of them were so content in the majesty of their new world that they walked directly past the alley where, hours before, Étienne and the blond brothers had gathered. So at first they did not see the strangled water dog, whose body had been hanged from a length of lead drainpipe jutting out of the wall. They did not see its bulging eyes, or the flowers-by-night that had been torn from the earth and turned into chains to garland the butchered beast. And it was not until the first light of morning was filtering into the alleyway that anybody realised how the water dog's belly had been opened up and its gore scraped out to daub, in crude letters across the shop wall, the three words that would, in the coming weeks and months, appear wherever the winterlights had erupted or the lightjars made their nests: 'PARIS NEW RESISTANCE', dripping with the effluent of a dead dog's heart.

*

A ghost crossed Paris-by-Starlight each night.

They knew his coming by the water dog that walked at his heel. He was wandering, they said, in search of people. Not his family, for he'd found them already. No, he was scouring Paris-by-Starlight for something else. 'His own landlocked sea,' they said in the bazaar where he came to drink each evening. 'The dogs found it in him, but he's still searching.'

He'd found Milena first. Down in the Khanate Beneath, where she'd built herself a home. She was surprised to see him, but she and her husband sat with him and gave him food and helped him clean the grit out of the gills of the dog that followed him. 'Do you know,' Milena said, 'when we set out together, I thought you were taking me along like you would a butcher's knife, or an old revolver ... or a bar of gold, stitched into the lining of your pack. Insurance. A sacrifice. In case you had to make one, to get through.'

Hayk laughed. 'There were people like that out there, weren't there?'

'It got so you didn't trust anyone.'

'Well,' said Hayk, 'now we can trust again,' and he left, trembling, without another word.

There were others he hunted for. People he'd been holed up with in camps. The man he'd felled when they tried to scale the barbed wire into the black forests of Hungary. Stitching together the pieces of his own story, if only to force it to make some sense. Some he discovered. Some, he realised, had never made it through. Then, though it took him a month and a day, he stumbled one night upon a sleeping man and, taking off the boots he'd worn for a thousand miles, laid them at his side. When that man awoke in the morning, he would think it a magic as miraculous as the seven-pointed star hanging above – for somehow his lost boots had tramped after him, a thousand miles into the west.

It was a penance, knew Hayk, but he knew another thing too.

He knew that penance never worked.

Now he tramped up a lonely stairwell, the echo of his naked feet his only companion. No shimmering pillars of light – not here. In this tower block there was only the cold clang of metal.

The rooftop grove was stark and wintry compared to the night garden where his mother had been laid to rest. Perhaps it was only because so few of the People lived in this block, too little of their magic leaching out of the stories they read. From a few terracotta pots, diamond-white flowers-by-night tumbled. A stark tree, in threadbare leaf, had erupted from the tiles in the centre of the roof.

In the roots of that tree sat another gnarled thing. The old man was dressed in a flowing black chokha, and inside it he seemed to have withered away. His arms were splayed out, his palms turned to the sky, and a cloud of lightjars made a fluttering haze about him. They darted from the boughs above, then down to the man's face. It was only as Hayk tramped around the tree, calling his water dog to heel, that he realised the birds were dipping their long beaks between the man's lips, depositing droplets of nectar there for him to imbibe.

'Master Atesh. They said I'd find you here.'

The man barely flinched.

'Hayk,' Master Atesh began, his voice rising as if in a question, then falling again with the certainty of an answer. 'Yes, I had a feeling you were not among the lost.'

Hayk said, 'They mentioned you, sometimes, in that place under the Métropol. The schoolmaster, they said. I looked for you there, but not one of them knew where you were. Then somebody said: "Atesh and his lightjars. He's seeking solitude."'

'Not solitude, boy.'

Hayk wanted to sit beside him, but he dared not interrupt whatever strange dance these lightjars were making, so instead he settled on the slates by the gutter's edge, and brought the water dog onto his lap. There followed a silence, as he tried to gather his thoughts. He liked the emptiness up here. He liked the peace.

'Do you remember, when I was a boy? I'd be sitting in your classroom, and all I ever wanted was to close this hand over your mouth and choke your words back into you. Schooling! What use did I have for schooling? I wanted the world.' Hayk paused. 'Well, now I want to hear you, Master. I didn't care for your lessons back then – because there was the landlocked sea, and I was going out onto it, captain of my own boat. But now ...'

Master Atesh made fists and, in a shrill burst of song, the dancing lightjars returned to the branches above. Now, at last, he could turn and look Hayk directly in the eye. Forty years ago, he'd taught this boy. A malcontent in the classroom, but only because his determination had led him in other directions. Now, his face had been shattered; the bulge around his eye would never heal. And yet ... the way his fingers ran through the water dog's fur, there was still, thought Master Atesh, compassion in the man.

'What do you want, Hayk?'

'I want to feel settled,' he quaked. 'I want to be back there. Not in the old country – I know it's gone. But back then I didn't think. I sailed and I drank and I fished ... and I loved. Yes, loved. Too much, or so Anahit used to tell me. And I felt at peace. I felt as if I were me. Now, I can't feel the ground under my feet. It keeps shifting. I'm dreaming of fire.'

Master Atesh said, 'Look at me. We're all of us feeling the same. I used to teach history, but now that history has ended.'

'Then what now?'

'Now,' Master Atesh answered – and, opening his palms, called the lightjars back to their humming dance, 'I do this.'

'What *is* this, Master Atesh?'

'How well do you know your Nocturne, Hayk?'

Hayk only grunted in response.

'In the elder time, Inkar the Star Sailor learnt the language of the Seventh Star.' He lifted his face to drink in its light. 'She spoke to it each night, and drank in its wisdom. But Hayk, there is a language more ancient still. In the apocrypha, they speak of it: the language of the very night itself. You won't find it written in your Nocturne. But the anchorites of old knew. They'd set sail for some woebegone island on the landlocked sea. And for long years that would be their life. The dew in the morning. The nectar that the lightjars brought them. Enough to sustain them while, whisper by whisper, they started to hear the language of the dark ...'

In Hayk's lap, the water dog whimpered sadly.

'If it's not in the Nocturne,' Hayk spat in suspicion, 'then how do you know it?'

Master Atesh just shrugged: 'The night whispered in my ear.'

Hayk had had enough. Magic tied you in knots. He'd known card sharps and experts in sleight of hand. He'd gambled enough to have learned its rudiments himself. Their enchantments were all just misdirection. One hand was caressing your thigh while the other drove a knife into your back. He got to his feet and stood at the gutter, looking down.

'I don't trust it, Master.'

'What?'

'All of this.' He moved his arms in great arcs, as if to envelop the entirety of Paris-by-Starlight.

'Why not?'

'Because it always ends in fire. Thousands of years ended in a day. And here we are: everyone in Paris-by-Starlight, dancing to dead music. Cooing and gasping and laughing in delight, when they should be …' His words had blazed a path ahead of him; when he finally caught up, they petered into silence. 'My son's having a baby.'

'But Hayk, this is such good news …'

'Is it?' he uttered. 'Of all the sons I had, all but the weakest one gone. And why? Because the old world was lazy. Indolent. A nation of fishermen and fishermen's sons. We've learned nothing. This Paris-by-Starlight, it's fledgling. It's fragile. One little push and it falls. The People know this. They feel it in their hearts. They want to call my son Ulduzkhan, but he just shrugs it off, as if it's nothing. But a new world doesn't exist just because there's a star in the sky, does it? It's right there in the final story of the Nocturne. The stars wink out, one by one …'

Master Atesh breathed some unintelligible word and the light-jars, which still trilled in the boughs around him, took off as one, enveloping Hayk, urging him by the flutter of their wings to step back from the building's edge.

'Sit with me,' he commanded.

Hayk joined him in the roots.

'I'm sorry, Master.'

'You're not at school, boy. You don't need to apologise. But …' Master Atesh gentled, as he tried to find his words. 'You need to calm down. Your body's here with us, Hayk, but your head's out there – still on the trail, still in the detention centres, still cramped up in the backs of lorries with a knife in your hand. You're looking for enemies, but the only enemy's in here.' Master Atesh lifted a finger and directed it first at Hayk's head, and finally at his heart. 'You didn't listen in school, but listen to me now. There are indeed things to fear in this new world, just as there were in the old. But the thing to fear most of all is fear itself.'

Hayk shook. 'I did terrible things out there, Master.'

Master Atesh looked at his naked feet. 'You're atoning for them here.'

He nodded.

'We get second chances, boy. The Nocturne isn't finished. The chronicle of our People goes on. We're writing a new chapter, here in Paris tonight. Be part of it.' For a time, they were silent together. A vibrant red lightjar ventured near Hayk's stubbled lips and, though his instinct was to reject it, he let it deposit its droplet of sapphire nectar there. The sweetness. The warmth. The submission of it. 'We all lost people, but we gained others too. Your son might reject his crown, but he has wisdom in him. I was there in the underpass when he said it out loud. *We are the People, and the People look after each other.* If I were you, Hayk, I'd heed those words. What was it you did, in the old world, that made you feel whole? What was it you did that made you alive? You sailed and you drank and you fished and you ...'

For a time, Hayk was silent. He closed his eyes to the stars wheeling above.

'I loved,' were the words he finally said.

'Well, there you have it. You can't fish or sail through Paris-by-Starlight, Hayk, but there are still people here to love. Find someone to commit to. Someone to focus all of your passions. By the Stars, we all need it. Find someone to love and protect, and, oh, the wonders you'll see.'

Later that night, when the stars were descending and dawn was but an hour away, Hayk lingered in the green arches of the night garden.

Arina had seen him as her lessons were coming to their end. Tonight, Mariam had been teaching them the shifting geographies of the world. As the aeons progressed, Arina had learned, not even the continents were constant. We live in an age of flux, Mariam had explained, so what happened to the old country must not be regretted nor avenged, just accepted as the turning of the world. Arina was content with this. It made her feel . . . safe, somehow.

But the eyes that watched her did not make her feel safe. They made her feel hunted. And, as the other children bound off for their parents and adoptive-parents, she helped Mariam pack her lessons away.

'I think he wants to see you,' Mariam said. The night garden was emptying, and Hayk stood alone, with only the water dog at his heel. 'Don't you want to go to him?'

Arina ignored the question. She bent down to help her aunt pick up the copies of the Nocturne's stories they'd been reading together in the midnight hour.

'Can I tell you a secret?' Aunt Mariam whispered. She glanced up and, in the corner of her vision, saw Hayk's eyes. If Arina was frightened, she thought, then he was frightened as well; they shared that same faraway look. 'He's here. That's what matters. He isn't running away. He isn't hiding. He's . . . your father.'

'But is he? He wasn't our father in the old country, not really.'

What man was? thought Mariam. She liked to think that Aram's father might have been different, but chances were that even he – good man that he'd been – would have spent more time on the sea than he would between his son's nursery walls.

'We get to do things differently here,' she said – and tried not to remember the times Hayk had made her sister cry with his cold indifference, nor the way he'd sashayed in and out of her life. 'Ana and Elen aren't truly your sisters. Nor Natia and Nino. But we think of them that way, don't we?'

Arina said, 'When we got to the boats that morning, he didn't come with us, did he? He wasn't my father then . . .'

Mariam had thought about this too much since Hayk appeared, battered and bruised, in the garden. She crouched and braced Arina by her shoulders. 'Were Aram's father to turn up – if some miracle had saved him from drowning that night, and he washed up here, scared and alone – well, Aram would be frightened too. There isn't any magic in the world that would make that boy remember his father. But ...' She paused. 'He'd still be Aram's father. Your father left us on the shoreline that morning. I don't forget it. Maybe you shouldn't either. But he also came here.' Two sides to Hayk, thought Mariam. It had been like that in the old country too. Loyal and devoted, and yet always raising hell. 'This is a world of second chances, Arina – and he's here, in the garden tonight.'

Arina emboldened herself, snorting noisily as she drew herself upright, and turned around.

Mariam watched as they settled by the water together. She marvelled as Hayk pursed his lips, trilled, and waited for one of the lightjars to flutter down and deposit its nectar on his lips. This was a trick Arina had never seen. No matter how she tried it, the lightjars would not obey, and perhaps this meant that her father had magical properties of his own.

He's going to need some magic, thought Mariam, if any of this is going to work.

'This is your bebia's garden, then,' Hayk ventured. 'I should have liked to have seen her face. She was always mad, your bebia. Chased me round the room with a slipper, but always with a sparkle in her eyes.'

'I miss her,' said Arina, and for a time that was enough. They sat in silence, until the glowing eyes of Hayk's water dog drew them both in. Unused to seeing its master commune with another, it was approaching slowly, its golden eyes alight.

'Did you bring him with you?'

'No.'

'Find him on the way?'

'I suppose,' said Hayk, 'that he found me. He comes like we all do. Out of the night. Do you want to stroke him? He won't bite.' He clicked his fingers gently and the water dog came near. 'They lived, just like us, on the landlocked sea. Great packs of them, hunting the shining fish and living on its islands. Following the boats out over the water. We looked after them, sometimes. Took abandoned or stray ones in. They'd sail with us, every dusk.'

Arina risked a glance over her shoulder. Aunt Mariam was still there, and that meant that everything was right.

'Here, let me show you ...' Hayk ran his fingers over the nape of the dog's neck. 'Gills,' he said, 'for breathing the water. Oh, the water dogs always came up for air in the end – but they hunted in the deeps as well.'

'Does he have a name?'

The question stilled Hayk. Yes, he thought, a dog should have a name.

'You may name him, should you like.'

The idea pleased Arina enormously. She sank into silence, for a task of this gravity required considerable thought.

'Gilly,' she finally announced.

Hayk threw his head back in laughter. Laughter like that was so out of place in the night garden. It shook lightjars and black-weathers, lace-winged bears and dragonflies from their rests.

'Gilly,' he repeated. 'Yes, a fine name for a dog of the sea.' Then, when his laughter had finally subsided, he said, 'I should like to hear about it. About how Levon got you here. About my mother. About yours ...'

His voice broke on the last words, so he would say no more.

Arina looked over her shoulder, where Mariam was still watching.

She'd heard it too: the way Hayk trembled when he spoke of Arina's mother. Something softened in Mariam, then: without something to love, without something to protect, Hayk seemed a peculiarly empty creature.

'Go on ...' Mariam's lips formed the words, though they made no sound.

It was enough. Arina turned back to her father. He did not seem so frightening now. Not with a dog named Gilly on his lap. There was a way, Arina thought, in which he didn't seem frightening at all – only strangely, mysteriously, sad.

Her mind was made up.

So she began.

11

* *

THE CITY AND THE STARS

The changing of the seasons brought fresh colour to the public spaces in Paris. By day the city's window boxes overflowed with zinnias and nasturtiums, begonias and cascades of vinca. But oh, the wonders of the night . . .

By spring, the bazaar in the Jardin des Tuileries was the most fêted of the wandering night markets. If the market pitched up here at fall of dark, the whispers went out. Meals were left unfinished, riverside cafés abandoned, relatives left to fend for themselves – as citizens of both day and night came to feast at its long tables, marvel at the lightjars flying in formation, watch the miniature light shows exploding over the corners where seamstresses wove shawls out of starlight.

Among the stalls, there was one around which the people of day and night always gathered. Here, behind a higgledy-piggledy mess of loose leaves and volumes stitched together, Mariam battled with one hand to keep Aram from making mischief and, with the other, to take the coin of her customers. Soon they would need more copies – for, no matter how hard Arina and her friends worked, their efforts would never be enough. There were scribes taking rooms in the Hôtel Métropol now, working with old typewriters and by hand – for what typewriter could ever capture the delicate spiral symbols of the elder world? – but it seemed to Mariam that, the more stories from the Nocturne that went out into the world, the more the world needed. French fathers telling

French daughters the story of Besarion at bedtime. Even the park-keeper, Emmanuel Caron, was enamoured of those stories; he took them home to read to his daughter at bedtime, and she in turn spread the stories around the schools of the day. Sometimes, Mariam thought, Paris-by-Starlight extended far beyond the dark.

'You're not teaching tonight, Mariam?'

The voice had reached through the crowd, all those eager hands flicking, curiously, through drawings of the moonlight world. Mariam watched as the great, hulking figure of Hayk cast his shadow over the stall.

'What can I say?' she shrugged. 'School-teaching doesn't pay for a thing, not in Paris-by-Starlight.'

Hayk picked up one of the books and tossed it in his hand. 'So the Nocturne provides.'

Mariam paused. He'd seemed broken, that night in the garden. He'd seemed gentle – if such a word could ever be bestowed upon Hayk – as he sat with Arina and the water dog and tried (at least he'd *tried*) to be a father. These things warmed her heart, but Mariam remembered Hayk from the old country too. The day Anahit had come home and spoken those four fateful words – 'I've met my soulmate' – to their mother had, on reflection, been her darkest day. Oh, there had been moments of light in it. There was Levon and, years later – when Anahit gave in again to Hayk's roughspun charms – there was Arina. But between those times, there was the sorrow and the gnashing of teeth and the months when Hayk was off, not on the sea, but in the hearts and minds and beds of some other. All those scattered sons, who'd come in and out of Anahit's house, calling Levon their brother. Hayk's face all over the shoreline, wherever you roamed.

Yet, after all that, thought Mariam, Anahit would have been with him now. The heart calls out to its own.

Which was why Mariam, in spite of how irked she was at his shadow, started smiling. Something Anahit used to say came back to her now. *By the Stars, he can be a bastard ... but, by the Stars, he can make you feel safe.*

'What do you want, Hayk? I've got my hands full, can't you tell? The stall, and Aram ...'

She looked down, but the boy was no longer at her feet.

'Aram?' she called out.

She turned in dizzying circles, trying to find some sign of her son between the crowded stalls – but instead of her beautiful boy, all she saw were lightjars wheeling and lines of Parisians snaking around while some enterprising stallholder made them necklaces of luminous blossoms. She called out again, and this time clambered to the top of her own stall, so that she might look across the entire bazaar. But the Jardin was an ocean of both Parisians and People, and all that she saw was a faceless mass.

Hayk had already taken off through the crowd. 'There!' he yelled – and, as he ploughed on, he pawed passersby out of his way.

By the time Mariam caught him, staggering past startled bodies as she crossed the starlit lawns, Hayk had the boy in his arms. They stood, together, in a courtyard, hemmed in by hedges taller than Hayk's head, where lightjars had turned the oak tree above into a symphony of colour.

'He's all right,' said Hayk. 'He was chasing the birds.'

The birds knew it as well. A silver-white one, no bigger than Aram's fist, exploded from the hedgerow and dived around Aram's face, trilling out its triumph.

'Aram,' Mariam snapped, angry and out of breath, 'don't you ever do that to your mother again!'

She had to wrestle him out of Hayk's arms; it seemed he wanted to stay there – and, like a fool, that thought dragged Mariam back to all the things Anahit used to say. *Those arms, you wouldn't want them against you. But when he folds you up inside them, Mariam ... Oh, Mariam, you old prude, you'd never under-stand!*

'You're to stay where I tell you!' She turned to heave him away. 'Three thousand miles and you never once went out of my sight. What on earth's got into you?'

'He thinks he's safe,' said Hayk.

Mariam was already retreating, but now she stopped.

She turned around.

'What's that?' asked Hayk.

She followed his gaze to the same tree in which the lightjars were making their symphony.

'You drummed the fear into him when you were out there. Now that you're here, you're ...' His words petered into silence. 'What *is* it?'

Still clinging to Aram, Mariam returned to Hayk's side. Up above them, knotted to the boughs, there hung a flag: thick stripes of red, white and blue sprayed unevenly upon a bedsheet. And emblazoned across it, two words: 'JARDIN NATIONAL!'

Scoured into the bark behind the bedsheet, chipped out in crude letters: 'PARIS NEW RESISTANCE'.

'It's nothing,' said Mariam. 'Stupid boys. They come into the bazaar sometimes. What is it they say out here? The devil makes work for idle hands ...'

Hayk lingered over it longer before he followed Mariam back through the crowd.

The stall she'd left behind was half empty. Readers were still browsing but, in her absence, half the trestle table had been relieved of its goods. She looked out into the shifting People, but not a soul was carrying a welterweight of Nocturnes over his shoulder. Broiling within, she started sifting through what was left.

'Bored boys again?' said Hayk.

'What are you doing here, Hayk?' she exploded. 'Isn't there some drinking den you ought to be lounging in? Some woman you ought to be romancing? Can't you see what I'm trying to do here? We've all got to build lives. I'm trying, I'm *trying*, Hayk, to do what's right for my son. He's three years old. His father's gone. All I want here is to …' Too late, she understood she was remonstrating against herself; as soon as she realised it, all the passion drained out of her. She sighed, 'Really, truly, what did you come here for?'

Hayk filled out his chest, straightening his long black coat as if that simple gesture might smarten him up.

'Well, isn't it obvious?' he said. 'I came here tonight to ask if you'd marry me.'

*

'Feel it,' she said, but Levon was uncertain. Isabelle snatched his hand and pressed it against her belly. 'Of course, he won't do it now. He knows what's expected of him. He's trying to make a point.' She laughed. 'He's just like you!'

Mariam said it was like the wings of a butterfly moving across your insides, but either Mariam's pregnancy had been charmed or she only remembered the romance of it. To Isabelle, it was the feeling of having eaten bad eggs: food poisoning, but with added personality.

Levon felt a tiny foot lash out, straining the contours of Isabelle's stomach.

'It's alive,' he whispered.

Isabelle rolled her eyes. 'While there's blood in my body.'

They'd reached the front of the Hôtel Métropol, an oasis of bright colours in the darkness of the boulevard. Sometimes, Isabelle thought, you could sense the enchantment radiating out of the place, like warmth from the embers of an unseen fire. She liked to think of the Khanate spreading out in the carrières underneath her, all its untold wonders rising up through asphalt and stone.

In front of the hotel, Levon kissed her. 'I wish I didn't have to, but ... I'll be there by the final songs. I promise.'

They'd talked a lot about the Hôtel Métropol. The Ulduzkhan, they joked, still scrubbing showers and scouring out toilet pans. There were those across Paris-by-Starlight who made their own work, in the markets and gardens, or cultivating patches of land that only blossomed by night. Paris-by-Starlight could provide for its People, they said. But it couldn't supply nappies. It couldn't supply formula and vaccinations. Isabelle, heeding the words of the Senegalese, had already made her visits to the doctors by day. And, 'We still need money,' Levon had said. 'But one day. One day soon ...'

That he scoured out toilets for their unborn son. She couldn't have been prouder.

After he was gone, she made her own way to Le Tangiers. It was early, and in the bar only a few scattered souls. Beyrek was polishing glasses at the counter but, as she approached, the old man indicated a figure sitting in one of the alcoves. His eyes, blue even in the dismal lighting, found her. His tangle of straw hair, just the same as hers.

Isabelle left the harp alone on stage and settled in the seat facing her father.

Shreds of serviette were scattered all about him. Isabelle did that too, whenever she was nervous; something in the wanton, petty destruction of it eased her. She stripped labels off bottles as well, and here were two bottles of some Belgian beer, scraped back to the glass. Beyrek must have scoured the store room; it had been six months since they last served beer in Le Tangiers.

'It's been two months,' said Hector. 'I wasn't sure you'd see me, if I called ahead.'

She thought: if you'd called two months ago, you wouldn't have been so nervous. This she dismissed as a poisonous thought – for wasn't he here, right this second, trying to make amends? But, three seconds later, she'd started imbibing the poison all over again. Two whole months, and he'd made the decision not to seek her out every single day. That was the way seventeen years had once passed.

'Look,' he said, 'it's for you.'

He'd reached under the table and, from the dark, produced a package wrapped in brown paper. Hector guided her, eager for her to unwrap it, until at last she saw the strings and curves of a lyre harp start to emerge.

The rosewood was dark, preserved with beeswax and lacquer, and into its grain had been carved interlocking spirals of intricate design. She looked through the hole in its heart, across which ten evenly spaced strings were stretched. From where she sat, the strings divided her father's face into narrow columns. He was waiting for her to speak, but when she remained silent, he blurted out, 'It's a Greek design. Do you remember? How its music soothed Apollo's wrath?' He paused, because the silence was inscrutable. 'It's for you.'

She ran her fingers across the strings, allowing each note to ring out.

'Look,' Hector said, 'I know I'm a shit. I didn't think I was, but here I am. You were only a girl.' He paused. All of it, she realised, was unplanned. This was Hector: he didn't plan for a thing in his life. Where she had quests, he just had wanderings. Not even the hero in his own story, she thought. Just a comic fool. 'I got the coach once. I rode it all the way to Saint-André. You'd have been seven. And I got off it and it was hot and dusty and the road so long into town. Seemed about as far from our little apartment as it was possible to be. And I thought ... why ruin it? You'd stepped into another world. Your mother had taken you there. And …'

'Don't blame it on her,' she snapped.

Hector lifted his hands in entreaty. 'That came out wrong.' He paused. 'I got back on the bus.'

Isabelle took the lyre onto her lap and started to tease a melody out of it. He'd have played songs on it first, she realised. She plucked one of the old People's laments and tried to blot out whatever melody Hector himself might have played – but, she realised now, it would always be there, lurking in the instrument's past. You couldn't unsing a song.

'I'm pregnant,' she said.

They stared at each other, oceans apart.

'Isabelle …'

'Just … be a better grandpa than you were a father, won't you?'

'I will,' he said, and in his eyes – so frustratingly like hers – was the look of an errant boy who'd been told Christmas wasn't really cancelled after all.

'Pregnant?'

The voice had come from the darkness of the dance floor. Isabelle was slow in turning, so at first she did not see Alexandre standing there. How long he'd been waiting there, Isabelle did not know. He came to the edge of the table and, finding there was no seat, forced his father to share.

'Isn't it wonderful?' Hector began. 'Alexandre, you'll be an uncle.'

Soon, Le Tangiers was full, Beyrek making music of his own as he rattled bottles behind the bar. It was then, as the dance floor heaved, that the Rose of the Evening stepped out onto stage. Tonight, the spectators saw, she was putting her trust in a new instrument. Some wondered if, perhaps, this meant that the

melodies of their old world would not come to her. But they need
not have worried, for the lyre she was playing took her to starscapes unseen, to nebulae unexplored.

'See, Alex?' Hector said. 'She spins it out of nothing. Just out
of the air. That's why I used to play as well.' He stopped, for the
refrain she was chasing was both mournful and beautiful, rising
from its minor key to explode into something fragmented, dis-
jointed, discordant – and then suddenly reassembling itself, buoy-
ant and bouncy and light. 'That feeling. You won't know anything
like it …'

Alexandre said, 'Well, I never learned to play, did I?'

The melody soared. From complexity to simplicity, in only a
few short bars. It made the hairs on his arms stand on end.

'You must be very proud,' came a voice.

Hector looked up. The old man Beyrek, who busied himself at
the bar, had threaded his way through the crowd to the table, and
onto it he placed a small pot, overflowing with a hundred minis-
cule blossoms.

'You are her father, no?'

'I am.'

'She is a revelation, sir. Her music stirs all our souls. If I
close my eyes, I fancy she is Besarion himself, setting sail into the
constellations … and leaving us her songs, so that we might
follow.'

Alexandre stood. 'I'll wait outside,' he muttered – and was
gone through the crowd before Hector breathed a word in reply.

Beyrek was still hovering above him.

'I taught her to play.'

As soon as he said the words, he felt the shame of it. To claim
it as his own, even the narrowest sliver of it, was wrong. And it
occurred to him, then, that to claim *her* as his own, even the narrowest sliver of her, was wrong as well. The memory was lodged
in his head – of the way he'd first sat her down, arranging her

fingers at the strings – but the person she was now, the Isabelle up on stage, that was not his doing. If you robbed an egg from a songbird's nest and warmed it until a tiny beak poked through the shell, you could hardly take credit for its flight. And there was his daughter, like the old man had said, setting sail for the stars.

The sagacious look Beyrek gave him made him burn with pride – but the falsity stung him like a hornet, so he closed his eyes and listened to her music instead.

He opened them again only when Le Tangiers filled with applause. On the other side of the People, Isabelle was descending from the stage. He saw her come down the steps, and there she fell into the arms of the boy he'd first met at the Hôtel Métropol. Levon, he thought – to whom he would now be connected by blood.

Alexandre had been waiting outside for too long. Poor boy, he hadn't wanted to come in the first place. Hector got to his feet. He meant to head straight for the staircase, but halfway there it occurred to him that leaving without goodbye was what he'd always done. It was becoming the speciality of a lifetime. So he threaded his way back to find her.

'Congratulations,' he said, reaching out his hand to take Levon's own. 'I'm going to get up and into our eaves. Dig out the things we kept from when Alexandre was small. Adaline's a hoarder. Cribs and blankets, we'll have the lot.'

Levon, who seemed dumbfounded at the idea, only nodded.

'You don't have to do that,' Isabelle cut in.

'Oh, but I want to!' Hector, who was still holding Levon's hand, paled suddenly and said, 'I suppose you'll be making an honest woman of her now.'

'Honest … woman?'

'Walking her up the aisle, or … whatever it is the People do.' When Levon still did not react, he grinned, 'Marrying my daughter!'

'Oh, but I ...'

Perhaps Hector realised he had said too much, for he quickly slid his hand out of Levon's. 'You'll make the best mother, Isabelle,' he said as he turned to disappear – and Isabelle, who watched him go with a relief that would, moments later, transform into a paroxysm of guilt, thought: I know I will. I'll make damn certain of it. But how would you know?

She had shed that thought, as poisonous and truthful as it was, by the time she'd spoken to every well-wisher and lost soul, but as she and Levon climbed back up the steps of Le Tangiers, he said, 'Have you thought about it, though?'

The night was turning towards dawn, the stars winking out, one by one.

But the seven-pointed star was guiding them home.

'About marrying me,' Levon said.

'No,' Isabelle replied.

They'd reached the scrublands along the railway sidings, where groves of flame fruit trees glowed with all the colours of a hearthfire.

'You haven't thought about it? Not even for a second?'

'Oh no,' Isabelle grinned. 'I've thought about it. I'm just not going to do it.'

Levon stopped dead.

Isabelle was still smiling. She ran her fingers in his thick, knotted hair. 'Being married didn't stop your father leaving again and again, or having children all over the landlocked sea.' They began to walk again, past the hearthfire glow of the trees and further north. 'Not even having a child together was enough to keep Hector and my mother under the same roof. By the Stars,' she said, and Levon grinned at hearing the old country's saying in her voice, 'there isn't a thing in the world to tell you what's coming. You can tie yourselves up with marriage contracts. Tie yourselves up with babies and blood. The old world still ends, doesn't it? It still comes crashing down.'

Levon had let his arm fall out of hers. He stood, with his feet rooted to the ground, and watched her walk on.

'I'll tell you how we'll know what's coming.'

'Go on then.' Isabelle turned and, on seeing Levon no longer at her side, baited him with a smile. 'Tell me what the rest of them never worked out. My mother and father. Yours. All the ruined lovers across all the ages. Every old time singer ...'

'I know because I love you,' he declared.

Isabelle only stared.

'And I know because I love that child – my child – in there, though I haven't laid eyes on it yet.'

She couldn't help it, then. She laughed, and laughed, and laughed.

'That's it?' She gambolled towards him, to kiss him as if it was the very first time. 'Oh, Levon! *They* all said that too. *They* all meant it. But the magic died.'

'Mine doesn't,' he breathed, into her lips. 'I'm Levon-by-Starlight. Even when you think it's dead, it isn't. It's just biding its time. And then ...'

'The Night of Seven Stars,' she laughed.

'Well, something like that.'

'I don't need to marry you, Levon. But I'd do it in a second, if that's what you asked.'

Knotting their arms back together, they set off up the road. A comet trail of aquamarine lightjars followed, flitting from tree to tree.

'Isabelle,' said Levon, 'not a whisper about marriage when we get home.'

By the tone of his voice, there was some other secret here. 'Levon?'

'It must be something in the air. Seems, even now, my father has more faith in the institution than you do.' This time, it was Levon's turn to laugh. 'Isabelle, there's been a ... development.'

*

They were to be married on the equinox.

In the old country, it was said that the strongest bonds were forged on the winter solstice, when nights were at their longest and the magic most potent. But a multitude of winter weddings had butchered that theory for Hayk, so the equinox would have to do. 'Equinox weddings were the pragmatic ones. Ones built on friendship and trust,' said Arina as she curled up with her bebia's Nocturne one twilight. 'That's what Ketevan tells her Second Maiden when the Ulduzkhan needs a new heir. She doesn't think she's in love, but she sees him in the starlit grove and it hits her ...'

'I don't think it's like that,' said Levon, 'not for Mariam. Beyrek said that, in the elder time, when a sailor drowned on the landlocked sea, his captain would take in his widow. It was a debt of honour you owed your crew. So that children didn't go without fathers.'

'I think we all went without fathers,' said Arina. 'The men were married to the sea.'

Sometimes, Levon could hear his mother echoing through Arina.

Isabelle, who was sitting by the window, said, 'He's ... trying.' Somehow, that seemed to matter. Her own father's lyre was at her feet. She picked it up, if only to feel its music. 'Trying to put himself back together.'

'He'll have to weave her a dress!' Arina exclaimed. 'Look!'

She turned the Nocturne round for all of them to see. There, daubed in old oils and dyes, was a painting of the centuries old

King of the Stars on his knees in a moonlit grove, a wooden loom at one side and a pile of harvested flowers-by-night on the other. In the picture, his face was screwed up while, in the background, a trio of handmaidens cupped their hands to their mouths in case they betrayed themselves by laughter. Half a wedding gown, glowing in emerald and sapphire, pooled around his feet.

And so it was in the night garden above.

'Mama, you old dog, you never taught me needlework. You never taught me stitches. I can knot rope a hundred different ways. Half-hitches and sheet bends, bowlines and round turns ... How hard can it be to make a bloody dress?'

Hayk sat in his own moonlit grove, surrounded by shredded flowers. The work of his daytime amounted to little more than a handkerchief. A thousand more of these and he might have a bedspread, but not any dress Mariam would wear.

It was hopeless.

'I don't know what you're looking at either,' he said to Gilly the water dog, who lurked by the rooftop lake, repeatedly submerging its head to snap at some wriggling eel.

'Do you want some help?'

Hayk looked up to discover Arina approaching him through the foliage.

Twilight was hardening to night. Soon, the grotto would be buzzing with the denizens of the block. Hayk knew they were speaking of him. They wondered what a woman like Mariam would want with a man like Hayk, whose face still wore the scars of his passage into Paris. What they did not know was that every one of those scars told a story: the story of his courage. Hayk wasn't oblivious; back in the old country, Mariam had barely pretended to hide her scorn when he waltzed into a room. But in the new world that courage counted. Everybody wanted to feel safe.

His hands were too big. He tried to thread one stem through the next, but instead he smeared it all over his hands. These he lifted up to show Arina, decorated in glowing amaranth pink.

'The flowers are fooling me.'

As he said the words, he heard another voice – *You're making a fool out of me!* – and felt the jackboot of some soldier smashing into his face. The pain of it was vivid, though the memory took him by surprise. He'd quite forgotten this one. Lying, face down, in an old country ditch, listening to the military transports roll on by, imagining he hadn't been seen ...

'They're not fooling you, Dad. They're just ... being flowers. You have to be gentle with them.' Hayk was bewildered by the ease with which she began feeding one flower into another. 'Aunt Mariam won't mind if one or two are crushed. She isn't dainty, is she? Not like mother used to be. Or maybe it's that she *used* to be dainty, just like mother. But Aunt Mariam got hard.'

Therein lay the answer, thought Hayk: Mariam was tired of being hard, tired of being strong.

Arina threaded yet more flowers together as, one by one, the families of the block emerged from the rooftop stair. As they fanned out into the grove, Hayk's eyes darted suspiciously around.

'Work for a woman,' he said, grinding the tiny patch of cloth he'd woven into mulch.

Arina glared. 'Don't let Aunt Mariam hear you.'

She had appeared from the top of the stairs, ready for the night's schooling.

'Anyway, you think everything's work for a woman. Everything except stupid fighting.'

There was silence while Hayk let the admonishment sink in. Twice he opened his mouth in retort, and twice he thought better of it. When Arina said 'fighting' what she really meant was 'surviving'. There was nothing stupid about that. And that was the taint of the new world: they'd forgotten how easily the End Times came; they didn't realise that survival went on.

Mariam had drifted past. She took in Hayk's endeavour and made a secret look at Arina. It was meant to be bewildered but, in her eyes, Arina saw, she was pleased.

'Is she going to be my mother now? Not just my aunt?'

'Everyone needs a mother. Everyone needs a father.'

Arina, who had lived long enough without either to know that this wasn't true, nodded. 'You know, you're going to have to write vows as well.' She showed him the Nocturne. 'To tell the host why you pledge yourself so ...'

Hayk shrugged. 'I'll read what's in the book.'

'Oh, but you can't. These are the Ulduzkhan's vows. The Starlight Proclamations. The vows of a king.'

Hayk picked himself up, preparing to drag the loom out of sight. 'The vows of a king, for a world without kings,' he said. 'At least, in the old world, there were kings to count upon. Write them out for me, won't you?'

Then Arina watched him go, cradling the loom as if he was carrying all the weight of the old world itself.

'I know you think I'm foolish, but I know who I am, and I know what's right.'

He'd had the argument with her before, and every time the contortions Mariam made to explain it were more elaborate than the last.

'We're all in a new world now, Levon. We're all changed. He's changing too. I see the thaw in him. Listen to me, child: you're still young. You still have romance. I dare say you still notice the scent when Isabelle wafts into a room. But ...'

'You're not old, Aunt Mariam.'

'I feel older than mountains. You wait until that child of yours is hurtling around, liable to kill himself every second step.' She stopped, put her hands on Levon's shoulders. 'After three thou-sand miles and nearly three years since Aram's father ...' She drew back, waving her hands as if to bat away some insidious thought. The guilt of it, thought Levon. And the hate that she should still feel guilt. 'I thought about it long and hard, Levon. I didn't answer him straight away. But I want to feel my feet on the ground. Don't we all deserve that?'

Levon whispered, 'I did my best, Aunt Mariam. We got here in one piece.'

She folded her arms around him. 'You were the best of us, Levon. You are the best. But you can't carry us forever, and you don't have to. You have Isabelle to think of now. Your own child. And ... I need to build something for myself, here and now.' They fitted each other perfectly, Levon and his aunt, like two sleeping infants. 'He doesn't love me,' she said, 'but he needs his feet on the ground as well. It will order him. It will order me. A family, built on honour. There are worse things.'

They released each other.

'Aram deserves a father, doesn't he? And Arina – she's old, after her years ...' She hoisted up a preposterous gown which shimmered in lines of mauve and pink and diamond white. 'So you'd better help me into this monstrosity, before I change my mind.'

Levon: the handmaiden at his aunt's second wedding. Some-how, this seemed the most ordinary thing in the world.

The equinox had stolen upon them with a sinking inevitability. In the staff lounge at the Hôtel Métropol, Levon and Isabelle hoisted Mariam into the gown Hayk had sewn. Then, as Isabelle braided Mariam's hair – 'What's left of it. Just wait until that babe of yours is suckling all the goodness out of your body!' – Levon peeked out into the dining hall. M. Fortier had been uncertain when they'd first petitioned him for the use of the hall, but the promise of a hundred guests was enough to make up his mind.

Now, the glimmering hall – bedecked in floral garlands, with a seven-pointed star hanging above – was filling up with people. Most had come for Mariam, but there were rags here for Hayk as well: a doctor who'd accompanied him on his trek west, and a group of men he'd taken to gambling with on the riverbank each night – all the manifold People of Paris-by-Starlight.

The water dogs that shifted in the Rue Castex were here for Hayk as well.

Levon had spent too long watching the assembling crowd. Natia and Nino had appeared, surrounded by new friends, and for a moment this buoyed him. They sat with Arina, who wrestled with a squirming Aram on her lap.

'There,' declared Isabelle, and when Levon turned, he saw Mariam as he had never before seen her. She looked, he decided, like a birthday cake in braids.

'Mariam, are you … sure?'

'Tradition,' she shrugged, and squeezed alongside Levon so that she could see the starlit hall. 'By the Stars,' she said, pulling the dress where it nipped her with sharp stems and thorns, 'they must have had tougher skin in the elder days. In the Nocturne, they make it sound like you're sailing on light.'

'He's here,' said Levon.

Out there, Hayk prowled the head of the hall – where Master Atesh, tempted down from his rooftop anchorage, stood in a haze of lightjars.

'You'd better go to him,' Isabelle whispered.

So Levon did.

Up close, Hayk looked anxious. His hands were balled into fists – and, although he looked resplendent in his jet-black chokha (like an imperious sea captain straight out of the Nocturne) there was no disguising the stumps of his fingers where the wedding band ought to have been worn, nor the hunkered way he still held himself, as if ready for a fight.

'You disapprove,' Hayk finally said, marching back and forth.
'I don't.'

'It would be braver if you just said it.'

'I don't disapprove,' Levon whispered, with new rigidity in his
voice. 'But ...'

Hayk smiled his crooked smile. 'Is this the part where you tell
me you'll hunt me down if I don't treat her well? You'd do well
to remember, son. I'm *your* father.'

'Three thousand miles,' said Levon, and straightened himself
up – for he could hear the tinkling of Isabelle's lyre, and a hush
was descending over the hall. 'Aunt Mariam at my side every step
of the way. I think that earns me the right to care, doesn't it,
Hayk?'

For a time, there was silence between them. Then Hayk lifted
his butchered hand, as if he might strike Levon – and pawed him,
bear-like, across the shoulders instead. 'I hear you, Ulduzkhan!'
he laughed, and Levon was disturbed to see a look like pride
ghosting across his face. 'Never front up to a mama's boy,' Hayk
said as he stiffened, sensing Mariam's approach. 'They'll gut you
in your sleep, you so much as look at their women wrong.'

Isabelle's music filled the hall. She had taken to a pedestal at
the back of the hall, and the music sailed up and all around them.
The wedding march of the Ulduzkhans of old, thought Levon.
He could see it now. Stars were wheeling through the sky at
night.

He saw Mariam too. She had taken Arina's hand and, together,
they wended their way through the crowd until they reached the
place where Hayk was standing. Aram, who trailed from Arina's
other hand, wore a look of such confusion that, soon, Natia had
reached out from the crowd and swept him up. Glad to be
reunited with a fellow voyager, his confusion turned to delight.

Moments later, Mariam reached the head of the hall. Levon
wanted to mouth the words 'Are you certain?', but the certainty

was there in her eyes: the certainty of a decision being reached, an arrangement being made. The People made families in all sorts of different ways, here in the new world, so he kept his lips sealed.

'Shall we begin?'

Every eye in the room settled on Master Atesh. A whisper of a man, now, he saw the world through a veil of beating wings and streaks of rainbow light.

'Begin,' ordered Hayk.

So, as midnight approached on the night of the equinox, two lost souls became one.

'Raise your glasses, and your spirits, you dogs! Raise your glasses to my wife!'

Le Tangiers was alive.

The procession had made its way from the Hôtel Métropol, first down into the wine cellars and the Khanate Beneath, and then up again, until eventually the People had wended their way down the basement stair. Now, Isabelle took her place on stage, stretched her fingers and leaned into the music. Tonight, she was not the only one. The ancient melodies of her harp were joined in chorus by fiddlers and drummers. On the dance floor beneath, Natia and Nino turned wild waltzes with their partners, while Hayk draped his arms around two old seadogs he'd discovered in the night markets, and cajoled every figure standing in the shadows to dance.

Levon found Mariam at the bar.

'You're going to ask me some fool question, aren't you?' She had a tankard – by the Stars, it was too big for her – and she used two hands to tip it, like a chalice, to her lips. 'You're going to make sure I'm all right ...'

'I'm going to wish you all the love in the world,' Levon said, putting his arms around her.

Together, they looked out across the heaving bar. Beyrek, who had somehow kept the nectar flowing, heaved past them, an empty barrel cradled in his arms, and picked his way to the basement stairs. Up there, empty barrels sat, attracting multitudes of lightjars and city rats alike.

'I think Aram's father would be happy for you.'

Mariam scoffed, 'He *hated* Hayk.'

'Still went to sea with him, didn't he?'

'Oh, you don't have to like someone to respect them. That's the way he told it. Hayk's a scurrilous dog, but Aram still admired him. So I think, maybe, he'd understand.'

The air was split by a single scream.

The music was too loud, the dancing too wild, Hayk still roaring out his stories for all his scurrilous old seadog friends to hear. But Levon heard the scream too vividly. It was the strangled cry of an old man. The hoarse exclamation of a man whose voice is no longer robust enough to contain his panic. He'd heard a lot of cries like that. So he turned his head to the basement stairs, up which Beyrek had only just laboured, and everything else seemed to fade away.

One scream, but in a second there were more.

A confusion of shadows erupted at the bottom of the basement stair. Then, out of nowhere: smoke. The shriek of a rocket, the percussive crashing of a hundred miniature bombs going off – and everywhere was smoke.

Mariam dived for Aram. Until moments ago, he'd been dancing in the arms of one of the mothers from the block, but now he was being held aloft in a crush of bodies as the dance floor, already too crowded, moved en masse, as if it might escape the smoke. By instinct, Levon looked at the stage. In the same instant that the explosions had fired, the music had stopped. Isabelle's eyes locked with his, over the ocean of heads. 'Go!' he screamed at her, though she could not hear. 'Go!' His eyes were on her belly. His eyes were on her face. She took a step towards him – but the smoke was rising like a wall between them, and at last she turned around, dived instead for the door at the back of the stage.

The ear-splitting shrieking went on.

Lights flowered, but these were not the lights of the People. They erupted upward, geysers of sparks forcing their way through the smoke. Like corrupted winterlights, casting their seedpods up into the Parisian night, the sparks fountained across the People. But they did not give birth to lightjars; they only rained down cinders, scorching the People where they stood.

The screams became impenetrable, and so too did the smoke.

Levon staggered forward, joining the fray. 'Arina!' he called out. 'Arina!'

Something caught his foot. He tripped, stopped himself from falling only because of the crush of bodies up ahead. By now, the smoke was in his throat. He gulped at it, couldn't breathe, gulped again. 'Arina!' But the word wouldn't finish itself. All he could taste was ash.

Then: a hand on his neck, hoisting him upright, barrelling him back into the corner of the room. He crashed against the bare brick wall. At least here, by the bar, there was air.

Hayk loomed over him. 'On your feet, you dog! Don't pitch over now!'

Levon forced himself to his feet, hawking black phlegm onto the floor. 'Where's Arina?'

Hayk turned, taking in the cellar room. The smoke was thinning, the interminable shrieking stuttering to an end. Some of the People had found sanctuary in alcoves set into the walls, where the smoke had not reached. But the screaming went on.

Somebody was lying propped against the outer wall. His wife was on her knees, trying to make him open his eyes.

'Come on, Levon. You call yourself the Ulduzkhan?'

Hayk forced him bodily back into the smoke. By the time they reached the basement stairs, it was already crowded. Hayk heaved somebody by the shoulders, pushing them behind. 'You fools,' he spat. 'Go up there, would you? It *came* from there ...'

The People on the stairway relented. 'What came?'

Hayk waved back at the dance floor. 'Fire, and smoke,' he spat. 'Now, out of my way.'

Something in his voice would not be ignored, so he came between them, up into the night, Levon following close behind.

The empty barrels had been upturned. Golden rats lay gutted at the doors of Le Tangiers. The flowers-by-night that had grown in a perfect arch above the entrance had been ripped from their roots and scattered around. Remnants of dying light marked the pathway along which the cowards had fled.

Hayk thundered after them, but soon the fragments they'd left behind became too disparate to follow. A water dog appeared out of the night, and Hayk dropped to his knees to take hold of it. 'Which way?' he uttered, and in reply the dog set up a whimper.

It was only as Levon turned back to Le Tangiers that he saw the body lying in the road. In Hayk's haste to follow the shattered trail he had not seen the man lying in the dark. It was the crown of flowers that drew Levon's eye. Strange, because – even though they were intact – they were not radiating light. He faltered as he drew near, then dropped to his knees.

Beyrek was lying spread-eagled in the dirt, and the flowers around his head were not flowers-by-night from the old country, but only irises: simple French flowers, already wilting on the stem. Beautiful, perhaps, but they could not hide the undoing of his face. It was bloody and raw. His nose was a pulp of cartilage and flesh, and where his shirt had been ripped from his breast it revealed dark welts the colour of the night.

'Beyrek,' Levon whispered, 'please ...'

He felt a shadow on him. Hayk had appeared.

'He's alive. There's breath in him. I can feel the beating of his heart ... '

Levon's hands had been searching for it, and they found it now: the distant pulse, the will to survive.

'Look,' uttered Hayk.

A leaf of paper was lying on the ground at Beyrek's side. Perhaps Levon had brushed it off the old man in his haste to make certain he was alive. Hayk held it up for Levon to see.

'PARIS NEW RESISTANCE' were the words that it said.

'We need to get an ambulance,' said Levon. 'There's a phone in the bar. Dial 112.'

'An ambulance?' Hayk breathed.

'Go!'

'From *them*?' Hayk snapped. 'You'd call for help from the same people who ...'

Levon exploded upwards, barrelling his father back. 'I'll do it myself.' He marched past. 'You stand there, Hayk, and seethe, for all the good it will do him. He's dying. He's my friend.'

Levon exploded back into the bar, to a mortar attack of questions.

'It was fireworks,' somebody said. 'Somebody threw fireworks down the stairs.'

Levon clawed forward. The reef of grey smoke was dissipating now, but in the air was the hard, acrid stench of gunpowder.

'We need an ambulance,' he said, with a faraway feeling settling over him. 'Somebody call an—'

'We already have.'

That voice: Isabelle's voice. He looked down and found her crouching in the middle of the dance floor, the remnants of fireworks at her feet.

Too late, he realised who she was hunching over. He rushed forward, dropped to his knees beside her.

'It's coming,' Isabelle promised him, and took hold of his hand. 'They said they'd be here in moments.'

'Levon?' croaked a tiny voice.

The figure on the floor had been hoisted into Mariam's lap. His aunt was gently brushing the hair out of her eyes. Not that it mattered. There were, it seemed, no eyes there any longer – or, if there were, they were caked in such blood and dirt that they might never see again.

'Levon?' Arina trembled. 'Is it you?'

'It's me, little one.'

'Levon,' she breathed, 'I can't see you. Levon, I can't see.'

Somewhere up above, the sirens had started to wail.

12

* *

BORDERLINE

'You remember where you were on the day the old country ended. You were down at the shore, readying to haul in the morning catch. Or you were tucked up in bed, dreaming whatever it is we dreamed of back then. Fighting your children into their school clothes. Tramping into the foothills, feeding your livestock.

'Then, suddenly, none of that mattered. You were crammed onto the boats, taking flight across the landlocked sea. Or you were trapped in your houses while the soldiers swarmed outside, trying to save pictures of your bebias, in case you never saw them again. You didn't know, in those moments, that photographs didn't matter. That clean water and good boots were what you were going to need. You didn't know, but, by the Stars, you found out.'

A hundred faces faced Hayk. Two hundred. More. All the way into the furthest recesses of the Khanate Beneath, the People gathered.

'And you told yourself, didn't you: I'll never be caught wanting again. I'll never take my loved ones for granted. I'll never close my eyes and drift off, safe in the knowledge that the world will still be there when I wake up. Because I've seen it now. I've seen how fragile it is.

'Well, remember where you were last night, you dogs. You lazy, indolent, dreaming *dogs*. Remember where you were when

ROBERT DINSDALE

the new world ended – because, by every star up above and every
one we, the People, brought down to Earth, I will.'

He stopped, surveyed them all, found them all – every last one
of them – wanting.

'It's written in blood.'

He could hear the ambulances coming – and this, more than anything else, more than the broken old man who still lay in the gutter, filled him with fire. Blue lights, advancing through the night.
They'd give with one hand and take with the other, would they?
They'd run teasing fingers up the inside of his thigh while draining
his blood with the others? Well, no, Hayk thought. Not this time.

So he bowed down, put his arms around Beyrek, and bore him
aloft.

Smoke was still curling up from the basement stair – but, as
Hayk stepped back into it, he knew it for what it was. They did
not really have incendiaries. Their weapon had been panic, pure
and simple. Rounding the corner of the crooked stairway, he
ducked back into the bar. Reefs of grey still shifted across the
dance floor, but for now the chaos was finished.

'Milena!' he yelled. She'd been at the ceremony, so by rights
she was somewhere here. 'Where's the doctor?'

There she was: down on the floor, down where his son and the
French girl were crouching.

'Well, get here! Don't give up on him yet.'

From the floor, they turned to face him. It was only then, as
they parted, that Hayk saw the figure over whom they'd been
looming. He stuttered forward, bent under his burden, and laid
Beyrek down. Then he stepped over the prostrate body, his eyes
fixed on Arina.

She was so pitiably small. He wanted to tell her 'Daddy's here',
but he had no voice.

There were footsteps on the stairs.

Two figures emerged from the parting smoke: paramedics, white masks over their faces as they descended into the grey.

'Here,' Levon called out – and Milena, who had crawled to Beyrek's side to run her hands across his beaten body, seeking out ruptures and hardnesses, the signs of internal wounds, added, 'And here!'

But the paramedics stalled when they saw Hayk.

He'd put himself between them. He was rocking on his heels, and both his hands were turned to fists. 'It's your people did this,' he uttered. The paramedics tried to fan out around him, but Hayk was too vast; all he had to do was open his arms to hem them in. 'Don't touch a hair on her head.'

'Sir, please ...'

It was the paramedic on his left who'd spoken. The one on his right had simply tried to step around him, heading for Beyrek on the floor.

The first punch was a feint.

It was the second that sent him sprawling.

In the silence of the Khanate Beneath, Hayk held up his hands. Though they'd long since been washed clean of blood, there was no mistaking them for what they were. He flexed the stumps of his missing fingers as he whispered the words.

'Perhaps I shouldn't have done what I did. Perhaps it's like they're saying in those news rags of theirs, and I really am an animal.' He paused. 'Or perhaps it's like all of this. Lightjars back in the skies. Packs of water dogs lurking in the shadows. Flowers-by-night and winterlights and the Rose of the Evening. Just the rage of the old world coursing out of me.' He paused. 'Because it's like I've been trying to tell you people, those of you who'd dare to listen.'

His eyes cut into them: the countless faces he knew, the countless he didn't.

'From the east to the west, from the north to the south, under the sun and under the stars, wherever men walk this blasted Earth – if you don't look after what belongs to you, somebody else will come along and take it.'

'Hayk!'

It was Levon who was first onto his feet. Levon who hurled himself into his father's path, so that the third punch Hayk threw caught his own son full in the face, toppling him where he stood. In Le Tangiers, the screaming had started again. This time, it was the People screaming at one of their own.

Nursing his jaw where he lay, Levon saw his father turn to the paramedic still standing. 'By the Stars, Hayk, there'll already be gendarmes on their way. How many cages do you have to be in ...'

If his father heard it at all, the words didn't touch him. He had kicked the fallen paramedic aside, was moving in on the second – when, out of the smoke that remained, Master Atesh appeared. Hayk could have swept him aside with the back of his hand – and that was precisely what he intended to do. But then the old man spoke. 'Hayk, have you learned nothing?' And whether it was the echo of the schoolroom, many aeons ago, or something deeper that touched him, nobody knew. But his fists curled back into hands, his face softened – and, when his eyes darted around the room, Levon thought he saw the fear that his father had been hiding. Open and raw, like the wounds on Beyrek's face.

As Levon got back to his feet, he tasted blood and spat it, thick and black, onto the floor.

'Get him out of here,' he said. From above there were yet more sirens, pulsing through the Goutte d'Or. 'There's a crevice, under the stage. He can go by the Khanate Beneath.'

'I'm not going anywhere,' Hayk breathed, 'not without my daughter.'

There were footsteps. Footsteps on the stairs.

'Go!' Levon roared.

Hayk was gone by the time the gendarmes appeared. By then, the paramedic was back on his feet, strapping a mask over Arina's face, Beyrek already ferried to the ambulance waiting above. In the shadowy darkness of Le Tangiers – where dead lightjars crunched underfoot, and the scent of gunpowder and urine was still strong – Levon and Isabelle watched as the paramedics secured Arina to the second stretcher they'd brought down. Up above, between the police cars with their swirling lights, the ambulances were waiting. Levon and Isabelle climbed into the first, where Arina now lay in perfect stillness, and were carried off, into the night.

The chaos of the emergency room. The remonstrations at the theatre doors. The long, bitter hours pacing outside, until some doctor came out and told them, in a paternal tone he'd practised over many long nights, that she would live – but that she'd never see again. Then: the agonising walk to her bedside on the ward; the touch of her hand as she lay sleeping, and the terrible thought of the lands into which her nightmares might be dragging her, even now. Later, when there came a tap at Levon's shoulder – and a hospital administrator told them that, General Amnesty or not, there were still costs that needed to be settled – neither Levon nor Isabelle was lucid enough to understand. They sleepwalked through the forms, then returned to her again, neither daring to believe that she would never again see the majesty of multi-coloured lightjars in flight; never again see unnumbered rainbows erupting over the city when the winterlights grew ripe; never again see the light of the seven-pointed star, to remind her that this was home, that the People had made it, that she was never alone.

Some time in the night, another doctor told them that Beyrek was dead. And, after that, death was all Levon knew.

Dawn had returned to the world when Levon stood again in the shadow of the horseshoe-shaped block and contemplated his return. He fancied he could still feel Isabelle's hand, though she remained at the hospital, determined that she should be there when Arina awoke. The nurses had taken a special request: on waking, Arina's first meal would be pancakes, smothered in whipped cream and honey. That, and the cocktail of drugs she would be taking in the days and weeks to come.

Levon listened to the echo of his own footfall as he rose through the glimmering strata of the block. His head had grown heavy with sleeplessness. His body a ruin.

He remembered the touch of the shovel, the smell of the earth, as long ago he put his mother in the ground.

The block was still, but Mariam would be waiting. He was certain of that. Clothes in a bag, books to read to her, their bebia's copy of the Nocturne – just so that she could feel the embroidery of its seven-pointed star – and then he would find Mariam and tell her.

As he neared the top of the stairs, he felt the tremors in his body and decided that, before all this, he would slip inside the back bedroom, stuff the bedsheets into his mouth, and cry. By the Stars, he needed to cry. It had been too long.

He was bracing himself to hold it in – and doing a terrible job of it, by the tears that streamed down his cheeks – when he reached the final landing and saw daylight flooding down the rooftop stair. From here, he could smell the scents of the night garden. Perhaps it should have buoyed him, for here was his bebia, all around him. But, for the first time, he was thankful that she was dead. Better that she was a star in the heavens than alive to acknowledge the lasting truth: that he'd kept them safe for three thousand miles but, in the end, he'd failed them all.

Before he went into the apartment, he climbed the stair. He'd tell his bebia first. Sit there in the grove, though it was daylight, and beg her forgiveness.

But when he reached the top of the stairs, he stopped.

The first sign that something was wrong was the flesh of the flame fruit trampled into the top steps. Blades of uprooted grasses, the stems of bulrushes ripped out of the earth and tiles, were scattered about his feet. Levon ducked through the door and knew, then, that this was no idle devastation. It reached into the heart of the rooftop grotto. The vines that had once tumbled over the edges of the building, making hollows and hideaways in which the lightjars lived, had been torn up – and with them lengths of gutter. The scaffolding, around which vines had grown in glorious arrays of colour, had been smashed, so that it stood crooked and buckled, bound together only by the few vines that had not been torn up. The flame fruit tree that once cast its star-light shadows over the lake lay on its side, its exposed roots caked in shattered roofing tiles. And in the air: the smell of smoke.

Levon came falteringly forward. What fires there had been had not been vast, but in places embers still sent columns of grey into the air.

And there was Hayk.

He was standing on the precipice, with Mariam beside him, gazing down into the freight yard.

'What happened here?'

Hayk revolved slowly. In reply, he simply turned to lead Levon on, around the concrete sarcophagus that had once been cloaked in colour – but was now naked as stone.

On the concrete wall, where the vines had been ripped away, words dripped in red paint.

'PARIS NEW RESISTANCE.'

'They knew the block would be empty last night. They knew there was a celebration.'

Levon just stared.

'It can't be the same people,' he finally whispered.

'Explain it a different way, boy. No, they came to Le Tangiers last night because they knew the People would be there. They came here, because they knew we'd be there too.'

'But how would they know?'

Hayk turned his face to the alien, blue sky. 'That, Levon, is what we have to find out. But is it any wonder? Paris-by-Starlight's a free-for-all. By the Stars, we invited it in.'

Mariam said, 'They were long gone by the time we got back. But Levon, is Arina …'

'She'll live,' was all he had the strength to say. His eyes roamed from one devastated corner to another. The gazebo they'd built – of that there was no sign. The bastards who'd come here had heaved it over the edge, down into the freight yard below. 'Bey-rek's dead,' he said.

Hayk barely condescended to look him in the eye. 'Now will you listen?'

'Excuse me?'

'I've been trying to tell you. You think I'm just some butcher come late to the party. That there's too much blood in my eyes to see the beauty. But I was right. There's people out to get you wherever you are.' Intermittently, he started shaking. 'And what have you been doing? You've been dancing and singing and glorying in it. And not one of you stopped to think what might happen when it stopped being beautiful. Not one of you – you foolish, foolish dogs – looked back at what was lost and thought it could happen again. Because you thought you'd reached the end of your rainbow. You thought you could luxuriate in it for-ever.' He spat into the bog where the lake used to be. 'Well, tonight you found different.'

Levon turned on his heel, felt the sickening crunch of some desiccated lightjar under his boot. 'I haven't time for this, Hayk. I've got to ...'

'I sent runners out.'

Levon turned.

'To every block I could think of. To the night marketeers. Up onto every rooftop where the People gather. There'll be a gathering tonight, under the Hôtel Métropol. You're going to address them.'

A new sensation touched every corner of Levon's body. It took him some time, feeling it tingle along every sinew, before he could place it. Rage, he thought. Rage was coursing through him. Because tonight he would not be beneath the Hôtel Métropol. Tonight he would not be with the People. He would be at a hospital bedside, and he would be holding a hand, and he would be forcing himself to stay awake – hour after hour, after long, long hour – so that he was there when she called out, blindly, for her brother.

'Me?' he uttered.

'You're the Ulduzkhan. It's you they're looking to. You that they need.'

He took two strides back towards his father. 'There isn't any Ulduzkhan. I didn't ask to be Ulduzkhan. We don't need an Ulduzkhan, Hayk. We need ...'

We need last night not to have happened.

We need to have been in a different place, in a different time.

Words, he thought, that might just as easily have applied to that morning, three years in the past, when he'd sat between his mother and Arina, holding fast to both, as the overloaded fishing boat pitched across the unforgiving ocean.

An image from that night, when all around was wind and ice. His bebia's face had peered into his. 'The age we live in,' she used to say, 'is not ours to decide. Our decision is only how to use the few fleeting moments the Universe has given us.'

Well, Levon already knew how he was going to use his. There was a little girl who needed him.

She was only nine years old.

'She's blind,' he said as he turned back to the stair. 'The firework scoured across her, and she'll never look on us again. She'll never see the seven-pointed star. Of course, you could go and hold her hand yourself – but you attacked the paramedic who'd come to help her. So there's a warrant out for your arrest, and gendarmes all over the hospital, standing guard.' He ducked back through the stairs. 'So go to the Khanate Beneath tonight, Hayk. I'll look after her when you won't. I've been doing it since the beginning.'

The police had been at the bedside twice before Levon's return. There Isabelle sat, Arina's tiny hand (fed by a catheter, hooked up to a bag of fluid hanging above) resting on her own. She'd slept, though she hadn't meant to. One moment she was there in the hospital; the next she was dreaming of the shrieking of fireworks. Once, when she woke, the lieutenant was hovering at the end of the bed – but he soon drifted on. The second time, two of them pulled up chairs so that they might sit beside her.

'What is she to you?' the first one asked.

'Did somebody bring you food? You've been here so long – a woman, in your state ...'

'The nurse says you were the singer, in the bar.'

'The Rose of the Evening. What is it, your stage name?'

'I'm sorry, mademoiselle, but we need to know what you saw.'

So she told them, what little she could.

'We need to ask about the man who was at the scene. He assaulted the paramedic.'

'He's her father,' Isabelle pleaded. 'He wasn't in his right mind.'

'That's right.'

'What can you tell us about him?'

Isabelle dared not raise her voice. 'Well, what can *you* tell *me* about the people who did this?' She could feel Arina's fingers twitching, and pleaded with her eyes that the officers might stop.

'An investigation is ensuing,' the first officer said. It was the first moment that Isabelle rose through the miasma and heard his concern. 'This has become a murder investigation, you understand.'

Into the silence came Isabelle's stifled sob. She told herself she was better than this, that she would not cry. But then she relented. If a woman couldn't shed tears over a friend, then what was the use of crying? Beyrek had been good to her. None had done more than the old man, with his feathery voice and his eyes so grateful for the wonders, to make her feel a part of their world. She remembered the end of the Nocturne. The stars winked out, one by one.

'Help us understand,' the other said, not unkindly. 'How does a nice girl like you end up embroiled with this lot?'

Isabelle was gathering herself, trying to put together the pieces of her reply, when the first officer's gaze settled on her swollen stomach. 'It's one of theirs, isn't it?' The two men shared a look. 'There are places we could take you, if that's what you wanted. Places we could talk in private.'

'I can't leave. She's nine years old.'

The officers stalled again. Yet more looks darted between them, as some silent conversation went on.

'Tell me, do you ... live by night, with them?'

'What's that got to do with—'

'We just want to build up a picture. It goes to bigger concerns. Why somebody might have targeted Le Tangiers tonight. Tell me, when did they first suggest you should start living by night? Was it after you fell pregnant? After the show they put on at Christmas?'

Isabelle rubbed her head, as if trying to shake off the question. The weariness of the night was catching up with her at last. 'It wasn't a show they put on. It's their Night of Seven Stars.' She looked down at Arina, but the bandages that covered her eyes made her feel a continent away. 'She's the one who discovered it, in their Nocturne. She loved it.'

'What I'd say is it's easy to love beautiful things,' one of the officers began, his voice dropping to a gentle, practised whisper. 'You must have found that, when you got to know these People. People draw you in with beauty. Well, it's so hard to say no, isn't it? Do you remember, when we were children – what was our parents' biggest fear? You'd get those pamphlets: don't talk to strangers. And pictures of a nice, handsome man standing outside school to offer you sweets. Well, you grow up knowing those sweets could be poison. And it's the same thing here.'

'What's that other thing they used to teach us?' the second officer chipped in. 'Beauty is only skin deep.'

'The thing is, you never really know what's lurking underneath.'

There was a simple silence, while Isabelle tried to stop herself from shaking.

'Madam, we're going to need to take a statement.'

A third voice came out of the darkness of the ward:

'You can take one from me.'

Isabelle looked up – and there was Levon, weaving between the two officers, setting his satchel down gently by Arina's side. Out of it he pulled two clean sets of clothes – one for Arina, and one for Isabelle herself – and his bebia's Nocturne. This he set beneath Arina's free hand, placing her fingers on its embroidered star.

'Your name, sir?'

'My name is Levon. I'm her brother.'

The officers nodded, as if they were one. 'Then I must ask you: the man from the basement bar, we're given to understand that he is your father. Do you know where he might be found, sir?'

'He's our father by blood only. Neither of us knew him when we were small. He isn't in Paris on our account, and nor are we responsible for him. Whatever he did last night, it isn't on us. She's nine years old, and she's lucky to be alive. All I ask is that—'

'Sir,' one of the officers interrupted – and Isabelle was unsurprised to hear the harder tone that had supplanted the cajoling, caring one of moments before. 'That matter, as tragic as it is, is being handled by officers from a separate division. My colleague and I have a different responsibility here. And we need your help. I don't know what it's like where you People come from, but in Paris we respect our civic servants. Our doctors and paramedics and ambulance drivers: these people are important to us. So I'm sure you'd agree that, when they're summoned to the scene of an attack, the last thing they deserve is to be ambushed by the very people they're coming to help.' He paused, if only to let the sentiment seep in. 'I'll ask it one more time. Your father – do you know where he is?'

Levon thought of the devastation in the night garden. He thought of his bebia's spirit uprooted and torn to shreds, scattered over the tiles like so much confetti. He thought of those three words – 'PARIS NEW RESISTANCE' – daubed upon Beyrek, daubed upon the night garden wall.

Then he thought of the runners that were going out. 'Come to the Hôtel Métropol,' they were saying. 'The People need to know. The People need to be together. There'll be a gathering tonight.'

He fixed the officers with a look like he was lost and did the one thing that, no matter what he'd learned across three years and three thousand miles, he'd never truly known how to do.

Levon lied.

'I haven't seen him since the basement bar. Wherever he is now, whatever he's doing, it's not for me, and it's not for my sister. So leave us alone,' he whispered. 'We're finished now.'

*

In the Khanate Beneath, a cry went up.

Hayk let it wash over him. It was like the crashing of a great wave, and he the prow of the ship that broke it. He looked into the ocean of People. Perhaps the whole of Paris-by-Starlight had not gathered here, but it was enough to make him hope. He'd been in want of hope for so very long. How many had made it? he wondered. Ten thousand. Twenty. More. Enough for a city to flourish when the sun went down. There was hope in this too.

'Three words,' he roared out. '"PARIS NEW RESISTANCE." I saw them stapled to my friend's breast. I saw them painted in my mother's night garden. The first night garden in Paris-by-Starlight, defiled while I was being wed.' His eyes found Mariam, standing on the closest shore with Aram in her arms. 'My only daughter ...' This time, he choked on the words. 'It's not the first time I saw those words. They were scored into the bark in the Jardin when it hosted the night market. "JARDIN NATIONAL!", across one of their flags. How many more ...'

'We've seen it too,' came a voice from the throng. Hayk's eyes sought it out: a man whose hair was bound back in a braid, threaded with strands of silver. 'I run a school for our block, right there in Saint-Denis. Somebody came into our stairwell while we slept. "PARIS NEW RESISTANCE", painted on the walls.'

'I've seen it on the Métro,' somebody else declared.

'Us too.' Hayk saw the girl they called Natia, standing behind Mariam. 'There were men, handing out leaflets.'

'I have one here!'

A figure emerged and handed Hayk a crumpled page. 'PARIS NEW RESISTANCE', it read. Apart from that, there was only one simple line: 'WE USED TO FEEL SAFE.'

'I used to feel safe too,' one of the women cried out. 'You spent a year transported from camp to camp, not knowing where you'd end up, not knowing whether you'd have to wander the Earth until the end of your days. Then they welcome you. They see that you're good.'

'And all the while,' the man beside her chipped in, 'they're waiting to take it from you.'

'They kill our dogs,' somebody said.

And so it went on. 'PARIS NEW RESISTANCE': stencilled in chalk across the square beneath the Tour Eiffel. 'PARIS NEW RESISTANCE': blowing in the wind over the bridges of the Seine.

'Somebody came to the bazaar,' a new voice cried out. 'Said that I was selling poisons. Poisons to make French girls fall in love.'

'They're just boys,' somebody said. 'Just stupid, stupid boys.'

'Until last night,' somebody else snapped.

Then the waves of noise returned. From one stand of glowing stalactites to another, invective and counter-invective flurried up and flew. Piece by piece, moment by moment, it grew louder, like the escalating sides of a war.

In the crowd beneath Hayk, Aram was crying. He was not the only one, because Hayk was crying too. By the Stars, it felt wrong. He began shredding the leaflet in his hands, but it assuaged so little of the feeling. They'd been given a second chance. And none of them, not a sorry one, had seen it for what it was. The world did not make recompense for its suffering. The world only kept turning. From day to night and back again. From suffering to survival, to respite and back round. He realised, then, that it was not anger he was clinging to. He'd picked his way here, wary of any police that were on the streets, with the fire of hate burning in him. But seeing them now, he realised he was wrong. It was not hatred but pity that burned in him. It was not their fault that they were too blind to see. They'd been through the dark; all they wanted was the light.

'*Just stupid boys?* No, not just boys. Never *just* boys. This word,' he went on, his voice getting fuller, richer, filling the cavern again. 'Resistance. I was part of a resistance, once. So were some of you. While the People fled, some of us stayed. We tried to make war on those who came to take the old country from us.' He started shaking. 'So I killed. I destroyed. I burned them down in their barracks. I did everything I could, because I wanted my old world so much. I'd have burned every one of them, just to sail my boat in peace upon the landlocked sea. Look at me, you dogs. LOOK AT ME!' He reached out with his butchered hand. He lifted his misshapen face to the spectral lights. 'This is how much I wanted it back. So don't tell me that these are *just boys*. Because boys with fire in them aren't *just boys*. They're proud. They're righteous. And they believe, with every passion within them, that they've been wronged.'

Silence in the Khanate Beneath, as the echoes of Hayk's voice guttered away.

'So what now?' a lone voice asked.

Hayk saw that it was Master Atesh. A family of diamond-white lightjars had returned to him tonight. In the dark: always the light.

Master Atesh, he thought, asking *me* what's next.

He looked at the thousands of expectant faces.

This was why Levon should have been here. Levon, the Ulduz-khan of old. The People needed a voice like that. Somebody to lift and restore them to the night.

All at once, he remembered being on the rooftop anchorage, alongside Master Atesh. What was it the old man had told him?

Words that Levon himself had spoken to the vagabond People. He closed his eyes and let the sentiment flow back into him. When he opened them again, he was ready. They needed to hear it tonight.

'Now? Well, now we start writing our own story. We don't sit back until somebody comes to take it away, all of the beautiful things the world gave us and us alone.' He paused one last time, for the emotion of it was turning his voice to a tremble. '*We are the People*,' he cried out, '*and the People look after each other.*'

*

The Senegalese set off the moment he was summoned.

In the darkness of the hospital ward, Isabelle brought him to the bedside. There lay Arina, in and out of sleep.

'Oh, my sweet child.' Dr Senghor took the clipboard at the bottom of her bed and lingered over its notes. 'They'll have told you she's been fortunate, no doubt. That a fraction of a moment, a sliver of time and space, and things might have been worse.' He slipped the clipboard back onto the bedframe and came to stand beside her, touching her brow gently where the bandages gave way to clean skin. 'Well, let them say it. This is no good fortune.' He looked up. 'The light exploded across her. Whatever was in its comet trail touched her. There was burning, but the eyes didn't rupture. Poor girl, she stood no chance. They're filling her with antibiotics to keep infections at bay. But I can help with those. The rest is just fluids …'

Isabelle said, 'I don't want to do this, but …'

The Senegalese grappled for her hand. 'I understand.'

'Levon signed all the forms, but there's no way he could pay them. And the police …'

'They'll use her, to get back to him. To her father.'

'Dr Senghor, it's all so …'

He lifted a finger to his lips, and all the fury drained out of her, just as if he were lancing a wound. It was enough that somebody understood.

'You have to go, child. This isn't a choice.'

'Levon thinks they'll take her from us. That she'll be back in some camp.'

Dr Senghor busied himself, inspecting the catheter in her hand, the trailing bag to which she was connected. All of it he could source himself; the black leather bag at his feet was already filled.

'Perhaps not a camp, but it would feel like one. A new home in a new part of the city. Compelled to live by day.' Carefully, he drew the tube out of the catheter, leaving it taped to her hand. 'She's still weak. Her body has to acclimatise. It has to ... understand. She'll still need rest.'

Isabelle nodded. 'Maybe, in her own home, with all the People around ...'

'She's going to be scared.'

So are we all, thought Isabelle. Every last citizen of Paris-by-Starlight.

She drove the thought from her mind. These were thoughts for another hour. Right now, there was only the girl.

'Levon went to the Métropol. M. Fortier's away for the season, so he's borrowing one of the cars.'

'Then we must work fast.'

Isabelle went to put her arms around the fitfully sleeping girl, but the Senegalese stopped her. 'In your condition?'

'She needs me.'

'And you'll be right there, right at her side.'

As the Senegalese lifted her, the bedsheets sloughed away. In his arms, she was so small.

Two hours past midnight. Three. Four. There had been police officers in the ward throughout the day, but only one prowled the corridors at night, and he was easily evaded. They took a back corridor; then, ignoring the elevator, came down echoing iron stairs until they emerged into the frigid night. Here six stone buildings sat around a great courtyard, with colonnaded walkways where crowns of radiant flowers-by-night had taken root. It was not the cold that made Isabelle shudder, then; it was the guilt that she could see the splendour when Arina could not.

The girl was awake. 'Please,' she said, and bucked in Dr Senghor's arms. 'Levon?'

'I'm here,' said Isabelle, taking her hand. 'Arina, it's me. We're taking you home.'

How did you cry, with bound, blind eyes? It was another thing the world had taken from her.

Their path took them across the courtyard and through one of the further buildings. Only on its furthest side could they emerge, past the hospital railings, to the barren street beyond.

A car was waiting. Levon killed the engine, clambered out into its dipped headlights and hurried towards them.

'We need to move,' the Senegalese said. 'Get her to a bed. Get her warm and safe.'

'It isn't far,' said Levon, and hurried them back to the car.

It wasn't. The Hôpital Laribiosière sat on the same railway tracks that they followed north, tucked away behind the Gare du Nord. At this hour, save for the ambulances ploughing their circuits, the roads were barren. So northward they coursed.

The block still wore its crown of light, and the blaze of colour at its zenith filled Isabelle with hope. Levon drew the car around in its shadow. Through the building's open doors, they could see the cauldron of colours that would take them up the stairwell. 'Be careful,' he said as the Senegalese opened the car door. 'They were long gone last night, but watch to the shadows in the stairwell.'

Holding Arina together, they entered the block. The strata of colour, the bejewelled vines that dangled down – all of it was an insult to Isabelle. But at least Arina could hear the maelstrom of tiny wings. At least she could breathe in the sweetness of the blossoms' nectar. This was a bitter kind of consolation, but at least it was something.

They rose slowly, lest they exhaust her even further, stopping on each landing to console her in their arms. Another hour had passed by the time they reached the very top. Here, Levon led them through the apartment doors.

Hayk was waiting.

He was not the only one.

So many faces were here, so many Levon scarcely knew, that at first he did not notice that Mariam and Aram, too, were in the apartment. He stopped in the doorway, Isabelle and Dr Senghor cradling Arina behind him, and saw Master Atesh, fluttering in a fresh haze of lightjars. Other than this, his home was a paradise of strangers. Three men played cards at the table where Levon ate breakfast. A fourth, an elderly soul with the air of a disgruntled soldier, waited in the corner by the kitchenette.

Hayk's bass voice was already rising. 'Did you bring her?'

'She needs to rest,' said Levon. 'We brought the doctor.'

Levon stepped aside, inviting Isabelle and Dr Senghor into the apartment. As they crossed the threshold, the sputter of old conversations fell silent.

Hayk crossed the apartment in two great strides, opening his arms to take Arina.

'My girl ...' Isabelle did not resist as he took her into his arms. She felt the scrabble of the girl's hands but, after that, all she could do was watch. 'I've cleared the back bedroom for her. Arina, my princess, you're going to be OK.'

Dr Senghor moved to follow, but the fire in Hayk's eyes rooted him to the spot.

'She needs antibiotics. Just to stay the course. The dressings will need changing. The wounds are light, but not insignificant. Were they to weep ...'

Hayk motioned silently to the corner of the room, where a woman – one of the People – rose to her feet.

'This is Milena. She's the one who'll look after Arina.'

The Senegalese darted a look at Levon.

'Only the People, for the People,' Hayk breathed, then turned to duck through the door into the back bedroom, Milena following behind.

They were gone for some moments, while in the apartment the silence remained. When, at last, Hayk returned, leaving Milena with the girl, not a word had been spoken.

'She's going to be OK,' Hayk whispered.

Into the uncertainty of silence that followed, Dr Senghor said, 'She's not going to see again. She'll need—'

'We'll see what the medicine of the People can do. If the old world can serve up Paris-by-Starlight, it can work other wonders. *Only the People, for the People*. I'm done with the rest of Paris. I'm done with your quackery. We don't need it.'

'Sir, I studied at—'

Hayk dismissed it with a wave of the hand. 'Levon, get rid of your lackey. We need to talk. You were missed in the Khanate Beneath, but the People will understand it, given time. It's your love they'll admire. They're feeling it too. An attack on my daughter was attack on them all. Here, look at this.' He snapped his fingers, and one of the unknown men tossed him a newspaper, then a second. These he pushed into Levon's hands. 'Tell me, boy, what do you see?'

Copies of *Le Monde*. Copies of *Le Figaro*. Copies of *Libération*.

'Well, boy? Don't you see it? Not a whisper of what happened last night. Not a whisper of Le Tangiers. Not a word of this Paris New Resistance.'

He was right, thought Levon. He passed the newspapers to Isabelle, but they just hung in her hands; all her heart was set on venturing through the back bedroom door.

'Don't you see? They don't care,' Hayk spat. 'Oh, they'll take the magic. They'll bask in their enchanted city. They'll rhapsodise about it, when it suits them. But they'll look the other way as well, when it's one of their own.'

Levon said, 'Who are all these people, Hayk?'

So he introduced them, one by one. The three at the table were Samvel, Narek, Arman. 'The Faithful Three,' Hayk said. 'The very last to leave the old country, nearly three years after it fell.' The fourth in the corner was Mr Andonian, though he neither made a greeting nor looked the other way when Hayk introduced him. 'They're the People. They're here to help.'

'Help ... what?'

'Why,' said Hayk, wearing the same air of disbelief as his last-born son, 'the defence of the city.'

'Mariam,' Levon ventured, picking her out in the crowded apartment, 'you're not—'

'They killed a man, Levon. They near killed Arina.'

'I haven't brought her home at all, have I? I've brought her to a council of war.'

'Not war,' Hayk uttered. 'We've seen enough of it. But they'll not find us wanting again. Do you remember, Levon, that morning on the shore?'

'You know I do.'

'Do you want to feel like that again? By the Stars, what they've given, they'll take away. General Amnesty? We're here at their forbearance, and it's starting to fade. There isn't enough enchantment in the world to keep them addled. The magic wears thin. Come next Night of Seven Stars, do you think they'll marvel at the winterlights exploding and the lightjars being born? Or will they start fuming that nobody speaks of their Christmases any more? Start sniping about the rot the winterlights leave behind, once they've cast their seedpods up and over the city? No, Levon, last night was a blessing. We'll come to see it like that. It told us to wake up. It shook us out of this dream. This time, we can be ready when—'

'A blessing?'

She had not dared speak until now, but Isabelle could hold it in no longer. The scent of the hospital antiseptic was still all over her.

'Beyrek's dead. Your daughter's ...' Even the word was too much; she choked on it. 'And you call it a blessing?'

Hayk stared.

'Isn't it enough that you left them to cross half the world on their own? Isn't it enough that you ditched them when they were children so you could fuck your way around the landlocked sea? Fathers like you, they're hardly fathers at all! By the Stars, Hayk, a blessing? A *blessing*?' She reached for Levon, and found him there.

'By the Stars?' Hayk's misshapen face had contorted further as it strained to imitate her voice. Then he, too, reached for Levon. 'You see, boy, this is what I've been trying to explain. *By the Stars*, she says, as if she's any right to say it. As if she knows the centuries and generations that used those words. The glory that flourished and fell, in the age before we were born. *By the Stars*, as if it's the Seventh that drew her home. And all over Paris-by-Starlight, Parisians wandering into our night markets. That dog at the Hôtel Métropol, turning the Khanate Beneath into some sort of attraction to line his pockets. And you, Levon, helping him do it! And *this*,' he crowed, 'what's *this*?' He reached for the table, where copies of the Nocturne were piled up. 'Scribes in hotel rooms, turning the Nocturne – *our Nocturne* – into French, so that they can devour it, like any old bedtime story. It came back for *us*. You shared it with them. By the Stars, you welcomed them in. And how do they repay you? They butcher your sister. They score my daughter's eyes from her head, so that she'll never see her father again. And—'

'*Father?*' Isabelle cried out. 'You're barely to fit to speak the word. You're—'

Hayk shook himself: exasperated, vindicated, lost. 'You can't call yourself Ulduzkhan, boy, not while this goes on. The People deserve more. They lost too much. They can't lose it again.'

Levon said, 'I never called myself Ulduzkhan, Hayk,' but his words were lost. Around the room, Hayk's strangers were on their feet.

It was Master Atesh who spoke. 'Your father is right, Levon. We've been foolish. Paris-by-Starlight isn't a playground. The magic isn't our reward for survival. It's a gift, given to us, so that we can start again. We should have been protecting that.'

'And we will,' said Hayk. He had fought his way to the window, where the inky-black sky was beginning to show the first traces of day. 'There are two cities here. Let them have their day. We have no need for sunlight streaming through the trees. Why bask in one star, when you have the whole night sky? But if we have no use for their day, then they have no right to the night. Not any longer. They forsook that in Le Tangiers. They forsook it in every crucified water dog, in every catcall and slight, in every ruin they made of our grottos, every time they daubed those words up on walls. Send a message to *Le Monde*. Send a message to *Libération*.' He waved a hand at the newspapers Isabelle had cast onto the floor. 'From this night on, they're not welcome in our markets. They're not welcome in our ...' He stopped, for the thought that had been hardening in him all night had finally taken form. 'They're not welcome in our city. If I have to patrol the border, I will. But pray that it doesn't come to that. I'll not take war back to them – but, by the Stars, they'll know it if they come into my city.' At this, he stopped. The light of the last stars of night was on his face, and he drank it in. Slowly, he turned around. 'You're not the Ulduzkhan, Levon. I see that now. But it had to manifest somewhere, and here I am.'

A tiny voice came from the back bedroom. 'Isabelle?' Arina was saying. 'Is Isabelle here?'

She took a step towards her, but a mountain was in her way. Hayk had stooped to lift her harp, her father's lyre, and these he pressed into her arms.

'The border rises at dawn.'

Levon chased her down the stairs.

'Isabelle, please!'

On the seventh landing, he caught her arm. The lights here were pink and gold, the lightjars glistening with the same vibrant hues. But they scattered as Isabelle wheeled around, straining to be free of Levon's hands.

'Don't,' she breathed at him. 'Don't you dare. You have to stay with her. *You have to.*'

'Come back, Isabelle. I'll sort it out. It's my apartment. It's ours ...'

'It's nobody's. It's whoever pays off the superintendent. It's ...' She stopped. 'He's right, Levon. If you don't look after what's yours, somebody just comes along and takes it. That's what he says, isn't it? So the apartment's his now. So Paris-by-Starlight's his. What's the use of me ...?'

There was footfall on the steps above. Soon, the Senegalese appeared, lit up in the ethereal silvers and whites of the flowers above.

'But where would you go?'

The fury was fading. She put her arms around him, curled onto his shoulder.

'I still have family of my own.'

Letting her go did not seem right. He wanted to keep his arms folded around her. He wanted to feel her arms closed around him. And yet going back above, dragging her through those doors, that did not seem right either. The only right place was here, in this moment, stranded between storeys. Stranded between cities. Stranded between worlds.

The Senegalese had come alongside them. 'I'll see her safe, Levon.'

It was only the thought of Arina that stopped him following them down the stairs. 'I'll come for you,' he called after her.

She did not need to reply. He knew that she believed it too.

Outside, the night paled towards dawn.

There was no key left in the car, so instead they tramped the southern road. Only once did Isabelle look back. At a conflux of roads, she stood in front of some dilapidated shopfront and saw, over her shoulder, the seven-pointed star fading as the nocturnal world beat its retreat. All across Paris, one city morphing into the next.

'Is she going to be OK, Doctor?'

Headlights were approaching through the gloom: a taxicab, looking for its final fare. The Senegalese put his fingers to his lips and let out a shrill whistle.

'There's nothing they can't do for her there. Keep her hydrated, fill her with antibiotics, keep the dressings changed. She has people who love her, doesn't she?'

Only the People, for the People, thought Isabelle bitterly.

'I was going to make her pancakes.'

The taxicab had pulled to the kerb some distance ahead. They hurried towards it now.

'He can't do it, can he? Put up a border, just like that?'

Dr Senghor said, 'My people keep to themselves as well. So do others. The thing you have to understand, Isabelle, is there aren't two cities in Paris. There are hundreds.'

Imagine the world, he said as the cab driver wound down his window. Imagine two Empires on two continents. There's order in that. Something to understand. But now look closer. In each of those Empires: nations. And in each of those nations: city states. Then ... look closer still. See the districts where the rich people live. The districts where the poor. See the places they touch and transform. Tiny worlds, all nestling inside one another, overlapping, touching, bleeding one into the next. Once, there were ghettos. Not any more. The world's too full for ghettos now. So instead we ourselves become the ghettos. We live on top of, in and around each other – easterners and westerners, northmen and south, rich men and poor men and all the infinite shades in between – and, instead of building walls, we just pick and choose which bits to see and which to neglect. So a city hosts a thousand different worlds, and they snake around each other, their atlases like the scribbling in a child's notebook. Geographies of madness.

Paris is no different from those two Empires. From a distance, it's all one. But look a little closer: here are worlds overlaid upon worlds, overlaid upon yet more worlds. Go smaller still ... Each family is a world of their own. Each household. A garden fence becomes a border between countries. The markings on every road, a new frontier. You don't need mountains and rivers to put up borders, not in this Modern World.

'No,' Dr Senghor went on, 'the only border you need is the one you imagine.'

'But Hayk's border, it's not real ...'

Dr Senghor shook his head. 'Isabelle, you haven't been listening. Imagination *is* what's real.'

By now, they had reached the waiting cab.

'I thought it was going to be different. You were there, weren't you, on the Night of Seven Stars? How do you go from that, to this ... Paris New Resistance?'

'Oh, Isabelle,' Dr Senghor said softly as he helped her into the cab, 'don't you know this yet? Everyone's heart goes out to a refugee – until they have to look him square in the face, day after day.' He stopped. 'Look after yourself, Isabelle. And look to the child within you, always. That's what matters to you, now.'

The taxicab was coursing down the barren Boulevard de Sébastopol, night still clinging on above the rooftops, when the driver checked his mirror and said, 'You want to look after yourself, love. This is no hour to be out, not in your condition. What, thrown you out, has he?'

Isabelle said, 'No, nothing like that.'

'There are brutes who'll do that, you know. It won't matter to them that the child's their own flesh and blood. They'll just up and run, and all on account of her having burned the dinner, or talked to another man too often at the bus stop. Yeah, you mark my words, he's no good for you, if he's that sort. Now, I've got two children, and them I barely see, all on account of me driving this cab. But ...'

Isabelle had started to let the words wash over her, for weariness was coming to whisk her away, but something compelled her to pay attention again. Everyone's living in a different world, she thought. All of us in a whirlpool, choosing what to look at, choosing what not to hear. So she listened to the cab driver's tale of his beautiful wife and their not-quite-beautiful children ('That's my fault, I'm afraid') until they reached the boulevard's end, and came finally to the river.

The bridge took them out onto the Île de la Cité, deep into the shadows of Notre-Dame.

They were still in the glow of the cathedral when the world shifted on its axis.

'We're not moving,' Isabelle said, scouring the window glass. 'Why aren't we …?'

The driver could feel it too. In the rear-view mirror, Isabelle saw the horror light up his eyes. She saw him wrench at the steering wheel, heard the roar of the engine as he pushed his foot on the accelerator; but, though the car vibrated around them, the world had stopped flickering by the window. There was Notre-Dame, standing as close and imperious as it had moments ago, and moments before that. But the car they were in: just spinning on the spot.

Isabelle dared to look up. By the Stars, she thought, Notre-Dame had never glittered like this, not even on the most starlit of summer nights.

She saw it blossom.

Trees erupted from its highest turrets. Vines tumbled out of the cracks in the stone. The great stone flower in its face had become a flower of such light that it seemed a star had been brought down to Earth. She counted its points: *one, two, three …*

It was happening before her eyes. Something let out a jubilant call, and an eagle with feathers of flame soared out of the cathedral's northernmost belfry.

Four … five … six …

The bells began to toll, but this was not the counting of the hours. It took only seconds for Isabelle to recognise the music they were making. Simple and joyful: the music of the old country.

Seven.

She craned her head out of the window. The rush of air against her face told her that something was still moving. It could not possibly be the car, because Notre-Dame remained above, ringed in myriad colours. But somehow the wheels beneath them were spinning.

They *were* still moving, she realised. But the rest of the world was moving too.

The riverside, which they had left only moments ago, was receding. The riverside, to which they were heading, was receding further still. The world was being stretched out of proportion, rejigged and rewritten. Waters surged into the abyss the parting riverbanks made, broiled up and frothed and raged. The waves of noise were like an ocean in the frenzy of a storm.

Then, in a second, they were silent.

Calmness restored.

The car lurched forward.

Caught unaware, the driver wrestled it back to the bridge. Slammed back into her seat, Isabelle looked through the mist forming on the rear window. The buildings on the riverbank appeared untouched. No earthquake had brought them down. No tremors had moved through them. The city had simply grown, reordering itself around the edges. The world went on.

The taxicab burst over the edge of the island, out over the water again. The next bank seemed a dozen furlongs away, and receding further still. We're not crossing the Seine, Isabelle realised. We're crossing the landlocked sea.

'By God,' the driver said, 'what's happening?'

And Isabelle thought: it's Hayk's border going up …

The magic being wrought, all over again.

She looked out upon the ocean, and now she could see sailing ships bobbing along its shores. The wide, ramshackle jetty with its moorings, and inclines of rippling sapphire reeds that rose to the boulevards above. All of it, there where there had once been open sky. As the car burst off the end of the bridge, she looked back. The waters were not inky and black, but nor was it merely the reflected light of the stars that they caught and crystallised beneath. Great golden shoals were moving through the elongated river. Sometimes they arced up, cresting the surface, and then vanished again, back into the depths. What had Levon called them? The bakhtat, she thought. Extinct through the centuries, and now ...

The People were being drawn down to the shoreline. Some of them were already on the boats, looking up in wonder at the sails that filled with wind, begging to be taken out. Water dogs, scenting the changing of the world, had given up their urban heartland and started coursing towards the sea, gills aching for the taste of its depths. As the taxi disappeared into the buildings of its southern side, Isabelle saw them lolloping through the streets.

'What was that?' the driver gasped, straining to control himself, just as he'd strained to control the car. 'What did we ...'

She reached out, put a hand on his shoulder. 'We were in the eye of it,' she said. 'But we're OK.'

'No, no,' he stammered, 'this isn't OK. But it's our own fault. We'd have seen it coming, if we weren't so blind. That's what being good does to you, isn't it? It blinds you. It was there all along, if only any of those blinkered idiots in the mayor's office had dared to see. How could you put your trust in people like that? Like vampires, living at night!' He paused, shaking his head. 'And by God, we invited them in!'

By the time the cab deposited her in the crescent outside M. Chabon's house, daylight was stealing out into the world. It was only a short walk from here. Isabelle retraced the steps she'd taken on that midwinter night, until at last she stood in front of her father's house.

She knocked on the door.

It was Adaline who answered. She appeared some moments later, dressed in her smartest blazer, ready for a day ruling over her unruly class.

'I'm sorry, Adaline. Is Hector here?'

There he was, in the darkness of the hall, struggling his feet into his boots with as much grace as a two-year-old tasked with getting himself dressed for the very first time.

'Isabelle?' he ventured.

There stood Isabelle, as tired as if she'd crossed continents herself. And it occurred to her, then, that she'd come just as far. The shoes she was walking in might not have tramped three thousand miles – but, though she knew not how, they had carried her from one world into the next.

'Hector,' she said. 'Dad,' she whispered, with a hand on her belly. 'I need a place to stay.'

13

* *

THE DECREES OF THE NIGHT

She opened her eyes to the unfamiliar dark.

Mouth parched, body knotted, Isabelle saw the digital lights of the clock on the wall. Midnight had not come, and this was the most sinking feeling of all. She reached for the bedside lamp and sent the glass of water that had been sitting there spinning to the floor.

The baby was straining inside her. Evidently, he still lived in Paris-by-Starlight, even while Isabelle was in exile. But it was not the baby that had woken her. There was shouting, rising up from below. Two bitter voices trading blows.

Something was squeezing her insides. As she turned her head to the voices, two hands closed their fists inside her, and there was nothing she could do but breathe. Two weeks she'd slept in this room, pretending this was home, and in those weeks she'd swollen further still. The nightdress she was wearing clung too tightly. Her body rearranged itself each time that she slept. All of her organs, bruised and out of place. But there were still two months to go, and these pains – just phantoms of what was to come – came and went. It helped if she stood and walked in circles, so she did that now, tramping to the door.

It wasn't just voices from below. There was music too. Hector liked to play her old harp, as if it still belonged to him. He tinkled with it even as Adaline screamed.

'They'll be fighting about us again, little one,' she whispered to the second heart beating inside her.

The baby turned a somersault in reply.

'You'll be too big for that soon.' When he turned, she could see tiny hands, tiny feet, making ridges in her flesh – like the dorsal fin of a shark, warning of its approach. 'We'll be gone soon. As soon as your father's ready, we're going to find a way.'

She opened the door, so that a sliver of light spilled in. The voices were stronger now.

'*Put it down, Hector.*'

That voice: shrill and slurred.

The music went on. She was just like him, Isabelle thought: picking out the simple refrains was centring him, bringing him quietude even as Adaline sniped.

'*You're not taking this seriously. What do I have to do make you take this seriously?*'

'*I'm listening to you, Adaline.*'

'*Haven't you thought about what happens next? That's always been your problem – you never think about what happens next …*'

Isabelle rubbed her belly and whispered, 'She has that right, at least. That's your grandfather all over.'

'*What happens when the baby comes? We can't have a baby here, Hector.*'

'*Why not?*'

'*You didn't even think to ask me, did you? Sixteen years we've been together. Who pays for this house? And you didn't even think to—*'

The music stopped.

'*Adaline, she's my daughter. What would you have me do?*'

This she hadn't expected. She drew back from the door – yet, try as she might, her fingers refused to let go of the handle. She imagined him on his feet, staring at Adaline, defiant. *She's my daughter. I left her once. I won't do it again.* All those nights she'd lain awake in far-flung Saint-André, with its terracotta rooftops and cracked, baked roads. Imagining that he'd turn up. Imagining that he'd say those very things. By the Stars (she caught herself using the words, remembered the sneering disbelief on Hayk's features), this was foolish. She wasn't a child. She was to become a mother herself.

And yet where was her own child's father?

Ten miles away, in another world.

'*Well, I'll say this – if you were half as interested in your son as you are in your daughter, maybe we'd know where he is tonight. If you spent half the time you do with these instruments with our Alexandre, maybe his schoolwork wouldn't be in the state it—*'

'*Oh, Adaline, by God! It's schoolwork. When did schoolwork mean a thing?*'

'*Yes, well, a man who collects refuse for a living would have to think like this . . .*'

Isabelle recoiled.

'*The house is too full, Hector. That – that's why Alex isn't here, and you know it! And I . . . I don't like these friends of his . . .*'

There was silence. Then: the tinkling of the lyre again, as Hector retreated into the music.

'*Do you know,*' he said over the arpeggiated chords, '*I never once complained that the house might be too full when your father came to stay. I never once said it, though I know what he thinks of me. Me, a refuse collector, and him with his glory days of Resistance.*'

'*Our son, Hector. Out at night. And you don't even care.*'

Adaline's voice had grown softer.

'*Hector, do you even love me any more? You haven't said it in months.*'

Silence, everlasting.

'*Hector, don't you see it? I'm scared.*'

After that, though the voices continued, Isabelle made out not a word. Closing the door, she tramped back across the squelching lambswool rug, then pulled back the curtain so that she could gaze out into the night. The house along Rue Alfred was not visible from here – but, if she craned her head out, she could see the halo of its glow, through a gap in the buildings. Sometimes, she saw fat bumblebees, dripping with sapphire pollen, sailing giddily over the gardens. Sometimes a lightjar flittered into sight, and she would follow its foraging with her eyes.

But that was another world, one that, by the dictums of its people, she was no longer permitted to see.

*

See the River Seine ...

After midnight, its harbours teemed with life. People thronged the wharfsides, where fresh night gardens had burst into colour, to see the ancient fishing vessels turn their sails to the wind. Packs of water dogs gathered on the Île de la Cité, where emerald reeds vied for dominance with sapphire and bronze – one moment coursing off into the waters to follow the boats, the next returning to shore to explore the forest that deluged the cathedral. The night markets no longer moved across Paris-by-Starlight, for the very moment the sun went down, the bazaars opened here, bringing noise and laughter, fire and story, back to the shores of the landlocked sea.

But, if you truly wanted to see splendours of this seascape that we once called the Seine, you would come to its shoreline just before dawn. There, when the People returned from their voyages and hauled in their nets, every new jetty was piled high with the shimmering radiance of their nightly catch. The golden fish of the old country, restored to the world.

Midnight on the south bank. Alexandre and Étienne emerged from the Métro at Saint-Michel and saw the rainbows erupting out of Notre-Dame. The Métro had been empty, rattling along with barely a Parisian soul in its carriages – and this, now, was the story of every night. Tonight, Alexandre knew why. The wind that hit him in the face was full of the spray of the sea. The air around him throbbed with that language he had never been able to understand. A single motorcar rolled past, flowers-by-night bursting out of its bonnet, and trailing behind it a barrow over-flowing with their golden fish. 'Bound for another of their markets,' Étienne uttered as he urged Alexandre into the shadows, while a pack of water dogs cantered past, rising and falling through rippling ruby reeds.

They followed the shoreline at a distance, sticking to the shelter of the Parisian buildings. Somewhere, out there, other Parisians must have been abroad, but those foolish enough to step out at night did not venture down to the landlocked sea. 'So keep your mouth shut,' said Étienne. 'We don't want to get noticed. Not when you're about to meet him …'

Turning from the shoreline, they disappeared between the ramshackle hotels of the old town. Most of Paris was keeping its shutters closed tonight. The face of every apartment, every shop-front, every hotel remained pitch black – all except for one.

The Hôtel Hugo had a grille across its doors, but lights still glimmered in its basement bar. From the street, narrow stone steps, down which barrels had once been rolled, led below. Étienne cajoled Alexandre to go first, down into the buzzing electric light.

Only a few souls remained in the bar. A middle-aged man had propped himself at the counter. In alcoves, other stragglers sat. The place was ripe with the smell of old spillages, wine worked deep into the woodwork that panelled the room.

'There,' said Étienne, compelling Alexandre towards one of the alcoves.

Here, Lucien was waiting.

The blond boy had cropped his hair in the weeks since Alexandre last saw him. In the shadowy vault he sat facing a man some years his senior, whose own head was shaven so closely that it had the appearance of a hard-boiled egg.

A Tricolore flag was pinned to the wall above them, so vast that it drew every eye in the room.

Étienne grabbed Lucien's hand as he sat down, then began helping himself to the olives on the table – but, hesitant to step within, Alexandre remained outside the alcove. The older man's eyes were appraising him slowly.

'Alex,' Étienne said, 'meet Maxime. Maxime, stop looking at him like he was dredged out of the river. This one's good. He's already done you a service, hasn't he?'

Alexandre stiffened. Étienne said he should feel proud about the thing he'd already done in the name of the Paris New Resistance, but pride was such a difficult feeling to hold on to. The boys had never understood why he didn't like coming out to lay traps for water dogs. They didn't know why he got squeamish when they talked about ripping lightjars out of their nests. But there were other ways to prove your worth – and Alexandre knew things, impossible things, that neither Étienne nor any man here had a chance of knowing. Alexandre had connections to the People; it made them suspicious of him, but it made him valuable as well.

'Yeah, I remember what he did,' said Maxime. 'And it's good to put a face to a name. Helps to know he's one of us.'

'And he is, Maxime, he is!' Étienne turned to Alexandre. 'Look, Alex, go and order us some beers. Then, when you're back, Maxime here'll slide up, and you can set yourself down. How does that sound?'

It sounded like an order. It sounded like there was no other choice. And, by the way Étienne was glaring at him, it sounded like he ought to do it now – or else go back up there, into

Paris-by-Starlight, alone. Alexandre did not like the idea of that, so instead he did as he was told.

As he was waiting for the glowering barkeep to fill a tray, he risked a look back. Étienne was still pontificating about some matter of (seemingly) grave importance, while Lucien nodded sagely and Maxime breathed them silently in. Then, out of nowhere, the table between them had been cleared, and Étienne was clasping Maxime's hand, so that one might wrestle the other into submission. Maxime, whose forearms had three times Étienne's girth, had smashed Étienne's arm into the table three times by the time Alexandre had crossed the bar. A cigarette had been lit and, as Étienne nursed a sore hand, Alexandre shared the beers around.

'Well, sit yourself down, Alex.'

There was an inch of space alongside Maxime, and into this crevice Alexandre forced himself down. The man beside him barely gave way. His scent, of wine and sweet sweat.

Not for the first time, Alexandre wondered at where he was, what he'd done.

'Do you know what that is, boy?'

Maxime had pointed to the Tricolore up on the wall.

'Of course.'

'Well?'

'You don't need to trick him, Max.'

'That's why I'm sitting here, right now. Because not a soul tells me where I can and can't go, not in the city where I was born.'

Alexandre nodded. 'I know it.'

'See, Maxime. He's one of us. Found your people, haven't you, Alex? He's gone and *proved* that, hasn't he?'

'I guess,' said Maxime, 'I expected someone a bit ... bigger.'

'Brawn he doesn't have, but Alex has got brains.'

'So,' Maxime said, 'come to give us more information, has he? More news from the Other Side?'

'Not today, Maxime. Not quite. Well … go on, Alex!'

Étienne was kicking him under the table, and it was this that startled him into action. With Maxime's great thigh crushed up against him, it was difficult to force a hand into his pocket, but somehow he managed it. His hand came back clasping a long sleeve of leather. Setting it down on the table, he opened it up.

The three bronze medals inside were hanging from silk ribbons of alternating red and black, and on one of those ribbons a crinkled rosette.

'Resistance medals,' Étienne began. 'Well, it's what you're after, isn't it?'

That nobody spoke around the table was answer enough. This was not just silence, thought Alexandre. This was reverence.

'May I?'

Alexandre nodded. No sooner had he laid the medals back on the leather, one of them was in Maxime's hand. With the ribbon entwined between his fingers, he lifted his hand. For a time, he let the bronze disc dangle, then tipped it to the guttering candle. Where the flame caught it, letters glittered. '"Patria Non Immemor",' he read out loud. 'Do you know what that means, boys?'

At one side of the table, Étienne and Lucien shrugged – but, when Maxime opened his mouth, meaning to humiliate them with his knowledge, Alexandre piped up, 'It's Latin. "The nation does not forget."'

In the second that followed, Maxime seemed perfectly balanced between barracking Alexandre and taking him into his arms. In the end, he simply placed the medal around his neck, with a touch as delicate as a father. '"The nation does not forget."' He enunciated each word carefully, then flicked the dangling medal with his forefinger. 'Up there' – he pointed to the street above with practised disdain, '—they'd say the same thing.

Their old world, desperate to be remembered. Well, we have an old world too. Why shouldn't we remember, as well?'

'Paris New Resistance,' whispered Étienne – and Alexandre, seeing the order in his friend's eyes, did the same.

'And this,' said Maxime, 'a date, written the old way. The eighteenth of June 1940. Do you know why that date lives, boys? Well, do you?'

'Alexandre will,' said Étienne.

'It's when it began,' said Alexandre, growing braver now. There was, it seemed, a use for boys with booksmarts after all; to hell with Raphaël and Antonin, and everyone like them. There were still places where using your brain mattered. If Alexandre hadn't already proven that, he wouldn't be here right now. 'After we lost the Battle for France. There was a government in exile, and they made an address. M. de Gaulle said—'

'"Nothing is lost for France."' Maxime smiled, with the wistful air of a veteran soldier who had once heard the words being broadcast for real.

'"Has the last word been said? Must hope disappear? Is defeat final?"'

'"NO!"' Maxime joined in.

Alexandre was warming to it now. The words had become manifest in him, though he knew not from which book he had learned them. '"There are, in the world, all the means necessary to crush our enemies ... The flame of French resistance must not be extinguished ..."'

There was silence around the table.

'Well, come on, Maxime,' said Étienne, at last. 'Alex didn't bring you these for free, did he? Fair's fair.'

Maxime grunted, 'A Frenchman keeps his word.' Then he pulled out an envelope and dropped it onto the table.

Soon, Étienne had torn it open and, on inspecting its contents, looked directly at Alexandre. 'Well, this is nice and all, but ...'

'But what?'

Étienne rolled the envelope, fat with banknotes, back towards Maxime.

'It isn't what we come for, is it, Alex?'

Alexandre shook his head.

'See, we've already done good work. And we don't need money. We want to ... help. Again. After what we already done, it might be we could be of some use. So no, we don't want money. We just want in – but properly this time, Maxime. Not just kept on the outside, like before. Me and Alex, we're worth more.'

A certain calibre of man needs to drink as he ruminates. This, Maxime did. There were dregs left in the carafe, and these he swirled around his mouth, making sure he could taste every last vinegary drop.

'Can you get more?' he asked, lifting the other medals to the light.

Alexandre felt the sharp jab of Étienne's boot under the table again. 'Well, Alex?'

Alexandre looked, mutely, from Étienne to Lucien. Then, 'Yes,' he said. 'I even think I can get you a Liberation Cross. There aren't more than a thousand of those in the whole of France. They were for the real heroes. The ones who went down in history.' He lifted himself where he sat, filling out his breast. 'I'm just going to need a little more time.'

*

THE STARLIGHT PROCLAMATIONS
There are two Cities where once there was one

~

While the flowers-by-night shine, the People have dominion

~

When the flowers-by-night fade, the People will abide

~

In dusk and in dawn our paths may cross

~

But violent acts will be met with violent ends

~

FOR WE ARE THE PEOPLE, AND THE PEOPLE LOOK AFTER EACH OTHER

Isabelle was labouring to pull on her boots when Adaline's father appeared in the kitchen doorway, brandishing a newspaper in his hand. The old man might have been one of the People himself, so early did he rise each morning.

'You won't believe this.'

When he handed her the newspaper, she read the headline, folded it and handed it back.

'Alexandre's going to take me up to see the ruin they've made of Notre-Dame. It's my Reunion again tonight. They'll want to know. Well, listen to this ...' He unfurled the newspaper again and began to read.

'The editor is given to understand that every Parisian news sheet has received the same communication. The Starlight Proclamations appear to address all citizens of Paris, to define a border between those native to our fair city and those who were welcomed here as refugees. Few good people of Paris can have failed to be enchanted by the arrival of the People and the joy and wonder they have brought to our City of Lights. Indeed, it is scarcely six months since this newspaper celebrated, along with all others, the festival they call the "Night of Seven Stars". Yet these so-called "Starlight Proclamations" ...'

The rest, he could not read out loud. Where, at first, he'd been simmering, now the old man seemed given to rage. 'Well, I'll see it for myself – you see if I don't. It's been fifty years and more since there was curfew in this city. I'll not live under curfew again. Certainly not one thrown at me by these ingrate vagabonds ...'

The pain that took root in the small of Isabelle's back each night reached a new intensity as she bent to fasten the last buckle on her boots. By the Stars, she thought, this baby had to come out soon. 'Well,' she snapped over her shoulder, 'it's us "free French" who murdered one of them, isn't it? Who blinded a little girl – as if she hadn't been through enough. But that's not in the papers for you to bitch over, is it, Victor?'

With the last word, she looked at him directly – and saw, then, that Hector had appeared, hanging in the darkness halfway down the stairs. The old man, his face creased in indignation, brandished the newspaper like a baton.

'As if it isn't bad enough we have all these interlopers in the city, now there're interlopers in my own house. My own home, Hector!'

Hector wore the look of a small boy coming down to watch his morning cartoons and instead stumbling into some parental battle he did not understand. It would be just like him to say nothing, thought Isabelle. Anything, she thought, for a quiet life . . .

'That's a matter of perspective, Victor,' Hector said, reaching the bottom of the stairs. 'Why, six years ago, there was another interloper in this house. And now he struts around, acting like he's a native.' Victor's face, already flushed crimson, turned darker still. 'We've all got to live in this house, Victor. This is a family. So go and put another pot of coffee on, won't you? I can hardly get going this morning . . .'

After the old man had stuttered back into the kitchen, Hector came to her and said, 'I'll take you. I can sack off work.'

There was, Isabelle had to admit, a tiny fragment of her that would have welcomed that. But: 'Levon's going to be there,' she said. 'Hector, thank you.'

A thought struck her. Brushing past Hector, she strode into the kitchen – where Victor was manfully doing battle with the cafetière. The newspaper had been dumped on the table. She reached for it, only to find that the page had been ripped away. There it lay, a crumpled ball by the edge of the kitchen bin.

'THE STARLIGHT PROCLAMATIONS', she read as she straightened it out. Such innocent words, in the once upon a time . . .

The nurses were kind at the Hôpital Laribiosière. By the time they'd taken her bloods, and told her that the phantom contractions were normal, she felt as light as she'd done in days. Kind words: the very best medicine. She came out of the consulting room with a sugary drink in her hand – and there was Levon, pacing up and down as if it was fifty years in the past, and the day of the birth itself.

'I'm sorry,' he said, rushing to her (and spilling half of her drink in the process), 'I wanted to be here before, but the Nexus ...'

It was what they'd started calling the Hôtel Métropol, though Fae and the concierges had fought to resist it. The problem was: you didn't get to choose your own name.

'It's OK,' she said, taking his arm, 'you're no use here anyway. You'd be sitting in the corner of the room, averting your eyes.'

'But I wanted to be here.'

'I know,' she promised him. Every joke she attempted was fraught now; they hit raw nerves, or they exposed some weakness, when all she'd meant to do was make him laugh. Was it really possible that things could be lost in translation, between the day and the night? 'Everything's fine. I'm huge, but I could be huger. That's the headline.' She stopped. 'You're tired, Levon. Look at you.'

'It was a long night.'

'Are you sure you don't need to go ...?'

'Home?' said Levon. 'No, not yet. All we have is dusk and dawn.'

'Does your father—'

'He'll think I'm at the Nexus. I've been crashing there. Look, I can take us there. I have a room.'

'To the Métropol?' she exhaled, because such a thing was scarcely credible.

'They'll all be sleeping. Isabelle, there aren't barbed-wire fences – not yet. I don't have to cram you in the back of a truck. There's the tradesman's entrance. The back stair.'

The walk was not far, though Isabelle could feel her feet swelling further with each step. Paris-by-Day had already returned to full life, and grew busier with each passing boulevard.

'Mariam wanted to write to you, but she's been so busy with Arina. She wants to see you. She just doesn't know how. I guess she wants to say sorry. For that night in the block. She was frightened. She feels ashamed. That she should have ... stood up for you.'

'There are too many things to be frightened of,' said Isabelle.

They'd found a bench on one of the park edges and sat together now. Levon reached down to feel the movements of his child – but, exhausted by the morning's inspections, the baby slept on. It had, he reflected now, been weeks since he'd felt it flutter.

'Are you frightened of …?'

'Of giving birth? I should say so. But, Levon, it's what comes after that frightens me more.'

'We're going to find a way.'

'I know it.'

'I didn't plan for any of this.'

She rolled her eyes. The future was always accidental. She was learning that fast.

'And Arina? Is she …?'

'She's out of bed,' Levon said. 'Mariam takes her to the night garden. There are sounds and smells and she still wants to learn. Gilly sits with her. But Isabelle, if you could see the night garden now …'

It was flourishing, he said. They'd come and upended it, slopped their slogans across the wall and ground lightjars to glitter under their heels – but, on the night that Hayk had cast her out, the garden had burst forth, as untamed and unexpected as what had happened down on the Seine. 'You'd hardly know it was a rooftop at all. I swear: you could wander for miles. All time and space, out of joint. We had to cut down some foliage where it was growing too wild. There we were, scything back sapphire and emerald vines – and, right there, there in the middle of the roof, the hulk of some sailing ship, as if it had been sitting there since the elder days. A great carved serpent at its prow, and everywhere mosses and lichens and shining barbed thistles. Hayk found the ruins of some stone anchorage, even deeper in. The kind of place the Star Sailors used to go …'

There was a time, not long ago, that the wonder of it would have brought Isabelle such joy. Now, she just said, 'And Arina won't see any of it.'

'She knows it's there. There's magic in that.'

'This Milena, are you sure she knows what she's—'

Isabelle felt Levon's hand grow tense in hers. Then, quickly, he snatched it back. 'By the Stars, Isabelle, of course I'm sure. She's a doctor. She studied and trained, just like any doctor in the rest of the world. The People did live in the twentieth century. She's not a witch doctor.'

His voice had risen to a pitch, but now it died down again.

'I'm sorry,' he breathed, hands beating at his thighs.

'I didn't mean to say ...'

'I know.'

'Your own bebia had us rushing around for ingredients from the Nocturne. Tariel and his tincture.'

'I'm tired,' he said. 'I haven't slept properly, not since you left. Isabelle, if you only felt what's happening at the block. You wouldn't think there were as many men like Hayk in the whole of Paris-by-Starlight, but somehow he seems to find them. Those Parisians came back, trying to trap lightjars. Hayk's men, his Faithful Three, sent them on their way with broken ribs and black eyes.'

Isabelle held him. 'You need to rest. *I* need you to rest.'

He nodded, regathering his composure. 'How long have you got?'

'Three weeks, they're saying. But it could come any time.'

Three weeks could be an aeon in Paris-by-Starlight. Who knew what the nocturnal world might look like then?

'I need you, Levon. I need you thinking straight. And ... I need you with me.'

His hand was softly retaking hers. 'Let me take you to the hotel.'

The scents in the Hôtel Métropol were almost tropical in their intensity. The scent of nectar, the mineral tang of the waters that flowed in the Khanate Beneath, the different notes in the sweetness that, by instinct, she could identify as sapphire, as diamond, as amber or emerald; all of this wrapped itself round her as Levon helped her in.

The room he'd taken was small, but lit in fire by the vermilion flowers-by-night that grew on the ledge. In here, blackout blinds shut out the day. Levon went straight to the chipped sink to douse his face in water.

'Lie down,' she said.

They went, together, to the bed.

'We've been clearing out the Khanate Beneath. Driving every last trace of Paris-By-Day out of it. M. Fortier's still out of town. When he gets back and realises what we've done ...'

Isabelle thought: By the time M. Fortier gets back, we'll likely have other things to think about. But she did not say a word.

'I'm sorry,' he said, 'I'm letting you down. Has your father ... I mean to say, has he been good to you?'

'Better than I'd thought.'

'That's good.'

He was already closing his eyes, but as dreaming pulled him in, he hit a moment of lucidity, and clawed his way back out.

'I wanted to be with you, just for a few hours.'

So she lay beside him and, with the child sandwiched between them, started stroking his hair.

'We'll make it work, Isabelle. Things have to change ... and they might.'

She said, 'You will be there when it happens, won't you?'

The very fact she had to ask startled him into wakefulness. He propped himself up. 'It's like we said. You'll put in a call to the hotel desk. They'll find me, wherever I am. I'll come running.' There was a silence between them; to Isabelle, it seemed to be swelling around them, just the same as the landlocked sea had swollen around Notre-Dame. 'Don't doubt it, Isabelle. I'm not my father. I'm not yours.'

She wanted to believe that, and part of her did. It was the other part that she hated. The part that was prodding at it, looking for weaknesses, daring it not to be true.

'So why not make the crossing? Come and live by day. You did it once.'

'Oh, Isabelle, you know I can't.'

He meant to go on, but every sentence was stillborn. Others remained half finished, too wearied to reach their peaks. Even when he completed one, it didn't reach her, just curled around in the air and dropped, dead, onto the bedsheets.

'Because of Arina,' Levon said, at last. 'How could I—'

'And the rest of them too.'

Levon nodded. 'It's my world, isn't it? I couldn't just walk out on it. Isabelle, I brought them—'

'Yes, I know,' she said, in a tone she would later despise, 'three thousand miles. But it's our baby, Levon. How can we not be together for our baby?'

He could have spent the night explaining, and none of it would have mattered. She remembered how she'd first felt on seeing their written language. All those sentences carved in spirals, intercutting each other; how could anyone make sense of a language like that? How, when every sentence intersected with the rest? It was like that, in the hotel, right now.

'I used to think I could separate myself from the old country. Then I learned I couldn't. If I just forsook it now . . .' He stopped; down this way lay another argument, so he took another passage. 'It's going to work out.'

'I saw his Starlight Proclamations.' She pulled out the crinkled newspaper page. 'In the Nocturne, they were just wedding vows, weren't they? But he changed it. Turned it to a battle cry.'

'He thought it sounded like a declaration. The sort the people in Paris-by-Day might listen to.'

'"But violent acts will be met with violent ends",' she read.

'He wrote that for Arina.'

It was Isabelle's turn to start shaking now. 'I'm never coming back, am I? How could there ever be space for me in a world like that?'

'I don't know,' Levon conceded, 'but it doesn't change anything for us, does it? Well, how can it? I still love you. You still love me. We'll be the twilight people. We'll have dawn and dusk. Just the three of us. Still a family, even if we are on two different sides of the world.'

They lay down together and each in turn closed their eyes.

After some time, Isabelle whispered, 'Next time, I'll meet you at night. There's a family of the People on Rue Alfred, near where my father lives. I can meet you there, Levon. They'll want to help. A quiet place, just for the two of us. The three . . .'

She wanted to say more, but on her shoulder Levon was already asleep.

*

On a dark Créteil night, while the radio buzzed with talk of the Starlight Proclamations, Hector looked out upon the moonlit street. Not for them the incandescence of the old town, where the ships set sail each night – but, according to the newsreader and his guests, it wouldn't be long. Water dogs had been sighted roaming from Saint-Denis to Ivry-sur-Seine. The nocturne bakhtat were driven wherever the waters took them. The People themselves were setting out from the old town too. Wherever they told the stories of the Nocturne, the old world would follow . . .

A pair of aquamarine lightjars were feeding each other in the boughs of one of the trees out on the avenue – and there she stood, wrapped in the shawl he'd dug out of the trunk at the end of his bed, the very same one she'd been wrapped in as a baby. His eyes had been on her for an hour already.

Adaline turned in the bed behind him, heaving the blankets up and over her eyes.

'Just go down to her,' she said, muffled by the blanket.

Hector still hovered there.

'Hector, *please.*'

'I'm sorry,' he said, 'I didn't mean to wake you.'

'Wake me? I haven't slept a wink. I can practically hear you thinking.' Giving up on hiding herself away, she propped herself up and reached for the light. 'Hector, *darling*, she survived seventeen years without a whisper from you. I'm quite sure she can—'

Hector turned on the spot, marched past the bed, had almost reached the door before the urge to snipe back overpowered him. 'What can you hear me thinking now, Adaline?' Then he clattered down the stairs and out into the night.

'Isabelle,' he said, approaching slowly from behind. 'Issy. Come inside. I can make cocoa.'

She had her arms around herself, resting upon the bump in her belly, standing crookedly as her body redistributed the weight.

'What hour is it?'

'It's late.'

She set off up the road, towards the house where the flowers-by-night grew rampant – but she did not stray far. 'He's not coming tonight, is he?'

Hector cautioned himself before he breathed another word. There were no words of wisdom that he had any right to proffer, so instead he said, 'Come inside. If he comes, he'll know which door …'

It was the ache in her feet that made up her mind. Her body was bored of this now, putting up every protest it could muster.

Inside, Hector was true to his promise. Soon, they were sitting together in the salon with mugs of scalding chocolate, thick with brown sugar. She hadn't remembered it until that very moment, but this was how he'd made it when she was tiny. She could picture it smeared in a thick brown smile around her lips. The simple, giddy joy of it.

While she was drinking, Hector had brought the flower-by-night from the kitchen and placed it in the front window. 'So he might see,' he told her, and Isabelle – damning whatever cocktail of hormones was pumping through her body – felt the tears prickle in her eyes as she whispered her thanks.

She had drifted to the window, still finishing the sickly chocolate, when she heard a tinkling behind her and looked back to see that Hector was gently fingering the lyre that he'd made. He'd produced her harp as well. 'I'll wait up with you,' he said, and his fingers began to pick out one of the old canticles. Charlemagne songs, he'd once called them. 'To pass the time?'

It wasn't just Hector's eyes that were asking her to pick up the harp. The harp was practically asking her too. But, 'I don't want to be the Rose of the Evening tonight,' she said. She was thinking about the empty stage in Le Tangiers, the smoke and the ruin.

'Not the Rose,' Hector said. His fingers moved from the rising canticle to another familiar refrain: one of the lullabies of old. Then – yes, she was quite certain of it – the theme tunes from the cartoons he'd watched with her every Saturday morning. Dogs as musketeers, the Happy Things that lived in the old witch's cellar, lonesome knitted mice who made their home on the moon. 'We have music of our own, don't we? Could be some of that deserves to come back too. Well, couldn't it?'

She picked up the harp. The runs came easily to her fingers, more easily than she'd thought. She watched Hector's fingers, and soon she'd found the melodies that ran counter to his own. The music happened somewhere between them, in the middle of the room. Perhaps it did not bring back the rolling starscapes of some elder world. But it brought back Saturday mornings, sitting snugly in the crook of her father's arm with the taste of a contraband hot chocolate still on her lips, and for the first time she did not feel bad that this was exactly what she wanted.

She would have stayed there all night – but some time later, she knew not when, footsteps clattered in the yard outside, a hand scratched at the door, and when Hector broke off, the music disintegrated around her.

'I'll let him in,' Hector said as he watched her strain to get up. 'See, Isabelle, he was coming all along ...'

Ten miles away, two hours ago, Levon burst out of the Hôtel Métropol.

He'd set out too late. He knew that already. But the tumult in the Khanate Beneath had been going on for weeks, and he'd been swept up in it tonight. The chasm into the Greater Dark, that labyrinth even deeper than the Khanate Beneath, had opened its maw on the night Hayk issued his Starlight Proclamations – and now, as yet more passageways and staircases appeared, the wonder had turned to panic amongst the People. Some said they heard voices. 'They whisper at night,' somebody had said. 'They're tempting us down. We haven't been paying attention to the Nocturne. The Khanate Beneath, it's always been a land for the dead.' Ghosts, they said. There are ghosts down there. 'It's where Endless Night was born.' But there was life down there too. If you hovered at the top of those new staircases, you could hear the beating of wings. Things slithered. Mushrooms as big as a man glowed in iridescent shades. And, 'How deep does it go?' some of the foolhardy young men had started to ask. 'Didn't adventurers travel into the land of the dead in the old times? Well, we can be adventurers too. Just think of the treasures we'll find! The romances we'll have ...'

As if this tumult wasn't enough, Levon had emerged through the wine cellar tonight to hear one of the local guests remonstrating with the reception girl Fae. It was after midnight, she already ought to have been off shift – but the man had fixed her in place and was thundering, indignant, across the counter. 'Holy God, woman, what did you think I brought my family to Paris for? This is the new wonder of the world. It's why I've come to your stinking little cesspit of a hotel, and not the Shangri-La!' He hadn't been the only one in the days and weeks since the Proclamation. Levon had explained, vainly, to a hundred men and more. Tonight was just one more – but, by the time he was through, midnight had long since faded away and Créteil seemed much further than ten miles.

He took the hotel car – M. Fortier was still in foreign climes – and made to cross the river at Notre-Dame. The shores seemed to recede further the more strongly the stars shone down, the cathedral island isolated in the middle of the waters. Tonight, you could see the pull of the moon on the waters' edge. A pack of water dogs had come up, dripping, from the deep and lounged around on a sandbank where the sapphire reeds had gone to seed. Glow-worms poked their sightless faces out of the sand, then disappeared beneath.

From the bridge, Levon could see the ships coming back in. Though Isabelle had not left his thoughts (how could she? he had to keep reminding himself), he felt himself easing off the accelerator, allowing the car to crawl into the cathedral's radiant pool. Here, he wound down the window to the play of light. Three ships were returning to the jetties, the masts of each wreathed in vines – and, at the head of them all, his father's vessel. He'd called her the *Return of Night*. Even from this distance, Levon could see the way her decks glowed with the metallic light of their catch: like a miniature mountain range of molten gold. There, silhouetted against the catch, was Hayk himself. He stood at the prow, directing his quartermaster at the wheel, staring proudly – jubilantly, perhaps – at the People on the wharf.

Levon brought the car to a halt.

Just a few minutes, he thought, no longer. Stepping out of the car, he propped himself at the railing at the edge of the road and stared out, dreamily, as the ships came home.

He remembered this. By the Stars, he remembered …

People said they hankered for a world that was gone, and Levon had always thought he'd known what that meant. Well, watching the ships coming in, he *knew* it. Because twenty years ago, he'd hauled himself up on a railing just like this. After dinner each evening, hurtling through the village down to the seafront, waiting for the ocean mists to part and the first ships to appear over the landlocked sea. Looking for his father at the prow of one of those ships, telling the other children who'd come to watch, 'There he is! My father, my father Hayk!' Daring to be the first to hail him as the ships reached the jetties. The thrill when he'd reach down and cuff him about the head, before drifting on with his shiphands for the night's drinking and playing cards.

His childhood, rushing through him – and, for the first time, he did not feel bad that this was exactly what he wanted. What it would be like, he thought, for his own son to see the ships coming in – and, with them, all the magic of the night …

He was still hanging there when an engine exploded with life, somewhere on the southern bank of the river. He looked that way, just in time to see a van appear on the shoreline. Its doors exploded outwards, and into the night tumbled a glut of men dressed in black. One, two, three – there were more, but how many he could not say. There were cries. There was shrieking. There was the barking of an order. Then the men were knee-deep in the banks of rainbow reeds that plunged down to the water, bringing their arms back to let whatever they were holding fly at the passing ships.

From where Levon stood, all he could see were tiny comets, the size of a fist, arcing out and over the water.

Then: the shattering of glass, as the comets struck home.

After that, everywhere was fire.

Isabelle heard a key turning in the lock, Hector's voice as the door drew back. She didn't know whether to be angry or relieved. Weariness had dulled the edges of both. 'At least he came,' she whispered to the baby as it turned inside her, 'and at least you're awake to hear him.'

Hector's voice, out in the hallway: 'Oh, it's … you.'

'Who else, Dad?'

Isabelle turned to the empty salon doorway. That voice: not Levon at all, only Alexandre. 'So much for that,' she whispered, and sat back.

'I didn't know you were—'

'I've been with Étienne.'

'Étienne.'

'Yes, Étienne.'

'Alexandre, please,' Hector sighed, 'you know your mother's worried. Out after dark, and in the old town, no doubt. By God, Alexandre, what you been drinking? You smell like turpentine.'

'Dad!' he laughed, and Isabelle heard him staggering around as he tried to take off his boots. 'I'm not a vagrant!'

Silence, out in the hall.

'You've got to be careful. Now more than ever. What, after these Starlight Proclamations—'

'That's just like you. You're such a coward, Dad. Starlight Proclamations? You always told me to stand up to bullies, didn't you? When Raphaël and Antonin used to come round here and …' His words petered away, as if he'd troubled even himself. 'Grandpa wouldn't have stood for it back in the old days, would he? People coming in and telling us where not to go and when

341

not to go there. And I'm not the only one who thinks it. The city isn't dead out there. Not everyone's hiding away. My friends, at least they're not …'

His voice was growing louder, and Isabelle saw him appear in the salon door. It had been three days since she'd last laid eyes on him; she hadn't known, until this moment, that he'd shaved his head. Those feral locks, which had imitated her own in everything but their tar-black colour, were gone. It changed, completely, the shape of his head.

'We were playing some of our old music,' Hector said, reappearing beside him – and, though he deigned to come and listen, he was asleep and snoring upon the chaise longue within moments. After that, there hardly seemed any point playing any music at all.

*

She'd called the Hôtel Métropol six times before the runners brought him to the phone. Three a.m. and she'd woken from some dream, aching in places she didn't know she could ache, desperate for it to be over – or just to have him there and be told it was going to be all right. By the Stars, she hated herself for it – what kind of a weakness was love? – but the closer she got, the more she wanted him near.

'I heard about the fires. I thought …'

'Isabelle, I'm sorry. I am. I was coming. I was on my way. And then …'

'Is everyone …?'

His faraway voice buzzed down the line. 'Hayk's quartermaster burned in the water.'

He tried to tell her more. Glass bottles, filled with petrol and stuffed with burning rags. They'd exploded all over the fishing boats. Flames had rushed up the mizzenmast of the first, turned the sails of each to sheets of raging orange. 'I don't know how many bottles they let fly. Ten. Twelve. One was enough. They were back in their van and gone within seconds. But Isabelle, the screaming on the wharf ...'

'And Hayk?'

'He's a survivor.' Levon paused. 'The flames took so quickly, Isabelle. Two of the ships were scuttled. Listen to me: everyone's frightened.'

'They're frightened here too.'

'I was going to come tonight, but I don't think I can. I'm heading back to the block, for the People ...' There came the crackle of static. Momentarily, Levon's voice evaporated, then re-formed again. '... patrolling the shoreline. After nightfall every night, volunteers he's found ...'

Isabelle remembered the last of the Starlight Proclamations:

'Violent acts, violent ends.'

'It's just to make the fishermen feel safe again. Just while this lasts.' There was noise behind him, other voices, somebody calling his name. 'Isabelle,' he said, distracted, distant, despairing, 'I miss you.'

'I know it.'

'And I'm going to be there soon. Are you ...?'

She held the receiver near. 'I'm close, Levon.'

'Just stay the course. Please. And look to me in your night garden. I'll be there this time, I promise.'

*

But he wasn't.

This time, he called. When Isabelle cupped the receiver to her ear, she heard him frantic down the line. 'He wants us all down on the river, for when the ships come in. A show, he said.'

'Then tell him no. What made him the—'

'I can't. If he casts me out ...' He stopped. 'I can't leave them all, not when this is happening.'

'Levon, it's been days. Weeks. And here I am, on my own.'

'I know,' he said. 'By the Stars, I know. Tomorrow, Isabelle. I promise – tomorrow.'

Tomorrow didn't come. Nor did the next day. And though there were hours when they spoke, and times when they even dared to dream, each night the abyss opened wider; each night, the landlocked sea grew a little broader, a little deeper in the heart of Paris – rearranging the city streets around it, so that, by the time morning came, the only real sign that the world had changed was that the sweethearts who parted ways on the bridges still spanning the water, and gazed back at each other from the opposite shore, had to work a little bit harder, squint a little bit deeper, to know that their lovers were still there at all.

On the seventh night, he appeared.

She'd taken to pottering in the night garden on Rue Alfred, where the old couple, Russ and Ashkhen, had nervously shown her their grotto. In truth, they'd been suspicious of the French girl who kept wandering past their gate, watching the moon moths that turned their bewildering pirouettes up above. It was the baby they'd taken pity on. They'd had babies, too, in the once upon a time. Isabelle asked no more about it, and instead found joy in the story of two old lovers who'd crossed the world, and wanted only their quiet corner of it in which to die. 'On the same day, if you please,' they'd both said. And Isabelle thought: So there is enduring love – but where's mine?

He came in the second hour after midnight.

She'd never seen him with stubble before. It hardened his face, changing its edges, occluding his smile. One moment she was alone in the garden while Russ and Ashkhen clipped the flowers-by-night; the next, he was there, with his hands stuffed into his pockets and eyes circled in exhaustion.

'You look awful, Levon.'

This, at least, provoked a smile. 'You look ... huge.'

He put his arms around her. She wanted to melt into it, but that did not feel right. She told herself that her body was the wrong shape, now. It didn't fit him any longer. At least his scent was the same. She breathed in and, by degrees, started to feel like she was at home.

'Levon, I missed you. I miss you, right now.'

'I'm here.'

She nodded. There was a place beneath the flame fruit trees, and they sat in its hearthfire light together.

She had seen him tired before, but this was the weariness of ages. 'Have there been more ...?'

Levon shook his head. 'Nothing like that. But ...' He didn't want to speak about it, but there were things he wanted to show her. He'd brought a satchel with him, and he opened it on the ground. In its pool sat flowers-by-night whose petals were marked with elaborate designs, their veins forming an infinite tessellation of seven-pointed stars. 'They grow in fervour every night – ever since my father's Proclamations. It's intensifying.'

It was beautiful. There was no denying that. Isabelle cupped one and lets its residual glow wash over her face. The smell of its nectar was divine. Of cinnamon and brown sugar.

'What do you think your bebia would have made of all this?'

'I don't know.'

'She wouldn't recognise it, Levon.'

Levon said, sadly, 'I think she'd have been ashamed.'

Isabelle nodded.

'She wouldn't have exiled you, not for all the magic in the world. She loved you, Isabelle.'

Love, love, love, thought Isabelle – and tried not to say it out loud, for fear of chiding him too far. But what did love matter in a divided world? There were practicalities more pressing than love to attend to. It was love, thought Isabelle, that drove Hayk to his Starlight Proclamations. It was love, she thought, that drove men down to the river with Molotov cocktails in hand. Love that made her father open his home to her, even though it built a border between him and his wife. Making decisions on love only ended in disaster. And yet ...

'Levon, I want to come home.'

He nodded, fiercely, uncontrolled. 'I want that too. Because ... it isn't home, Isabelle, not unless you're there. There's colour all around – but there's no ... light. It's like we never arrived at all. It's like we're still out there, striving to get here. Oh, they all *say* they're feeling safe. Now that there are Starlight Proclamations and rules and orders – but it doesn't take much, just a wrong word, before you start seeing the cracks in it. Because, if you really did feel safe, why would you need Starlight Proclamations at all? If you really did feel safe, why do you need to look the other way, pretend Paris-by-Day doesn't even exist? As soon as you start thinking like that, you can't get it off you. Safety's only skin deep. The Starlight Proclamations breed fear, just the same as this Paris New Resistance. I can feel it, all over Paris-by-Starlight.'

Isabelle said, 'Except here.'

'What?'

'Russ and Ashkhen,' she said, and as if on cue the old couple appeared around the corner of their house, secateurs in hand. 'A quiet little corner of the world, just for them. That's what I want for us.'

There was silence as the old couple drifted on.

'I didn't want to come here and turn it over, have another conversation about what we're going to do. I wanted to come and look on you. I want the scent of you. Just to sit in it, with you, and remember.'

'I have to think about the future, Levon.' Her hands were on her belly. 'You're fractured. You're in fragments. None of this is your fault. But what happens next, surely that's up to us?'

'Well, what does happen next?' he said, with more fear than Isabelle had anticipated. 'What happens when they come with fire bombs again? Or throw fireworks into another wedding? What happens to Paris-by-Starlight when they march up to the block – *our* block, Isabelle – with pitchforks and torches and start smoking us out? Laying poison like they would to any other vermin. Because that's what they think of us, isn't it? Vermin, corrupting their city. What happens then, if I've left Paris-by-Starlight far behind? And Aunt Mariam and Aram, and Arina. My whole People. My world.'

'Can I say something?'

Levon's face creased up in confusion. He said, 'You've never asked permission before.'

'You're not a ship to carry their lives. You can do what's right for you as well.'

His face had been bewildered, but as he listened to her, its lines hardened. She thought, for a moment, that he looked like Hayk. Well, she thought – picturing her own father's face next to hers – there was blood in it.

'That's fair, Isabelle. That's kind.' He started threading his fingers together, then unthreading them, over and over and over again. 'That's just the way someone from Paris-by-Day would talk. You *know* what I did for them. You *know* how much we did, just to get here. We didn't do it to ditch each other at the other end. How could I give up on them now? I couldn't. Not without just shredding myself to pieces first. How could I be me if I—'

'We're having a baby.'

He said, 'I'm going to be there for the baby.'

'I've been living to see you. But my days and nights, they're all out of sync. I go to sleep, knowing you're rising. I stay up into the small hours, as long as I can last, just to know I'm in the same city as you, just to make me think the three of us are one. I come down here, just to breathe it in. It makes me think I'm still next to you. By the Stars, I never used to be this way. I left everything in Saint-André to come to Paris. I near broke my mother's heart, but that didn't matter to me. I knew what I wanted. And now ... You undo me. I can't feel my edges. It's like when I used to play, up on stage. I'd reach for something and it just wasn't there.'

There was silence.

'It shouldn't be like this.'

Isabelle lay back and stared up through the boughs of the tree. Where the canopy parted, she could see the seven-pointed star. It guided the People home, she thought – but, she had to remind herself, she wasn't of the People. The star wasn't for her.

Some truths were more terrible than others.

'I think we're going wrong.'

Levon lay back too. Through the boughs, he saw the same star – and oh, the feeling of strength that it gave him.

'Hayk unleashed something with his Starlight Proclamations. I didn't know it would go like this.'

It took some time for Isabelle to whisper, 'I didn't mean Paris-by-Starlight.'

Then, at last, Levon understood. 'What are we going to do?'

'Come away with me. Leave Paris-by-Starlight. Leave Paris-by-Day.'

It was like asking him to step out of his own skin. 'No,' he whispered.

'Then you have to talk to your father. I want to come back to the night.'

He might have made the same exclamation, but this time he held his tongue.

'I need somewhere to have my baby, Levon.'

'Our baby,' he whispered.

She wanted to tell him: hell is limbo. Hell is not knowing. Hell is having half your head in one world, and half in another. Every thought gets torn up. Every dream cut in two. A mind can't last long, balanced on such a narrow ledge. It has to fall, one way or another.

He rolled over, laid his head on the roundness of her belly. It was, he decided, like listening to the sea. In there: their child, the god beneath the waves.

'I love you,' he said. 'We can make this work. Dusk and dawn. Our own little tribe. The twilight People.'

Sometimes, though you say the same words, they don't mean the same thing. Their edges are dulled, or their points blunted – or else language itself has spiralled away from you (the spiralling language of the People, she thought). Words change meaning the moment they leave your lips; they become like winterlights, casting out seedpods and giving birth to lightjars – winterlights, except without the beauty.

'I love you too,' she told him.

'Every family has a world of their own, don't they? And the People – they make families however they can, however it works. That's what you do when the world falls apart.'

She did not know if he was trying to convince himself or convince her – or perhaps it was just a plea he was making, to two worlds that used to be one – but, after that, neither of them had the words to say anything at all. So they lay there together, and Isabelle slept upon his shoulder, and Levon stayed awake all the long night through, with his arms wrapped around her, their three hearts beating in syncopated time.

And in the morning, the world had moved on.

AN INTERLUDE

ONE NIGHT IN PARIS

See the small girl: she is waiting, as we all once waited, for her father to come home from work.

Esmé Caron spends her afternoons in the apartment downstairs, playing with Élodie and her bichon frise, waiting – just waiting – until her father saunters home from the Jardin des Tuileries. Each night he brings her a book, or a bear, or a paper parcel of the salt-water sudjukh that they sell in the night markets. Esmé loves the tastes of the 'old country'. She was allowed, last Christmas, to bring a box of their little honeyed pastries, with their molten glowing cores, into school. This summer, at the school fête, they told her these things were no longer allowed (it is a new school edict, and all on account of a parent's complaint), so to Esmé the sweet treats from the night market have become a marvel for bedtime alone.

But tonight, when the knock comes at the door, Esmé's father has not brought a paper parcel of salt-water snakes. He has brought a roll of black felt, a pot of black paint, masking tape and drawing pins and more. He gets down on one knee – 'I've missed you, *saucisson*' – and kisses Esmé over the top of the head, in perfect imitation of the way she kisses him at bedtime. Then, making his thanks to Élodie's mother (Esmé has sometimes wondered if her father might marry Élodie's mother one day; this, she thinks, would be a very fine thing), he takes Esmé by the hand and leads her above.

Teeth brushed, hair combed; Esmé is the very picture of a model child. Once she is dressed in her unicorn pyjamas, she waits on the end of the bed for her bedtime treat and stories. Her father, who seems wearied with work again tonight, takes some time to tramp through. Tonight, instead of a luminous wonder from the night market, there is only a plate of the macarons he used to make; instead of the copy of the Nocturne they've been reading, her father has dug up the old story he used to write for her alone – of the children who venture into their cellar and find another cellar beneath it, and another beneath that, a universe of wonders hidden beneath their ordinary house, filled with enchanted peoples and runaways; such a thing seemed fanciful, once.

'Papa?'

'One moment, *mon chaton*.'

He disappears momentarily, and when he returns, he is carrying the roll of black felt, the paint, a pair of kitchen scissors. He kisses her on the cheek. Then he begins.

At first, Esmé does not understand. She watches as, with the curtains opened up to let in the splendours of Paris-by-Starlight, he paints each corner of the windowpane with glue. A pair of scarlet lightjars tumble past, tussling over some luminous root they've unearthed – but then her father fixes a square of felt into place, and it blocks out the night-time world. Around this he paints a border of black.

'Enough for tonight,' he says. Tomorrow, though she doesn't know it yet, Esmé will come home from Élodie's to discover new shutters as well, so that not a twinkle of Paris-by-Starlight can penetrate her room.

Together, she and her father settle on the bed. In the crook of his arm, she eats one of the macarons (which is not nearly as delicious as a salt-water sudjukh, though she wouldn't dream of telling her father), and listens as he begins the tale. Tonight, the children are lost in the cellars, and have fallen prey to one of the roaming bands of child-herders who live down there.

'It's like the Khanate Beneath, isn't it, papa?'

'Esmé?'

'Well, a magical world, right under our own ...'

Her father, who began imagining this story when he too was a child, stalls. The magic of the night, so much more powerful than his own imagination. His own stories are eclipsed. Probably Esmé would prefer to hear about Tamaz and Ketevan, Besarion and the Ulduzkhans, the pauper boy Vache who fell in love with the moon. He has a sudden idea, slips out of the room, and returns moments later with his own childhood copy of Chrétien de Troyes. This ought to do it, he thinks. There are enough stories in here to romance a little girl's mind – stories of Yvain, the Lion Knight; of Perceval, who searched for the Grail; of Erec the fallen knight and his impoverished love Enide. Let's get lost, he thinks, in the enchanted Brocéliande forest. French stories for a dark, French night.

But Esmé's mind just wanders. Her eyes keep going to the new blackouts in the window.

'Why, papa?'

So Emmanuel Caron lays back, his arms around her, and says, 'A little girl needs her sleep. Esmé, you mustn't go to the window any more – not after dark. Do you understand?'

She does not.

'I know it's beautiful, little one. But so is this, you and me, in our own little world. We can have our own magic here, can't we? All the games we can play. All the stories we'll tell. You and me, in our own little fortress.'

'And am I not to go to the Jardin any more?'

Emmanuel shook his head.

'But I liked it, Papa.'

So did Emmanuel. He remembers last Christmas, the first Night of Seven Stars, marvelling at what the winterlights were, then being there, right there in the Jardin, as the constellation conjoined and the lightjars were born in a wonder of soaring rainbows and comet trails.

But he remembers, too, the nights of this past season. The men who came into the market in the Jardin and pulled its stalls apart. The lightjar nests he'd found littering the approach to the Louvre, ripped from the trees and ground underfoot. The dead water dog left as a trophy at the foot of Theseus and the Minotaur. And, more than any of this, the man he'd seen fleeing the garden, three proud Parisians on his tail, until he either lost them in the boulevards, or found himself cornered in some alley with no way to get out.

He kisses his daughter goodnight, turns the lamp out as he leaves – and, ever after, Esmé stares at the new blackouts in the window, wondering what might have happened in the world beyond that grown-ups no longer love magic as they should.

Stories like this, all over Paris-by-Day.

BOOK FOUR

PARIS, IN THE DARK

One by one, the stars winked out. One by one, they died. One by one, the sailors drowned, until no man survived. One by one, we spilled our hearts, until each soul was free. And one by one the lights went out across the landlocked sea.

From 'The End of Night', final story of the Nocturne

14

. . . .

THE FAR AWAY WORLD

Another night, another world – but this time, no flowers-by-night to illuminate the world's darkest corners, no seven-pointed star to guide a lost soul home.

The coach that pulled up on the scrubland road had already lost most of its passengers since it set off at noon, and the girl who stepped out onto the tussocky grass was tired and alone. Taking pity on her, the driver helped her down to the dirt and, though she had little to carry with her – just a small overnight bag and a musical instrument draped in cloth – he carried these down too.

'Are you sure?' he ventured. 'I can take you into town.'

'Quite sure,' she said, and breathed in the scent of the fields, where goats were huddled up together against the night. 'It isn't far.'

The driver thought twice before climbing back into the coach. 'Then good luck to you,' he said, and watched in his headlights as the girl tramped away, heaving her unborn child with her.

The night was vast enough that, as she walked, she did not see the outline of the mountains that hung above. The darkness impenetrable enough that the only thing guiding her was the memory of roads she'd known since she was a girl. Eight hours south, the night had a different texture. It was closer here, and in the fields the cicadas were in full song. She found she was grateful for the dark.

It was good when things were absolute.

The house was where she had left it, not yet two years ago, sitting in one of the squares on the outskirts of town. Though there were no lights in its face, she knocked all the same; there were balconies out back where you could drink wine of an evening and gaze up at the mountaintops. Over there, somewhere, was Spain. It was not until she'd knocked three times, each time a little more fiercely, that she knew the house was empty. She felt her insides strain and knew, then, that she should have accepted the coach driver's help. It was a mile and more into the middle of town.

Some time later, the night still deepening, she was walking the narrow stone streets of Saint-André. Past the Roman abbey where baskets of flowers, quite devoid of any light, smelt summery and sweet. Past the shuttered windows of the *boulangerie* and *bureau de poste*. Into the square where tables were arrayed outside the delicatessen with its restaurant in the annexe, and old men were playing cards.

She was drawn to the voices more than the light. Some of the old men followed her with their eyes, but she did not mind; there was, perhaps, a scathing look or two among them, for they had last seen her leave as a girl and now she was returning alone and with child, and men like these had forgotten the follies of their own youths. But Isabelle had heard another voice, inside the restaurant, and she floated that way now.

The restaurant was homely and small, and in the air the smell of the morning catch. Isabelle, who had eaten only breadsticks and almonds all day, did not know she was ravenous until she was breathing in those smells. Inside, the baby awoke.

At a table on the restaurant floor, a woman with flame-red hair crowed with laughter at the stories her partner was telling. Isabelle had not seen this man before – but, she supposed, two years was enough for countries to end, for magic to be made and babies to grow, so there was nothing very wrong with that. He was younger than the woman and so rapt that he did not see her at all, not until Isabelle was hovering over the table like a total eclipse.

Only then did the laughing woman look up.

She stopped laughing, then.

'Isabelle!' she exclaimed – and, standing to embrace her, took in every contour of her body. 'Oh, Isabelle.'

*

The same hour, a different world:

The letter was waiting when Levon arrived at the Hôtel Métropol. Fae was long gone, but the night girl Emi – who came to the city in the back of a trafficker's truck, just like so many among them – rushed to give it to him. She always rushed, whenever Levon arrived.

Levon hadn't been anticipating any letter, but the curl of the handwriting made him stutter. He opened it, there and then.

Dear Levon,

If I'm right, you will receive this letter at the first fall of dark. Your world will only just be waking up. By then, I will be gone.

He broke off reading. He looked up. There was the Hôtel Métropol, still pulsing and shining in its myriad colours. There was Emi, still lingering with her eyes on him. All of the old, familiar things – but everything had changed. This time, when the world ended, it wasn't like the morning when the old country fell at all.

Please don't think badly of me. What I do now, I do for the baby bursting to get out of me. But I cannot have a child in

ROBERT DINSDALE

Créteil – in that place that, no matter how much Hector strains to make me welcome, I know I cannot stay. And if I cannot come back to Paris-by-Starlight so that we can raise our child together, then there is only one other place I can go. And go I must – before it is too late. It might, I suppose, be too late already. What the chances that I give birth on a Flixbus heading south? It would, I confess, be a fitting entrance for a child of ours: born between towns, with no one place to call his own. But our child deserves better. He deserves to belong to a world, not an edgeland between the two. Not to be shuttled backward and forward. Twilight and dawn, twilight and dawn ...

I think you know this too. I think I heard it in you last night.

When you left this daybreak, something else was leaving too. It is not your fault. Cling on to this, Levon, because I mean it with everything that I have. But the bridges between worlds keep getting longer, the longer we don't cross them. And, when you spoke of the world we could build, together, last night – our dusk and our dawn – for the first time I didn't see it in your eyes. And I realised, then: it hasn't been in mine either, no matter how much I thought it was. Sometimes, when you spoke of it, I'd feel it reflected on me. I could believe in it – or, at least, I tried to. But that vision of a world between worlds, it was never really mine. And as soon as it started fading from you, as soon as you needed reassuring that that world could still exist ... it was gone.

I am sorry, Levon. Sorry because I know I am letting you down. Sorry because love, whatever that word might mean, isn't enough. I don't think I need love for what comes next. I think I need rigour. I think I need my feet on the ground. And I think I need the 'knowing'. I need to know the shape of life, and my baby's, or else lose everything in the void.

My father has brought me here, to the coach station, and I have asked one last favour of him: to deliver this letter to the Hôtel Métropol, so that you are not left wondering. I think it is playing on him, too, that I am to leave Paris again. To him, I am six years old and boarding the same bus, away from the city. No doubt, in the once upon a time, he received a letter much the same as this, sent by my own mother. The lives we make for ourselves are but echoes of what has gone before, and long may we echo in the hereafter. But he has agreed to help me, and this, I think, is his way of making an accommodation with what happened when I was small. Or maybe I forgive him now because, soon, I will need to forgive myself.

I might be gone from Paris-by-Starlight, and I might be gone from Paris-by-Day, but you can write to me, care of the bureau de poste in Saint-André, near Perpignan. There isn't a number (my mother rid herself of the telephone after my stepfather left – the lovestruck fool just wouldn't stop ringing) but if you call the payphone in the village square, Santiago, who runs the restaurant there, will find me. The world is smaller here. For now, I think that's right.

All the love that remains,

Isabelle X

Some time later, Emi found him sitting in a corner, straining at the letter in his hands. She brought him nectar, tried to sit beside him, but Levon was howling, howling into the night.

*

Nothing was as she'd left it.

There was no bedroom any longer. In the time that she'd been gone, her mother had taken up watercolour painting, then sewing – and now, in the place where she'd once slept, there was both an exercise bike and strings of Polaroid photographs, hung around the room like garlands. It mattered not. Her mother busied herself making up a bed in the living room, while Isabelle sustained herself with fresh coffee and toast, and oranges from the basket.

The house was narrow but tall, three storeys stacked on top of one another with the attic crawlspace above (how she used to love hiding up there with her harp!), and on the second storey a terrace looking out onto the Pyrenees. The kitchen and salon were on that same storey, and in summer the windows never closed.

Her mother barely stopped for breath as she hurled herself around, battling bedsheets onto the bed that popped out of the sofa, then lighting candles and arranging them around the room ('in a design Matthias taught me – you remember Matthias? He knew everything in Heaven and Earth!'). When she was done – and the room half transformed – she took a wine glass from the cupboard, poured a full measure, and flopped into the stool alongside Isabelle.

'So, are you going to tell me?' Her mother was eyeballing her over the top of her glass, but it was not in reproach. The glint in her eyes was that of an old girlfriend, hunting some libidinous rumour. 'Well?'

The day had been long. The orange was unsettling Isabelle's insides. By the Stars (she had to stop using the phrase), she wanted rid of this thing. Good mothers would never think such a thing, so she supposed she was not going to be one of those, but she was quite certain her own mother would understand. 'I'm bored of being pregnant. I'm tired, mother.'

'Yes, well, that's what nine months of being cannibalised by this' – she spiralled a finger over Isabelle's belly – 'thing will do to you. But that's not the reason you rocked up here in the middle of the night.' Setting down her wine glass, she took Isabelle's fingers. 'Are you going to tell me, or not? You always cut your own way, Issy. But all this time, with barely a whisper of that life you've got up there. Paris! I swore I'd never go again … But we small-town folk are still part of the world, you silly girl. I've seen the pictures from that moonlit world of yours. I know what goes on at night. I read about the old country and its lost People.' She faltered. Then, more tenderly now, she said, 'Has he thrown you out, Isabelle?'

'Nothing like that,' she replied.

'It's something like that, Is. Because, if it wasn't, you'd be up there with him, huddling down. Nesting, that's what they call it in my magazines. Like songbirds!' She paused. 'Isabelle, all I've had is fragments. Letters and cards. So … it's time to tell me it all, isn't it?'

Isabelle supposed that it was.

Dear Levon [she later wrote],

By the time I'd finished, it was after midnight. 'That's quite a tale,' she said. Those were her exact words. And then she said that, if I thought it was a secret that I was in Paris looking for Hector, well, I was as bad at keeping secrets as she was at keeping men. That she'd always known I'd go. That Paris is made for people like me. People with dreams. And when I told her about how they called me the Rose of the Evening, and of the People who came to Le Tangiers, just to hear me play – Levon, I don't think I've ever seen her prouder …

She didn't know why she was setting it down, but there was value in letting the words out. There was value, too, in the things she didn't write. 'If he loved you, he'd have followed you,' her mother had said, 'as simple as that.' But Isabelle wasn't sure that anything in life was as simple. If it was, why then this clawing guilt that she felt?

'It's what they did in the old country. The fathers left their children to be raised by mothers and aunts, while they went out onto the landlocked sea. And besides, if I'd loved him, well, then I'd have stayed.'

'Then maybe that's it. Maybe it wasn't love. Issy, darling, I remember *that*.'

But that wasn't right either, so she told herself what she'd been telling herself since that night: some things mattered more than love. A border had gone up, and cleaved them apart.

Tell Arina I'm thinking of her, she wrote, *and I'll write to her soon. She can write to me too.*

But in the days that followed, not a letter came back. The only thing waiting at the bureau de poste at all was a tiny package and, in it, a pair of badly made booties. And with them, a simple note.

Her father had taken up knitting.

Four days later, in the middle of the night: a knock at her mother's chamber door.

Caro slept lightly and was already reaching for the light when Isabelle came through. 'Well,' she said with a prompt clap of her hands, 'we're on, are we?'

Isabelle, who was clinging to her cardigan, said, 'I think so.'

'How long have you …?'

'I thought it was phantom, and if I went back to sleep…'

'Oh, wishful thinking! Wishful thinking, my girl! Look at you – you've been fit to burst since you got here.' Caro wrapped a dressing gown around her and joined her daughter at the door. 'If he's ready, Issy, you'll have to be ready too. There's precious little you can do to change it.'

Caro pushed past, darting to the top of the stair.

'Is it going to hurt, Mother?'

'Don't ask me,' she grinned, flicking lights on as she scurried down the stairs, 'I've only done this once. Once does not an expert make! So let's do this together, shall we?' At the bottom, she looked up. 'You're a big girl, Is. You're my big girl. And in a couple of hours' time, you're going to be a mother. That's life! Just . . . embrace it!' She stopped, wearing a look of preternatural horror. 'I'm going to be a grandmother. It'll call me *grandmama*. Good God, Isabelle, you didn't think of that, did you? I'm not yet fifty years old!'

Isabelle wasn't laughing. When Caro looked, she was braced between the doorjamb and the wall, barely in the room.

'We'll need to go to the square.'

'The square.'

'The payphone. So we can call the—'

Not for the first time, Isabelle seethed, 'It's the twentieth century, Mother. You should have a—'

'What, and have it ringing at all times of the night? No, come on, Is, it isn't far. Just prop yourself on me. We'll get there.'

And they did – though whether they were mother or daughter by the end of it, or enemies sworn against each other for life, neither could say.

In the nocturnal stillness of the square, Caro settled Isabelle in one of the chairs outside the bar and dashed to the payphone. There was a hospital in Perpignan, half an hour away at least. 'So we'll just have to wait,' she said when she was done. Then, taking her daughter by the arm, she led her to the restaurant doors and fished a key out of her pocket. 'Worse places we could wait.'

'You have a key?'

'From when I worked here,' she said, mysteriously, 'for Santiago.'

Asking anything further might open the pages of a story Isabelle had no desire to read, so instead she followed her mother across the empty bar-room floor.

'I'll pour the wine, shall I? One can't hurt. It'll steady you. Bring this baby into the world with some joy, that's what I say.'

367

'I don't need wine, Mother. I need ...'

Caro saw how her eyes had returned to the square, and the silhouetted payphone waiting there.

'You want to call him, don't you?' Outside was the deep of night. 'He'd be awake in that Starlight of his.'

She did. And yet – what kind of cruelty was that? She had to remind herself about the landlocked sea: the lovers on either side, fading fast from each other's sight. There were no second chances now.

She shook her head.

'Sit with me,' she said.

Then, after they sat:

'I can't sit.'

They walked together, up and down.

'Mother,' she said, 'I want to push.'

'You silly girl,' Caro laughed, still coaxing her on, 'you've hardly started. You don't need to—'

'What do you know?' Isabelle snapped. 'You've only done this once.'

Caro rolled her eyes. 'Once an expert does not make. Well, come on,' she shrugged, and helped her into the furthest recesses of the bar, 'if your body wants to push, might be you should just ...'

So Isabelle's baby was born in the back of the bar where her mother and her stepfather used to fight, and to Isabelle this seemed the most ordinary thing in the world.

Gravity gets the best of us, in the end.

*

The letter came with a Polaroid picture, and in its tiny frame all the love in Creation.

Dear Levon,

He is here, and I do believe he looks like you.
I haven't heard from you. And I understand. But he is here,
and he is beautiful.
Isabelle X

At dawn's approach, he left the Nexus and returned to the block. Hayk's men were busy demolishing walls in the uppermost storey, making one grand apartment where there had once been three, and for a time that meant Levon and Arina bunked together on the floor beneath.

'I wish you could see him.' Levon sat with her, cross-legged upon the bed.

'So tell me,' she said.

She liked to touch the edge of the Polaroid. It made her feel closer, somehow. It made her remember Isabelle and pancakes, in a time before the night-time came alive.

'He's bunched up and ugly and red. He has hair on his ears. A turned-up nose.'

'He sounds like you.'

'He's mine,' Levon shuddered.

He had his own eyes closed, and now he felt Arina's hand creeping out, trying to find his. 'She did love you, Levon.'

He said nothing, just opened his eyes and stared at the baby in the frame. If she'd still loved him, he told himself, she'd have sent a photograph of them both. There would have been a signal in that. This? This was consolation.

By the Stars, he had to snap out of it. Feeling sorry for himself – while there she sat, sightless and alone. He wrapped his arms around her. Lay down with her, just as they'd done through countless long nights.

'You know, Levon,' she said, with her face buried in his shoulder, 'you could go to her. You don't think, if you turned up there, she'd tell you to go, do you? *You*, Levon. So you could ...'

He whispered into her ear, 'I could never leave you.'

Not even for Isabelle, were the words he didn't say. Not even for my own son, whose name I don't yet know. And here was the secret. Here, the mystery revealed. Isabelle was right: some things are more important than love.

'But, Levon, you don't think I wouldn't come with you, do you?'

I'd thought of it, of course [he later wrote]. *The moment Hayk exiled you from Paris-by-Starlight. You'd hardly reached the bottom of the stairs before I was thinking it. But I thought – how could I take Arina now? Now, when her world's already ruined?*

But she's strong. You knew that, from the start. Hayk and Mariam, they'd made her feel safe since the fireworks in Le Tangiers. Walls can do that. But now I know: walls do other things as well. They become prisons, in the end. I thought Arina needed home, but all she really needed was me. So we sat up, and she made me see: we already made it three thousand miles. All you've gone is another six hundred. Six hundred miles of straight highway, me and her and one of the cars from the Nexus. It wouldn't take much to steal one. I'd borrowed them before.

So, by the Stars, we made a plan ...

It was midday in Saint-André, and on the terrace, looking up past terracotta rooftops at the summer haze on the mountains, Isabelle nursed her unnamed child. Two weeks – all of it a blur – and still she couldn't decide. Sometimes, she hovered on the edge of one of the old French names, Alain or Achille, but every time she stalled; you could see, in his look, that he was of the People as well. By the Stars, he was more Levon than Isabelle, and this made her both proud and despairing. She had so little idea how the People might have named him. Tariel, she thought, with a dismissive smile.

The letter was in Caro's hand. She turned around the terrace, sloshing coffee like a sot with her wine, and read it out loud.

That night, I went to the Nexus so that I could fix up the hotel laundry truck. I changed its oil and filled it with water. I siphoned what fuel I could from the hotel generator. Then I went Beneath, into the bazaar. Food and water was easy enough. I filled the trunk. I visited doctors and bartered for fresh dressings and painkilling tonics, tinctures in case infections set in, the dust of the emerald reeds which put a princess to sleep in the Nocturne, so can surely do the same again. I was being over-cautious. This, I admit. But she is my sister, and in the end I was not cautious enough.

When I emerged from the Nexus, it was still the heart of night – and all the ships of the People still out on the Seine. This was our hour. My father's men, and so many others like them, would all be down on the river, patrolling against further attack: an army of fishermen and fishermen's brothers. The Militia of the Night, to stand against this Paris New Resistance. But it meant that all was quiet in the block.

By the time I got there, school was in full swing, but Mariam was easy to fool, and I asked for just a moment to speak with my sister. Besides, Arina was tired. She gets tired easily, now. I took her by the hand and she pretended (I had not instructed her in this – the flourish was all of her own!) to loll upon my shoulder until we were out of sight – and, from there, the thrill of adventure propelled her. She had packed a satchel, and this we collected from her quarters. With this in hand we hurried down through the rippling colours in the stairwell, and out through the doors below. I'd hidden the truck in a backstreet, and only once she was settled in the back did my heart stop pounding. I had given her the Polaroid of our son to cling on to, and though she could not see it, she kept asking, 'Does he have a name yet?' and it killed me to confess that I did not know. 'Ari's a good name. That's who I'd have been, if I'd been a boy. When we get there, if he doesn't have a name, do you think Isabelle might let me name him Ari?' This was the first thing that made me smile all night. 'You can ask her,' I told her, 'when we get there.'

Of course, since this letter is in your hands, you know already that we did not get there.

It was my foolishness to go by the river. We crossed by the bridge through the entangled cathedral – but, by the time I propelled the laundry truck across the last expanse of water, it was already too late. They were waiting for me on the other side.

No sooner had I reached the end of the bridge, a car erupted out of the reeds on the shoreline. Then: figures I recognised from the block. Samvel, Narek, Arman. The thugs he calls the Faithful Three. Mr Andonian, who looks as gentle as Beyrek, though he fought and killed with my father when the old country fell. My father was not the last to appear. That was Master Atesh, who stood back from the rest, clouded in his consort of lightjars.

If I thought I was being cunning, they told me I was wrong. If I thought I was heroic, all I'd done was confirm the cowardice I'd shown on the day I fled the old country with the women and children. They ripped me from the car, and out came Arina too. She was crying, and men with missing fingers, the callused hands of war, sat her on their knees and told her that everything was all right. She would be safe, here, in Paris-by-Starlight. She begged them not to beat me, but nor was this in their nature. For an hour afterwards my father sat with me on the bank, and though there was anger in him, there was pity too. 'You've been through much, boy, but it's time to stand up. We won't run again. We are the People, and the People look after each other.' My own words, come back to haunt me.

I had only one question for him. How, I asked him, did he know what I had planned? 'Master Atesh has learned the language of the night,' he told me. 'He has accomplished what the sooth-sayers of the Nocturne could not. The night knew you planned to betray us, and it whispered to him. By the Stars, boy, don't you know how fortunate you are? We have a world ...'

He said more, but I heard not a thing. A language of the night. Whispers in the ear. There must have been some other way that I was betrayed, because these things I cannot believe.

Now it is dawn and I am writing this, sequestered in quarters in what was once the Hôtel Métropol. Like you, I am exiled: not from the night, but from the home I built for my family when we first arrived. From the block and my bebia's night garden I am banished, so that it can become my father's fief-dom. When darkness next falls, I am to be taken down to the wharfs to go out onto the landlocked sea with my father. I am to learn to captain a ship. I am to learn to be a man.

I am sending this letter with Khazak. You may remember Khazak. You met him, once, below the motorway bridges – when Paris-by-Starlight was but a fledgling dream. He has agreed to ferry letters from the Nexus, should I be being watched.

I don't know if you love me. I don't know if what we had was but fleeting for you. I don't truly know if, after everything, you believe in long, lasting love at all.

But I know, too, that this doesn't matter. I love you whether or not you love me. And this, to me, is like revelation. It isn't an act that demands return. And nor, Isabelle, is this letter.

Your son's father,

Levon X

In the same moment that Caro finished reading, the baby set up a squall.

'So he doesn't give up easily, this Levon of yours?'

Isabelle thought of him, cornered. The look of triumph that must have been in Hayk's eyes. The look of dominion.

'He told me once he was like Levon-by-Starlight.'

Caro said, 'Now, *that* you're going to have to explain …'

'He meant the magic doesn't die. It just gets forgotten. Then it has to be reborn.'

She named the baby Ari.

*

There was so much to learn. Her mother helped but, in the end, it was Ari who taught her. She learned that she could not make him feed, no matter what the hour on the clock. She learned that whether or not he slept was not down to the vigorousness with which she rocked him, nor the tunefulness of the lullabies she picked out, but to the vagaries of his own will. She learned that babies could be as pig-headed as the most argumentative adults, but that they got away with it because of their dimpled cheeks and innocent eyes. And she learned, through all of this, that guilt was to be a presence in her life for now and ever after. She would no longer have any dominion over her own heart.

Writing helped. So did staying up into the small hours of night. It was then that writing came most easily, so for long hours she would sit on the terrace and write down almost everything she could. Not the chronicle of the People, she knew, but the chronicle of a person. She sealed it in envelopes, and sent it to her father with instructions for onward delivery and yet more Polaroids of her son. Then she felt the rush of guilt again, as if she was taunting him, and waited nervously for reply.

Dear Isabelle,

What a difference is made in a month. He has grown! His eyes seem darker. He has no hair upon his ears. Such a strong, handsome boy you have made.

Levon put down his pen and stalked to the window. What a difference a month made for a child – but what a difference a month made for the world itself . . .

It was the height of summer, when days lasted longest and the splendours of Paris-by-Starlight dwindled to only a few short hours each night. And yet . . .

375

*The rooms I am sequestered in are the old chambermaids'
quarters. You can reach here by a crooked stairway, or not at
all. It is small in here, with but enough room for a bed and a
writing desk alongside. What need do I have for anything else?*

*Things are changing, Isabelle. You and I know how quickly
things change, but I venture out each night, and I am not
certain it is the same Paris-by-Starlight as it was the twilight
before. Let me tell you, first, the story of how I received your last
letter.*

Each twilight, when he awoke, he ventured down to the glowing
heart of the Hôtel Métropol, where his father's deckhands were
waiting to accompany him to the wharfs. They said it was easiest
to make the journey together (you never knew when delinquents
from the Paris New Resistance might be lingering outside,
regardless of any Starlight Proclamations), but Levon knew this
for what it was: it was his escort. It had been a week and more
since he'd tried to make his flight with Arina. He hadn't seen her
since, and knew not when he would again. And this injustice was
broiling in him as he trudged into the hotel reception – and
walked straight into Isabelle's father.

'Have you time for a drink?' Hector said.

*That was how, some moments later, we found ourselves in what
was once the Métropol bar. No guests here now, of course. Only
citizens of Paris-by-Starlight, breaking their fasts before venturing out for the night.*

*Your father gave me the envelopes you'd sent, and we spent
some time, together, looking at the Polaroids. Ari. If I ever get
the chance to tell Arina, she will be so proud. And I believe*

your father is proud, too – to see what you have made of your-self.

He didn't write what came next. He didn't tell her how Hector had said, 'I remember when Caro took Issy down to Saint-André. It sticks in you. You think life's sweeping you one way, then it beaches you in another.' There were other things he wanted to say, so he said them instead.

We were almost finished, when the deckhands arrived. We were saying our goodbyes, and suddenly they were arrayed around us – all four of them. 'Who's this, Levon?' they said. 'Doesn't he know what hour it is?' 'Only the People, for the People.'

I can barely describe what happened next. Your father is not a fighting man, and perhaps he has his life to thank for it. For in a second they were dragging him out of his seat. In the next, they had cast him onto the ground. If he had fought back, I wonder if they would have fought more fiercely still. Even so, I cannot say that their boots did not connect with his ribs as he lay there. I cannot say he did not, finally, find himself ejected from the Nexus with a bruised and swollen face. I wish I could say that I protested more, but when the deckhands turned on me, and said, 'Levon, how can you tell he isn't one of their Paris New Resistance? And you brought him straight into Starlight!', I understood a little of what they meant. Because, while your father certainly does not march with the Paris New Resistance, there is little doubt that their movement spreads. Nightly, I see slogans daubed on the wharfs. The Tricolore flag, into which black letters have been stencilled, hangs from lamp posts along the Champs-Élysées. Le Monde and Libération publish editorials on the demonstrations held at the Place de la

377

Bastille, when a thousand Parisians listened to orators hold forth on the meaning of 'amnesty' and 'refugee'. Emi, who works here at the Nexus, opened a package this morning, only to discover the cinders of countless dead lightjars wrapped up in brown paper. They tell us to go back from where we came, though they know that world is gone.

My father sees the same things. But Hayk is not like Hector. He does not lie down. 'It used to be beautiful,' I told him last night, as we stood together at the prow of the ship. 'You should have been here, Father, on the Night of Seven Stars. Every last person, from day and from night, finding rapture in this magic we brought …' But he wasn't. He was here for the night in Le Tangiers. He was here when they rained fire on him from the shore of his resurrected ocean. How can anyone be expected to see the light, when they've lived too long in the dark?

I miss you, Isabelle. I would like nothing more than to hear your voice.

Yours still, in love,

Levon X

She would have liked it too, she thought. So that night, with Ari sleeping, she made the trek into Saint-André. There, in the village square, she called the exchange operator and asked to be connected to the Hôtel Métropol in Paris. For a time, the line went dead. Then, a dour voice said, 'This line is no longer connected,' and brooked no further argument as she asked to know why.

In Paris-by-Starlight, the border wall was still going up.

*

Dear Levon,

It has been four months since I last saw a flower open itself to the stars, but something happened tonight that I must set down.

Ari is well. Seventeen weeks is enough to have finally taught his mother that babies are like your starlit world – not to be controlled. As soon as I stop trying to marshal him, he lets himself be marshalled. And that is how, tonight, I was able to settle with him just as the dark was rising over the mountains.

Out on the terrace, while my mother cooked (believe it or not – she cooks!), I took out my harp. I have been playing him the old lullabies, the medieval canticles of which my father was so fond. I don't know why. These felt safer, somehow. But tonight a different mood struck me. I let myself venture into the music of your old country ... and found that, without you near, my fingers are as disobedient as they used to be in the bars of Pigalle. The last time I was the Rose of the Evening was the night we clung on to Arina to keep her slipping away. So perhaps it is just that the music does not live in me any longer. Or perhaps it slipped out of me on the night I was sent into exile? 'Only the People, for the People ...'

But our son is of the People, and he deserves his history too. If it wasn't to be music, well, I could still remember stories out of the Nocturne. So I told him the story I have always loved best: of Tamaz, who wanted to know what was beyond the horizon, and so voyaged far from the old country, among unknown men. I thought, perhaps, that this was the story that fitted Ari most of all.

It was as I neared the end of Tamaz's first odyssey (for aren't there so many, weaving their way in odd interludes and foot-notes through your bebia's wonderful book?) that something caught my eye. My mother's roof terrace looks out directly into the fields beyond Saint-André, and in the undergrowth down there, something sparkled.

I tried to ignore it. I told myself it was only a bottle top, or a piece of broken glass. But no – the glittering lingered. By the time Ari slept, it seemed more vivid still. So I picked my way down, through the scrub country where the wild goats graze, until I could touch it with my hand.

In the middle of a cluster of cowslips: a single, diamond-white flower-by-night, no bigger than the nail on my thumb, a pin-prick of starlight brought down to Earth.

Can it be that, wherever the stories of the Nocturne are cher-ished, the magic of the old world begins to remember?

Levon was not certain. Nor was he certain whether the idea was one to be marvelled at. Worlds could not be destroyed if they did not first come into being. Hearts could not be broken. He lifted his face from the letter, stood to look out of the window. Down in the boulevard below, People were running.

There was a clatter of footsteps outside his door as well. Feet flailing. Hands knocking. He did not have time to answer, for already somebody was pushing through. 'Emi,' he said – it was always Emi, with some new excuse to come and see him – 'I'll be—'

'Levon, you'd better come.'

He faltered.

'*Now*,' she said.

In the reception hall, clots of the People had gathered, families Levon recognised from the rooms, and others who had taken up residence Beneath. Spread between them were cases and haversacks, trunks on wheels, all the ill-fitting luggage in which they'd once ferried their lives.

A van was pulling up on the Rue Castex. Its doors slid open, revealing a small family – mother, father, six-year-old son – already inside.

'What's going on?'

At first, nobody answered. One of the waiting families was already pushing through the Métropol doors, throwing their packs into the transit van and helping each other up. Soon, others followed.

'They're leaving, Levon.' Emi threw her arms up in the air, her eyes imploring him. 'You're going to have do something. Call for the Ulduzkhan, or …'

One of the men was brushing past Levon on his way to the doors. Levon reached out, as if he might take him by the arm – but the man feinted back, refusing to be touched. 'It's a free country, isn't it?'

'But …'

'You've been a good man, Levon. So I'll give you one chance. Step out of my way.'

Levon stepped aside.

'We'll not stick around any longer. Not waiting for something to happen. There's too many lost already. I'll not lose another member of my family. Another friend.'

'They painted Paris New Resistance outside the Nexus today. Big white letters, right there on the Rue Castex.'

'And the Nocturnes. They burned them all …'

This Levon did not know.

'Yes, that's right. Robbed them out of the night markets and burned them in canisters, right there on the Place de la Bastille. Well, go on. You tell me that's where it ends.'

'It's like this,' somebody else chimed in. 'Imagine you can go back. Back, when the old country still prevailed. If some wise man called you over, told you that in a week – two weeks, three weeks, four – it was going to end, what would you do? There's not one of us, here, who would stay. Give us the miracle of foresight, and we'd hit the road – before the tanks, before the soldiers, before the wharfs going up in flames. Before starvation and dysentery and fever. Well, look at us now. Different world, but it's the same old story. Only, this time, we've been given that second chance. We *know* what's coming. So we're getting out.'

'The Ulduzkhan says different,' Emi called out. 'He says, if we'd known, we could have stood together. We could have saved the old country if we'd been strong. Couldn't we ... Levon?'

Levon didn't want to wound her pride, but he shook his head sadly. 'Stop calling him the Ulduzkhan.' Then, to the families crowded at the door, 'Where will you go?'

'We were trafficked in,' somebody said, hoisting his daughter onto his shoulders, 'but we'll get ourselves out. There's no Starlight Proclamation telling us to stay. So we'll find somewhere else. There's a whole world out there. Live by night or live by day, it's all the same to me. All I want to do is live.'

After that, Levon watched them flocking through the doors. He hadn't seen, until now, that there were two transit vans with their engines idling out on the Rue Castex. The first, packed full of families, was already taking off. The second was only just opening its doors.

Emi, beside him, with her hands on her hips: 'Well, Levon? What are you going to do?'

He didn't know it until she asked. But then it seemed so clear that it was as if invisible hands were guiding him.

He followed them through the doors.

It was cold out on the Rue Castex. Autumn was drawing its veil over Paris. He looked up to see the seven-pointed star – a gleaming guardian over the rooftops. The others in its constellation had been growing in vividness over the past nights. The Night of Seven Stars, still some weeks distant, was approaching nevertheless.

The families had boarded the van, but as one of the men reached out to shut them within, he saw Levon standing in the boulevard.

'You'll not convince us, Levon. We know our minds.'

Levon forced his way aboard.

The families reeled back. But Levon begged them with his eyes, and in the end it was Levon himself who reached back to heave the sliding door shut. The last thing he saw was Emi, staring in horror at him through the fogged-up glass of the Hôtel Métropol. Then, it was just the darkness of the van's interior, lit by criss-crossing torch beams, the rattle as the driver took off. The smell of sweat and diesel and apprehension.

For a time, Levon simply braced himself: the cold exterior of the van against one shoulder, the hard muscle of somebody's arm against the other. He tried to sense where the van was going, but the streets were a labyrinth and it was a relief when he stopped trying. A release, of sorts, as well. He remembered this. The old, familiar feeling washed over him. Your destination in somebody else's hands: if you could cope with the terror, it really wasn't so bad. There was a numb beauty when you gave up trying. You started believing in Fate.

The thought struck him that they might go by the river. He lifted his hands to pound on the driver's cab and warn him, but there was no hope he would be heard, so instead he closed his

eyes and let himself be buffeted around. He'd been being buffeted for so long. Buffeted out of the old country. Buffeted into
the new. Never, except in rare moments of grace, in charge of his
own life. By the Stars, that had to change. He'd start making
decisions soon. Go wherever they took him, then find a way
south. He'd done it before. He could sleep in hedgerows. Steal
from convenience stores. Beg for an afternoon's work at farms. It
would be easier to do it alone.

Alone ...

The word was all wrong. He cocked his head to listen to the
swirl of conversations going on around him.

'We started out in Kreuzberg, Berlin. Only came to Paris
because of the magic. But Kreuzberg was as good a place as any.
We'll head there, all three of us ... together.'

'Oslo. My wife studied in Oslo. If there's a way across, we'll do
that. But anywhere, I don't care, as long as we're together ...'

When he opened his eyes, he could only see the People in silhouette, but he knew they were holding one another: each family,
a silhouette of its own. And no sooner had he realised that, he was
thinking of Arina. He remembered the last time he'd been in the
back of a Transit van. He'd been holding her hand, back then.
He'd been holding her hand in the back of the ambulance too.
And now where was she? A princess in her tower. Locked away
from the person who'd carried her three thousand miles. The
person who, even now, was leaving her behind.

'Stop!' he bawled out. 'Stop the van!'

He pounded his fists at the cold metal wall that separated them
from the cab. At first, nothing happened. Somebody took him by
the arm, ordered him to control himself – 'You're panicking, boy!
Don't you remember what it's like to panic?' – but Levon shook
him off. One of the younger girls was crying. He was sorry for
that, but still his fists rained down.

The engine guttered. The van slowed. Levon reached out before it had come to a halt and heaved the door open. One of the men was remonstrating with him, fearing perhaps that this was some trap. But no – Levon only begged apology, then staggered out into the dark. They had come to a stop on the edge of some dual carriageway. So few flowers-by-night flourished this far from the old town, but if you looked south you could see the cauldron of colour that was Paris-by-Starlight.

Hands reached out to heave the door shut again. Levon did not stop them. He slapped the flat of his palm on the van, as if to tell them it was all right to make their getaway – but the driver had needed no such instruction; it was already careering back onto the empty carriageway.

Levon looked up at the seven-pointed star. It was there to guide him home, yes, but it was there to watch over him as well. It was there to see all and know all. Like Master Atesh and his language of the night.

When did the walls you put up to protect yourself become the walls that kept you in, the very same walls you had to tear down?

He screamed and screamed and screamed.

Dear Isabelle [he later wrote],

They were not the only ones to leave. I later discovered that the People have been leaving since summer's height. Even now, as the nights grow longer, their minds are made up. How much my father knows I cannot say. Paris-by-Starlight is populous enough that a few families slipping away changes nothing. But if a few families beget a few more, and they beget yet others, what then? Hayk would call it desertion. Letting the Paris New Resistance win. I admit to an incalculable fear at what his remedy for desertion might be.

I have been thinking about what you said to me. A single flower-by-night opening up for my son, upon his first hearing of the Nocturne. Well, what would happen to a city without its People? What if half of them were gone? What becomes of our magic, if there are fewer of us left to remember?

I want to come to you. For months now I have been thinking that I needed a sign, my own seven-pointed star to tell me it was right that I should come. Maybe it would come in a letter from you. But looking for signs is hopeless. Portents are unreal. A star might hang in the heavens, but it is we who decide what it means. There is no language of the night whispering into Master Atesh's ear.

For too long, I have allowed myself to be swept along by the circumstances of this world. Now, the time has come when the world must bend to circumstances of my own. So ... I will bide my time a little further. Earn their trust, so that my father no longer sends his deckhands to escort me to the wharfs. Then, when they finally believe I am a citizen of this world, I will take my chance again. I will find Arina and we will come for you.

Wait for me, Isabelle? The landlocked sea is between us but I believe I can still see you on the other side. Look for me there. I am begging you.

I remain, your

Levon-by-Starlight

When Isabelle put down the letter, Caro could see her frustration. Out on the roof terrace where they sat, Ari looked at his mother too. For a moment, there seemed opprobrium in his eyes.

Then, with the perfect serendipity of a child, he vomited out his morning milk – and, after that, sat beaming once again.

'It's what you want to hear, isn't it? That he's coming for you.'

'It isn't that.'

'Then what?'

'It's that … he's said it before.'

Caro looked up at the early winter sun. 'Come on,' she said, 'you need to take the baby out anyway.'

And so they walked. First, into Saint-André, where they provisioned themselves with bread and oranges; then, further, along the back road towards the seaside sprawl that was Argelès-sur-Mer. Sometimes, when the road rose, they could look down on the ocean, glittering yet grey. Sometimes, when it threatened rain, they waited in the bus stops, or for the land train, idling the hours away as the day grew old.

'He asked me to marry him once. I don't think he'd planned it. Just blurted it out, like we were in some grand romance.'

'And you said no?'

Isabelle just stared, as if to say: well, here I am.

'Isabelle, you sorry girl! Look at yourself; listen to yourself! And you think you're *not* in some grand romance?'

'You don't believe in romance, Mother.'

And Caro said, 'No, Issy, my problem is I believe in it too much.'

Nobody in life is with you constantly, she said. Nobody, truly inside your own heart and mind. But what does that matter? You fall in love regardless. 'It's like this,' she said. 'Imagine you can go back. Back, before you stumbled on his sister and shepherded her home. If some wise man had called you over and told you that in a week – two weeks, three weeks, four – you'd meet someone and fall in love, but that there'd be trial and tribulation up ahead, that it might end beautifully or it might just … end, what would you do?'

Isabelle looked at Ari. There was her answer.

'There's not a person in this world who'd take the other road. The only thing you have to decide – really, truly decide – is if you're still on that same road. Sometimes, you never were. Me and your father, we were a little like that. Others, well, they're tramping down that same road together and, one day, they decide they're done with tramping. They'll build a little home instead. So they go out and find timbers and stone, start building four walls and a roof to keep them safe. Then they can focus on each other. Don't have to think about the rain and the snow. Don't have to think about where they'll rest their heads each night. It's … bliss. For a time. But, soon enough, those walls they put up, well, they aren't doing what those walls were built to do. They're not keeping you warm and safe. They're keeping you pinned. They're telling you where you can and can't go. And those very same walls you put up with love, now they're the ones you need to tear down.' She stopped, as if suddenly remembering herself. 'The world is full of impossible questions, Isabelle. You can't hope to get it right. You just have to get it least wrong.'

'I know he still loves me, but what was I supposed to do?'

'Well, then,' Caro said with an absolute finality, 'he loves you and you – whether you'll admit it or not – love him. That's just the most ordinary thing in the world: a complete and utter mess. You can either tidy it away, roll the dice and see what comes next. Or you can … find another way, and have your grand romance.'

'He'd have to show up first.'

'I've read the letters, Isabelle. He's a lovesick fool, in an impossible world. He's going to show up.'

But he didn't. For two weeks afterwards, she let herself believe that one morning he'd be standing right there on the doorstep. But one after another, the days – joyous and empty, frustrating and fulfilling – tumbled by. She wrote a letter, and it went unanswered. She wrote another, and dared not post it until December was approaching. In return came silence: long and strained. And at last her son was five months old, still without a father on whom he'd ever laid eyes in this world.

It came, at last, on the second day in December.

Isabelle was spinning Ari around the salon, rising and falling according to the vivacity of his giggles, when the front door opened and her mother appeared, clutching not a letter, but a copy of *Le Figaro* to her breast.

Setting Ari down (he quickly put up a protest – he was that kind of child), Isabelle took the newspaper and knew, straight away, that something was wrong. The image on the front was of the radiant façade of the Hôtel Métropol – and, arrayed around that, a horde of people carrying placards.

The demonstrations at Paris's Hôtel Métropol spilled out onto the Place de la Bastille yesterday evening when the city mayor-alty confirmed that seven men arrested last month in the investigation into the disappearance of nineteen-year-old Mme Lisette Chastain have been released without charge. Mme Chastain was last seen dining with her paramour, an unidentified man of the People, on the night of 17 November, in the vicinity of the Boulevard Bourdon. Her last contact, prior to her rendezvous, was with her school friend, Étienne Turgot, who alerted the authorities to her disappearance on 18 November. Though the investigation quickly identified the Hôtel Métropol as the likely destination of Mme Chastain and her partner, the investigation was hindered by the so-called 'People' and their Starlight Proclamations, which seek to pro-hibit entrance to proscribed parts of Paris within the hours of darkness. Officers have persistently been declined entry to the Hôtel Métropol (this in spite of the intervention of its prior owner, M. Fortier, who – it has been revealed – this summer forfeited a majority shareholding in the hotel to an unnamed body of the People), sparking localised protests – which yesterday saw a thousand Parisians marching in the Place de la Bastille.

Sources close to the investigation have revealed that the People under arrest were last night released without charge, after no CCTV footage was identified to show Mme Chastain's admittance to the former hotel. Rumours that Mme Chastain may have been taken into the Khanate Beneath – the vast, interconnected system of catacombs and caverns excavated beneath Paris by the hand of the People – were last night rife among the protestors who still swarmed the Rue Castex. The demands of the protestors are simple: they promise a blockade of the Hôtel Métropol until Mme Chastain is returned.

Isabelle stopped reading. Her eyes were drawn to the photographs instead. She had seen the Rue Castex thronged before, but not like this. Everywhere: Parisians with placards. Only a police cordon kept them away from the front of the Hôtel Métropol itself. Some of their faces were blurred and indistinct, but in others she could see their righteous indignation. She could read the placards, too. 'PARIS NEW RESISTANCE' daubed on every one.

'Do you think it's him they arrested?' Caro asked.

Either that, thought Isabelle, or he was trapped behind that cordon.

She let the newspaper drop from her hands.

'Mother,' she said, 'I have to go back.'

Her mother followed her, up the back stair to the chamber that had, five months ago, become her bedroom again. There she watched as Isabelle forced clothes into a haversack, dug out old boots and crammed those in as well.

'Two days, mother. Please. Can you stay with him for just two days?'

Ari, who was suspended upside down in his grandmama's arms, gurgled with pleasure.

'What will you do?'

'I don't know. I never did.' Isabelle hoisted the pack onto her shoulder. 'Find him. Give him his sign. Drag him out of there by the hand, if I have to. Bring him here so that he can meet his son and we can ...' She tailed off, for she saw that her mother was already nodding. 'I have to, mother. You see that, don't you?'

'I do.'

'If the world cleaves you apart, well, it's down to you to put it back together ...'

Back in the salon, Isabelle took her son in her arms and kissed him on the brow. Perhaps the solemnity of the occasion disturbed him, for a moment later his jaws were yawning open and he was straining to take Isabelle's nose between his lips. She wrestled herself out of his arms, passed him back to her mother. 'Thank you.'

It wasn't too late to make Perpignan and, from there, the coach to the north. The hard December dark would have fallen by the time she reached Paris, but she would cope with that. The Rose of the Evening did not have her own story in the Nocturne, but perhaps there was time left to write one tonight.

'Isabelle,' her mother said, when the taxicab pulled up and Isabelle rushed out to meet it. 'You'll be safe, won't you? You'll ... go straight to your father's? Not into whatever's happening at the Place de la Bastille?'

Isabelle was already clambering into the taxicab when she looked back. 'I'm coming back in one piece, mother.'

Her heart was thundering as the taxicab pulled away. Once she had mastered it, she turned back and saw Ari's hand tucked inside her mother's, both of them waving as the taxicab turned a corner and disappeared out of sight. Only then did she look down. The copy of *Le Figaro* was on her lap, and slowly she opened it up.

She did not like lying to her mother. There had been too much of that. But she could not go straight to her father's home, no matter how unsafe the streets of Paris-by-Starlight. She could not return there, no matter the sanctuary they had given her once before.

There, caught in the photograph on the newspaper's front page, his face one of the few made up of crisp, defined lines, was Alexandre. A 'PARIS NEW RESISTANCE' placard raised up above his head. His mouth open to join the chorus. And beneath it, the caption: 'Drive the People Out!'

15

. . . .

THINGS FALL APART

It did not begin with the medals, but this is as good a place as any – so let us begin there.

Look at Alexandre: there he is, sitting in class, rigidly ignoring the whispers from Raphaël and Antonin in the row behind. There's only one thing that focuses his mind enough to shut them out. On the page in front of him, he scours three letters: 'P', 'N', 'R'. He's tired and distracted – a late night out on the Rue Castex will do that to a man – but scribing the letters brings him peace. He realises, now, that his mother was right: it's focus he's been lacking. Only now he's so focused that he doesn't notice when the tutor hovers over him and sees what he's writing. He only looks up at all when the tutor touches him on the shoulder. There's no doubt about it: the tutor's seen. He lingers over the letters. Then, with the tiniest incline of his head, he marches on.

It's only when he reaches the head of the classroom that the tutor fixes his eyes on Raphaël and Antonin and snarls out, 'Are we boys, Raphaël, or are we men? Antonin? Don't think I haven't seen you, all day, all year long. Get out of this classroom.' When the bewildered boys put up a protest, the tutor only smirks. 'Out! We're here to learn. It's boys like you who don't deserve free education. I won't have you undermining the other students in this class a moment longer.'

Alexandre is as bewildered as any when he watches them leave. But, by God, it's a good feeling.

That day, he scores his best ever marks.

It was the medals that did it. Didn't matter what he'd done to get a meeting with Maxime in the first place. There is nothing like hard currency, in this or any other world. When Maxime saw them, his eyes glistened with envy. 'You can get more?' he asked. That was because the true heroes of the Paris New Resistance needed recognising. If they weren't recognised, Maxime said, then the Paris New Resistance was just some rabble. What they needed was order. Organisation. 'The People have their Ulduzkhan. We'll need our generals too. It's time to get serious.'

It felt good to have a quest. Good to be needed. But Alexandre was a good boy, too, and didn't like the idea of stealing yet more medals from his grandfather's collection. So, one night, he came clean. 'I didn't take any of yours, grandpa. Just the ones you'd collected.'

'They belonged to friends who've passed.' This wasn't strictly true; some he'd bought from second-hand sales, to show at his reunions.

'It's the good work, grandpa. Please?'

And Victor, who was proud of his grandson, acquiesced. It was good to see Alexandre developing principles. Good to see him ... impassioned. Passionate boys made good lives for themselves. Young men, these days, were listless. What they had to understand was: you had to embrace a cause.

After that, Victor even convinced some of his old compatriots to dig out and donate. He had to pick and choose, of course. Some of them would balk at the suggestion. But they were the ones who lived in the past. You had to fight for the present as well. No good could come from burying your head in the sand.

'They're so grateful, grandpa. They gave a medal, tonight, to a man named Bale. He's the one who scuttled the boats on the river.'

Alexandre had been there to see it done. There he'd stood, in the back of the basement bar, while Maxime made toasts to the bravery of their comrades. He'd felt a thrill of pride, too, when Bale took the medal over his head. One day, Étienne said, that would be them.

They took to attending the meetings, whenever they could. Sometimes that was down in the basement bar, after fall of dark – because defying the Starlight Proclamations was the first order of the Paris New Resistance. Other times, they met in the daylight – out on the Place de la Bastille, or in the Jardin des Tuileries. The vagabond People owned neither daylight nor starlight. The fact was, Parisians could meet wherever they wanted – and if that just happened to mean ripping up the fragrant orchards in the railway sidings, that was the business of no-one but them. Sometimes, it was just likeminded souls being together. They'd talk about how their overseers were bitching at them at work, or about the football, or how the world wasn't what it used to be. Sometimes, they barely talked about the People at all. Alexandre learned to play pool – and this he impressed them with, because playing pool was just a kind of sleight of hand, and he'd developed so much of that with his magic set. But other times, when somebody's discontent was reaching its zenith, they'd come in with swinging fists, and say, 'We need to do something. My kids want Christmas this year. They don't want this Night of Seven Stars. They want Père Noël, not birds being birthed up high.'

That was when Alexandre first heard the whispers. 'We Own the Night,' somebody said. 'Christmas Restored,' said another. 'The mayor's office ought to know. Not everyone cooed at their fireworks. Some of us hid indoors. We've been hiding all year.

And can't we have something for ourselves? For our kids? I sup-pose that's not allowed, now. God forbid we look after each other! *We're Parisians, and Parisians look after each other.*'

Alexandre liked the sound of this. It made him feel safe, some-how. He'd heard his mother fret about the Paris New Resistance (when she wasn't fretting about his father). She said there was hate in it, but she couldn't possibly understand: what was so hateful, Alexandre thought, about people wanting to look after each other?

'Maxime, I got an idea.'

Winter drawing in. Summer long gone. Étienne and Alexandre had been playing pool all day, but now that the night fell earlier each evening – flowers-by-night opening in the verges, at least where the Paris New Resistance hadn't ground them into the dirt – they gravitated back to the bar.

'Étienne, you've always got an idea.'

'Want to hear it?'

'You know, we have ideas of our own. You're here for the numbers.'

'That's right,' said Étienne, 'but I still got two brain cells to rub together. It's not like me and Alex have been short of ideas before, is it? Wasn't it Alex's idea that brought us to your atten-tion in the first place?'

Maxime looked Alexandre up and down. These were the looks that still made Alexandre feel dirty, that still made him wonder if, perhaps, he'd be better off at home with his magic set and his silent, seething parents. But then Maxime nodded, and Étienne went on:

'See, the Hôtel Métropol, that's the place.'

'What place?'

'They've kicked good Parisians out of the Hôtel Métropol. Tried to give it a new name. See, there's this girl. Fae. I been chasing her for ages ...'

Maxime laughed. 'It's a weak man that chases. You ought to be hunting. A hunter just wants a haunch of venison on a camp-fire that night. Doesn't care which deer it is. It all eats the same.'

'Well, Fae lost her job. Been working at the Métropol since we done with school, and then – bang! Along come the People, and she's finished. So I figure – we should run them ragged. Show them what being frightened really is. I've been ruminating on exactly how. And it come to me last night.'

The bar was filling up. Maxime waved at the bartender, who began uncorking fresh bottles of red.

'We file a missing persons report,' said Étienne, with triumph. 'For this girl of yours. Fae.'

'No, not Fae! We go to the gendarmes, put up a sob story. Tell them my friend Lisette's been stepping out with one of the People. Make them think she went back to the Hôtel Métropol with the bastard, but she never ever came out. Who knows, maybe they took her into that underworld of theirs. God knows what they'd do to her down there, People of the night like that. No time at all, there'd be police all over that building. It'd be in the newspapers. They'd be talking about it in every café in Paris. Then we'd see whose side everyone was on ...'

By now, Maxime was swirling wine around his lips, painting them in violent colour. From the look on his face, Étienne judged that he liked this idea. But one thing still rankled. 'This girl of yours. Lisette. She's going to play along, is she?'

'Oh, well,' Étienne grinned, 'that's the beauty of it. See, Lisette doesn't exist. That's just a name I saw on a poster. But who's going to care about that? By the time the gendarmes find out, it won't matter. Everyone will know the People for what they are. Mud sticks.' Étienne thought for a moment. 'Well, that's all you want, isn't it? We got to show these People how to stay where they belong.'

*

December coming on. In the bar, a group of men Alexandre had not seen before. Étienne said they were from out of town. And here they were, with a sports bag open on the table, lifting crossbows out and handing them round.

'You coming, boys?' one of them called, eyeing Alexandre and Étienne.

When neither replied, the crowd laughed.

'Off for some sport. Big game. Well, our friend Maxime told us you got a stray-dog problem in this city.'

The next item out of the bag looked the same as a crossbow, but its bolt was tethered to the mechanism by a long black cord. Alexandre recognised it easily enough: a harpoon gun. 'Heard they liked the water, these dogs, but we like game fishing too, so we're well prepared. You girls in for this, or not?'

'Come on, Alex,' said Étienne, draining his drink. 'This we ought to see.'

He couldn't not go, not with all the men looking on – but later, when the sport began and one of the men tried to put a crossbow into his hands, his whole body started trembling and he declined to take it. They wouldn't shut up about that, not until it was nearly dawn.

It took an aeon to win a man's respect, and only a moment to give it away. That was why, when Alexandre returned to the bar and saw Maxime holding court, he hovered on the edges of the group until the older man noticed. Bale, who'd joined them out on the hunt, took Maxime to one side and started pontificating about what they'd seen. 'The star's getting brighter, Max. There are those ... winterlights popping up everywhere again. Something's got to be done.'

'And we're doing it,' Maxime seethed in return. '*We Own the Night*, remember? *Christmas Restored* ...'

When Maxime's eyes landed on Alexandre a second time, he left the pool table and sidled over.

'I'm glad you stuck around, A. I been thinking about this – you and that sister of yours ...'

Caught off-guard, Alexandre uttered, 'She's gone.'

'Gone?'

It was important to tell it properly, before Maxime heard about his reticence out on the hunt. 'Months ago. Ran off back to her mother. Had her baby there. Well, I told her she wasn't welcome. Couldn't just set up in my house like that. Told her she was as bad as the People – just rocking up where she wasn't invited, making out like it's her own ...'

Maxime clapped him on the back. 'For that, young man, I'll stand you a drink.'

At the bar, Maxime went on, 'You done good, A. A man's got to stand up for his family home. If you don't look after what belongs to you, somebody else just comes along and takes it. That's just the nature of man. But, listen to me, you talked to her, didn't you, before you sent her packing? I know you did, because how else would you know about that night garden of hers?'

Alexandre could hardly meet his eyes. Silently, he begged for him not to say more about that night garden.

'Blood's blood,' Maxime went on. 'Probably, you even liked her a bit.'

'I didn't,' Alexandre interjected, with more passion than he'd meant. 'One day, everything was good. Then, there she was, on my doorstep with—'

'Easy, A! Calm down! What I'm saying is – you probably got to know something about the People, didn't you? Something more we could use? Look, A, it's not that your loyalty to the cause is ever questioned. You proved that, before I ever laid eyes on you. It's your ... thirst.'

Alexandre tremored. This brought Maxime mirth as well.

'What are you asking, Maxime?'

'I'm asking you to use that brain of yours again – like you did the last time.' He closed his fist, rapped his knuckles on Alexandre's head. 'You haven't got the balls to be out on the streets, doing the good work. There's no use in pretending. It's written all over you. But you've been good with information before. Well, haven't you?'

Alexandre nodded.

'So be good with information again. Dredge something up from that little head of yours. Your boyfriend Étienne's good at that. See what mischief he's stirred up at the Hôtel Métropol! It's time for you to do the same.'

It took him two weeks. Two weeks later, he stood in the Place de la Bastille, watching columns of smoke rise into the air while a thousand loyal citizens gazed on, and it hit him like a revelation.

Later, when the incinerators had burned out and the crowds were moving on, he followed Maxime down to the Rue Castex. There, the protestors had been gathered around the doors of the Hôtel Métropol for more than a week. Tonight their numbers were swollen by drifters from the rally out on the square. A tide of them moved down the boulevard, crowding the doors, momentarily spooking the gendarmes who'd been stationed there. Étienne hailed him from the crowd, but Alexandre moved on, picking his way through the protest until he reached Maxime's side.

'Maxime,' he said, 'I got it.'

The man was like a bulwark in a shifting tide. The protestors moved around him, but he remained resolute.

'I watched you up there, by the Bastille. All that smoke going up into the air. All those burned books. That'll pain them, but there's more. It's like you said – something my bitch of a sister threw up. Because, when the People first turned up in Paris, they didn't have copies of that book everywhere. There was only one of them. That's the book that started all ... this. It's a relic to them, you see. It's a symbol.' The roar of the crowd was surging around them, but Maxime seemed to hear every word. 'And I know where it is.'

'You do?'

'I could take you there. It would be like burning their Bible ...'

Soon after that, Maxime took him by the hand. 'I knew I was right about you, A.'

Then the crowd was shifting around him again. Somebody had seen a flicker, up in the windows of the Hôtel Métropol – one of the People, peering back down, wondering how, by the Stars above, Paris-by-Starlight had come to this.

Maxime remained resolute, but somehow the tide turned against Alexandre, driving him back towards Étienne and the rest. Moments later, a placard was being pushed into his hands. He looked up, but couldn't see the slogan slashed across it. It didn't matter. Whatever it was, it made him burn with pride.

'Drive the People Out!' the voices around him were chanting. 'Drive the People Out!'

It would have been difficult not to get swept up in a chorus like that, even if he hadn't wanted to. But the words meant some-thing to Alexandre tonight. He was certain it wasn't just the belonging, because he'd been feeling that for months. This was something more – and, as he lent his voice to that glorious song, he finally knew what it was.

He was changed.

From good boy to good soldier in less than a year. Yes, worlds were collapsing and being remade all of the time.

But so too were people.

*

Paris, from the southern approach. After fall of night, you could see the glow from the old town hanging on the horizon like a haze. The motorway strip lights were like channels leading you there.

Isabelle's nerves set in somewhere outside the city, so that by the time she wandered through the coach station at the Pont de Créteil, they were all she could feel. At a news stand, she picked up a copy of *Le Figaro* and looked at the grainy images on the front page. Columns of smoke hung above the Place de la Bastille.

It hadn't been like this the last time she'd arrived in Paris. Back then: the wonder of the new, the thrill of adventure. Now: only the gnawing dread – and the inalienable feeling that she'd left a piece of herself back in Saint-André. She needed to get to a phone, and quick.

The darkness was absolute when she left the coach station, to the touch of a bitter winter night. Few Parisians, she was given to understand, cared much for the Starlight Proclamations out here. But the local bus she took, down through Champeval and over the Lac de Créteil, was still empty, and by the time she was hurrying along the old avenues, she began to imagine that this, now, was the entirety of Paris: a dead city, as dead as the catacombs underneath.

She hadn't meant to walk down her father's street but, in the end, her feet took her that way. Lights were on in the windows. Shadows moved across the shuttered blinds. *He* was probably in there too, she thought. Alexandre. Unless he was still out on the Rue Castex, with a placard in his hand. There could be no bed for the night here – but there was, at least, a place she could go.

A winterlight had erupted through the asphalt on the Rue Alfred, right outside the Chabons' house. Isabelle approached it cautiously, for its light was pale, the colour of stagnant water thick with scum. Where light rippled along its thick veins, it did so only intermittently. Perhaps, she thought, it was like Christmas last year, when the neighbours had sought to hack it from the ground. But she could see no bite of an axe in its leathery exterior. No grapple marks where locals had to tried to uproot it. It had not been touched, and yet it glowed with the colours of rot.

When she got there, so did the night garden.

Russ and Ashkhen's garden had once shone with such radiance that you could see it beyond the curve of the street. Upon your approach, you might hear the song of lightjars, or see them chasing each other in stylish pirouettes up into the sky. A dance of colour, and a dance of love. But tonight everywhere was dark – punctuated only by the faintest whimperings of light. The flowers-by-night that had once grown around the garden's edges were scarcely luminous at all; their bells hung limp, betraying only the merest flicker of colour, and in the trees above them fruits hung grey and spoiled. Even the grasses were dying. Tiny shapes, silhouettes of grey and black, pecked between them – and it took Isabelle some time before she recognised them as lightjars. Without the vivacity of colour, they were just husks. She watched as one tried to take flight, barely reaching the top of the grass before it somersaulted back to earth. There it lay, unable to right itself, until its brethren came pecking around and, quite by accident, set it back on its feet. Then, the desiccated husk staggered onward, desperate for nectar that wasn't there.

When Isabelle knocked at the door, there came no answer. Nor was there any resistance. The door fell inwards at her touch. 'Russ?' she called out. 'Ashkhen?' She dared to take a step into the shadowed hall and, through a doorway, saw the kitchen table laid out for breakfast.

They'd left in a hurry.

Shaking with the fear of it, she dumped her haversack in the hall and lit up each room as she staggered from one to the next. Nowhere were there signs of violence. Nowhere the signs of struggle. She came, at last, to the bedroom the old couple had shared – and, daring to open the wardrobe, found it empty of everything but a single cardigan, hanging forlornly against the wall. In the end, this was the thing that eased her panic. It seemed they'd planned to leave.

There was a telephone on a stand in the hall. With fingers still trembling, Isabelle dialled a number and listened as it rang. As she waited, she looked down. Another newspaper was lying here. Across its front page was the banner: 'THE PROCLAMATION', and underneath that a legend in smaller letters: 'BY THE PEOPLE, FOR THE PEOPLE.' There were only a few pages, and one of those torn out. The People had started their own news sheet, she thought. Reaching down to her haversack, she brought up the copy of *Le Figaro* she'd brought from the station. The pictures on both were near identical. Above one, the headline screamed, 'PARISIANS DEMAND ANSWERS'; above the other, 'THE PEOPLE'S SANCTUARY UNDER SIEGE'.

A voice buzzed down the line:

'Hello?'

'Santiago?' Isabelle stammered.

'It is he.'

'It's Isabelle. I'm looking for my—'

'Not here, mademoiselle. Where are—'

'Can you send for her, Santiago?'

She was shaking. She wanted to hear the gurgle of her baby, or else to whisper into his sleeping ear.

On the other end of the line, there seemed much rumination. 'It will take some time. Wait by the phone.'

'That's OK,' she whispered. 'That's good. Santiago, thank you.'

There was time. She could wait. This was where she would be staying tonight. She needed daylight for what she had planned.

Out in the garden, lightjars were still reeling through the grass. Perhaps there was nothing she could do – the People were leaving, and taking the intensity of the old world with them – but even so she bent down, opened her palm and waited patiently until one stumbled aboard. Then, cupping one of the ailing flowers-by-night in her other hand, she drizzled what nectar was left into its beak. A single drop of radiance beaded there. In her palm, the lightjar's wings beat less furiously, its feverish heartbeat stilled.

'Look up above,' she said, and angled it so that it might see the constellation already coming together. 'The Night of Seven Stars is nearly here. You can last that long, can't you? Maybe the wonder will make them see. What the magic used to be like. What it could be again ...'

Inside the empty house, the telephone was ringing.

*

The water dog was good to her. Ever since she'd lost her eyes, he'd stayed with her with the loyalty endemic to his kind. Sometimes, the others said, you could see him venture to the very edge of the night garden and look forlornly into the city, as if still pining for others of his kin. But if Hayk ever took him down to the wharfs, out onto the water where the wild dogs roamed, he pined for Arina instead.

So with the girl he stayed.

Tonight, she wrapped her hands around his muzzle, while Mariam read from her bebia's book. Now that the winter months were here, the time had come for her favourite story: the lost princess, and the sailors who set out into Endless Night to deliver her home. They had just reached the passage where one of the sailors, carrying the crestfallen princess in his arms, looked up to see the seven stars aligning, when the apartment door opened and the new arrival announced himself with the sound of lightjar song.

In the back bedroom, Mariam put down the book. 'Master Atesh is here.'

On the bed, Arina drew back. 'Aunt Mariam, do I have to?'

'It's what your father wishes, Arina. We've been through this.'

'But what about what *I* wish, Aunt Mariam?'

Mariam said, 'I'm sorry, Arina. We've been through this as well. Just try. Your father wants you to ... try.'

It was Mariam who went, first, into the apartment. Arina, who remained on the bed with her face buried in Gilly's fur, listened to their voices through the walls. 'Stay with me, Gilly,' she whispered – though the dog needed no such direction.

She heard the toll of footsteps again, smelt the distinct scent of Aunt Mariam's perfume. 'It's time, Arina.'

This time she had no option but to follow.

She could find her way, by memory, into most corners of the apartment. Since Levon had left, their father had refashioned the block's upper storey, so that the walls were further apart, with eight chambers where each of the family's members, and their closest compatriots, slept. Sometimes, she would sit up and listen to her father and his fellows talk about the midnight hour, out on the sea, the catch they had pulled in, the hustle and bustle of the city-by-starlight. She tried not to listen to them speaking of those other things – the night markets desecrated, the water dogs slain, Paris New Resistance slathered in fish guts across the wharfside walls – because this made her think of that morning in the old country, her mother and Levon, all those countless nights on the road. There were some things that, sightless or not, you couldn't unsee.

Gilly led her out onto the top of the stairwell and, at last, up to her bebia's garden. It was only the heady scent of the place, the warmth radiating from creeper and vine, that quelled Arina's discomfort.

Here Master Atesh was waiting. She could sense his presence in the beating of wings.

'My girl,' he said.

'Master,' she returned.

Taking her by the hand, he led her to one of the night garden's many groves. 'Listen,' he said. 'Arina, what do you hear?'

She took a breath. Remembered Aunt Mariam's instruction. 'I hear the whispering,' she said, swallowing the lie. 'But I don't hear the words. Just voices, on the edge of everything. Master, is it really the language of the night?'

Master Atesh said, 'I believe so.'

Arina wanted to cry out: It's no such thing. I made it all up, Master, just to please you, just to please my father, just to give you what you want. You can't force magic into the world where it doesn't belong. Some things are beyond your control ...

'What do you sense around you tonight, Arina?'

She sensed the night garden, flocks of lightjars in the boughs of its trees. She sensed warmth and sweetness and swathes of vivid colour; each colour, she had begun to understand, had a different scent. She fancied she could find her way, stumbling, from emerald to mauve, from crimson to aquamarine.

'My bebia's garden, it's wilder than ever.'

'That's because our block is still the beating heart of Paris-by-Starlight. This block, still host to a thousand of us, reading our Nocturnes each night. But out there ...'

She sensed that Master Atesh had wandered from her, that he'd stepped through the veil of ferns – encrusted in diamonds, just like the dew – to the edge of the garden itself. Here, where there used to be gutters, was just the eternal emerald cascade.

'There are some things you are fortunate not to see,' came his fading voice.

Master Atesh stared out into the northern environs of Paris-by-Starlight. Once upon a time, when a citizen of the People stood here, they would see a hundred other rooftops, each one of them the crown to a vibrant block where the People were making their homes. But in Paris-by-Starlight tonight, the cauldrons of colour were few and far between. The few that remained glowed with the faint luminescence of a lonely death. The nightscape of this city had once seemed an atlas of stars brought down to Earth, but now the blackness was spreading. The stars were winking out, one by one.

'Do you know why, Arina?'

They'd spoken of it so many times. 'It's because the People are running, like they ran before.' Just thinking of it cast her back to that morning they'd fled out onto the landlocked sea. She did not want to feel that way again. How much worse would it be to be cast out now that she was blind? 'Somebody should do something,' she whispered, unable to shake away the image. 'Tell them ... together is stronger.'

'Somebody already is,' Master Atesh intoned. 'Just pray that it isn't already too late.'

The cars spun out into the outer lanes of the carriageway, dividing around the minibus in the centre lane. Now that they flanked it, the driver of the bus knew that something was wrong. Grinding the accelerator down, he banked in front of the car on his inside lane. If he could make it to the next junction, perhaps there was a way he could shake them off, continue the journey undisturbed. He'd been told it might happen. Hadn't believed it. A city as big as this, how would anybody know about him? But now, here they were: lights flashing in his mirrors, dazzling him with their brightness. In the back, one of the older passengers had already started to cry.

He reached the junction, but made it no further. Somehow, one of the cars forced itself in front of him – and, without a second lane to circumvent it, there was nowhere left to turn. The minibus slewed to a stop.

It was the Ulduzkhan himself who boarded the bus and ordered them out onto the hard shoulder where the scrub grew tall. One of the younger runaways tried to take off into that scrub, but the Ulduzkhan had brought his retinue with him, and soon the boy was brought back and cast down into the sodden earth. These thugs were as bad as any border guard, the minibus driver thought.

A single winterlight was already dead at the side of the road.

Hayk hated the texture of this night. The night was supposed to be paradise, but here were only the naked trees and cold, lancing rain. The People he'd pulled out of the minibus had their arms wrapped around each other, guarding against the cold, and as he marched up and down he ripped coats and shawls and blankets out of their suitcases, wrapping them personally around each. Some of them cringed from his touch, but that was OK; that was only fear, and some modicum of fear was good.

A diminutive old couple stood at the end of the line. Hayk lingered over them, remembered his mother, whose face he would never see again.

'Where were you going?'

'Anywhere but here,' the old man whispered.

'And you?'

The old lady trembled, too. 'Wherever he goes, always and forever.'

'Your loyalty to one another is admirable' – he raised his voice so that the others might hear – 'but your loyalty to the rest of us is at fault. Look back,' he said – though there was nothing to look back into, for the lights of Paris-by-Starlight flickered so intermittently now. 'The Paris New Resistance seeks to divide us, but we don't have to let them. They seek to undermine the very fabric of what we are. I was there when they killed the first of us. I was at sea when they rained down fire. I've seen what they're doing. The envy they hold for the wonders of our night. The envy they have that we are the ones who brought magic back to the world. We are the People,' he said – and if any noticed the sob that he choked back, none of them dared show it, 'and we survived. But now? Now, we're giving up on each other. All of you here gave up on me tonight. Back there lies your world. If the rest seek to destroy it, well, that's on them. But that we seek to destroy it ourselves? How could our children ever forgive it? And all the children still to come?'

'It isn't us who destroyed it,' the young runaway, still spread-eagled on the ground, cried out. 'It's you, and your Starlight Proclamations. You gave them reason. Reason to hate …'

Hayk marched to him, glowered down into his eyes.

'I protected the People. They were coming for us long before that. It is man's nature to hate. But, by the good grace of our biology, it is man's second nature to protect.'

Without further word, Hayk reached out his hand to draw the boy back to his feet. For a fleeting moment, the young man thought about resisting; then, with nowhere else to go, he took the Ulduzkhan's hand.

'My friend,' Hayk said as he helped brush the worst of the earth from his anorak, 'I think you're beginning to see. But what of the rest of you?' He marched back along the line. 'How many of us have to die before the rest of us understand? The magic dies when we don't stay together. *Family dies, when we don't stay together.* We are not a People if we're scattered across the Earth's countless corners. We are not a family if we live under different roofs.' He reached the centre of the line, where the minibus driver stood with his head hanging down. 'People, I know you're scared. I'm scared too. But our loyalty outweighs our fear. *We are the People, and the People look after each other.* So, please ...' It was the first time that he'd stopped to take a breath. His voice was softening now. '... let us look after each other tonight.'

Hayk turned over his shoulder, to where his retinue were waiting in the dark. 'Get them back on the bus. Take them back to the block. My mother's night garden still shines the strongest in Paris-by-Starlight. These People nearly lost the will to go on. They need reminding of the splendour.'

The People put up no protest. One after another, they picked their way back onto the bus.

The driver was about to follow, when he felt Hayk's meaty hand on his shoulder. 'My men will drive.'

The engine in the minibus had already fired. Banks of harrowed faces looked back out of the windows.

'I'm not angry with these People,' said Hayk. 'It isn't their fault they're afraid. The instinct to fight or flee – there's barely a hair's breadth between them. You can't be angry with a fearful old man, who only wants to tend his garden for the rest of his days. You can't be angry with his wife, who would follow him to the end. But when other men come along and round them up, and take their coin, only to profit from and propagate the end of our world, well, that seems a thing a man of honour might get angry about.'

'You're making a mistake. You're not these People's keeper ...'

'We're all each other's keeper, now. Haven't you been listening?'

Hayk's hand was still on the driver's shoulder. It was, he realised, holding him down.

'I've known men like you all my life.'

Both men said the same to each other.

It was just the driver's misfortune that Hayk was the bigger man. As the bus pulled away, the last thing the trembling People

saw was a fist coming back, their Ulduzkhan's face being show-
ered in another man's blood.

*

Dawn in Paris-by-Day. She'd watched from the window as her
father set out for work. She'd watched, later still, as Alexandre
lolloped along the avenue, making for his morning bus. From on
high, there seemed nothing about his demeanour to suggest the
nights he'd spent marching with a placard in his hand. He was
just Alexandre, slouching to school, and perhaps this was the
most unnerving thing of all.

Now, she stood at the end of the Rue Castex, watching the
clot of protestors that still obstructed its furthest end. Not long
after dawn, the crowd seemed smaller than it did in the grainy
pictures she'd seen – but the closer she drew, the more confident
she was that there was no way in along the Rue Castex. The cordon around the entrance to the Hôtel Métropol was being
manned by three gendarmes – but, even had they been summoned away, there would be no breaching the front of the hotel.
Its doors had been barred from within, and up against every window barricades had been constructed. She saw tables and chairs,
upended to become walls; vending machines braced against the
doors. Only its upper storeys appeared undefended, and even
here stones and pieces of brick had shattered glass. Most of the
hotel's shutters remained locked. Paris-by-Starlight was being
sealed within.

But there was, she remembered, another way into the Hôtel
Métropol.

The doors to Le Tangiers were boarded up, the back street on
which it sat as barren as the scrub roads outside Saint-André.
Isabelle stood for a time, remembering the age when

flowers-by-night had flourished around the entrance. In the springtime, well-wishers had sat out here, basking in the melodies drifting up from below. Now there was only silence. Joy rotted too, just like the flowers, when the People no longer came together.

It was a simple thing to pull back the loose plywood boards across the doors and slip into the darkness beyond. Many months had passed since she'd stepped into this little hall, but she fancied she was still breathing in the gunpowder scent of that final night. Indeed, as she stepped out onto the dance floor, her foot sent some piece of detritus skittering – and, when she crouched down, she saw it was the stub-end of a rocket, perhaps the very same one that had scorched its path across Arina's face.

She approached the stage. It was difficult to remember what it had felt like to be the Rose of the Evening. Difficult to remember what any of life had felt like, now that Ari was a part of the world. She closed her eyes, tried to will the music back into being – and was grateful when it came. It calmed her. It made her feel in control. She was going to need that, where she was going.

There was a crevice under the stage. She pulled back the front boards, got to her hands and knees – and, though she recoiled in horror at the scuttling of rats, she felt herself lifted, too, by the soft cyan glow coming from the cavity ahead. Hayk had gone this way, after he felled the paramedic – and there was the path opening before her.

There were tables and chairs stacked under the stage. Coils of cables, old amplifiers, a single stage light. Past all of this she came on hands and knees, drawn like a lightjar to the luminescence below.

The fissure was just a place where the floorboards had rotted away. Out of its maw grew a magnificent outgrowth of vines, sparkling with clusters of fruit, tiny as bilberries, each emitting pulses of pure, crystalline light. She'd seen tangles of Christmas lights like this, but never before had she lowered herself through them. That was what she did now. The rocks were uneven below, but when she ducked her head through the halo of light she could see steps – rough-cut, hewn out of the bedrock itself. She followed them down.

The scent was heady and sweet – enough, she thought, to intoxicate or bewitch. The stairway spiralled in on itself, seeming to grow tighter with every revolution, and more than once the instinct to turn and scramble back to the hollow shell of Le Tangiers overcame her. It was only the thought of Levon that made her hold true to the course she'd set. Somewhere down here was the Khanate Beneath. Somewhere, the bazaars where the people of Paris once came to mingle. Beyond that, she would climb the wine-cellar stairs and into the hotel's interior.

She had not yet thought what she might say to him, when she found him there. That would have to be like the music; it would have to manifest in her, unbidden.

Some time later, the stairs narrowed to another fissure – this one vertical – through which she forced herself to go. It was darker here, where the Khanate levelled out. Pockets of blackness punctuated the outbursts of light – so she plucked a bouquet of flowers-by-night and used these to guide herself on. Where the flowers did not grow, the tunnel was cold; but where the flowers dominated, so too did the warmth. And, by the time she came to the first fork in the tunnel, she had got to thinking that, perhaps, it wouldn't be so hard. From the Goutte d'Or to the Place de la Bastille was less than an hour on the surface; perhaps the Khanate Beneath would be kind to her, and show her the way.

She took the wrong fork.

She knew she had because, soon, she found herself standing above a small, subterranean lake, where a shoal of golden fish turned in circles. There was no way to progress from here, so she turned back – only to discover that the tunnel had forked behind her, and that she knew not which path she should follow. She tried to judge by the colours, tried to picture Paris Above, but these tricks were useless. She thought she heard the rumble of some Métro train, grinding its way through the rock, and it was only this that reminded her she was in Paris at all.

Wild things chittered in the blackness.

Panicking now would be the worst thing. Though her legs told her to take flight, she steadied herself by remembering the music. There was no harp in her hands. Perhaps that had been a mistake. But she had her voice, frail and unpractised as it was. So she sang to herself, under her breath, and picked her way further on.

She developed simple rules: in choices between up and down, she always took down; choices between left and right, she alternated, seeking to preserve her passage further south. The first sign that she was heading in the right direction were the caverns where campsites had once been erected. She saw bedrolls and mattresses; the remnants of a long-dead cookfire. There was a rough-hewn table, around which the People had perhaps gathered – and, on its surface, a copy of the Nocturne, with faintly glowing mushrooms feeding on its pages.

It was here that she first saw the rot. In places, great thickets of briars no longer blazed with light. The People, she decided, were leaving here as well.

One hour. Two hours. Three. Darkness and further darkness. Time had so little meaning down here. The only way she could track it was by how heavy her legs felt. The Khanate Beneath had certainly turned her in circles, because by the surface she would have reached the Hôtel Métropol in only an hour.

The idea of those beds, abandoned and being slowly consumed by radiant lichens, was too tempting. It played on her as she advanced – until, distracted for too long by the thought of her own weariness, she doubled back to find them.

One hour. Two hours. Three.

Perhaps there would be some message in the dreaming.

She awoke to voices on the very edge of the alcove. There was control enough left in her that, at first, she did not startle. She kept her eyes closed, feeling the play of lights against their closed lids, and listened.

'There's somebody there.'

'She's alive.'

'By the Stars,' said a third voice, the first woman among them, 'she isn't even of the People ...'

That was the first moment her terror was unassailable. *Not of the People.* That meant something, now. She thought she could sense the terror in their voices too.

She opened her eyes, just in time to see the hand closing over her mouth. Others were already hoisting her out of the bed, pinioning her arms. There weren't just three of them, she saw. There were four, five, six. Yet more lingered in puddles of radiance in the tunnels beyond.

She needed the music now, more than ever. But with the man's hand closed over her, she couldn't even sing. So terror was all that she had.

They left her in a pit.

Ten fathoms along the tunnel, through caverns whose waters thronged with bulrushes and tiny birds, they dropped her into a pit with sheer walls, seven feet high. She tried to tell herself: they didn't cast you down; they lowered you gently, though you clawed and scrabbled at their arms. Perhaps that meant there was reason in them yet. But for long hours they left her there, until she began to think that their reason was just a mask for cowardice. They hadn't been able to kill her, so instead they left her to die.

Occasionally, one of them returned. They barked at her in the French language, and she replied in the spiralling language of the People – but this only seemed to provoke their ire. 'You break the Starlight Proclamations,' one of them uttered. 'What do you want from us?' She tried to tell them she was here searching for a friend. But none among them listened. 'We don't come into your city, but you come into ours. You come with fire and guns. You come to steal and ruin. The People have known your kind before …' And then, after an hour in the darkness, another voice snapped, 'Are you her? The girl Lisette? By the Stars, if it's true, and you wandered down here alone … You fool, you don't know what you've done!'

After that, she could hear voices above the pit, but never what they were saying. Sometimes they flurried up, urgent and wild. Other times, the silences stretched on and on. 'I'm not her!' she called out, in both languages. 'My name is …'

A face appeared above the pit. Lit up from one side, she saw a young man, his crooked teeth the sign of some skirmish of the past, his long black hair tied back in a braid.

His eyes, in which she thought she saw both fear and kindness, opened fractionally wider upon seeing her standing there. 'You fools,' he whispered, 'this isn't Lisette Chastain. This is … the Rose of the Evening.'

They escorted her further, to a cavern with Métro trains rumbling above, where the People had erected a semi-permanent camp. There, the man who'd recognised her showed her to a camping stool, and ordered another to bring her food and water; the water must have had a magic of its own, for it revived her in seconds.

'I'm right, aren't I?' the man said. 'The Rose of the Evening?'

'Who are you?' she asked.

'You know me.'

In that second, she did. 'Khazak,' she whispered.

He looked older than the last time they'd met. Scarcely a year had passed since she stood with Levon under the flyover, but Khazak's features looked more defined, somehow – as if he'd finally grown into his body. She remembered him, beaming and sparkling even as the snow strafed down.

'Some of my friends here,' he said, indicating the arc of People standing behind him, 'don't believe you're who I say. They say you're the missing girl, Lisette. I tell them Lisette does not exist. She is a phantom. A ploy of the Paris New Resistance to turn us into demons and root us out. *They* say even this does not matter: they sent us a phantom, but let us deliver back to them a woman of flesh and blood. That, perhaps, would end the madness. Strip the Paris New Resistance of their story. Lisette Chastain – just a poor girl who got lost, and was rescued by the good folk of Paris-by-Starlight.'

'It wouldn't stop them,' she said. 'It couldn't. They have to finish what they started. Anything less—'

'Did they start it? Or did we?'

Who started hatred? she thought. Where was it born? Not in any Starlight Proclamations, she thought, for there was hatred enough before then. Not in fireworks, or dead dogs, or lightjars burned to a cinder. Hatred was a thing before all that. Its seed was in all of them. The only decision was whether or not you let it grow.

'You can help me,' she said. 'I need to get to the Hôtel Métropol. That's why I came into the Khanate Beneath. I came to find Levon.'

Khazak was silent – until, finally, he said, 'You left Paris-by-Starlight.'

'I was cast out.'

'Then you left Paris-by-Day. I know this. I delivered his letters.'

She nodded.

'Why?'

For the same reasons, she realised now, that Hayk sought out a border between night and day. For the same reason, perhaps, that the Paris New Resistance marched. People were putting up walls all of the time. Mostly it wasn't to keep other people out. Mostly it was only so that you could say that *this,* this little corner of the world, this is *mine.* This is where the people I love will always be safe. This is ... home. Everything else was temporary – even, she feared most of all, love itself.

Isabelle had needed some permanence – so she'd issued a Starlight Proclamation of her own.

'I need to see him and explain. Can you take me there?'

Khazak looked over his shoulder. 'They're not going to let you leave, not unless you can convince them.'

'Convince them what?'

He crouched and started sorting through the packs that littered the campsite floor. Then, finally, he came back with a small silhouette in his hands. As he pressed it onto her, her fingers found the strings of an old, ragged lyre.

'That you're the Rose of the Evening.'

She'd taken to the stage before. The months might have passed, but that feeling of anticipation, or of being watched, never truly left you. At Khazak's insistence, the People gathered round. But this was not the feeling of being in Le Tangiers. The eyes that gazed upon her had a different expectation.

They were expecting her to fail.

When she first reached for the music, her heart was beating too fast; its rhythm disrupted her, and the melody she sought slipped away. After that, she focused on her breathing. Get the body under control, and sometimes the heart and soul followed. She let her fingers caress one string after another. One arpeggiated chord followed the next, but this was not the music she was searching for; this was not even its prelude. In the end, she had to close her eyes. She had to remind herself: she was not in La Cave de Denis. She was the Rose of the Evening, and the music had chosen her.

She dove towards it, fingers working like a spider spinning silk.

The music lifted itself out of the lyre, and took her with it. For a time, she herself was one of the Star Sailors, and the night sky opening up around her. Stars wheeled past. Spirals of interstellar dust. Below her lay the glittering waters of the landlocked sea, where the breakers crashed like cascades of diamonds. The magic might have been turning to rot all across the nocturnal world, but in the Rose of the Evening it was still manifest.

Some time later, she opened her eyes. The People were still staring – but this time, they understood.

'Well?' she said to Khazak. In the darkness, he was drying his eyes. 'Is it far?'

'And still farther,' he said, 'now that the Khanate Beneath plays us false. Come, I'll explain on the way.'

They rose out of the outer tunnels, into expansive caverns where Khazak punted them across stagnant waters, and an under-world glade where the flowers had started to rot. 'It isn't every-where like this,' he tried to explain. 'It still beats as strongly as it ever did at the heart of it – the Nexus, underneath the Hôtel Métropol. But …' The Starlight Proclamations had brought yet more magic, for a time. Perhaps there was something in the purity of it. Or perhaps it was only the celebration of the night as a place for the People alone. 'It opened up the sea. It brought back the bakhtat, and everywhere across Paris-by-Starlight the night gardens flourished with new wonders. But then …'

'The People started leaving,' said Isabelle as they glided across an ocean of dead bulrushes. 'And when the People started leaving …'

'The wonder just withered and died. People had gone exploring, deeper into the Khanate Beneath. Romantics on quests, delving into places the magic had opened up. But when the People started leaving, the world seized up. The passages those People had followed, they just weren't there any more. You'd go to the places they'd set out, and there'd be dead stone. Some People said they heard crying in the rock. Our People were still down there, cut off, with the world contracting around them. People's daughters. People's sons. After that, more left every night. Some of the boys here set up a convoy and the word went out. The world ended once. Now it's ending again. So the People abandoned Paris-by-Starlight.'

After some time, they came to caverns where wild lights still shone. There were other People here. At the site of the old bazaar, a veritable town had arisen. It wasn't quite dead, thought Isabelle. There was still hope.

'That's what we were doing out there, where we found you. You can still trust in the inner reaches, but the farthest lands, they're changed. We've been trying to chart it, or bring in stragglers who wandered too far. All of the old openings to Paris above, they're closing up, just like wounds scabbing over. The Khanate Beneath retreating, all around us ...'

They beached themselves, at last, on a shore Isabelle recognised, and together tramped through scarlet reeds until they reached the passageways above. The flowers had surged up here, turning the rock faces to strobing walls of diamond, but she knew these steps for what they were. She had been here before.

'I can find my way from here, Khazak.'

'It is better that I show you. The hotel above, it's no place for somebody not of the People.'

Together, they climbed into the cavity that had once been the wine cellar. Then, through the glittering oubliette they rose.

The hotel lobby was a demolition site. As they crossed the floor, she could hear the chanting of protestors out on the Rue Castex. The lobby windows had been barricaded with tables and chairs dragged out of the restaurant, and the vending machines that fortified the doors were themselves fortified with pieces of old scaffolding. Along the barricades, a glut of the People moved miserably up and down – silent, drawn, exhausted.

'They've had supplies enough to last. But the hotel's larders aren't infinite, and there are too many People here now. Some of them came up from the Khanate Beneath. Too fearful of being entombed, I suppose. But …'

They'd reached the bottom of the staff stairs, steel steps echoing above.

'Where is he?'

'If he's not at the barricades, he's in his quarters. Come,' Khazak said, 'we're almost there.'

Up and further up. It was not as she'd pictured it in his letters. The crooked stairs, the gabled roof, the passageway along which, once upon a time, chambermaids had carried their guttering candles. The reality was so much starker. She had to palm her way off walls of flaking plasterboard, and shuffle around the missing steps. You could trick yourself into thinking that almost anything was beautiful, if you looked at it from a distance.

At the very top of the stairs, there was a door. She paused in front of it. She was tired. She was parched. There was the dust of the underworld in her hair. She wanted nothing more than to be back in Saint-André, with Ari on her lap, and Levon at her side.

But to do all that, first she had to go through this door.

So she knocked.

*

College was the ultimate endurance test, but somehow Alexandre had survived. It wasn't until the end of the day that he saw Raphaël and Antonin at all. If they'd been cowed in the last months, it was only whenever their language tutor was near; the rest of the time, they were as committed as ever. Now, when Alexandre hurried through the college doors and down the sweeping stone steps, he saw them heaving into view. By the looks of them, they'd been out on the rugby field. Raphaël was smeared with more of the wet winter earth than Antonin – but, if they were tired by their exertions, the sight of Alexandre renewed their vigour. Though he tried to ignore them, they lapped around him as he followed the path through the staff car parks and down to the tall school fence.

'We haven't been seeing much of you, Alex. Look, Antonin, he's been muscling out.'

It was true. Maxime's brother owned a gym in Petit-Montrouge and, sometimes, Étienne convinced him to go there. Étienne said that manhood was measured in how many hours you spent at the chest press machine, or what weights you could bench press without breaking a sweat – and Alexandre himself had to admit that it felt good when, after weeks of going unnoticed, the other men in the gym had started commenting on his achievements, or taking him to one side and showing him how he might approach his training better. You buzzed with pride, after something like that.

That pride was gone now. Raphaël had put his earthy arm around his shoulder, and every time he shook it off, Antonin's appeared instead.

'Yeah, Raph, he's pretty solid. Feel these deltoids.'

'No, Antonin, feel these pecs!'

They'd followed him out of the gates and were haranguing him up the road, when a gleaming black car slowed to a crawl beside them and a voice called out, 'Jump in, A.'

ROBERT DINSDALE

'Tell your sugar daddy you'll be home later, Alex,' Raphaël grinned.

At this, the car stopped dead.

There were parked cars between Alexandre and the road, but he watched as Maxime's face appeared at the window – and was not certain whether it made him feel bolder, or more chagrined. Not wanting to appear weak in front of Maxime, he shrugged Antonin's arm off and called out, 'It's OK, M. They're from college.'

Maxime looked them up and down. 'Who are these couple of losers, A?'

Raphaël grinned, sidelong, at Antonin. 'Cruising outside the college, picking up boys, and calling us losers? This guy's got to be joking ...'

But he wasn't. When Maxime unfolded himself from the car, the back doors opened too – and out stepped Lucien, Léon and Bale.

'Let's leave this one to Alexandre, should we, boys?'

The others shrugged.

'But maybe I'll give him a helping hand.'

Maxime was through the parked cars in an instant. His fist flew, catching Raphaël in the side of the jaw. Antonin was already flailing back towards the college gates when Maxime said, 'Go on then, A, hop after him.'

Alexandre remained rooted to the spot.

'Or is this the one you're after?'

Raphaël was nursing his jaw up against the tall iron railings, his kit bag lying open at his feet.

'Craven,' laughed Maxime – and, striking out suddenly with his boot, toppled Raphaël to the ground. 'Don't you know you're messing with a hero of the Resistance?'

Raphaël looked up. 'Hero?'

'Not *me*,' Maxime laughed. 'Go on, A. The rest is up to you.'

424

Maxime was already dusting his hands as he waltzed back to the car.

Hero, thought Alexandre.

He'd never punched anyone before. He didn't know if he could. But that didn't matter, because Raphaël was still on the ground, still puzzling over the word 'hero', so when Alexandre stamped on his face it came quite out of nowhere. The second time was rather more expected, but by then Raphaël was so dazed he could do little but lie there and take it. And, by the time the third blow came, it was so predictable that he just let it wash over him. He would think about the pain much later. Now, there was only the blood.

When Alexandre finally got into the back of the car, his hands were clean, but his heart was racing. It wasn't until the car had started, and Raphaël vanished from the wing mirrors, that it started to still. It was, he reflected, easier when the blood was not on your hands. Easier when there was a bulwark between you and it. And no sooner had he thought this than he was thinking about the reason Maxime was calling him a hero even now: the information he'd provided to buy his way into the Paris New Resistance.

He would throw out his boots later. Right now, he did not want to look.

'Ingrates,' said Maxime as they cruised further north and the old town erupted around them. 'The problem with boys like that, A, is they're spoilt. They don't see how easy they have it. It's other people doing the dirty work, keeping them safe. They used to put people like that in prison, back in your grandpa's day. Called them objectors. Happy enough to let someone else take up a gun and die in a ditch for their country, but couldn't bear the thought of doing it for themselves.'

'Maxime,' said Lucien, 'stop here.'

Soon, the car had pulled into the side of the road, and Alexandre followed the others into a small parkland where a winterlight had risen up through the sod. Maxime, who knew sport when he saw it, produced a baseball bat from the car and walked around the winterlight methodically. There was something sorrowful, Alexandre thought, about its appearance. The light it emitted was dishwater grey.

'Things are stepping up, A. That's why we come to get you.'

'Yes?' Alexandre shivered.

'My brother got word the gendarmes are going to force it. Protestors been out on the streets too long. It's a drain for them. So they're gunning for a curfew of their own. Take everyone off the streets, they think, and then things will simmer down.' Maxime twirled the bat.

'But that's just … their own Starlight Proclamations,' said Alexandre.

'*Exactement!*'

Maxime drew the bat back and cut an arc straight into the side of the winterlight. The veins flurried with ugly colours, the outer flesh buckled, leaking sap, and he drew the bat back again.

'But it's a Frenchman's democratic right to protest. They don't understand that in Paris-by-Starlight, of course. They're medieval. They have … kings. But our own lot ought to get it. We got rights.'

He swung again.

'A curfew from Starlight, that's one thing. But a curfew from our own? Well, that's collaboration. And it's like this: revolution, it's in a Frenchman's blood. It's my birthright. So this march of ours. *We Own the Night. Christmas Restored.* We're bringing it forward. It's coming tonight. Once the People see we aren't giving up, then they'll get the message. The whole lot of them will leave …'

He swung the bat for a final time. This time, when it hit, the winterlight erupted. Its leaves furled back, the seeds flew out – and, when Alexandre watched their parabolas, he saw them not as the pure balls of starlight of last Christmas, but only dull, furred, grey little orbs that landed with heavy, wet thuds. Léon and Lucien ambled over to tread on them, as if they might snuff out the lightjars that hatched from within – but there was nothing to hatch, for inside was only rotten, grey mulch.

Maxime cleaned the baseball bat in the long winter grass. 'They're gathering, right now, on the Place de la Bastille. A, it's time. This book of yours. The one they worship. The original. We're to march on it tonight, burn it so that they all can see. There can be as many laws as you like. As many edicts and amnesties as the mayor's office can write. But you're not welcome in a place until its people say you are. And we, the people, say they're not.' He paused, began to lope back towards the car. 'Time for you to be a hero of the Resistance again, A. Tonight, when that seventh star of theirs shows up over the rooftops, we're going to tear it down.'

*

Levon woke to knuckles rapping at his door. He thought, at first, that he was still in some dream. There'd been too many of those – but, ordinarily, he was the one hammering on some door, begging to be let back in, so he roused himself, staggered wearily across the room and opened it up.

She was standing there, looking as depleted as he felt – and, in that way, it was like looking into a mirror.

'Isabelle, you're … '

'I'm here,' she said. And she scrambled for his hand, snatched it up and held it against her.

She could hear Khazak retreating down the stair, but on the threshold Levon did not shift. She could tell, by his eyes, that he was in some dreamland. Beyond him, the attic windows were shuttered up – but, around their circumference, she saw the paling light of Paris-by-Day. She'd been in the Khanate Beneath too long. The day, already growing old.

'Where is he?' Levon breathed.

She still had her green woollen coat with her. From its pockets, she produced Polaroids – handfuls of them, spinning out the story of Ari's life. 'He's with my mother. He's waiting for us.'

Still, Levon blocked the way ahead. He lifted a hand, kneaded at his eyes and said, 'Come.'

He took her to the window. Unshuttered now, he bade her look down upon the Rue Castex. The protestors had swollen across the day. They thronged the boulevard from side to side.

'That's the difference between you and me,' Levon sighed. 'They let you pass, but were I to step out there ...'

She tried for his hand again. 'They didn't let me through. I came through the Khanate Beneath.'

'You shouldn't have done that, Isabelle.'

She knew. She nodded. 'I had to,' she whispered.

After that, they closed the shutters again and sat together on the bed, trying not to listen to the protestors below. Sometimes, it was just mindless noise. Sometimes, words in the cacophony: *Drive the People Out! We Own the Night!* Levon himself seemed inured to it. He lost himself, instead, in the Polaroids through which he leafed, cycling through the same ones over and again. It was all so useless.

'I've been trying to get to you,' he finally said. 'I almost had it, once. But every time I was on its brink, I'd think: She hasn't once asked you to, not since she left. It's hard to cling on to, without a sign. And by the time I thought to hell with signs, they've been steering us wrong all our lives, *this* ...' He waved his hand, as if to take in the hundreds of people swarming the Rue Castex.

'I didn't leave because I didn't love you. I came back because I did.'

He nodded. You had to roll over, he thought. It was like taking a beating. The illogic of love could leave you just as battered, just as flayed.

'I understood what you meant, in the end. I remembered Aunt Mariam, with Aram on her breast, in hostels and roadside camps, on the boats and in the lorries. You needed a home.'

'I didn't want him to be ...'

'... living between the worlds,' Levon said.

'We wouldn't have been a family,' she said, 'not like that. Not under separate roofs. Ari, spinning between us. Waiting all day and all night, just so that we could be together a few short hours. He needed more than that.' She paused, uncertain whether she should say the next. 'I needed more.'

'Hayk says the same about Paris-by-Starlight.' Levon stood, returned to the shutters. 'If the People don't stay as one, they aren't a People. If they're scattered to the winds, every corner of the Earth, finding homes wherever they can – in night or in day ... He couldn't countenance it. So he heads them off, wherever he can. He terrorises them into staying. Just so the stars light up at night. What he doesn't see is, if the People don't want to stay, *that's* when they're hardly a People. If they just cower and live in fear, trying to pretend. And all the time, the Paris New Resistance, finding new ways to spread fear in us ...' Levon paused. He was still holding one of the Polaroids of Ari in his hand, and for a time he lost himself in it. 'It's the same with us, isn't it? Only, I'm not my father. I couldn't terrorise you into staying, love or not. I'm sorry, Isabelle. I am. But I look back on it and, by the Stars, I don't know if I'd have done it any different. I couldn't leave them to it. To him ...'

'That's why I came.' She stood, and joined him at the shutters. It was too soon to touch him so instead she just propped herself at his side. Behind them, the chanting in the street seemed more distant than it had. Night was coming on. 'We'll get her together,

429

ROBERT DINSDALE

you and me. We'll take her and be a family together – all of us,
Arina included, all under the same roof. Saint-André, or Barcelona, or Carcassonne – wherever it has to be. By day or by night,
but together. For always.' She hesitated. 'If it's what you want.'

Levon said, 'You don't need a sign from me.'

'No,' she whispered, 'but I'd like to hear it.'

Levon nodded, still staring at the photo. 'Is he a good boy?
Did you tell him about his father?'

'I told him he was the most stubborn, pig-headed, wise and
beautiful man in the world.'

'He'll already know it about his mother.'

Isabelle dared to touch him now. It was, she sensed, the right
time.

'I haven't seen Arina, not in weeks. They used to let me back
to the block, but I had to have an escort. Even then, it was just
fleeting. Hayk had me out on the boats ...' He turned, reached
for the shutter clasp. 'We'll have to get through this first.'

It was only as he opened the shutters that she realised why the
noise from the crowd had faded. In the Rue Castex below, only a
few solitary stragglers remained. The chanting still filled the air,
but it was duller now, perhaps out on the Place de la Bastille.
They looked at each other, then again into the night. If they
opened the window and craned their necks out, they could see
what remained of Paris-by-Starlight coming to life.

And, in the air, the first few flakes of December snow.

Khazak was in the hotel lobby when they came down the crooked
stairway. The People, waking at fall of night, had disgorged themselves from the suites where they slept. Now banks of exhausted
faces filled the lobby, crowding around a tinny little radio that the
girl Emi had set up. Children were up on shoulders, others nes-
tled in their mothers' arms; an old man, propped on the shoulders of his children, strained to hear.

Khazak looked up from the crowd, saw Levon and Isabelle together on the stair.

'They're marching.'

Levon's eyes took in the barricades. 'Where to?'

'North,' someone said. 'They're calling it "Christmas Restored". "The Rally Against the Night".'

Khazak lifted the radio to his ear. The voice of the newscaster was breaking up, bursts of static punctuating her speech. 'A thousand of them, and picking up more on the way. Levon, your father . . .'

There was a way through the crowd, and Levon found it now. Soon, he and Isabelle stood at the barricades. He bent down, strained at one of the lengths of scaffolding holding the vending machines in place. When he could not shift it, Isabelle too put her weight against it.

'My father might be down on the wharfs by now. Might be he's already set sail. But when he finds out . . .' The scaffold shifted, and Levon struggled for purchase on the first upturned machine. 'He calls them his militia – the Militia of the Night. Ever since the ships were scuttled, he has them as guards. I was meant to be with them – but I'm weak, aren't I? Just like on the landlocked sea, all those years ago. I couldn't stand up for us then, and I can't now.' Inch by inch, the vending machine moved. Some of the People were rushing to help; others hustled back, fearful of what they might find out on the Rue Castex. 'When Hayk knows, he'll rally them. He'll—'

Isabelle cupped a hand around his jaw, angled it so that he was compelled to look into her eyes.

'We're going to get her now, and we're leaving tonight. Paris-by-Starlight, Paris-by-Day, we're . . .' She stalled. Behind her, hundreds of faces were watching on. And she thought she understood, then, the reasons Levon had stayed. A hundred different histories were here in this room. A hundred different stories, each one of them spinning around the rest. These People had been here before. They'd rushed, in panic, down to the wharfs and crammed themselves aboard boats and, from there, taken off across unforgiving waters, onto unforgiving shores, across thousands of miles of unforgiving lands – until, some benediction from above: a home at the other end.

But what then?

The world was full of impossible questions. It was just like raising a child. You never got it right. You just hoped to get it least wrong.

Out on the Rue Castex, where Paris-by-Starlight was coming to life, not a soul could be found.

16

* *

THE DYING OF THE LIGHT

Adaline was shaking when they sat her at the kitchen table. Hector was worse than useless; all he could do was share cups of coffee around, as if this was the most ordinary thing in the world. Three police officers on the doorstep might have been ordinary for some, but to Adaline it was barbarity. She knew the sorts of homes police officers had to visit – she taught enough of those kinds of children at college – and this was not one of them. Here there was a welcome mat at the door, freshly cut flowers in the salon.

'It must be a mistake. Alexandre couldn't hurt a fly.'

'Madam, three separate witnesses testify to the assault, and this quite apart from the victim himself. His father is very upset.'

'He's always been a good boy. Hasn't he, Hector?'

It was Hector's silence that infuriated Adaline. The man had no backbone. All he did was nod along. That was what came, she thought now, of marrying musicians. All their conviction was spent on melodies and refrains; they had none left for the things that truly mattered. By God, he'd already let one child go to seed – and look at what had become of her, abandoned and pregnant and running from one end of the country to the other.

Hector said, 'I think, perhaps, he's in with the wrong crowd.'

This seemed to attract the attention of the lead officer, who had accepted Hector's offer of cream (what did he think he was, an American?) and had, until now, been focused on drizzling it into his coffee.

Adaline said, 'They're his friends. It's good to have friends.'

'What kind of friends, sir?'

Two sets of eyes were on Hector, and both burned into him: Adaline demanding his silence (why, when he bothered to speak at all, was it always to say the wrong thing?), and the police officer his elaboration.

'There's a young man named Étienne. I don't know ...'

'This is it, sir?'

It shamed Hector to admit that it was. 'It's been quite a year, gentlemen.'

'He became a grandfather,' snapped Adaline.

The officer nodded.

'To a child he hasn't seen, from a child he doesn't know.'

It was evident, by the look the officers shared, that they knew there was nothing more to glean here – nothing except that most ordinary of crimes: a husband and wife, ill at ease with each other, ill at ease with the world. At least, the lead officer mused, the coffee had been good. 'Does he return each night?'

'Every night of his life,' Adaline lied.

'Then it's your civic duty to notify us of his return. You have our number.'

It was Hector who showed them to the door. After he'd ushered them through, he stood alone on the welcome mat and braced himself for whatever argument was to come. Nine times out of ten, he could see the storm approaching.

As he lingered there, Victor appeared in silhouette at the top of the stairs. He would need helping down. He so often did.

'Police?' Victor said, as Hector steered him into the kitchen, where Adaline had set about skewering sausages. 'Adaline?'

'It's Alexandre, Papa.' The tears running down her cheeks were not only because of the shallots she'd so fiercely chopped.

'They're saying he started a fight. They came to … arrest him, I think.'

'Arrest him? Our Alexandre?' The old man's indignation was ripe. 'But, by God, he's a … hero, that boy!'

'Well,' she said, 'we've no idea where he is. But when have we ever?' She had her bleary eyes on Hector now. 'Darling,' she said, and for the first time without any bile, 'what are we doing? Fighting so much, sniping so much, we've just … let him go.'

'You haven't let him go at all!' the old man announced. 'You've done the very best job, Adaline. Alexandre's a boy to be proud of. He's taking his first steps in the world, that's all. It's a rite of passage for any young man – isn't it, Hector? Alexandre's a man of principle. He's found his cause. And …' He leaned forward, as if to share a secret. 'I happen to know where he is this very second. He's with his brothers in arms. He's standing up for what's right. Why, it's all over the radio right now. They're gathering by the Bastille and marching north, to show this city who we really are. To show them we're not afraid. Whatever happened in Paris this year, whatever black magic they worked, this city's survived two thousand years of hardships, and it can survive one more. Starlight Proclamations? They just don't know who we are. But Alexandre does – and he's with all the rest, showing them, right now.'

*

He'd been at the wharfs at the true fall of dark, stood on the jetty and watched as his deckhands brought in the *Second Return* – for so he'd dubbed his vessel, now that the wreckage of the first lay somewhere in the deep. But he'd known, already, that something was awry. It wasn't only the winterlights on the jetty, which pulsed with the same rotten light as they did in his mother's night garden. Nor was it the way the water dogs, ordinarily so eager to course through the waves, lounged instead on the Île de la Cité, seemingly indifferent to the magic of night. It was the feeling that had hummed in him since that long-ago morning when he'd harried his family to a wharf just the same as this. It was the recollection of that afternoon, not so very long ago, when he'd watched the rally on the Place de la Bastille. It was the knowledge of the present, stacked against the knowledge of the past.

It was crackling in the static of the shipboard radio. As he boarded, he could see the disquiet on the faces of the deckhands who gathered round, but it was the look in his boatswain's eyes that told him he ought to be afraid. They'd been standing together, on the deck of the *Return of Night*, when the flames rushed up the mizzenmast. This was not a man meant for panic and despair, but it was here all the same.

'Where?' Hayk demanded.

'They left the Nexus. Near a month of blockade, and they abandoned it tonight. They're marching from the Bastille. North, they think. But looping around, collecting more on the way.'

Hayk looked up. The darkness above them was vast.

'Cast off,' he said. 'Get out on the water. You'll be safest there.' But, as he said the last words, he strode over the deck rail and back to the jetty.

The Paris New Resistance hadn't come to the wharfs, not since that night when he'd watched his quartermaster burned alive. They couldn't. They'd got lucky once, caught the People by surprise, but they wouldn't get that chance again. Hayk looked up and down the wharf, and saw his militiamen stationed there: clots of them, at waystations up and down the very breadth of the landlocked sea. As he thundered down the jetty, he put two fingers to his lips and let out a shrill whistle. That caught the first militiaman's attention.

'Find the Faithful Three,' he said. 'Samvel, Narek, Arman. Listen out for the radio and send them north, wherever the march has reached. And you,' he cried out, gesturing at one of the marketeers who'd arrived at dusk, anticipating the golden catch the ships would bring in, 'I'm going to need your car.'

The engine strained underneath him. He hadn't driven in so long. At least, as he crossed the bridge that spanned the land-locked sea, the golden shoals glittering underneath him, the roads were empty. He turned one of the dials on the dashboard until the voice of the newscaster was crackling in and out, and focused on the French language. If he understood every second word, it was enough. There was some other curfew tonight. The mayoralty had issued an edict of their own. The Daylight Proc-lamations, he wryly thought. But their people had disobeyed it, just as they disobeyed his own.

The Place de la Bastille was barren. As the car slewed to a stop, he stepped out and ran across its stones, arms wheeling. They'd gone north from here. But what was north? And why? By the time he got back in the car, cursing its German engine, the whole of history seemed to be moving in him. He thought: It takes an aeon to raise an empire, and only a moment for it to fall; a lifetime to raise a child, and only one ill-timed blow to end its life.

The Boulevard du Temple was barren; so, too, the Boulevard de Magenta. Yet, sometimes, as he drove, he saw flickers of light – and, when his eyes were drawn that way, he saw that it was not the flowers-by-night marking out the places where the People lived and prayed; it was only that the people of Paris-by-Day were opening their shutters, stepping out onto their balconies to peer out at Paris-by-Starlight. One, even bolder than the rest, appeared on a doorstep, portable radio in hand, listening out no doubt for news of the march.

Hayk found it soon enough. The boulevard arced past the ter-minals at the Gare du Nord, and there he saw the ragged tail of the marchers, twenty abreast as they moved up the street. Hayk left the car in the middle of the boulevard and stepped out into the sweetness of night. There had been winterlights where the train station opened up to the city, but no longer. All that had been left was a leathery mulch. Looking back along the barrel of the boulevard, he saw, now, what he had missed before: everywhere the flowers-by-night had grown, in the verges and beneath the trash cans, cascading over the shop awnings and bus shelters, there was ruin. One by one, the stars winking out.

The march was still headed north – and he realised, with a sinking inevitability, the place they must be bound. For what else was north of here, but the place he called home, the cradle of this starlit world, the tower where his daughter and wife remained?

The Paris New Resistance, he reflected, had been there once before.

He'd let his people down once, he thought, but he was stronger now. This time, he understood. This time they wouldn't have to run. This time they wouldn't starve and freeze and die on the way to somewhere new. There was no new frontier. Paris-by-Starlight, for here and ever more.

In his mind, he was back in the old country, listening to the report of the first tanks, and pounding the back lanes down to the jetties.

He was older than that, now. He was battered and tired.

But, by the Stars, he could run.

*

Levon braced his sister by the shoulders, looked into her sightless eyes. 'I'm sorry, Arina, but it has to be now.'

They'd found her alone in the apartment, sent down to conserve her strength by Master Atesh, with only Gilly the water dog at her side. Ten minutes later, as Isabelle piled clothes and boots and trinkets into a haversack, she was buried in Levon's shoulder, while the water dog turned in distressed circles around them.

Levon snapped every time it emitted one of its shrill barks, but only Arina's softness could calm it down.

'Oh, Levon,' she said. 'But what if it's like last time? It's what he does now. If he thinks the People are leaving, he ... brings them back in. There's a group of them up there in the night garden. He brought them back last night. Just old men and old women, but somebody turned them in, told him they were getting away. Well, it's the law, isn't it? We are the People, and the People look after each other.'

Levon kissed her on the brow. 'It's why we have to go now, Arina.'

'Where to?'

'Isabelle has a place. Far away from Paris. We can be a family again.'

He would have said more – but, as he picked her up, there came the crash of footsteps from the night garden above. Through the roof, something shattered. Isabelle's eyes lifted to the ceiling.

Still holding his sister, Levon approached the window. From here, he could see south, down the long barrel of boulevard running parallel to the railway tracks. The clusters of lights bobbing down there did not manifest from memories of the old country. Those, he thought, were the lights from the Place de la Bastille – and many thousands more.

Isabelle had seen it too, this tide of lights. 'They're not really coming this way, are they?'

'Why would they?' Levon breathed, but the way he continued to stare – as if daring the tide to get closer – was admission that he didn't know. 'We've still got time. We can get out before—'

A muted cry from up above, another muffled crash, and Levon watched as parabolas of silver light, darkening to grey, arced out from the night garden above. Upwards and outwards they flew, trailing glittering dust behind them. A winterlight giving birth, he thought – but that did not make sense, for Christmas night, the Night of Seven Stars, was not yet upon them. He set Arina down, tried to crane upwards so that he could see the cascade of green tumbling from the garden's edge – and, beyond that, the seven-pointed star. The stars in the constellation were almost aligned, but not yet.

There came another crash, and yet more arcs of dirty light erupted, casting their net over the apartments. Levon waited for the seeds to arrest mid-flight and the hatchlings inside to slough off their shells. This they did. A multitude of mottled green and grey fragments rained down around the block, and in the air around them a generation of lightjars were being born.

None of them shimmered. None of them shone. Some of them dropped directly out of the air, and those that didn't flapped feebly for uplift, then turned in panicked eddies, just to stay aloft. One cut an arc across the window out of which Levon was star-ing, and he saw it defeathered except along its spine, beak mal-formed and eyes out of balance. No wonder it could not fly. It wasn't truly a lightjar at all, just some paltry imitation of one. For some time it careened in circles, then crashed headfirst into the window. If it had ever truly been alive, it died in that moment, pirouetting down, out of Levon's sight.

It was a mercy Arina couldn't see. 'Something's going wrong,' he whispered, and his eyes lifted again to the roof.

After that, trying to shake off the sadness, he carried Arina out into the empty apartment, Gilly at his heel.

'My book!' Arina cried. 'Have we got …?'

It was in the bag slung over Isabelle's shoulder. She'd picked it up from the bedside table, and now she pressed it into Arina's hands. Instantly, her fingers started tracing the star embroidered on its cover.

'Ready?' Levon asked, shifting her onto his back. She was so much bigger than when he'd last carried her, but tonight she seemed as light as a feather. She clung on tight. 'Ready,' she promised, soft and wet in his ear.

On the other side of the apartment door, the stairwell was empty.

There was still time, Isabelle told herself, leading the way to the top of the rainbow stairs. If the march was coming here (and she realised, with some dread, that the Paris New Resistance had been here once already) they were still some furlongs away. By then, the three of them could be lost in the labyrinth of the old town. Or perhaps they'd find some quiet place to linger until the Métro started running again. By fall of next night: Saint-André, and Ari, and home.

She realised, too late, that she was the only one rushing ahead. She'd been so lost in her thoughts, leaping ahead in time, that she hadn't heard the screaming.

It was coming from above.

Levon was peering up the rooftop stairs, Arina on his back and Gilly the water dog at his heel.

'Levon, we haven't time. We need to go now.'

He knew that. Deep inside, he did. But, in his head, he too was back on the landlocked sea. His father was thundering at him to get off the boat, to leave Arina with their mother and join him back on the wharf. Together, they'd head for the hills. Rally all his disparate brothers. Fight the good fight, wage the unwinnable war.

But that was different. Back then, all he'd had to leave was his father. Everyone else was taking flight too.

He felt Arina's heart beating, rapid percussion against his back.

He thought of Aunt Mariam and Aram. He thought of Ana and Elen, still somewhere in this block. He thought of everyone else he'd welcomed into the city, back when there was joy.

'Levon?'

Isabelle's voice came at him through the haze of his recollections.

He nodded, though his heart ached to do it. Took a stride in her direction.

Faltered only when he heard more voices from above.

Any other voices, he could have ignored. It wasn't even as if he'd recognised any words.

But the one thing he did recognise changed everything.

The man screaming up there, he was screaming in French.

*

They were calling it a march, though an ill-assorted collection of men like this could hardly walk in step with one another, nor keep to formation as they went. More appropriately it was a 'tramp', and it had been tramping north since the onset of night.

Hector darted from one side of the column to another. He'd found the march somewhere east of the Sacré-Cœur and, though he'd picked his way between them since then, there was no sign of Alexandre in their midst. This, at least, gave him hope. Every time some element of the march stopped, to bring back their baseball bats and pulverise the winterlights they found, he tried to imagine Alexandre among them, and found that the images did not fit. Alexandre, focused on his magic set, or Alexandre, scoffing when his father brought out his old mandolin – these were the things that made sense. He stopped one of the few women marching, asked her if she knew a boy named Alex, was quickly battled back by the towering man at her side, and moved on.

And, all the time, the chorus of different voices, assailing him from every side:

'Christmas Restored!'

'Pull Down the Stars!'

'*Drive the People Out!*'

Words like those, he felt certain, could never come from Alexandre's lips.

Sometimes, the rally split. Elements of it vanished into side roads, then reappeared later on to strengthen the column again. What they were doing out there, Hector could only guess – but some of them came back seeming to be sated, and perhaps that meant they were ripping up more of the nocturnal flowers. Hector was not sure how he felt about that; fingernails rimed in earth were not rimed in blood, but somehow the two seemed to match each other tonight. He was happier, a mile further north, when the march ahead slowed, and he followed them through the gates of a freight yard where coaches and delivery trucks framed an expanse of broken asphalt and earth. Here the march had come to its end, the protestors spreading out to fill the expanse. On one side of the vast yard, warehouse roofs glowed in the patches where yet more flowers grew. Some of the protestors were already scrabbling up to snuff out the lights. On the other side of the yard, a tenement building, sixteen storeys high and shaped like a horseshoe, towered above. The lights at its zenith were the most incandescent Hector had seen all night. They were, he reflected now, the brightest he'd seen all year, ever since the Night of Seven Stars.

It was only as he made that realisation that he knew he'd been here before.

He turned on the spot, taking in the freight yard and the amassing protestors, then looked up again, at the crown of lights. Yes, he was certain of it. The last time he was here, they'd approached it from a different angle, but this block was surely the same. A year ago, he'd stood up there proudly and watched the winterlights make their spectacle over Paris.

What a night that had been, he thought, and was buoyed to find it still thrilling inside him.

But then he looked around, listened to all the baying voices. Some of these people must have felt like him. They'd have carried their children out into the gardens and balconies and watched the glittering trails of the lightjars being born. They'd have been touched by it too. The rush of love enchantment could bring. It was funny how it withered. Funny how you forgot how it used to feel. And as soon as he thought of this, he was thinking of Adaline: the rancorous looks she gave him, and the rancorous looks he gave in return. Or he was thinking of Caro, Isabelle's mother, and how, at the beginning, his heart had filled at the end of every night, knowing he'd get to go home to her, that they'd wake up and waste their hours together, the rapture of mindless nothings. If loves like those just rotted away, well, was it any wonder that the mob around him had forgotten the majesty of last Christmas?

He trembled. Somewhere, some of the protestors were sparking fires inside tin trash cans – for what purpose he did not know. But at least the flickering warmth was something.

'Drive the People Out!' The chanting had coalesced around this one simple phrase. 'Drive the People Out!' It crashed in waves around him.

Perhaps the only love that really sustained itself was the love you had for a child. Why else, Hector thought, would he be here, in air that ruptured with such violence? Why else listen to the chanting, the braying, the ridiculous voices that rose in the horde? Why else deny that his son was really and truly one of them, if not for love?

'Étienne!' a voice called out. 'Come see …'

Étienne. That, at least, was a name that Hector knew. He sought out the voice in the crowd, and saw one man reaching out for another. The man named Étienne turned, and Hector saw his face for the first time. It was so very ordinary. He was tall and rangy, his hair a black fuzz, with eyes that, had he looked away for a second, Hector might not have picked out again.

By the time Hector reached him, he was making his way to the head of the assembly. Hector snagged him by the arm.

'I'm looking for Alexandre.'

Étienne shook him off, continued on his way to the front of the throng. Here, beyond banks of parked cars and coaches, the walls of the apartment block towered. When Hector looked up, he could pick out the cascade of glowing green, amber and blue that poured from its edges. The seven-pointed star seemed to hang directly above.

A rising wind was snatching away his breath. 'Please ...'

'Who's asking?'

Perhaps it was not right to say it. Perhaps Alexandre had denied he had a father had all. There was always a chance he'd filled their heads with stories, terrors, madnesses of his life at home – anything to make it seem as if he, Alexandre, belonged among this bruised and hateful people. But when Hector looked around, none of them seemed very different from him.

'I'm his father.'

Étienne's eyes widened. 'Then you're here for his finest hour! And better late than never, if you don't mind me saying ...' Hector tried not to wince when Étienne put an arm around his shoulder and, in that way, shepherded him to the line of cars, as close to the apartment walls as the protestors could reach. 'Alex isn't here. He's gone on ahead. Look up, old man.' Hector did. All that he saw was the mountaintop, blazing with lights. 'Your son's been fighting the good fight. He's quiet, that one. Intense. But he's always thinking. That's why I'm not jealous, see. I don't think I'd be here without your Alex at all. Oh, we helped each other along the way, that's a fact, but the truth is, it was your Alex and that brain of his that helped us into the *proper* Resistance, back when it was just me and him kicking around, doing what we could. I might have had the contacts, but your boy had the brains. And he's being rewarded for it tonight. He's on a mission, you see. It's your Alex who found out all about that book of theirs, the very first. He's up there right now, snatching it from under their noses, with three of our best. Any minute now, they'll be bringing it back down here – and then? Well, then it's time to watch their world go up in smoke.'

*

Levon reached the top of the stairs.

He had to venture a few strides into the forest of lights, still hidden behind fronds of glittering ferns, before he saw them. The night garden was wilder, deeper than he remembered – and, for the most fleeting of moments, it reminded him of what the majesty of Paris-by-Starlight could really be like.

Then he saw the People hunched together on the far side of his bebia's lake. He saw the three men looming over them and the fourth parading the lake's near side, a baseball bat in his hands.

The winterlights that had been growing on the lakeside were obliterated, all except for one. As Levon watched, the fourth man – thick and round, his head like a hardboiled egg – brought the bat back and cut into the winterlight's side. The light in it flared, the thick petals convulsed – and, a second later, its seed-pods erupted into the air. So that, thought Levon, was why they were exploding before the stars had properly aligned. He watched, with horror, as the bat swung further, carrying the man with it, and – by sheer chance – caught one of the seedpods mid-flight. There, the fuzzy grey orb cracked open – and its lightjar, already defeathered and deformed, died in a sickening crunch.

Levon felt Isabelle at his side. He set Arina on the ground between them, then pleaded for her to stay where she was. Gilly the water dog snaked protectively around her legs.

'We're not the people you think we are,' the man with the bat was saying as he studied the viscera on his bat. 'We're not going to hurt a soul among you.'

'That's if you People have souls,' said one of the other men. Levon inched into the glowing greenery and saw him, gangly and blond and smiling sweetly as he stood guard over the People. The man at his side was bigger, broader of chest and with the Teutonic features of some comic book hero. The fourth he could barely see. He stood at the precipice itself, looking down into the freight yard beneath.

There were People here that Levon did not know. The refugees, he supposed, that Hayk had dragged back. All of them aged. All of them afraid. And then ... Aunt Mariam, with Aram on her lap. All the children who took their schooling up here, huddled in the crooks of her arms. Master Atesh was on the edge of the huddle, his head bowed and trembling like all of the rest.

'We're just not the sort of people who'd do that to another,' the first man said as he carefully wiped his bat clean. 'Not the sort of People, say, who'd march into a city, enchant everyone with their parlour tricks ... then stab them in the back. But that's OK. Nobody needs to get hurt. Not any more. The People's time in Paris is over. We all know that. Paris-by-Starlight never really existed. This city of yours is a figment of your imagination. It doesn't belong to you at all. It's mine, and it's my children's and ...' He stopped, the bat dangling in his hand. 'I didn't come here to hurt you. Live or die, it's all the same to me. Just live or die in someone else's parish.' He stopped. 'We came for your book. Your Nocturne. And one of you's going to give it to me now.'

Isabelle folded her hand firmly over Levon's. 'Be careful,' she whispered, and clung on to Arina as Levon strode forward, out of the glittering ferns.

'Put it down,' Levon said, 'and we'll talk.'

All of the faces in the night garden turned to him. The man with the bat. The cowering People. The rangy blond boy and heavy-set hulk who hung over them. The younger man, with his military fuzz, who'd been peering over the precipice, divorced from the rest ...

Before any of them could reply, Levon heard the ferns behind him scissoring apart – and Isabelle's voice sounding out as she stepped through: 'Alexandre?'

The boy who'd been at the grotto's edge was barely familiar to Levon at all, but he thought he saw it now. How long had it been? Nearly a year? His hair was cut short, and he'd grown into his body, and he looked with disbelief across the glistening glade at his sister.

'Alexandre, what's going on? Why are you—'

'Who is this, A?' asked the man with the bat.

Alexandre's head dropped, as if he could bear to look at her no longer. 'She's my sister, Maxime.'

The man named Maxime's eyes were all over her. 'The bitch who betrayed her own people?'

To this Alexandre did not reply. 'They call her the Rose of the Evening.'

Isabelle hurried forward, faltering halfway between Levon and the man named Maxime. If she heard Arina begging her not to, she did not show it. Levon had caught hold of her, somewhere behind.

'Alexandre, what are you doing here?'

'What am *I* doing here?' he said, voice suddenly rising in pitch. 'Isabelle, what are you doing in Paris? You ran away ...' He stopped. 'They just want the book. *We*,' he said, catching himself too late, 'just want the book. If they give us the book, it's all going to be OK.'

She tried to take a step closer, but Maxime had lifted the bat again, and this rooted her to the spot. 'Alexandre,' she breathed, 'how?'

His shoulder lifted, his face opened up, and she thought she saw in him the same person who'd sat in the salon with her, late at night, and listened to the story of her life. Perhaps he was thinking of the same thing too, for when his eyes settled on her they seemed to beg for understanding. He said, 'I found my people, Isabelle. You, of all people, would understand that.' If there was a moment where he might have sloughed off whatever skin he was wearing, it was now. Isabelle thought she could see into his eyes. She thought he was scared. But then he said, 'They're good people, Is. There are good people everywhere. That lot down there' – and he beckoned Isabelle over to look at the rally in the freight yard below – 'they're good people too. You don't know them like I do. All they want is … things back the way they were. Back when they were good. Back before all the fighting and the anger and the … arguments, night after night after night …'

Isabelle tore her eyes from the rally. They'd started building pyres down there, fires spilling out of old trash cans. Their placards still flying, their chorus still strong – but, when she heard Alexandre, it might have been that he wasn't speaking about the city at all; it might have been he was still shut up in his bedroom in Créteil, listening to Hector and Adaline and all the ordinary, everyday venom of a family at war.

'Back when things were good?'

Levon's voice: loud and stark. Isabelle turned back to him. She hadn't realised, until now, how far across the garden she'd come.

'Back when things were good, and my People were starving? Back when life was good, and they were dying of dysentery? When we were in cattle trucks, pushed from one camp to the next? When they told us there was no home? That home was gone, that we had to …' Breathless, he looked from one man to the next. There were scales in the world, he thought. Things had to be balanced. One man's Golden Age was another man's Hell on earth. The only thing that separated the two was the

449

imagination of men, building border fences or raising Starlight Proclamations, scrabbling for what was left of their worlds.

He was still.

What else was left, but to tear it all down?

'Give them the book,' he breathed, and turned to Arina, who huddled with Gilly somewhere behind.

He went to her, sank down on his knees. 'It's OK, Arina. I'm here. Just give me ... let me give them the book.'

'Levon, no!'

He recognised the voice of Master Atesh, somewhere among the cowering People, but he did not look back. He was gently touching Arina's face, running a finger along the line of her jaw, promising her it was going to be OK.

'It's just a book,' he said, with words meant for everyone in the garden. 'So let them have it. Let them burn it, if that's what they want. What does it matter to us? To you and me, little sister?' He knelt down, pressing his brow against hers. 'Those stories, they're in our hearts. We know them, inside and out. I know about Tariel and Ketevan. I know about Davit the Daydreamer and all the Star Sailors there ever were. I don't need it written down. I've got a star in the sky. The Nocturne isn't paper. It's ... hearts and souls.' He stood and looked around, at the People imprisoned. 'It's the memory of being together, even when we're apart.' At this, his eyes strayed to Isabelle. 'And it isn't even finished. Our history's still being written. So let them burn the book. What do we care? As long as our lives can go on.'

He was done. He turned back, to take the book from Arina's waiting hands.

He'd almost done it by the time the glittering ferns parted. His fingers were on its cover, tracing the embroidered star, when the shadow fell.

'Stay where you are, Levon,' came his father's voice.

Isabelle watched as the man named Maxime wheeled around, baseball bat in hand. A moment later, the two men standing over the People had rushed forward as well. Of the Paris New Resistance, only Alexandre did not move. Isabelle tried to take him by the arm, stop him from joining them on the edge of the lake. By some strange mercy, he let her.

Neither was Hayk alone. Though he was the first through the ferns, the stairway behind him was swollen with shadows. One after another, it disgorged Samvel, Narek, Arman. His Faithful Three.

'Give them your bebia's Nocturne?' Hayk breathed, stepping aside and allowing his followers through. 'I've taken you for a coward, my son, but never for a fool. Give them the Nocturne, and what do they want next? You still don't see this for what it is. One person cannot make a peace. If only one chooses peace, it is still war.' He shook his head. 'You abandoned your People once before, Levon. Took off, when you could have made a stand. Well, here we are, on the landlocked sea again. All that's happened in the world since then, all the magic that's been revealed, and you haven't changed.'

'No,' said Levon, 'and I never wanted to. I didn't abandon my People back then. They lived, father.' He stopped. 'And they'll live again tonight.' Softly, he said, 'The book, Arina.'

Hayk moved imperiously forward, brushing Levon and his sister aside. Across the glowing expanse, he faced Maxime.

'Who are you, you dog?'

Both men spat out the same words.

'I'm the Ulduzkhan,' Hayk declared, 'and you're here, in my mother's grove, at the sufferance of my People. So I'm laying it out now, as clear as I can. I'm giving you ten seconds to ...' His words petered into silence. Perhaps it was only that he was struggling to formulate the sentence; the French was so ill suited to his tongue. But then he nodded, as if reaching some silent arrangement with himself. He needed no language any longer. When he spoke again, it was in the spiralling language of the People. 'Ten seconds? Why, these dogs gave our People no warning at all on the wharfs.'

Maxime was too slow. The baseball bat had already been wrenched out of his hands, lost in the untold depths of the rooftop lake, by the time he realised what was going on. The fist that found his face was not enough to fell him, not straight away. The second turned the world to a haze, and somewhere between the third and the fourth he found himself on the earth, with the man they named Ulduzkhan above him.

In the same moment, the Faithful Three surged past Levon and into the heart of the garden. There, Samvel fell upon the blond boy, pummelled him into the earth. Narek was smaller than the third man, with his jet-black hair and comic book jaw, but what he lacked in girth he somehow made up in spirit. The Frenchman might have killed water dogs in the streets, but he didn't know how to take a blow. In a second, he too was on the earth, the air being choked out of him until he begged, with flailing hands, for it to stop.

The third of Hayk's men had further to go. While the fists flew behind him, he cast himself forward, making for the boy at Isabelle's side.

Isabelle threw herself between them.

'Stop,' she said – and, when she put up her hands, something in it seemed to quell the man. 'He's my brother,' she stammered. 'My brother, you understand? Whatever they've done to him, whatever they've said, he's a good boy. He is. I know it.'

She danced left, danced right, certain somehow that this man would not touch her.

'A good boy?'

It was Maxime's mangled voice. Underneath Hayk, he lay bloodied, one eye swollen shut, the other clenched tight against the lights.

'I should say he's a good boy! This brother of yours, he's a hero. Tell them, A. Tell them how it is.' When Alexandre did not speak, Maxime choked out the blood that had pooled in his throat and went on, 'Alex, well, we didn't think much of him. Not at first. Just some mother's son. We'd barely even heard his name. But that snivelling friend of his, Étienne, always turning up, always wanting in. Didn't know where he wasn't wanted – just like the lot of you People … Until, one day, he comes up to me and he says: I know how you can do it. I know how you can make your mark. My friend Alex, he says there's a garden, a forest on top of a rooftop. That's where it started. That's where the magic comes from. Get up there and desecrate it, he says. Well, as ideas go, it wasn't bad, was it, A? But it wasn't what I wanted. So I told that shit, Étienne: find me something better. Do that, and then we'll talk about you signing up. And he comes back, not two days later, with the right stuff. Leave the rooftop to me, he said. I got you something better. See, there's a bar A knows, a place where the People go to play. There's going to be a wedding. And it's all going to happen at this little cellar, Le Tangiers…'

If stillness could be a magic, in that moment it cast its spell over the night garden.

'Our proudest moment, and all because of little A here. You know, when I finally laid eyes on him, I thought: he may not look like much, but at least he's got the brains we need. Yeah, you don't know our Alex. He's a bona fide …'

Hayk's bloodied fist met Maxime's face for a final time. After that, there were no more words. The Ulduzkhan hoisted himself from the prostrate body and looked across the garden at where Alexandre stood.

'My wedding day?'

He uncurled his fists, closed them again.

'My daughter?'

Alexandre was already looking at Arina. The girl had started to cry. The tears were pooling in her sightless eyes – and, in that moment, Alexandre understood.

Isabelle's hand was still on his arm. As she released it, he reached out for her again. 'It isn't like he said. Isabelle, it isn't. Étienne was so desperate for an idea. Something to prove who we were. I thought we'd come here, make a mess of the garden. Just to put the frighteners up the People, I thought. Show them not everyone's enchanted. After that, maybe we could ...' The words were exploding out of him. His eyes, darting between Isabelle and Hayk. 'It was Étienne who'd gone to tell them. He said, with a plan like this, they'd think we were good enough. Then we could finally go to the bar. Then we'd have a place to *be*. All we'd have to do is come here and paint a few slogans.' He stopped, desperate for breath. 'I didn't know he'd told them about the wedding as well, not until it was already done. We went back to the bar afterwards ... and the paint was still on my hands. Isabelle ...' Now that Isabelle had reeled back, Alexandre stood alone at the edge of the lake, his body a stark outline against the endless night sky. '... you have to believe me.'

Across the night garden, Hayk's huge hands had come together in applause. 'And the little pup begs.'

'Nobody was meant to get hurt. That's why we came when no-one was around. I didn't know they'd go to Le Tangiers. When I heard what they'd done, I was sick, Isabelle.'

'But you still ran with them,' Hayk breathed. 'You still came here tonight, didn't you, you dog?'

Levon had seen that look on Hayk's face before. He'd seen it on the shores of the landlocked sea. He'd seen it in Le Tangiers, when a paramedic wanted only to help his wounded sister, and found himself smote upon the cellar stones instead.

'Father,' he said. 'Hayk.'

The man was teetering on the edge of some abyss – not fighting the gravity that was pulling him down, but only the urge to cast himself over.

'What happens next?' Levon asked in the language of the old country.

'Next?'

'That night in Le Tangiers. I know what it meant. I was there as well. But what happened next, Hayk? I'll tell you, shall I? It was Starlight Proclamations. And ... ships being set aflame, down on the Seine. It was your quartermaster burning in the water. Water dogs hunted in the streets. It was blockades at the Hôtel Métropol, and rallies on the Place de la Bastille. It was you – you, Father! – driving out and rounding up people who'd been rounded up like cattle too often in their lives. It's ... this.' He crouched and picked up what was left of the dead lightjar. 'Who knows where the rot starts? Maybe it's in here' – and he held his hand, still clasping the dead lightjar, over his heart – 'in every last one of us. I don't know. But I know where it can end. Paris-by-Starlight isn't meant to be a war. By the Stars, it's meant to be a home.'

Hayk had listened patiently, but now that was done. He hung his head, and the lines on his face deepened, and he started whispering to himself, a litany, over and over. 'You haven't been listening. I've been trying to tell you, ever since I arrived. All I wanted was for you to see. To learn, just a little of what's left of me. Then, perhaps, I wouldn't have to do this alone. I'm not a ship to carry your lives. I won't last forever. Paris-by-Starlight *is* meant to be a home, Levon. But if you don't look after what belongs to you, somebody else will just come along and take it ...'

Before the last word had been exhaled, Hayk threw himself forward.

Levon threw himself forward too. He was roaring out for his father to stop, roaring out that none of it mattered, that if he didn't stop it was already lost – but there was a border between them now, and no words, no pleas, no desperate cries could breach it. Instead, he caught his father's shoulder as he rampaged past. For a second, that was enough. It slowed him, staggered him – and Alexandre, who'd understood too late that the older man was coming for him, ducked aside just in time.

It was Isabelle who picked him up, but she too was too late to stop the rest. Levon was still hanging from his father's shoulder as Hayk staggered on. Where Alexandre should have been, there was only thin air. He crashed into it with all the force that had been meant for Alexandre, all the fire that came from the old world. All the years of not knowing, the years of hope, the years of devastation.

He was staggering still as he reached the green cascade at the outer limits of the night garden. Staggering still, with Levon hanging from his shoulder, as together they lurched off the edge and into Endless Night.

*

Hector was back in the heart of the rally when he heard the crash. Even then, he did not turn round. He wanted only to be gone. Back across the city. Back to Créteil. Back to Adaline – whatever she meant to him now. The chanting was still pounding in his ears. The words, like some blemish you could never scour away. But when the crash came, all of that ended – because, moments later, the alarm of one of the parked lorries was sounding, drowning out all other noise.

It was the alarm that made Hector turn back. He wasn't mistaken; he could hear screaming too – far away, and far above.

As he picked his way back through the throng, it hardened around him. Too many people, all coursing together, and in moments there was little room to move, little room to breathe.

Somehow, he reached the place where he and Étienne had been standing. Some of the protestors were hauling themselves up, first onto the line of cars, and from there onto the tops of the lorries beyond. Étienne was up there. Hector reached out a hand, as if the boy might help – but no such luck; evidently, Étienne had already forgotten the older man existed at all. After that, with the hard press of the crowd behind him, Hector had no choice but to scrabble up of his own accord. By the time he'd picked his way along the lorry roofs, others were rising up beside him. He clamoured so that he could see.

A man was lying face down in the depression on the top of the lorry, the metal buckling to the shape of his body. His life's blood was pooling around him, filling up the fractures he'd made when he fell.

'Help me,' Hector said, dropping to his knees and taking the fallen man's wrist. When he found no pulse, he ran his hands across the broken body, not knowing what he was searching for, let alone what he might find. 'Help!' he snapped over his shoulder.

'He's one of them,' Étienne breathed.

'He's a person, isn't he? Help me turn him. He's a person ...'

'I'm not touching it,' Étienne said. 'It fell from the sky. That's divine.'

He was too heavy for Hector to move alone, so in the end all he could do was angle the man's jaw so that, if there was life left in him, he might still breathe.

It was useless, of course. His face was as ruined as the winterlights the protestors had been destroying. That was the reason that Hector didn't realise who he was looking at. Because the truth was, he'd seen this face before. Now the eyes were sealed shut, and his nose smeared across what was left of his face. Cracked white shards rained out of his lips as Hector rolled him. Probably his insides were as ruptured as his out; probably he'd

ROBERT DINSDALE

broken his back when he landed, or else perished in terror somewhere above. But Hector bowed his face to what was left and
pursed his lips. It was difficult, from this angle, to make a seal –
but whatever air he breathed into him had to be worth something. The taste of his blood was the same as the taste of his own.
Above Hector, some of the protestors were recoiling in disgust.
Étienne was crowing, 'You degenerate, what are you doing?'
Some of them clambered back down, because the sight of one of
their own, coming up for air with his lips turned crimson by the
blood of another, was too distasteful to bear. 'Let it go,' somebody said. 'It isn't up to us. What is it these ingrates always say?
We are the People, and the People look after each other ...'

Hector took a breath. 'Yes,' he nodded. He thought of Isabelle and he thought of Alexandre. 'We're people, and people
look after each other.'

'The old man's lost it,' somebody said. 'The alarm's addled his
mind. You've got it wrong.'

But he hadn't. By the Stars and screaming up above, he had it
right.

He cleaned his lips and bent back to his task.

*

Isabelle was the first to the edge. She clamoured for purchase in
the green cascade, but was too late to see the impact far below.
There came a crash and, in the same instant, the screaming of
some alarm.

'Levon!'

She looked over her shoulder. The Faithful Three still pinioned the intruders, the last one looming over Maxime's prostrate form. Mariam and the children still huddled with Master
Atesh. The screaming was coming from Arina – for, even sightless, she seemed to understand.

And there was Alexandre, suspended in time between them all.

There was nothing stopping him now. In the time it might take to reach him, he could have plucked the Nocturne from Arina and been off down the rooftop stair.

But he wasn't. He was staring at her, begging to be told what to do.

She had no time for that, because down below she could see a host of the dark, corrupted lightjars – blots of blackness against the luminous cascade – beating their wings in a fury. She clawed the trailing vines apart and saw nothing. She tore at them again, opening a ravine into the foliage below. There she saw a hand.

It was there one second, and the next it was gone. She ripped at the vines again, felt one uproot. This sent panic coursing through her, for perhaps it was the very vine onto which the hand had clung. 'Levon?' she called down. 'Hayk?'

She turned back. 'Alexandre? Please ...'

He could have taken the book. One of the beaten men, still pinioned by Hayk's followers, was bawling out for him to snatch it. 'What do you think we came here for?' he thundered, before a closed fist silenced him. But Alexandre was shaking. Perhaps it was the sight of Arina's face in front of him. She was still scream-ing, into the night.

Alexandre nodded.

He was the first to Isabelle's side, but soon the others were coming. Mariam picked herself out of the children and rushed to the green cascade. Gilly the water dog rose onto his hind paws, sniffing frantically at the winter air. Somehow, Arina picked her way through as well.

'There!' Isabelle cried, parting the hanging vines again until she could see the hand, and another hand, rising. The desiccated lightjars turned frenzies around him, still sounding their own alarms, until at last the hands drew near. She reached out to take the first, but there were still inches between them. She reached out again – and, for the first time, the figure looked up from beneath its untamed black hair.

'Levon …'

Levon's eyes focused on hers. There was fear in them, and there was incomprehension, but there was stubbornness too. She allowed herself a small flicker of hope at that. Stubbornness: such a sorry, deplorable trait. It was stubbornness that lifted one hand over another, even as every muscle in his arms screamed out to be released. It was stubbornness that made him use the breath he did not have to call out her name. It was stubbornness, too, that meant he kept his eyes locked upon her even as, realising at last that they would never connect, his hand flailed for the one that had reached down at her side.

After that, it wasn't stubbornness at all. It was Alexandre holding on to him, braced against the edge of the roof – and somehow, in a confusion of arms and legs, Levon found himself hauled back over the side. There he crumpled, his body fatigued beyond measure, into Isabelle's arms, until Arina found her way between them, and Gilly the water dog leapt up, desperate to be a part of the majesty too.

On the rooftop, all was silence – while, in the world around, the night moved on. In the freight yard beneath, the security alarm had burned itself out. The protestors of the Paris New Resistance were fanning back to the streets, just as the Faithful Three abandoned their positions and took flight down the rainbow stair.

Levon opened his eyes and saw, through a veil of Isabelle's tangled hair, that Alexandre was the only one of the intruders that remained. He tried not to think of his father, the Ulduzkhan, slipping past him, spiralling down into Endless Night, and thought instead of the question he had asked before the fall, those three simple words: what happens next?

In the distance, there came the sound of sirens. Turning blue lights were advancing through the night – but whether they were coming for the citizens of Paris-by-Day or the citizens of Paris-by-Starlight not a soul could say.

*

In the days that followed, obfuscation followed obfuscation.

In the testimonies the gendarmes took, not a soul spoke of the Paris New Resistance (though some had to surreptitiously fold their arms, the better to hide the tattoos that had been inked there). In the interviews, not a soul mentioned the Militia of the Night – and though investigators asked after the man they called 'Ulduzkhan', all they ever heard was of the last King of the Stars, who had fallen from a blazing mountaintop in the fairy tales of the Nocturne. 'But that was thousands of years ago,' somebody said, 'and perhaps not real.' After that, there was just the ordinary, everyday business of arrests and restitution. December grew old – and, though the gendarmerie puzzled over the two men, one named Maxime and one named Hayk, who lay in the city morgue, no arrests were made in the case of either. After a little while, the only thing the morgue attendants remembered about the peculiar case of Paris-by-Starlight were the tiny flowers, glowing ruby red, that flourished on the bigger dead man's body, lighting up wherever his bones had ruptured through flesh.

Without the Ulduzkhan to protect them – or corral them, as the People began to say – the wayfarers from the old country could follow the trajectories of their own hearts. One by one, in families and groups of friends – forged in the old world, or forged in the new – they made plans to set out from Paris. Some remembered the places they had first tried to settle, and decided, perhaps, there were still second chances in the world. Others looked to the oceans and thought: there are yet further places to go. So in the days and weeks and months that followed, families loaded the possessions of their lives into wagons and cars, coaches and trains, and set off to new lives in new worlds. And with each family that left, the lights shone a little less brightly in Paris-by-Starlight. The stars never did get to align (they so often don't), and on Christmas morning, when walkers with heads heavy from last night's réveillon set out on their early promenades, they did not find Paris bordering an inland ocean, nor Notre-Dame swamped in tangle vine; they found the River Seine, devoid of golden shoals, and in the skies above it no moon moths floating on the early-evening dark, no water dogs coursing through the waves in their packs, no lightjars or nighthawks making comet trails of beautiful colour. By New Year, when the final flowers-by-night were receding to the few rooftops and suburban gardens where the People remained, a visitor to Paris might have remarked on the occasional flurry of sapphire and bronze in the Jardin des Tuileries – but they would not have stood in awe upon the plateau of the Tour Eiffel. There was a time, people wrote, when the magic of night existed in every corner of Paris – but that time is past. Now, only a few rooftop groves remain.

Somewhere along the way, somebody – History would not record who – breathed the words 'Paris-by-Starlight' for the final time. After that, Paris was just Paris. Where once had been two cities, now only one.

Of course, its fragments lingered on. In the New Year, when the refuse collector Hector kissed his wife goodbye (and meant it, with every piece of him – for, like the People, and perhaps even thanks to them, he believed in second chances as well), his days were filled with collecting the remnants of the nocturnal world. The winterlights rotting on the promenades. The tangle vine and flowers-by-night that had wilted clean away. The nests of mummified lightjars, who had burned so brightly and now burned no longer.

At least, in these endeavours, he had help – for there, at his side, worked his son Alexandre. The bracelet at his ankle, and the community service order that sent him out onto the same streets where his father toiled, were his punishment for the crimes to which he'd confessed on Christmas Eve when he'd walked into a police station to give them a list of his every misdeed. And though they'd cared only for the moment in which he'd hovered over Raphaël, Alexandre knew, in his heart, where his true crime dwelled. No prison sentence, no community service order, could atone for words whispered when they should not have been whispered; for careless talk that cost lives. This, he understood, was up to him. There were penances to be made, in private, to the few People who remained. He would go to them, when he could. He would find a way to help. If there was so little of their magic left in Paris, he would find a way to work his own – and one day, perhaps, if the fates were willing, find forgiveness for what he had done. Besides, there was, he was discovering, a simple joy in working with his father. He had a peaceful, easy feeling at last. His hair was growing back.

There was joy in it for Hector too. Sometimes they spoke, and sometimes not at all. He asked about his magic set, or he asked about what he might do after college was finished. And then, when the time was right, he asked about Isabelle. Because Hector had a plan. *Be a better grandpa than you were a father,* she had once told him, and this time he meant to honour the promise. He would go to her in the spring, and Alexandre too, and in his dream they would sit around a table together and, at night, play with mandolin and harp while Alexandre read out passages from the Nocturne to the blind girl Arina and the baby boy. Bridges built, where once borders had been raised. There was work to do until then, but this, at least, was the start: to build new worlds, you first had to dream them into being.

*

It took some months for the People to leave Paris, but the first among them left on the night that the Ulduzkhan fell. In a car taken from the ruined hotel, on the long road south – with Arina sleeping in the back, and Gilly the water dog lying like a blanket upon her – Levon held Isabelle by the hand. She slept often, but woke often too. Levon needed her directions; he liked the thought that, from now until the day he died, he would be taking directions from Isabelle. And this was a world he would dream into being himself: the one where he brought her coffee each morning, and wine after dark; the one where Mariam and Aram – who had promised to follow after – lived on the outskirts of the same town, and they came together each evening, so that their children could play; so that together, whether they lived by night or by day, they would never forget.

'There was a thing my father said, before he slipped away,' Levon said, with the night coursing past. 'I was holding on to the cascade, and him on to me, and he said ...' Levon drove further, before he could give voice to the words. 'He said: you can only hold on for so long.' He meant to the world, thought Levon. He meant to starlight itself. 'Then his fingers slipped through mine.'

Isabelle had sensed the trembling in him. The doubt.

'You hold on forever,' she said. 'You did for me. You're Levon-by-Starlight.'

They drove a little further, into the paling dawn.

'Just Levon,' he smiled. 'I don't think I need the magic any more. I think I just need the ... ordinary world.'

He would get his wish, in the end. There was enough that was ordinary in raising a child, in fixing the drainpipe and paying the rent, in putting food on the table and watching him grow from baby to toddler, to teenager and young man. Enough that was ordinary in listening to him laugh and cry, celebrating in his good times and sitting with him, finding the answers, when times got hard. Enough that was ordinary in waking up one morning, to discover yourself fifty years old and about to become a grand-father for the very first time, and looking back at years that had cartwheeled past with barely enough time for you to take breath.

Enough wonder, he would always think, in the ordinary world.

But the magic of the old country was not finished with him yet. Isabelle had already seen it: a tiny gesture in the scrubland, the faintest glimmer in the dark, little memories becoming manifest in the edgelands of life, wherever the Nocturne was told. Nor, in later years, would they be the only ones. For everywhere the People went, so did their enchantments go with them. So there became Saint-André-by-Starlight, Kreuzberg-Berlin-by-Starlight, Penrith-by-Starlight and Starlight-sur-Mer. Tiny cradles of creation, an archipelago of lights across the atlas of the world.

In Paris that Christmas, when the winterlights had blossomed, they had not sent arcs of glittering colour across the city sky. Families had not emerged from their houses, nor stepped out onto their terraces, to watch lightjars being born, and to be reminded – though they needed it, as all of us do – that there was still magic in the world. But in Saint-André a father met his child for the very first time. A mother brushed her hair in the mirror and went to sleep in the arms of someone she loved. Big worlds might end, but little ones are forever being forged.

La Fin

ACKNOWLEDGEMENTS

With thanks to my agent Euan Thorneycroft; James Clegg, for all the many sounding-board moments in the Fitzroy Tavern; Gillian Green, who first commissioned this novel; Sam Bradbury, Ben Brusey, and the whole team at Del Rey.